W9-AEB-642

PURE
EVIL

Also by Lynda La Plante

Jane Tennison series
Tennison
Hidden Killers
Good Friday
Murder Mile
Th e Dirty Dozen
Blunt Force
Unholy Murder
Dark Rooms

DC Jack Warr series
Buried
Judas Horse
Vanished

Widows series
Widows
Widows' Revenge
She's Out

Trial and Retribution series
Trial and Retribution

For a completed list of Lynda's works, please visit:
www.lyndalaplante.com/books

Lynda La Plante was born in Liverpool. She trained for the stage at RADA and worked with the National Th eatre and RSC before becoming a television actress. She then turned to writing and made her breakthrough with the phenomenally successful TV series Widows. She has written over thirty international novels, all of which have been bestsellers, and is the creator of the Anna Travis, Lorraine Page and *Trial and Retribution* series. Her original script for the much-acclaimed *Prime Suspect* won awards from BAFTA, Emmy, British Broadcasting and Royal Television Society, as well as the 1993 Edgar Allan Poe Award.

Lynda is one of only three screenwriters to have been made an honorary fellow of the British Film Institute and was awarded the BAFTA Dennis Potter Best Writer Award in 2000. In 2008, she was awarded a CBE in the Queen's Birthday Honours List for services to Literature, Drama and Charity.

✉Join the Lynda La Plante Readers' Club at
www.bit.ly/LyndaLaPlanteClub
www.lyndalaplante.com
🅕Facebook @LyndaLaPlanteCBE
🐦Twitter @LaPlanteLynda

Lynda La Plante

PURE EVIL

ZAFFRE

LONGWOOD PUBLIC LIBRARY

This is a work of fiction. Names, places, events and incidents are either the products of the author's imagination or used fictitiously. Any resemblance to actual persons, living or dead, or actual events is purely coincidental.

Copyright © La Plante Global Limited, 2023

All rights reserved.
No part of this publication may be reproduced, stored or transmitted in any form by any means, electronic, mechanical, photocopying or otherwise, without the prior written permission of the publisher.

First published in Great Britain by Zaffre in 2023
This edition published in the United States of America in 2023 by Zaffre
Zaffre is an imprint of Bonnier Books UK
4th Floor, Victoria House, Bloomsbury Square, London WC1B 4DA

Paperback ISBN: 978-1-83877-963-4
Ebook ISBN: 978-1-83877-964-1

For information, contact
251 Park Avenue South, Floor 12, New York, New York 10010
www.bonnierbooks.co.uk

Printed and bound in Great Britain by Clays Ltd, Elcograf S.p.A.

MIX
Paper from
responsible sources
FSC
www.fsc.org   FSC® C018072

Chrissie Most, for her friendship, kindness and fun.
You will be truly missed.

EUSTON STATION

He has wasted weeks, including a couple of nights, at Paddington and Charing Cross stations, trying to spread out the hunt so that it was safer, and remaining wary of CCTV cameras, knowing exactly how far away from the stations he needed to be before he was in the clear. He knew it was imperative that he never created any suspicion, but it's been frustrating.

And so tonight, he was returning to his old hunting ground. But with one new added dimension: saving the cash required to be allowed into Euston station's First Class Lounge, via the cheapest ticket he could purchase.

Choosing a table with a complete view of the station's concourse below the bay window, he helped himself to a free coffee and a pastry. Wearing rimless glasses, a black hoodie with jeans and sneakers, and carrying a non-descript canvas haversack, to all intents and purposes he appeared to be a university graduate. Sitting with his back to the rest of the lounge, he was relieved that it was virtually empty. From his position he could watch passengers coming and going, and all the train departures and arrivals were on screens clearly visible from his position. Taking out his mobile phone, he appeared to be concentrating on messages and texting, while in reality, his concentration was on Platform 1, awaiting the arrival of a train from Liverpool Lime Street. This had been very productive on previous occasions.

Finishing his coffee, he took an old takeaway coffee beaker from his haversack in readiness, as the arriving passengers began to stream out onto the station's concourse. Surrounded by cafés and fast-food stalls, newsagents and book shops, his focus was directed on the passengers with their trollies and wheelie suitcases. As groups of family and friends waited outside the platform's exit gate, he *began to feel very agitated that after all his planning it looked as if he was out of luck.*

The last straggling passengers had walked out of the exit gate when his antenna kicked into action. She was very petite, with blonde hair worn in a thick twisted knot. Wearing a short mini skirt with rubber-soled ankle boots and a cheap parka puffa jacket. Over her shoulder she had a large dirty white canvas bag with wide straps and what looked like a sleeping bag wrapped around with straps. He would have to learn quickly if she was meeting up with friends, intending to camp out somewhere with them. She seemed disorientated, standing by the exit gate as the grille was drawn closed. Looking around, she headed towards one of the empty seats available for passengers and paused by a stand offering various tourist attractions and free tube maps. Picking one out, she turned to look over towards the sign for the exit down to the tube trains, then concentrated on reading the tube station map.

From the First Class Lounge it took only a few minutes for him to walk across the concourse towards her. Prepared in advance was the takeaway coffee beaker, and as he made the last few steps towards her, he jolted forwards, virtually into her arms. To any casual onlooker it would look like a friend hugging her.

'I am so sorry, goodness, here let me mop this mess up.'

He had spilt the cold watery coffee from his beaker over her canvas bag, and quickly took out some tissues from his pocket to dab at the stain. She was much younger than he had first thought, a teenager with bad acne and bitten fingernails.

'It's alright, didn't get any over me.' She had a strong Northern accent.

He gently dabbed at the stain on her canvas bag. 'I don't think I've done too much damage, but I was hurrying for the tube station. Are you catching a train?'

'No, I've only just arrived. Don't worry about me bag, honestly.'

'Well, I've probably missed the train I was hurrying to get, so can I buy you a coffee? Or are you waiting for someone?'

'No, I'm on me own. I've never been to London before. In fact I was just checking out the tube station. Never been on one of them either.'

She gave a nervous laugh, then checked the stain on her bag. 'It's not too bad, so thanks.'

'What's your name?'

'Heather.'

'Well, I apologise, Heather. If you like I can walk you down to the tube. Whereabouts are you heading?'

Almost without any hesitation they began to walk towards the exit for the tube station. He'd picked up her sleeping bag by the strap, insisting he carry it for her, at the same time asking where she was staying. He had played out this routine so many times and knew his next moves would be eventually getting her onto the tube near to where he lived, then offering her not just a coffee but stopping off for a hamburger. It would not be too difficult to subsequently offer her a place to stay. Only once before had his instinct failed.

Heading down to the tube station it was imperative that he give her no hint of interest that might alarm her. It was important that he gained her trust. She was intending to go to Piccadilly Circus, telling him that she had been told by a friend that she might find her there, or over at the Embankment.

When he offered to accompany her and look for her friend, Heather appeared quite relieved. She was concerned that her old flip-top mobile might need to be charged as she had hoped to do it on the train but didn't have the right lead. By the time they had alighted at Piccadilly it was after ten, and they sat by the Eros Statue for a while before Heather started to become fretful. He looked at his own mobile, checking the time as if concerned about getting home, but at the same time saying he was worried about leaving her on her own, even though there were a lot of tourists around. He asked her if she had any other contacts, suggesting that perhaps he could call them for her on his mobile. She started chewing at her nails and shaking her head.

The offer of a hamburger and fries with a milk shake made her hesitate, even telling him that she should be the one offering as he had been so helpful. He didn't insist but said he was definitely hungry. He knew a cheap place they could get a burger from a street stand. It was important that by now he knew she had very little money, but there was one element he needed to find out before he wasted any more time.

They walked up Shaftesbury Avenue as the theatres spilled out their audiences. Already there were a few homeless people taking up their positions outside the empty theatre exits. He watched Heather looking towards one young man and he bent down towards her and whispered that he was glad he was not in that position as it was very risky sleeping rough.

The stall was close to the Shaftesbury Theatre, and sometimes there were other market stalls selling mostly tourist items. After they stood side by side eating their burgers, he gained the last important fact. She didn't explain it right away, but eventually, she said she might have been stupid but she could not take any more tirades from her stepfather, describing him as a bully and how her mother was afraid of him.

'I've run away. I mean not for the first time – I done it a few times before – but they always got me back. This is as far as I ever come before.'

'How old are you?'

'Fourteen, nearly fifteen.'

He wiped his mouth with the paper napkin that had been wrapped around his burger. He was pleased with himself. He had been right: she was perfect. He was beginning to really like her, anticipating that *it could be a few weeks or even more, depending on how she turned out. He doubted that she had even been reported missing yet.*

It took a little persuasion to get her to accept a room for the night, saying that it would just be until she made contact with her friend.

She looked dubious, chewing at her bitten nails again. Then she crumpled the ketchup-stained napkin into a ball and tossed it into the waste bin by the side of the stall.

'Are you sure? I don't know if I should.'

'I don't want you to think I'm coming on to you in any way, Heather. I just really need to get back as I have to do some studying and be up early in the morning. It's only a small box room, and you might have to use your sleeping bag, but you'll be safe until you decide what you're going to do next.'

'Do you live far away?'

'Two tube stops then a change and we're there.'

She smiled, hitched her canvas bag onto her shoulder as he picked up the strap wrapped around her sleeping bag. 'Are you coming?'

'This is really kind of you; I really appreciate it, thanks ever so much.'

They disappeared, heading towards Leicester Square tube station. Just another ordinary looking young couple stopping as he pointed out the hanging lanterns as they passed the entrance to China Town.

Nothing gave any hint of the horror that would come.

CHAPTER ONE

The entire team had been called together by DCI Ridley for a briefing in the boardroom of Kensington Police Station. Chairs had been placed around the large meeting table and along the walls in two tiers. Stacks of notebooks and pencils were placed in the centre of the table should they be required. Squashed in the corner was a trolley with tea and coffee.

The officers arrived in dribs and drabs; some dealt with crimes like assaults, robbery, burglary and fraud. Others were part of the safeguarding units, dealing with sexual offences, domestic abuse and offences against children. They helped themselves to refreshments then sat down at the table expectantly. Fourteen officers were already at the table by the time DC Laura Wade and DS Anik Joshi arrived, carrying their Starbucks coffees. Laura glanced at her watch. There was no sign of DS Jack Warr, and she suspected he would leave it to the last minute, so she placed her jacket on the seat next to her to reserve it. Anik eased the lid off his coffee, glanced towards the door and said under his breath, 'Jack's going to be late as usual. Any idea what the briefing's about?'

'No, I only got the e-mail last night. But whatever it is, it's got to be something big. I've never seen so many from other departments present in previous briefings.'

'Me too.'

The two chairs at the top of the table remained empty, as well as the one next to Laura. She glanced at her watch again. It was five to nine. Two female clerical staff hurried in. One squeezed past a seated officer and flicked a wall switch that lowered a large white screen at the far end of the boardroom. The other went to the top end of the table and switched on a laptop that projected the Met Police crest onto the white screen. They then left the room.

At exactly one minute to nine, Jack – still wearing his overcoat – strode into the boardroom. He went straight to the refreshment trolley and poured himself a cup of tea, heaping in sugar before turning to look around the table. Laura raised her hand to indicate that she had saved the chair beside her, and he beamed. He had just sat down as Detective Chief Superintendent Ian Henderson walked in, giving a brief nod to everyone. He hesitated before he spoke.

'Due to personal matters, which I can't go into at present, DCI Simon Ridley, will be stepping down from his position here for some time. I will be introducing you to an officer whom I admire greatly that will be taking over from him. He will decide how all the cases you are involved in will be handled in DCI Ridley's absence. As I said, I can't give you any details regarding the situation, it must be treated with the utmost discretion and not revealed under any circumstances to anyone outside this station.'

Nobody knew quite how to interpret what Henderson had just said. There was a strong sense of confusion, but no one wanted to ask any questions. There was a light knock on the boardroom door and the Superintendent walked briskly over to open it. DCI Nathan Clarke was ushered into the room and stood next to Henderson.

'This is Detective Chief Inspector Nathan Clarke. He has a full list of our ongoing cases for you to discuss with him. I apologise to everyone for having been unable to give any formal notice before this morning. It is imperative that we continue to practise the high standards and commitment the teams here have always had. Thank you, and I urge you to respect my request for the utmost privacy during this time.'

Henderson walked out leaving DCI Clarke facing everyone. If they had hoped to get some further insight into what had just occurred, they didn't get it. Nathan Clarke opened a Word document on the laptop, then, using a laser pointer, pointed towards the large screen at the end of the table.

'Ladies and gentlemen, when I indicate your names on the screen, please could you give me an update regarding the investigation you are attached to.'

Clarke was tall and had a deep voice. He was dressed in an immaculate grey suit with a pristine white shirt, and tie. Everyone around the table craned their necks to look at the screen. They were still bemused at the morning's development but followed Nathan Clarke's request and waited in turn as he passed from name to name.

After an hour they were all released and returned to the incident room. It proved difficult for anyone to discuss the situation or ask questions regarding Ridley's departure, as Nathan Clarke's secretary was already moving his computer and other equipment into Ridley's office. This was odd, as normally Ridley's computer and laptop would have remained there and anyone taking over in his absence would simply use a log-in code to use them, but nobody paid particular attention. Nathan Clarke instructed her to remove various personal items belonging to Ridley, including a large pot plant and a box of framed pictures and commendations. The team were then each handed a typed single page giving them details of Clarke's impressive career with the Met. It appeared he had been a serious high-flyer, excelling in IT and establishing a forward-thinking Guide to Digital Evidence program to help all Met officers to become computer literate. He had also led a team on an investigation into burner phones and mobiles to enhance tracking and arrests.

Lunch break was the first opportunity for the team to voice their concerns about what had taken place that morning. The consensus was that Ridley was ill, perhaps with some form of cancer, and had taken time out to have chemo. Amid all the frantic speculation, Jack kept his thoughts to himself, but inside he was upset and angry. Surely he had been a close enough friend for Ridley to have had a private conversation with him about what was going on. Unlike the rest of the team, Jack had been privy to Ridley's cancer diagnosis the previous year, but he had been assured that he was in the clear, in complete remission. He had already been absent for two weeks prior to this morning, telling Jack he was taking a well-earned break. What the hell was going on? Thankfully, Jack was able to avoid getting involved in any discussions with his colleagues, as Clarke was already arranging one-on-one meetings with everyone.

Jack's own meeting with him was quite lengthy. He had been overseeing the investigation of a violent knife attack at a local corner shop and officers had made an arrest the day before. Jack would have to go through a lengthy court process as the suspect, Rodney Middleton, had a long history of violence and had been refused bail. Clarke listened attentively as Jack outlined the entire investigation which resulted in officers tracking down the offender to his flat. Clarke looked over the statements and suggested that Jack delve further into the medical background of the assailant. From his previous record it had been suggested Middleton was a schizophrenic and he had been transferred to a psychiatric unit for assessment. He told Jack the CPS would want a full medical history, and it was best to get a warrant issued.

Jack had actually already arranged a meeting with a psychiatrist from the unit but told Clarke that in his opinion Middleton had 'acted up' after his previous arrest eighteen months earlier, to get a lenient sentence, serving only seven months before his release. He didn't mention that it was Ridley who had first suggested that there was something fishy going on.

'Jack, I'm not interested in your opinion. Please just get the necessary medical data as it appears his violence is escalating. I also suggest you re-interview his girlfriend.'

Jack had already arranged to bring in the girlfriend for further questioning, but he simply agreed with Clarke as he was eager to leave. Jack had not actually met the offender as the original DS who had been dealing with the case had gone on long-term sick leave. A forensic psychologist had been contacted to assess the defendant and judge whether he was fit to enter a plea, stand trial and participate in proceedings. It felt as if Clarke was being over-diligent, but he presumed it was due to the fact that he was taking over from Ridley at short notice. When Jack returned to the incident room, he found that most of the others felt as if they had been interrogated rather than asked for a summary of the cases to which they had been assigned.

When he left at five thirty, Jack and the entire team had no clearer understanding of what was going on with Ridley. Maggie arrived home shortly after Jack and, as soon as she saw him, she knew something was wrong. He was in the kitchen putting a casserole into the oven, and their daughter, Hannah, was upstairs being given a bath by Jack's mother, Penny.

'What's up?'

'How do you know something's up?'

'Well, you don't usually hover in the kitchen with a glass of whisky before six thirty. Did you have a bad day?'

'Not exactly. Something strange happened and none of us can fathom what's going on. Ridley's been replaced, with no reason given. So, we have a new DCI who's being very over-cautious with everything we're working on. Most of the team assume Ridley must be ill. You know he had that cancer diagnosis, and when I found out he was having chemo he made me promise to keep my mouth shut about it. He also told me he'd been given the all-clear and, to be honest, I believed him. He's been in great spirits lately, almost unlike him, telling me he'd started working out at a gym and asking my opinion about these new clothes he'd bought. I was surprised when he took off for a couple of weeks. I even thought he might have been lying about being given the all-clear but didn't want anyone to know. He didn't look that good either.'

'Why don't you call him?'

'I did. No reply. It went straight to voicemail.'

'Well, I'm sure he'll be in touch.'

'I guess so. I've become quite fond of the old codger . . . even more so with him testing out his new wardrobe on me, but this is so unlike him . . . it was just sprung on everyone.'

'What veg do you want?'

'What?'

'With the casserole. We have spinach or carrots.'

'Whatever . . . I'll go up and see Mum and Hannah.'

Maggie caught his arm. 'Before you do, can I have a quick word? Something's bothering me a bit. Does Penny seem alright to you?'

Jack shrugged, watching as Maggie took her coat off and handed it to him.

'I've been meaning to have a chat with you because I'm concerned. Penny seems to be a bit forgetful lately and I wondered, you know, if it's too much for her?'

'If what's too much?'

'Well, she has to take Hannah to nursery every morning, then collect her in the afternoon. She's only there for three hours before Penny walks her to the playground, then comes back home, feeds her, bathes her, gets her ready for bed. It's a lot for a woman in her seventies, you know.'

'She's fine; she loves it . . . and I haven't noticed anything.'

'OK, well I just wanted to mention it. If you could hang my coat up in the hall, I'll get on with setting the table.'

'I could just call round to speak to him, couldn't I?'

'Yes, you could.'

'Although the Super asked for complete privacy. What do you think?'

'Jack, it's up to you. Did you turn the oven on?'

'Oh, I might not have. I'll call him again and leave a message.' Jack walked out of the kitchen to hang up her coat.

Maggie shook her head and went over to turn the oven on. She then opened the fridge and took out the vegetables.

Although she had treated it lightly with Jack, she was genuinely concerned about Penny. She had noticed a few things that were unlike her: she had left the iron on a couple of times recently, and the washing machine was full of dirty clothes that hadn't been washed. They weren't terribly serious things, but they were niggling at Maggie. Also, the nursery had given Penny some dates for parent meetings and Maggie had found them left on the hall table under a duster.

When Jack went into Hannah's bedroom, she was wrapped in a soft bath towel, and his mother was opening a drawer to get out a nightdress for her. Jack gave Hannah a hug and a kiss, and then sat on the edge of her little bed with one of her cuddly toys.

'Has she been a good girl today, Mum?'

'Yes, apart from eating another little boy's biscuit, according to the new young nursery assistant.'

Jack watched as Penny put on Hannah's nightdress and some soft wool socks, saying that the nights were getting colder so if she tossed her blankets off at least her feet would stay warm. Hannah took the cuddly toy from Jack, saying 'dadda'. Penny then picked her up and Jack got off the bed so that Penny could tuck her in and pull up the sides. She was too big for a cot now, but still needed the sense of safety.

'The casserole's in the oven. Are you having dinner with us tonight?' Jack asked.

'No, dear, I'm going to have an early night. After I drop Hannah off at nursery tomorrow, I'm going to meet up with some friends. We're arranging a bingo night so when I get the dates, I'll tell Maggie, as one of you will need to be here for Hannah.'

'That's good that you're making new friends,' Jack smiled. 'I sometimes worry about you leaving all your old friends back in Devon. It's about time you had some new interests.'

'Well, I don't know if you could call bingo a new interest! But we'll have dinner and make it a weekly date . . . if I enjoy it. A couple of the women are bringing their husbands, and then there's the caretaker from the nursery . . . he's up for a night out.'

'That's great, Mum! Just let us know when one of us needs to be here to look after Hannah.'

Penny pulled out a large story book and drew up a low chair to sit beside Hannah's bed. She lowered the brightness of the bedside lamp and glanced at Jack as he hovered.

'Everything alright, dear?'

'Yeah, yeah. See you in the morning, unless you want me to bring a tray of supper up to your room?'

'No, thank you, dear, but I appreciate the offer. You enjoy having dinner with Maggie.'

Jack quietly closed the door behind him as Penny began reading a story to Hannah. He went into his home office to call Ridley. It went straight to voicemail again, so he left a message asking if he could do anything and hoping that Ridley would get in touch with him. By the time he went back to the kitchen, Maggie had cooked the vegetables and was just taking the casserole out of the oven. Jack opened a bottle of red wine and fetched two glasses.

'Mum seems better than ever. She's joining some women to start going to bingo once a week.'

'You didn't mention anything to her?'

'No, like I said, she seemed fine. I left her reading Hannah a bedtime story.'

'I should have gone up to kiss Hannah goodnight,' Maggie frowned. 'Never mind, it's nice to have a quiet evening together and I'm feeling really pooped. We had a long day today, lots of new cancer cases taking up beds, and as usual we're awfully short-staffed.'

Jack nodded. 'I called Ridley again and left another message. It's all very odd.'

'Maybe he *is* ill again, and just wants his privacy?' Maggie suggested. 'You could always go round to his place and find out; although if he wants you, or anyone else, to know I'm sure he'll contact you.'

'Yeah, you're probably right . . . perhaps I'll pay him a visit at the weekend.'

Jack ate hungrily, and they drank almost an entire bottle of wine between them, before Maggie, her eyes drooping from tiredness, said she was going to have a shower and go to bed. Jack said he would clear up and then join her. He loaded the plates and cutlery into the dishwasher, washed up the casserole dish, wiped the work surfaces, then filled his glass with the last of the wine before switching off the lights and going upstairs to his office.

Opening his briefcase, Jack took out his notes on the investigation and listed his meetings for the following day. First thing he had the appointment with the psychiatrist, to discuss Rodney Middleton's previous medical history. He knew he would be given the usual blather about client confidentiality but was hoping that as Middleton was no longer a patient, he might actually be able to glean some information. He had checked, as Clarke had suggested getting a warrant, but had been informed he did not need one as Middleton had signed a statement saying police could access his medical records. This was unusual and made Jack feel as if Middleton might be adept at playing the system. Jack had also arranged an interview with Amanda Dunn, Middleton's girlfriend, at her hostel in Shepherd's Bush. Middleton's lawyer had informed Jack that she had moved out of the flat they had previously shared.

By the time Jack had showered, Maggie was fast asleep in bed. He tried not to wake her as he climbed in beside her. More often than not she slept so soundly that he joked it would take a bomb blast to wake her. He switched off the bedside light and lay down with his back to her. Just as he was dozing off, he heard low murmurs from Penny's bedroom above. He turned over, suspecting that she had probably left her TV on and fallen asleep. He lay on his back, eyes wide open, as the murmur continued, then got up with a sigh of irritation and crept up the stairs to Penny's bedroom, standing outside and listening. It wasn't the television. Penny was having a lengthy conversation with someone on the phone. Jack knew his mother had a mobile; in fact, he had insisted on buying her one in case of an emergency when she was out, but he had never heard or seen her using it. Jack paid the bills, so he knew that she very rarely, if ever, made calls. He heard her laughing, then felt as if he was spying on her, and quickly headed back down to his bedroom.

Jack slid into bed and lay back trying to listen but there was no more murmuring so he assumed she must have ended her call. He thought about what Maggie had said and knew that his mum's forgetfulness was a bit of a concern. However, Maggie had insinuated that Penny might have signs of dementia, in addition to the normal symptoms of old age. Jack felt that Maggie was probably being over-pessimistic as she had been dealing with a number of very elderly patients during the pandemic, many of whom did have dementia.

* * *

The following morning Jack overslept. Maggie was already serving breakfast to Penny and Hannah by the time he had got dressed and shaved. Jack sat at the kitchen table, buttered some toast and poured himself a coffee, whilst Maggie gave him a kiss on the cheek before rushing out.

Penny cleared the breakfast away and prepared Hannah's orange juice and cookies for her mid-morning break. Jack gave Hannah a bite of his toast whilst she sat in her highchair, noticing that it was getting way too small for her. She had also learnt how to lift the tray and slide out on her own.

'I heard you talking on the phone last night?' Jack said tentatively.

Penny closed the dishwasher and began wiping down the work surfaces, whilst Hannah chortled and kicked out happily.

Jack continued: 'I thought it was your TV, and that maybe you had forgotten to turn it off.'

'Oh yes. I was talking to my new friend about the bingo dinner. You know you shouldn't give her that seeded toast. It often gets stuck in her throat because she doesn't chew it properly. Here, let me get her out of there as we should be leaving in a minute.'

Jack finished his coffee and by the time he had put his dirty things into the dishwasher, Penny had got Hannah into her buggy in the hallway.

'Right, we're off. Have a good day, dear.' She leant in through the doorway and waved, and Jack blew a kiss to his daughter. He smiled to see her making the same gesture back to him, replete with kissing noises.

Jack collected his briefcase from the office, got his coat and went into the kitchen to double check that everything was turned off. He noticed that Penny had forgotten to take Hannah's orange juice and biscuits, which were still on the kitchen table in a zip-up food bag with her name printed in cartoon letters on the outside, and decided he would drop it off on his way to interview the psychiatrist.

Ten minutes later, Jack pulled up outside the gates of the nursery school, which were kept locked whilst the children were inside. He rang the bell and waited, putting his mask on. After a few minutes a pretty teenager came out and he was able to pass the bag through the railings to her. 'My mother forgot to bring this, for Hannah Warr.'

'Oh thanks, I'll take it in. I'm Carol, one of the classroom assistants,' she smiled, before walking back into the nursery. He checked his watch, realising that he had not seen Penny returning home before he left, but then told himself that she was probably doing some shopping before she met up with her friends.

By the time he had found a parking space near the psychiatric practice, just off Marylebone High Street, he was fifteen minutes late.

Angus Seymour's name was listed on the brass plaque outside the building. Jack walked into the small reception area. There was a rather elderly woman sitting behind a curved desk who looked up as he approached. She was wearing a mask and Jack quickly pulled his own mask up, as it was hanging from his right ear.

'I have an appointment with Dr Seymour.'

The receptionist put on her glasses and opened the appointment book.

'I am Detective Sergeant Jack Warr, Met Police.'

She pointedly looked at her watch.

'Sorry I'm a bit late . . . traffic.'

'Let me call through to him. He does have a rather a full morning.'

Jack waited patiently as she spoke to Seymour briefly then told Jack that he could go straight up the stairs to the second landing where Mr Seymour's office was behind the first door to his right.

The carpet was well worn, even though the clinic was in quite a prestigious location. Jack knocked on the door, which had Angus Seymour's name printed in gold on the outside.

The first room had three hard-back chairs and was obviously a waiting area, and then there was a door to another room which was ajar. Jack hovered for a moment before he heard an abrupt voice asking him to come in.

Seymour was about the same age as Jack, wearing casual jeans, a checked shirt and a thick tie pulled down to the third button of his shirt.

'Sit down and let's get on with it,' Seymour said briskly. 'I have a patient in fifteen minutes. You can remove your mask.'

Jack lowered his mask and sat down on a chair opposite Seymour. Positioned against a wall was a worn leather couch with stacks of files on the seats, so he doubted it was used in a Freudian capacity. The walls had numerous framed diplomas and a couple of Turner prints. The modern desk had a laptop, telephone and an anglepoise lamp. Seymour sat in a leather swivel chair and flipped open a large diary.

'I would like some information regarding a previous patient of yours by the name of Rodney Middleton,' Jack began. 'As he is no longer a patient, I am hoping you'll be able to assist me without worrying about client confidentiality.'

'Yes, I am aware of the reason you're here, Detective Sergeant,' Seymour replied. 'However, it would be unethical for me to discuss any patient with you, past or present. At my suggestion, Rodney Middleton was transferred to another practitioner; being only seventeen, he came under the umbrella of Child & Adolescent Mental Health Services.'

Jack was feeling frustrated. 'But it would not be unethical if you were just to tell me how you came to see him.'

Seymour flipped back some pages in his diary, then took his time before he sighed.

'He was referred to CAMHS by his GP, and they contacted me to do an assessment. He was with me for six months, having one session every two weeks.'

'Why did you refer him to another practice?'

'I suppose I can tell you that. I had grave concerns regarding his aggressive behaviour and his inappropriate interactions, not only with myself but with my staff. My receptionist in particular.'

'So, you felt you couldn't help him?'

Seymour nodded, then closed his notebook. 'I suggested that perhaps past-life regression, a form of hypnosis, might help. He was refusing to take his medication, was becoming very aggressive and had missed several appointments. He would not accept that he had severe mental health issues, and I was concerned – not only for his wellbeing but for anyone associated with him.'

'Was he schizophrenic?'

'Not to my mind. Though I considered a multiple personality disorder, and decided that he needed treatment. Do you have the details of the clinic I referred him to, as they would obviously be better equipped to discuss his condition?'

'Yes, but his current therapist is on holiday so I'll have to wait a couple of weeks. You said his GP referred him to you?'

'Yes, that is correct, via CAMHS. They contacted me as it was suggested that Rodney needed further psychiatric assessment after he was released. His GP also knew about the fire at his family home.'

Jack was also aware of the incident. 'Was he suspected of setting the blaze?'

'I believe so. He was only sixteen or seventeen. He had an abusive father and his mother was a drug addict. As a teenage boy it was clear that he needed help to recover from the tragedy.'

'Can you tell me more about it?'

Seymour sighed and glanced at his watch.

'I can only tell you that his young siblings died in the blaze. There was an extensive investigation. However, I'm sure this will all be on his record.'

'Well, I've read the case file and the SIO was of the opinion that Rodney could have been involved.'

'I believe that was never proved, but after it happened, he became very troubled and then began to get into trouble with the police.'

Jack made a few notes, and it was obvious that Seymour was eager for the meeting to end.

'So, Rodney was what age when you first met him?'

'Eighteen. Once he became an adult, and no longer under CAMHS, I didn't have any further contact with his doctor or the psychiatrist who took over his treatment. I'm afraid I'll have to finish now, detective, as I have a patient waiting.'

Jack stood up, pleased that Seymour had in fact given him more information than he had expected. Seymour scribbled on a Post-it note and handed it to him.

'That's where Rodney was referred after being here with me. There may be someone else that can see you rather than having to wait.'

Jack put the Post-it into his briefcase and headed for the door. Seymour pushed back his chair and stood up.

'Is he suspected of something serious?'

'Yes. Another violent assault.'

Seymour put his hands in his trouser pockets. 'On a young girl?'

Jack shook his head. He was slightly taken aback when Seymour moved from behind his desk to open the door for him.

'I would certainly be worried about any woman getting close to Middleton, especially very young females and by that, I mean underage girls. There was a lot of press coverage . . . ' He added.

Jack thanked him for his time. As he passed through the small reception area, he saw a young woman was sitting waiting, wearing a felt hat pulled down to hide her face.

Jack smiled at the receptionist and walked towards her. From Seymour's last comment about the press coverage, Jack thought that he had been hinting he should look through old newspaper archives. He would ask Laura to check through the case file on Holmes.

The receptionist gave him a small nod as he stopped in front of her. He spoke quietly.

'Do you recall a previous patient named Rodney Middleton?'

The receptionist pushed her glasses further up her nose and shrugged.

'I most certainly do, but I am obviously not allowed to discuss patients, past or present.'

'He apparently caused some trouble with the staff a number of years ago. If there is anything you could tell me, I would be most grateful.'

She sighed. 'He was a very troubled soul. But his aggressive attitude towards me, and another secretary who works here, was very unpleasant. That is all I am prepared to tell you.'

Jack didn't waste any more time and left to drive to interview Middleton's girlfriend in Hammersmith. On his way there he rang the station to ask Laura if she could search newspaper articles about Rodney Middleton and the house fire from about six years ago. He was certain there would have been a lot of coverage saved in the case file. Laura was a bit tetchy and said she had her own work cut out for her with the new DCI always being in the incident room.

'Well, if you can help, I'd be really grateful,' Jack said. 'And perhaps you could make a note on the incident board that I'll probably be out until after lunch as I'm on my way to West London. I've just left Marylebone and the traffic's a nightmare.'

Laura promised to help if she could.

Jack dug out Middleton's girlfriend's address in Shepherd's Bush. The girl had previously been questioned by uniforms as she had been at Middleton's flat when he was arrested.

After finding a parking space and leaving the Met Police vehicle log book on the dashboard, he approached the large semi-detached house. There was a discreet notice by the front door with the name of the hostel's caretaker and stating that privacy was essential. All callers had to ring a bell as the main front door was kept locked.

Jack waited several minutes before he heard an inner door opening. The main front door was eventually unlocked and opened by a woman wearing navy blue overalls and trainers.

Jack introduced himself and showed his ID before the woman removed the chain lock and stepped back for him to enter, then replaced the chain lock before ushering him into a reception area.

This was dominated by a large table covered with leaflets and self-help guides. On every wall were Social Services posters, details of various self-help programs, and a list of instructions for the residents. The rules were underlined in red: no visitors, no late entry, no food in bedrooms, and all residents had to sign in and out.

The woman introduced herself as Mavis Thornton, explaining that she was the hostel's official caretaker. She made it very clear that it was a Christian charitable foundation, with special care assistants and medical attendance when necessary. Amanda was in the day care unit and she said that she would call her out. If they needed privacy she would see if there was an interview room available.

Jack waited in the reception area for over ten minutes, glancing through the various leaflets and details about local churches and services.

Miss Thornton eventually returned and said that Amanda had gone into the interview room, then asked if he would like a coffee or tea. Jack said he would love a cup of tea, and Miss Thornton showed him the way past a wide staircase into a corridor with various doors leading off it. The interview room was the second door to the right. She slid across an IN USE plaque attached to the door and gestured for him to go in, saying that she would bring his tea shortly.

Jack gave a polite knock before he opened the door and entered the small room. It had two chairs and a table, with children's toys in a wicker basket and a bookshelf with some paperback books by the window.

Amanda was sitting with her back to the door and turned nervously as Jack entered. She was very petite, wearing a floral dress, trainers and a pink cardigan. Her long blonde hair was held back in a braid, with a heavy fringe that almost hid her eyes, but did not disguise the deep rings beneath them.

'Hi, Amanda, I'm DS Jack Warr.'

'Yes . . . ' Her hands were clasped in her lap.

'Thank you for agreeing to talk to me.' Jack pulled out the chair to sit opposite her and opened his notebook. He searched his pockets for a pen and had to rifle through his briefcase before he found one.

'How long have you been here, Amanda? I hope you don't mind me calling you by your Christian name?'

'No.'

'So, when did you come to stay here?'

'Three weeks ago.'

'Has your boyfriend, Rodney Middleton, been in contact with you since you came here?'

'No, visitors aren't allowed, and I don't want to see him again.'

'Can you tell me about the night you called the police?'

Amanda began to chew at her nails, and it was a while before she eventually explained that she had become afraid of Rodney. He had made threats because she had told him she wanted to leave him, and he had got very angry. The landlady had heard him shouting so she had come to the door and Rodney had spoken to her and apologised.

'But as soon as she left, he punched me in the face. When I fell down, he started kicking me. I began screaming so he walked out.'

'So what did you do then?'

'I thought he'd do something bad, so I rang the police. He came back and started punching me again. I ran out of the room and tried to get out of the front door, but he chased after me, and kicked me until I was on the ground. He knocked me against a wall outside, and that was when the police arrived.'

'Was he charged with assault?'

'No, I was on me feet when they came, so I never bothered.'

'You have called the police numerous times in the past, haven't you?'

'Yes.'

'I believe you've suffered abuse from Mr Middleton on four different occasions, and one time you were hospitalised. But you never pressed any charges against him. Why did you stay with him, Amanda?'

Amanda shrugged and continued to chew at her nails.

'You know, Amanda, your evidence will help to get him a lengthy sentence and he is in custody so cannot assault you. Did he threaten you?'

'Yes, he said he'd kill me if I caused him trouble. So I did nothing because I was afraid I would be sent back to my parents. I was a runaway; Rodney took me in and cared for me when I was in a really bad way. My father was abusive, and I met Rodney at Euston Station after I escaped from my parents. I was so scared when I arrived in London. He came up to me at the station. He was really nice and bought me a burger and chips, and then when he found out I had no place to stay he took me in.'

'When was this?'

'Four years ago.'

'How old were you then?'

'Twelve. I'm seventeen now.'

Jack was shocked at her age, and jotted a note to track her details with mispers. 'So, whilst you were living with Rodney, did you work?'

'No, just kept the flat nice and cooked for him.'

'What work was Rodney doing to pay for rent and food?'

'He was on benefits and never had a job. He was mostly at home, watching TV and playing computer games.'

'With you?'

'Yes.'

'Did you have any visitors?'

'No, Social Services came to see him once, but I hid in the bedroom.'

'So no one came from his family?'

'No, his mother died a while back and his father is in prison.'

'Was Rodney kind to you?'

'Yes, mostly, but he would just sometimes have these rages and then he was nasty.'

'Did he ever discuss his past with you?'

'Not really. He didn't like to talk about what had happened. I knew it was something bad as he had nightmares and would scream about being in a fire.'

'Did you know he had two young sisters that died in the fire?'

'No, he never said nothing about them. He had a few photographs but if I asked about who they were he would get angry, so I just left it. It was better to have him calm and being nice than have him get angry. Anyway, he took them and hid them somewhere, so I never saw the photographs again.'

Jack took notes as Amanda spoke with barely any emotion in her voice. He closed his notebook.

'Have you been told about the trial? As a result of you contacting the police, Rodney was arrested for a violent assault on the owner of a grocery store, who recognised him and knew where he lived.'

Amanda shrugged and continued biting her nails. 'Stupid, he done that before, got arrested for it.'

'Did you have a sexual relationship with Rodney?'

For the first time she showed some emotion, cringing back in her chair.

'I'm sorry to have to ask you these personal questions, Amanda, but you were underage when you first met Rodney.'

'Yes, we had sex, but not recently.'

'Did Rodney ever bring back other young girls when you were there?'

She nodded, shifting her weight in the chair.

'Sometimes, but they never stayed for long. He picked them up at the station, like he did with me. They were young girls and he wanted them to stay, but I didn't like it; that was often why we had fights.'

'When you were left alone in the flat, did you ever think of leaving?'

'I couldn't.'

'Why was that?'

'Rodney said I'd be arrested for running away so he locked me in, for safety. I started to complain about it and that's when the beatings started. He would tie me up so I couldn't leave when he wasn't there.'

'How long did this go on for?'

'What?'

'You being tied up and locked in?'

'Oh, it was ages, maybe six months or so the last time. I can't really remember it clearly cos he would give me some of his medication to make me sleep. He blames me for his arrest, but I didn't know that, before he started punching me, he had attacked that poor man in the local grocery shop. Like I just said, he was getting out of control with his violence to me.'

Jack was struggling to take it all in. Amanda remained completely unemotional whilst describing her trauma, while Jack was more and more shocked by her revelations. He decided that he had enough to make out a report and voice his concerns about Amanda's welfare, which would then involve Social Services and a safeguarding team. He thanked her for her time and left the room.

Miss Thornton was at the end of the corridor, and he signalled to her that his meeting was over. She hurried down to the room and fetched Amanda out, putting her arm around her as she ushered her past Jack and back down the corridor towards the day unit.

Jack waited until Miss Thornton reappeared. 'Is Amanda receiving therapy, or is anyone else interviewing her?' he asked.

PURE EVIL | 28

'Well, obviously she was interviewed at length before being brought here. I've not been given details regarding any therapy. She obviously has a low IQ and is subdued. She's as helpful as she can be when working in the kitchens. We're attempting to trace her family as this isn't a long-stay establishment.'

'You know she was a runaway?'

She nodded. 'Yes, we do have that information from Liverpool. She is also illiterate and obviously she may be required to be a witness at his trial. A police officer interviewed her but, as you may have discovered, she's not very forthcoming. We've been told to wait for further instructions; in the meantime, we'll take good care of her, and hope we can trace her family.'

'Thank you for your time. I'll be in touch if I need to talk to Amanda again.'

Jack turned to leave but Miss Thornton put a hand on his arm.

'She is a very troubled soul.'

It was the second time that morning he had heard that expression. The same phrase had been used about Rodney.

CHAPTER TWO

When Jack returned to the station, he completed his report. He wanted to discuss it with Clarke before he filed it, but the DCI wasn't in his office.

Just then Laura appeared, dropping a large envelope down on Jack's desk.

'They're the press cuttings I've printed out for you from the case file.'

'Thanks, Laura, I really appreciate it. You having a good day?'

'No, I'm not. Had to go to Battersea to see if this woman's poodle had been handed in. It's beyond belief how many poor little things are found wandering the streets.'

Jack looked puzzled. 'Why, if I maybe so bold as to ask, is an experienced officer such as you are, being assigned to look for a dog?'

'It's the woman who was found wandering the street outside the station.'

'Had she been handed in, too?' Jack grinned.

'Very funny. She's a witness to a hit and run and was coming in to be questioned. But she seemed disorientated and distressed because her dog had run off when it happened. She couldn't find him, so I was asked to check out Battersea.'

Laura sighed and returned to her desk. Jack picked up his report and went over to Anik, who was using antibacterial wipes to clean up some coffee he'd spilt on his desk.

'Any news about Ridley?' Jack asked.

'Nope, not a dickie bird; consensus is, he's sick. DCI Clarke seems to be pressing for all the ongoing non-serious cases to be put to bed and I'm tracing this punk that knocked an old man off his

bike and pinched his shopping and his wallet. The man's in inten-
sive care; if he doesn't make it, then it could be a murder charge
instead of robbery.'

Jack filed his report, deciding that he would interview Rodney
Middleton's father in Wandsworth prison. He returned to his
desk, but before e-mailing the prison authorities, he opened the
envelope from Laura.

The newspaper coverage was not extensive. The two little girls
had burnt to death in the top-floor bedroom but arson couldn't be
proved. Anthony Middleton, Rodney's father, had suffered extensive burns in an attempt to save his children. He had a long police
record for petty crimes and burglaries and was presently serving a
seven-year sentence for breaking into a corner shop and assaulting the owner. Jack found it strange that Rodney had now been
arrested for a second similar assault at his local grocery store, only
this time with a knife.

Jack e-mailed the appropriate forms to Wandsworth prison,
requesting an interview with Middleton's father. A short while
later he received a return e-mail informing him that the prisoner
had agreed to meet him. He could see him at nine the following
morning. Jack noticed Laura approaching his desk.

'Well, they've traced the poodle, and they want the owner to collect him. So that's me having to schlep over to her place and take
her to Battersea.'

'I'm going to meet Rodney Middleton's father tomorrow. I
might tell him that there's a chance I have to reinvestigate the fire.
That means I've got to read the full case report before I go.'

'What are you looking at me for? I can't read it for you.'

'More's the pity. Do you know where the DCI is? I want a word
with him about the case.'

'No idea. He was here most of the morning. Have you heard
anything about Ridley?'

'Nope, I called a couple of times but just keep getting his voice-mail. You know this investigation I'm on? I went to interview the girlfriend and his psychiatrist and from what I've gathered, I think he's a very twisted bastard. There could be a lot more to his case than we first assumed. CID don't usually handle this type of arrest. Basically, his girlfriend calls in to the local nick as he was abusing her, so they go round. Coincidentally, they're looking for a suspect who had just assaulted a grocery store owner a block away. He comes out, hands over the knife and admits he'd done it so is arrested. Open and shut case.'

Laura yawned.

'Sorry if I am boring you,' Jack said with a frown.

'I'm all ears . . . I'm totally attentive . . . open and shut case, right?'

'What do you know about the DS that was handling the case before it was passed over to me?' Jack asked.

Laura sighed. 'Not a lot. His name was Mike Poulson, big bloke, and I don't quite know all the details. I think he had an aneurism, serious, went up North to his family. What do you want to know about him?'

'Anything, really. I mean, I'd only just taken over the case when Clarke arrived, and I've got a lot of schlepping around to do tomorrow myself to try and find out what's going on.'

'Just make sure whatever you're doing is written up on CRIS. Clarke is a stickler for being made aware where everyone is and specifically what they're doing, via the crime report system. So, what's your concern?'

'Apart from Middleton being aggressive and keeping an under-age runaway locked in his flat, something doesn't sit right. I want to talk to his father to see what he has to say. According to his girlfriend, who was twelve years old when he picked her up at the station . . . twelve! I mean, she was dismissive about any kind of sexual abuse, but admitted to being knocked around by him. She's just turned seventeen and I need to get advice on who should be dealing with her at the hostel.'

'Is Middleton out on bail?'

'No, he's on remand. He's got this over-keen legal aid lawyer who has asked for a pre-trial psychological assessment. I reckon the lawyer's hoping Middleton isn't mentally fit to plead or may offer a manslaughter plea on the grounds of diminished responsibility.'

'Well, I wouldn't get your knickers in a twist; he's in custody, and you know the legal sods will try anything they can.'

'I don't want him released, though. I don't trust him. He bit one of the uniforms, but because he handed over the weapon they never even entered his flat. It's unbelievable! I'm not taking a swipe at that DS Poulson, but they should have searched the flat.'

Laura shrugged and started writing an update on the CRIS system, giving details of her day and proposed work for the morning. Jack remained perched on the corner of his desk flicking through the thick case file, banging his heel against the side of the desk.

'I really need a warrant to search his flat. Clarke's not around to approve one, and even if he was, a magistrate would then need to sign it, which could take ages if the courts are busy . . .'

'You can enter without a warrant if you think someone's life is in danger . . . like another young runaway's.'

'Good thinking, Laura!' Jack smiled.

'What else do you think Middleton's guilty of?'

'I don't know. I just have my suspicions, but I'll wait until I've sat on it for a while. I used to like to have a chat with Ridley about stuff – it's strange not having him here.'

Jack returned to his desk and as he sat pondering his meeting with Amanda, DCI Clarke walked in and went straight into his office, without acknowledging anyone. Jack got up and knocked on his door.

'Excuse me, sir, I just wanted to run something by you . . .'

Clarke nodded at him to enter, and Jack closed the door behind him.

'I had a meeting this morning with Middleton's girlfriend. Something about her concerns me. She said that she was a runaway aged twelve when she first met Middleton. She's been held virtually prisoner by him; he made sure she couldn't leave the flat, by tying her up, drugging her and locking her in. But she was afraid of being returned to her family. When I asked if he had ever brought home any other girls, she said he had. I think he picked them up from Euston, or other London mainline railway stations, and took them back to his flat.'

Clarke nodded, and Jack found his quiet staring unnerving. He wasn't sure if what he had just told him had even registered.

'How long has she been with Middleton?' Clarke said eventually.

'She's seventeen now so that's over four years.'

'And she has been held there for that length of time?'

'Yes, sir.'

'Did she complain about it? Or try to leave him?'

Jack frowned. 'My concern is how many other young girls he took back there. We haven't searched his flat as he was arrested on site.'

'Sergeant, there's no major crime here. He's been arrested for assault at his local grocery store, albeit with a knife. Right now, I don't think we should be attempting to uncover further criminal activities when we have no complaints or witness statements other than for the crime he was arrested for.'

Jack frowned. 'What about the fact that his girlfriend was under-age, beaten, scared he would kill her if she contacted the police?'

Clarke sighed. 'She was interviewed, Jack, by the previous officer handling the case and she refused to make any accusations against Middleton. We also have to take into consideration that in the four years she has been living with him, during which time he was sent away, she had the opportunity to report him.'

Jack was disappointed but continued. 'Yes, sir. The other matter was the possible arson when his family home was set on fire and his two young sisters died. This is one of the reasons I'm keen to talk to his father.'

'How did the meeting with his psychiatrist go?'

'Well, I could only interview Angus Seymour, and he'd referred Middleton to another therapist when Middleton turned eighteen and was no longer eligible for CAMHS. I can't speak to his current psychiatrist as he's on holiday, but according to Seymour, Middleton was prone to violence and it seems he couldn't wait to shift him on to someone else. One of Middleton's parole conditions was that he kept his appointments, but Seymour said he often missed them.'

'If Seymour reported Middleton's breach of parole he should have been returned to prison.'

'I don't think he did.'

'Sounds like he couldn't be bothered. Again, with the time lapse I doubt anything can be done about it now.'

'For my own satisfaction I would really like to search his home,' Jack pressed.

Clarke straightened in his chair. 'I'm sorry, but in my opinion, you don't have reasonable suspicion for a search warrant. Talk to his father if you want, but then I suggest you proceed with some of the more pressing cases we have under review.'

Jack returned to his desk, feeling deflated. He then jotted down his following morning's meetings as requested using CRIS and took off.

He was intending to go straight home, but instead he found himself driving to Middleton's flat. They had already taken a statement from the caretaker, Mrs Delaney, but Jack wanted to have a conversation with her himself.

The semi-detached property was in a side street, close to Shepherd's Bush Market. The building was divided into numerous flats and bedsits, and Middleton and Amanda had occupied the basement flat, which had iron railings and steps leading down to it.

Jack looked down into the area outside their front door. There were a few large rubbish bins on wheels, and several piles of dead leaves. Next to the front door was a small window with bars across it. Jack walked up the three stone steps to the main front door of the building, which had bells for the various tenants. Mrs Delaney was listed as being on the ground floor, so Jack rang her bell and waited. He was about to ring it again when the door opened a few inches.

'Mrs Delaney? I'm DS Jack Warr.' He was wearing his mask, but showing her his ID, which she studied before opening the door wider.

'You gave a statement to one of my officers when Rodney Middleton was arrested. I would like to ask you a few more questions. May I come in?'

Mrs Delaney was almost as wide as she was tall. She was wearing a stained wrap-around apron over a thick woollen jumper and tweed skirt. Her swollen legs were covered by thick, wrinkled stockings and she wore battered old slippers.

'I told them all I knew.'

Mrs Delaney shrugged as she ushered Jack into the hallway, with its ancient lino, in places worn down to the concrete. She walked slowly back to the open door of her flat and gestured for him to follow her into the kitchen.

'I was just getting dinner ready for when my husband gets home.'

The kitchen units were old fashioned, but everything had obviously been cared for. There were gleaming glass-fronted cabinets containing crockery, and a polished gas cooker with a row of pans lined up on the wooden draining board next to a large double sink.

The folding kitchen table had one flap down and was covered with a plastic, floral tablecloth, and two hard-backed chairs tucked underneath.

Jack pulled out one of the chairs and sat down, whilst Mrs Delaney stood at the sink and resumed peeling a pile of potatoes in a bowl of water while twisting to face him.

'I'm making a stew. I do it every week . . . keeps us going for a few days. My mother could make hers last all week!'

'What does your husband do?' Jack asked.

'He's on the Tubes. But he's due for retirement . . . should have finished last year but they was short staffed, and then with the pandemic there's been so many of them off sick or having to take time off.'

Jack took out his notebook. He noticed a photograph on the mantelpiece showing Mrs Delaney with a very tall dark-skinned man. She saw him looking and immediately pointed to the photo with her peeling knife.

'Before you ask, that is my present husband. My ex-husband was a right bugger and left me high and dry with two kids. He's now back in Dublin, with nine children and no teeth!' She laughed loudly and returned to peeling the potatoes.

Jack smiled. 'Can I ask you about Rodney Middleton, who occupied the basement flat?'

'Yes, his rent is paid by his benefits, same as a few of the other tenants. At one time some of the flats were rented out and there was no end of problems with them not paying, always being in arrears. Now the landlord gets the rent paid to them directly from the tenants' benefits.'

'What can you tell me about the young girl that was living with Mr Middleton?'

Mrs Delaney shrugged. 'To be honest, I didn't know she was living down there, but then I saw her a few times. I mean, it's not against his lease, I don't think. I haven't seen the landlord here for years; I believe he owns properties all over London.'

'What's his name?'

Mrs Delaney tossed another peeled potato into a bowl of water. 'William St Edwards. He's got to be getting on in years . . . his lawyers handle everything.'

'When you said that you had only seen Mr Middleton's girlfriend a few times, can you tell me anything about her?'

'There was an incident a few years back. Police came round – she had called them – but nothing came of it. In fact, they came a few times, but Rodney came up to see me and apologised. He said there had been an argument but it was just a misunderstanding.'

'What did you make of Rodney?'

'He was a hard one to make anything of, if you want my honest opinion. He was good about carrying all the bins up to the road, though. The bin men won't go down to the basement now, and there's no way I could do it, and Lionel has a bad chest . . . so I was very grateful that Rodney did it every week. You have to make sure you got the right bin out on the right collection day. In the old days coal used to be tipped into the coal hole at the side of the basement, but that was years ago now. And we no longer have a fire in here as it's against the law.'

'Did you talk to his girlfriend?'

'I was a bit concerned about the coppers being called, so I went down to have a word with her one day after I saw him going out. I mean, I wasn't scared of him. Like I said, he was always pleasant and helpful, but I'm the caretaker here and I need to know what's what and if I should tell the lawyers there had been an altercation.'

'I understand . . . and so you talked to her?'

'Yes, she was a frail little thing, very nervous. She said it was all her fault because Rodney had met another girl, and she didn't think it was right.'

'Did you ever see another girl there?'

'I didn't, but Lionel did. He said he thought she was Jamaican like him, but I never saw her. The only other time I went down to check things out was because there had been a bad smell coming from outside their front door. I thought the drains might have been blocked. Rodney came out and said he had found rats, and he was getting some traps set in the coal hole.'

'And did you find rats?'

Mrs Delaney shrugged her shoulders. 'I wouldn't go into the coal hole, but he told me he got rid of them and washed it down with bleach. From then on, he made sure there were traps set . . . you know, the boxes with poison in them? Some of the tenants put their food waste in the wrong bin . . . that's what attracts the rats.'

'Do you know anything about Rodney's past?'

'No, all I knew was that he was on benefits and didn't seem to work or have a job of any kind. He told me once that he had a family tragedy that had made him ill and unable to work.'

'Did you ever see him acting in an aggressive manner?'

'No, but he's very strong, lifting those bins up and down the basement stairs.'

'Did you ever hear any arguments, or fights, from his flat?'

'No, this is an old house with very thick walls. Like I said, I didn't know anything when the coppers came round those few times. The last time they never even had to go inside his flat. He came out and they took him away in handcuffs. That night was the first time I had heard a ruckus going on because I was at the front door taking in an Amazon delivery. I keep telling them not to ring my bell as I don't use Amazon, but the tenants up top are always getting deliveries and they leave them on the step. Round here that's asking for trouble.'

'This was the night Rodney was arrested?'

'Yes. I heard her screaming, so I went down and banged on the door. Rodney comes out and I asked him what was going on. He told me she had burnt his dinner. He was very sorry about causing a problem and seemed really upset, so I just went back up the steps and before I got to the main front door he was heading out.'

'This same night? What happened then?'

'I've already told the copper exactly what I know. They had a blue light flashing on their police car and two of them was down in the basement. Rodney was outside his door, and they was arresting him, and I was told to get back inside.'

'How long after you had seen him leaving did this happen?'

'About three quarters of an hour, maybe less.'

'Do you know when his girlfriend left?'

'No, I just know the flat is empty now. As his rent is paid directly out of his benefits, I have no reason to go inside.'

'So, who moves the bins now that he's not living there?'

'One of the other tenants agreed to do it, with Lionel.'

'Was Rodney friendly with any of your other tenants?'

'No, I don't think so . . . kept himself very much to himself.'

'But you have access to his flat?'

'Yes, I have the keys for all the flats in case there's an emergency, burst pipes or that kind of thing.'

'In the past, have you ever had any need to go into the basement flat?'

'No, Rodney was a very good tenant, and he didn't like anyone being admitted without his permission.'

Jack was itching to enter the basement flat but knew he would be in trouble without a warrant. He intended to get one, and as Mrs Delaney had keys, the sooner the better.

* * *

On the way home, Jack decided to take a detour and stop off at Ridley's. Jack had stayed there once, the night before his wedding, so he knew exactly where to go. He had been surprised about the dismal flat: the décor was all a dull cream, the furniture mostly G Plan, and the kitchen appeared to have hardly ever been used. He had slept in a cheerless box room with a small single bed.

He had also been moved when Ridley had told him that apart from his elderly mother he had no relatives, and he had also mentioned that should the cancer take over his life he would leave everything he had to Jack for his family. Jack had obviously been touched but then had joked about it; he said even if he was left the flat, it would be a hard one to sell as it hadn't one single redeeming feature. Ridley laughed, explaining that he had at one time intended to smarten the place up, but as always work was his priority.

There weren't any photographs or memorabilia around the flat and Jack had always found it difficult to draw any personal details from Ridley about his past, so it had been a surprise when Ridley, after a few glasses of whisky, appeared at the box room door.

'I was close to getting married a long time ago,' Ridley confided. 'We had been childhood sweethearts, and I was never sure who broke whose heart, but I think it was her who broke mine because I've not had what I would describe as a loving relationship since. I envy you finding Maggie. You're a very lucky man. Get a good night's sleep, Jack. I'll wake you in good time.'

Jack parked the car and headed up the path. He checked down the bells for the different flats. He recalled that Ridley had had no name plate, but he was sure it was on the second floor. Flat 2, however, seemed to belong to a TL Harvey. He rang the bell anyway, and a man answered who was clearly not Ridley. After a brief conversation, Jack dialled Maggie's number.

Maggie answered Jack's call sounding flustered. She was always concerned when he rang her at work, worrying that something had happened to him, but he quickly told her that he just wanted to ask her something.

'Mags, I went to Ridley's flat. You know, I spent the night before our wedding there, but I spoke to this bloke who told me he's bought the flat more than six months ago, and he has no address for Ridley.'

'Surely you can check at the station. They have to have his address.'

'Yeah, I know that, but I don't want anyone tipped off that I'm trying to see him.'

Maggie sighed and was about to tell Jack she had to get back to the ward when she remembered something.

'Listen, Penny got all the addresses for people who wanted wedding photographs sent and, if I remember correctly, Ridley asked for a couple as he was your best man. Penny was going to check with you, but you were in Ireland, so give her a ring and see if she has his new address.'

'OK, will do, sorry to bother you, and I'll see you later.'

'I won't be too late – love you.'

She ended the call before Jack replied and he immediately dialled Penny at home. The phone rang for ages, and he was about to hang up when she answered.

'Warr's residence,' she said using her posh voice.

'Mum, it's me, Jack.'

'Oh, hello, love, I was just running a bath for Hannah. Is everything alright?'

'Yes, everything's fine. I just wanted to ask you if you had Ridley's home address. Mags said you may have sent him some of the wedding photographs.'

'Yes, I did, one outside the registry office and one from the dining room or maybe it was from when you both left. Do you want me to check which photograph he wanted?'

'No, Mum, I just need for you to tell me where you sent them.'

'Didn't he get them?'

'It's the address I want, Mum. Did you make a note of it?'

'Hang on, it's in my notebook.'

Jack sighed impatiently as Penny said she would have to go into her bedroom. He waited and could hear her telling Hannah to go into the bathroom, and it was at least five minutes before she came back on the phone.

'I've got it. It's a Putney address. Is that the one you wanted?'

Jack jotted down the address on his phone as soon as he ended the call, then got back in his car and headed for Putney.

When he got there, he wondered if Penny had given him the correct address. The house was part of a modern, upmarket estate and each identical property had a neat front lawn and an attached garage. All the curtains of Ridley's house were drawn, but there was clearly a light on in the front room. Jack took out his mobile and was about to dial Ridley's mobile number when the front door opened. Ridley stood there wearing a thick turtle-necked sweater, baggy cord trousers and old, worn slippers, along with a woollen hat. He pulled the front door partly closed and walked down the path.

'We can talk in the car,' he said.

Jack unlocked the car and got in. Ridley opened the passenger door and joined him.

'Not many CID officers would drive around in a pea-green contraption like this. I knew it was you as soon as you parked up.'

'I've been worried – ' Jack began, but Ridley cut him off.

'I'm sure you mean well, son, but this situation is serious, I can't discuss anything with you.'

'Are you sick?'

'No, I'm touched at your concern, but I told you months ago I was in complete remission; truth is, past few months I've felt better and fitter than I have for years. I'm sorry, Jack, I have to ask you to leave now.'

Jack persisted. 'I went to your previous address. You never mentioned to me that you'd moved. I've just been trying to find out if you're OK.'

'I don't want to get into a lengthy conversation, Jack, but this was my mother's place. She died a year or so ago and left it to me. I sold the flat; in fact, it went within a week, not only did I get a good price, but the chap bought all the furniture.'

He gave a small shrug of his shoulders and smiled, almost like the old Ridley.

'Remember you said to me when I thought I was on the way out that it'd be a hard sell as it didn't have any redeeming features? Turns out you were wrong.'

'Well, I'm glad about that,' Jack said, beginning to lose his patience, 'but I still don't understand what the hell is going on. I'm relieved you're not sick, but there are things I need to run by you. You put me on the Rodney Middleton case, remember? You said it was low priority with CID but you had an intuition that it shouldn't be. I'm now having major concerns that something is not right but I'm not bloody sure what it is.'

Ridley sighed. 'Cross reference, cross reference – and if you can't go forwards, go back. Answer your own questions, Jack. I can't help you.'

'But what was it that made you suspicious?'

'Look,' Ridley said, 'it just didn't make sense. He's a very intelligent young man, so you can maybe excuse his first assault, but the second appeared to me to have some ulterior motive, that's all.'

Ridley looked back towards his house and reached for the door handle. Jack looked round too and saw it – just a momentary glimpse of a man wearing a dark uniform standing partly hidden by Ridley's front door. Ridley got out of the car and leant back towards Jack.

'I promise you, I will be in contact when I can, but please don't come round to see me again. Give my fondest to Maggie, and to little Hannah. Goodnight, Jack.'

Jack watched Ridley hurry back to his posh little house and saw the dark figure usher him inside before the front door closed.

CHAPTER THREE

Maggie was at home when Jack got back.

'Let's have a takeaway Chinese,' she said. 'Do you want to order, and see if Penny would like to join us?'

'OK, is the number in the book by the phone?'

'Yes, unless you'd prefer to have something else, like a burger or a curry?'

'Chinese sounds good. I'll order us the usual.'

Maggie opened the freezer section of the fridge and took out a 'cook in the bag' chicken for the next evening. She then checked the fridge for vegetables and began making a shopping list of things for Penny to get the next day.

Jack ordered the takeaway and went up to see his mother and daughter.

'Thank you for taking her juice into the nursery today,' Penny said, after declining Jack's offer of a takeaway. 'I left it in the kitchen.'

'That's OK. I met the new girl.'

'Anna is very sweet and all the children love her.'

'I thought she said her name was Carol?'

'Oh yes, that's right. Can you mention to Maggie that I'm going to bingo on Friday, so I won't be here to babysit? But I can get Hannah ready for bed before I leave.'

'Sure, I'll be home early on Friday. Are sure you won't join us?'

'Yes, thank you, I've already eaten with Hannah. You have a nice evening together. Oh, was it the right address for Ridley?'

'Yes. Thanks for that.'

Jack kissed his mother on the cheek, then read a story to Hannah for a while before going downstairs to wait for the food to be delivered. Maggie met him in the hall and said she was going up to say goodnight to Hannah, then have a quick shower before they ate.

Jack got the plates out to warm them, opened a bottle of wine and set the table. He had already drunk a glass before the doorbell rang and the food arrived. Maggie came downstairs in her dressing gown, just as he was opening up all the different cartons and placing them on the table.

'Perfect timing!' he said.

'Is Penny joining us?' Maggie asked.

'Nope, she said she'd already eaten with Hannah. And she wanted us to know that she has her bingo on Friday night. Are you on late shift this week?'

'No, next week. I might be on call this weekend though. We have two nurses off and it's starting to have huge repercussions. We're so tired out, and we've been having Covid cases lined up in corridors whilst we try to find beds. The A&E department is swamped and trying to make people adhere to the rules is very trying. Lots of us are beginning to lose patience.'

Jack nodded sympathetically as he ate, using his chopsticks to shovel the food into his mouth as Maggie jabbed at the noodles with her fork. He poured her a glass of wine, sensing her exhaustion.

'So, how was your day? Did you get to see Ridley?' she asked, taking a large sip.

'Yeah, it was the right place, but I didn't go inside; he saw me parked and came out. He said he was still all clear with his cancer being in full remission, but there is something going on. He wouldn't tell me what and he was on edge.'

'You think he was lying?'

'I don't know . . . I mean, he said he felt fine, but he didn't look it and just wanted me to leave and not to contact him again.'

'No doubt he'll tell you what's going down when he's ready. Maybe you just have to give him some space for a bit. How was it at the station?'

'A few things cropped up. The kid that assaulted the shop assistant has quite a record for previous attacks, but I interviewed his girlfriend. She's in a hostel, told me she had been with him since she was twelve. She was a runaway and he had virtually kept her prisoner.'

'She was only twelve?'

'Yeah, she's seventeen now, but she's very young for her age. I got a message from the carer at the hostel. They traced her parents to Liverpool, but I'm not sure if they're coming down to collect her. Thing is, we found no record of her being a missing person. I'm going to do some leg work tomorrow and get a warrant to search the basement flat where they were living. I think he had other girls there, but when he was arrested no one took a look. It was almost a perfect arrest. He admitted assaulting the guy in the local shop and handed over the knife. I was just brought in to oversee the final investigation and tick all the boxes. But my gut instinct is that something isn't right. I also spoke to the psychiatrist that his GP had referred him to a few years ago, when he had committed a similar offence. His secretary called him a "troubled soul". Apparently there was a fire at his family home and his two sisters burnt to death.'

'Did he do it? Was it arson?'

'Not proved. They had fire investigators examine the scene who concluded it was an electrical fault. I've not seen the coroner's report but reading between the lines there was some suspicion about the fire. Tomorrow I'm going to visit his father in prison.'

'What about his mother?'

'She died of a heroin overdose a few years ago.'

'Gosh, no wonder he's a lost soul!'

Jack emptied the rest of the fried rice onto his plate. 'I would really have liked to talk to Ridley about the case, but he just told me to stay away.'

'Surely there will eventually be some information about why he's been replaced.'

'There was someone at the house. I didn't see who it was, but I think he was in uniform. It was all a bit awkward.'

Maggie had her eyes closed and was falling asleep at the table. Jack pushed his chair gently back, took her in his arms and kissed her. He then helped her up and guided her out of the kitchen, saying he would join her after he had cleared up. She hugged him before slowly making her way up the stairs. Jack gathered all the empty cartons and put them into the waste bin. He then put the plates and cutlery into the dishwasher and wiped the table and the surfaces. He didn't feel like going to bed quite yet, so he poured himself another glass of wine and went up to his office.

He decided he would make a list of what he intended to do the following day, including applying for a warrant. He was also going to do what Ridley had suggested and go back and cross reference everything again. He stopped and listened, as he could hear Penny chatting, just as he had done the previous night. He got up and went onto the landing. He heard her laughing, and then speaking so quietly he couldn't make out what she was saying. He felt guilty as he listened, then he heard her saying goodbye to someone and the call ended.

Maggie was sound asleep when Jack went in, and he crept around so as not to disturb her. He didn't even put the lights on in the bathroom in case it woke her. He eased into bed beside her and gently drew the duvet up around himself as he rested his head back on the pillows. This was becoming their usual routine. Maggie was always so tired when she got home from the hospital and Jack was glad they had Penny. However, he decided that he would get Maggie to sit down and talk about the possibility of her taking some time off soon. She had been on the front line doing crazy hours for a long time, and he admired her for it, but if it was going to damage her health then he felt he needed to say something. They had spent very little quality time together recently, and tonight was the first time they had had a proper conversation in weeks.

By the time Jack woke up the following morning, Maggie was already downstairs and about to leave for work whilst Penny was giving Hannah breakfast in her highchair. Jack hurried down into the hallway still in his pyjamas as Maggie was putting on her coat.

'I didn't wake you, darling . . . you were in a deep coma!' she said, laughing.

'What time is it?'

'Almost eight. I have to get my skates on.' She wrapped her arms around him and kissed him on the lips.

'My God, I had better get showered and out as well. Will you be late tonight?'

'No, I hope not. Have a good day. I love you.'

Jack went into the kitchen. Penny was adding to Maggie's shopping list of the things she needed to get on her way back from nursery. She asked him to get out some shopping bags for her and put them under the carriage of Hannah's pushchair.

'I can easily get everything Maggie wants and wheel it back home.'

'Do you need some cash?' he asked.

She paused. 'Well, I am a bit short.'

Jack had to run back upstairs to get his wallet. He handed Penny a £50 note.

'Thanks,' she smiled. 'I usually use my debit card, but I need a top-up on that if you can organise it for me. They still don't like cash these days.'

'Right, I'll call the bank and sort it out when I get to the station.'

'Thank you, dear. You have a good day.'

Jack hurried back upstairs to shower and get dressed. He was pissed off at himself, as he had wanted to get an early start, and it now looked as if he would have to go straight to Wandsworth prison for his interview with Rodney Middleton's father. He collected all his notes from his home office, stuffing them into his briefcase, and went out to the pea-green car he detested so much.

Laura was working at her desk when Jack rang to say that he would be returning to the station as soon as his meeting was over. He asked if she could do him a favour, or get one of the secretaries to help with a further search into details about the fire that had occurred at Middleton's home.

'I got what I could yesterday, but I suppose I can do some further research,' she said. 'Lucky for you my case has been sorted, so I have some spare time. I should be able to pull up all you need on the Holmes/CRIS system.'

'I also want the names of the officers who reported the incident.'

'It was a few years ago, Jack,' Laura said doubtfully.

'Only six years ago, so you might find them, plus their contact details as well as the names of the officers who worked on Rodney Middleton's first assault charge.'

'Bloody hell, Jack, you don't half push your luck.'

Jack hung up and then made another call on his hands-free system, to the clinic that Angus Seymour had referred Rodney to. A receptionist answered and forwarded his call to Dr Natalie Burrows. By this time Jack was parking in a bay close to Wandsworth prison.

Natalie Burrows was abrupt but listened as Jack requested a meeting with her. She said that she could free a 'window' at twelve that morning, but if that was no good it would have to be the following day. Jack said he would be able to see her at midday and hung up. He finished manoeuvring into a tight parking bay where the vehicles on either side were over their lines. Sometimes the small pea-green car was useful, and he didn't really care if the bumper acquired a few more dents.

As expected, Jack had to go through lengthy security procedures to enter the prison. After completing all the relevant forms and having his ID verified, he left his briefcase and mobile phone with the duty officers and was led to the section used by prisoners for meetings with their legal teams.

It was a small, airless room with a table and two chairs under a high, cobweb-covered window that faced the outside wall. The floor was covered in worn lino and the door had square frosted glass in the top half. Jack sat and waited for over ten minutes before a uniformed officer opened the door and stood back to allow Anthony Middleton to enter.

He was a huge man with heavily muscled arms covered in tattoos from his hands to his shoulders. He was in his late forties with thick black hair and equally thick eyebrows, and his pock-marked face was covered in dark stubble. He had a stubby nose, and his mouth was pursed in a thin-lipped snarl. His only redeeming features were his striking blue eyes.

Jack stood up to introduce himself and shake Middleton's hand, thanking him for agreeing to talk to him. The officer looked at Jack then indicated that he would be outside the door. Middleton sat down.

'I don't know if you are aware that your son was recently arrested?' Jack began.

'I know. My sister wrote to me . . . said someone had told her.'

'I'm part of the investigation, and I just wanted to ask you a few questions.'

'I can't help you . . . I don't speak to him. I've not seen him in years.'

Jack nodded. 'I just need a bit of background from you. I'm sorry if it distresses you but . . .'

Middleton leant forwards. 'I hope they lock the little bastard up . . . ideally in here. I'd like to get my hands on him.'

Jack kept his tone neutral. 'It's about the fire. Can you tell me what happened?'

Middleton leaned back and shook his head. 'I been asked about that, over and over. Karen never got over it. It broke her . . . nearly broke me. She went back on the drugs, and I went and done a few stupid things and ended up in here. Not that there's anything for me on the outside now anyway.'

'Can you talk me through the night it happened?'

He nodded and let out a long sigh. 'I was in the pub. Karen and me had been rowing a lot. She had just come out of rehab, and was stressed out, and the two little ones were playing up a lot. She said she was going to see some friends. I didn't like it, because she had some friends that I didn't approve of, and I was worried she'd start using again. We had a big argument and she flounced out. So I told him, Rodney, to take care of the girls.'

'How old was he?'

'Seventeen. He was working at a local supermarket, stacking shelves. He agreed to stay home that night. He'd been in a bit of trouble, thieving, but he was going to try to get back on track and take some exams. He was quite clever . . . well, he thought he was. I was always at logger-heads with him, and Karen wasn't happy with him either. Kept saying he was messing around with the girls.'

Jack leaned forward. 'What did she mean by that?'

He shrugged. 'Said he was too touchy-feely with them, but I didn't really believe her. They were only five and seven years old. He was good with them, and they liked him playing with them.'

'So, on the night of the fire?'

'I was drinking and had a right skinful. Then someone come into the pub and yells that there's a fire in my street. It was my bloody house, and it was completely ablaze by the time I got there. Fire engines were already dowsing it with hose pipes, but the upstairs windows had smoke billowing out and the flames were blazing downstairs. Rodney come out with a steaming blanket over him. He'd tried to get up the stairs . . . well, that's what they told me. They wouldn't let us get near. I bloody tried . . . but it was burning so fierce. The windows were blowing out and this horrible thick black smoke was everywhere. My two little girls didn't stand a chance.'

Jack remained silent as Middleton bowed his head, twisting his big hands.

'Their bedroom was on the top floor. I never heard a scream or nothing, and by the time they got it under control and tried to get in, there was no hope.'

'How was Rodney behaving?'

'Crying, sobbing . . . they gave him some treatment in the ambulance. They brought the kids out as soon as they could, but you just knew the way they had the blankets wrapped around them . . . covering their heads . . . they were dead.'

'When did Karen find out what had happened?'

'Same night. Someone called her. She came in a taxi. She was screaming and then she collapsed. They took her into the ambulance. She saw Rodney and started kicking him and trying to beat him up. It was all just a terrible scene. She had wanted him to leave the house and that's what we were rowing about. She's not his mother. The bitch that was Rodney's mum ran off, leaving me with him when he was just seven years old. I was told she went back to Jamaica, but I've not heard a word from her since. Karen brought Rodney up, and then we had the two girls.'

'Is Rodney's mother Jamaican?'

'Yes. He found it tough as a kid being mixed race, and he got a lot of abuse at his school. But I always sorted it out for him. I taught him how to take care of himself, took him to a gym for boxing lessons. He was good, skinny but strong.'

Jack took a moment to absorb everything Middleton had told him. He had only seen a blurry photograph of Rodney, so he had no idea about his background. There had been no emotion when Middleton had described the night of the fire, as if he had repeated the story many times. It left Jack with more questions than answers.

Jack noticed the prison officer peering through the window in the door, so Jack thanked Middleton and gestured for the officer to take him back to his cell.

*　*　*

Jack drove from Wandsworth to Natalie Burrows' clinic, not far from Shepherd's Bush and Rodney Middleton's basement flat. He wondered if Seymour had chosen it because of the location, hopeful that Rodney might be more likely to keep his appointments.

The clinic was in a new build, hemmed in between two residential properties just off the high street. Once again Jack had trouble finding a parking space and drove around for a while until he found a single yellow line, then parked leaving his police vehicle logbook on the dashboard in full view.

By the time he had walked to the clinic it was just before midday and he was relieved that he was going to be on time. There was just a small desk with a young girl sitting behind it, using a computer. The clinic looked as if it had been built in the sixties and was definitely in need of refurbishing.

'Excuse me, I have an appointment to see Dr Natalie Burrows. I'm Detective Sergeant Jack Warr.'

The receptionist continued typing before looking up. She then opened a large appointment diary and flicked through the pages. Jack waited patiently before she reached for the phone and pressed two numbers.

'There is a Mr Warr here, for his twelve o'clock.'

She replaced the receiver and pointed to a glass door, telling Jack to go up to the second floor where he would be met and taken through to see Dr Burrows.

A threadbare ivy-green carpet ran up the stairs, turning into a brick red lino on the second floor. It looked very clean and there was a strong smell of disinfectant. The numerous closed doors all had name plates, and Jack stood looking around at the plethora of framed landscape reproductions. He could hear the murmur of voices before a door opened and a woman in a white coat appeared. He was surprised by how young Natalie Burrows was. She had shoulder-length silky hair and wide brown eyes, along with a rather prominent hooked nose.

'Detective Warr?'

Jack nodded and reached for his ID, but Burrows had already turned back to go through the door, gesturing for him to follow.

The small waiting area was painted white and contained four hard-backed chairs and a stack of magazines on a spindle-legged coffee table. Burrows had left her office door open and Jack followed her in. She gestured for him to take a seat. Filing cabinets took up most of the space around the room, and her modern-looking desk had a laptop and phone with files stacked to one side.

Burrows pulled out a comfortable desk chair and sat down, wheeling it close to her desk. Jack undid his jacket button and placed his briefcase down beside him.

'You wanted to talk to me about Rodney Middleton? Obviously, you are aware of patient confidentiality. I am his reserve psychiatrist. By that I mean he was transferred from CAMHS to this clinic to be a patient of Dr Donaldson's, who is currently on holiday. I'm listed as the reserve to see Rodney whilst Dr Donaldson is away, should it be required.'

Burrows opened a file, glancing at the numerous documents before sitting back and folding her arms. She looked at a small watch on her slender wrist before she spoke.

'I assume Angus Seymour suggested you came to see me. If I can answer any questions you have without breaching any confidentiality, then I will obviously do whatever I can to assist you.'

Jack nodded. 'Did Rodney Middleton come to the clinic for regression therapy?'

'Yes, Dr Donaldson is very much an advocate of regression when it seems appropriate.'

'What do you mean by that?'

'If the patient seems to be repressing emotions, regression can be a very valuable means of discovering what may be deeply buried.'

'Did Rodney Middleton benefit from this therapy?'

She pursed her lips and glanced at the file. 'I believe Dr Donaldson found the patient unwilling to participate. Also, according to his appointment book, Rodney persisted in missing his appointments. As we are an NHS clinic this is a huge waste of our over-stretched resources. We always have a lengthy waiting list, and we have to report lack of attendance to a client's probation officers where it is appropriate.'

'Was Rodney here via a probationary parole requirement?'

'Yes, he was. The reason I'm able to tell you that is because it was some time ago, and I believe Dr Donaldson sent in his report, as did Dr Seymour.'

'So, was he mentally ill?'

Natalie began to slowly turn pages in the file in front of her, then frowned, turning back a few pages.

'He was referred to Dr Seymour when he was seventeen, after a family tragedy. According to his GP he was suffering from depression and severe anxiety. He was prescribed medication, but it appears that this was not being taken, and he was therefore heading for a possible nervous breakdown. However, as you can see, this is quite an extensive file. Rodney Middleton was referred for further treatment a few years later, this time via a probation department.'

Jack saw Burrows glance at her watch again. Judging by the thick file there was a lot more information than she was willing to divulge.

'Was there any indication that Rodney was violent, or suffering from multiple personality disorder?'

Burrows hesitated. 'He was certainly angry and prone to aggressive behaviour. I found no suggestion of multiple personality disorder, though, having said that, it was reported that he did have an ability to quickly switch his moods from aggressive to charming. I suggest you might gain more information from the probationary department, as the details must be in his criminal records.'

Jack nodded. 'Was he ever sectioned?'

'Not to my knowledge.'

'Was there any reference to his over-familiarity with young girls?'

Burrows pursed her lips and closed the file. When she pointedly looked at her watch again, Jack leaned forwards.

'I am investigating a serious assault, Dr Burrows. I have discovered that Rodney kept a young twelve-year-old girl virtual prisoner for several years. He was also violent towards her, and his own father has told me that his wife was concerned that Rodney was "touchy-feely" towards his young half-sisters.'

Burrows frowned. 'Are you asking me if Rodney had paedophiliac traits? To my knowledge that has never been diagnosed, either by Dr Donaldson or Dr Seymour.'

'What about your own interaction with him?' Jack pressed.

'I don't think you quite understand my position, Detective Warr. I explained to you I am here as a reserve psychiatrist, to be available should Mr Middleton require an appointment when Dr Donaldson is absent. I have not had any direct interaction with Mr Middleton, but I am privy to his files in case I am required to have an appointment with him.'

'So, you have read his past medical history?'

'Yes, of course. And when you rang, I took the trouble to read over the files again.'

Jack leaned back and reached down for his briefcase. Burrows immediately stood up, eager for him to leave. Instead, he placed the case on his knee, opened it, and took out two pages of notes that he had made the previous evening.

'I am here to try and ascertain Rodney Middleton's state of mind when he attacked a local shopkeeper and used a knife in a threatening manner, causing serious injuries. I am also aware that he beat up his girlfriend before the attack. But I have grave concerns that he may have committed even more serious crimes.'

Jack waved the pages in front of Burrows before placing them back in his briefcase. Burrows chewed at her bottom lip, then sighed.

'I am sorry not to be able to be more helpful. It is unethical of me to have even given you my personal opinion. We have to adhere to a strict code of confidentiality.'

'But he's not your patient,' Jack snapped.

She sat back and flipped open the file again, then wrote something down in her notebook before ripping off the page, folding it and handing it to Jack. She stood up.

'These are the names of the probation officers, should you require more information.'

Jack pocketed the note, knowing he could easily get the names from Middleton's records. He thanked Burrows for her time and left.

By the time Jack returned to the station it was after two o'clock, so he went up to the canteen to grab a sandwich and a coffee. The CID office was half empty, with just a few probationary officers sitting at their desks.

'Where is everyone?' Jack asked.

'Board meeting with the DCI, for an update.'

Jack sighed, knowing he would get a few harsh words from Clarke. He grabbed his notes and went over to join the probation officers. He asked them to get moving on bringing up all of Rodney Middleton's previous records and to track down the fire teams who had handled the blaze at his family home, as well as the probationary records they had on file. He then asked a young female officer if she could contact mispers again in Liverpool, as they still had no confirmation regarding Amanda's time away from home. He told her to go back five years to see if they had any other information on Amanda Dunn, or if there had been any reports of a black girl, possibly Jamaican, who also went missing around the same time.

Jack picked up his coffee, logged on and typed in his report on his recent meetings, including the prison visit to Rodney Middleton's father. He saw, in large letters on the screen, that all members of the team should be in the boardroom at 1.15 p.m. for a progress report.

Jack wandered out and headed to the boardroom. He was just about to enter when the door opened and the team came out in dribs and drabs. He waited until Laura emerged and she immediately rolled her eyes at him.

'You are really in for it; you were supposed to be back here by mid-morning, and no one seemed to know where you were. I covered for you and said I knew you were going to Wandsworth Prison, but . . .'

She stopped as DCI Clarke appeared behind her.

'DS Warr. A few words. Now.'

Jack followed him back into the boardroom and closed the door. 'Sorry to have missed the meeting . . . I got held up at the prison, then had the appointment with Middleton's psychiatrist. I did make a note of my whereabouts and will make out my detailed report straightaway.'

Clarke frowned. 'You seem to be conducting your own investigation, DS Warr. You were allocated to oversee the forthcoming trial which, until my arrival, had simply been an arrest with the suspect pleading guilty at the magistrates' court. So why – after my discussion with you yesterday – are you giving priority to these meetings?'

'I just felt we had not got enough on Middleton's psychiatric background. On a previous occasion he has committed a similar offence and was put on probation due to mental health issues.'

'Yes, and . . .?' There was a deep note of scepticism in Clarke's voice.

'I felt it was important to interview his psychiatrists. In his case, at two different clinics.'

'So, what did you gain from these interviews?'

'Middleton did not attend all his appointments and refused to take his medication. Both National Health clinics and his GP were concerned about his mental state.'

'So, having had these meetings what is your conclusion?'

'I think this young man is very dangerous. If he succeeds in avoiding a custodial sentence yet again, I think he is a great risk. He is prone to violence and appears to prefer very young girls.'

Clarke looked up sharply, frowning. 'There has been no previous reference to this.'

'I know that, sir. But Rodney's father said his son had been told to leave their home as he had been over-familiar with the two little girls. I also interviewed his girlfriend. She has been with him since she was a twelve-year-old runaway, and she inferred that he had picked up other young girls as well. Perhaps I'm being over diligent in my investigation, sir, but to me there are alarm bells – '

Clarke interrupted him, waving his hand. 'Never mind the dramatics, DS Warr. If I understand correctly, your concerns are that Middleton might yet again avoid a custodial sentence due to his medical history.'

'Yes, sir, and that he may well go on to commit murder. In fact, he may have already done so. This is the reason I would like to get a search warrant for his basement flat. From the case file it appears to me that although a uniformed officer did actually do a search of the flat, it was not thorough. They weren't looking for any blood or other weapons as Middleton handed a knife over to them after assaulting the newsagent.'

Clarke nodded then glanced at his watch and gave Jack a long, cold stare.

'Right, I want a detailed report of the interviews you conducted today. I seriously hope you're not embroidering the facts of this case. I will need to consider everything before I give you the green light to continue your investigation. I understand your concerns regarding Amanda Dunn, and I'm confident that the right department is now handling the situation. I also need to know every officer's whereabouts at all times so make sure you and your team's daily duties are recorded on CRIS. That's all for now, sergeant.'

Jack watched him walk out and sat back to finish his cold coffee. He drained the takeaway cup and tossed it into the bin.

He missed Ridley.

CHAPTER FOUR

Jack worked on his reports for most of the afternoon. With Clarke's demand for detailed feedback, the entire team seemed to be glued to their laptops, and the clerical staff were endlessly typing and printing.

Laura had found some more information about the fire at the Middletons' family home, but nothing significant. Jack took a break at 5 p.m. and went up to the canteen, getting another coffee and a ham and cheese toasty. Laura was just leaving when she stopped by his table.

'You heard anything more about Ridley?' she asked.

'No, have you?'

'No, it's very strange, isn't it? I did ask an old mate of mine over at the Yard and she said she hadn't been told anything. He must be ill, don't you think?'

Jack didn't want to get into a conversation about going to visit Ridley, so he just shrugged and continued eating.

'I've just handed in my report. I really hope that tomorrow I can get onto something more interesting. It's strange, isn't it, not much going on but DCI Clarke is so intent on clearing up outstanding stuff that we're all typing our fingers red raw! Good night then.' She laughed, leaving Jack to finish his sandwich.

Any time now the night shift would be coming on duty and Jack wanted to get a bit more work done without interruption. He called home and told Penny that he might be late, and to tell Maggie not to worry about his dinner. She said she would leave some stew and he could just heat it up when he got back. He hung up, realising he'd forgotten to ask about Hannah, and thinking again how fortunate they were to have his mother caring for her.

Jack returned to his desk where stacks of files were waiting for him. The young female detective was just leaving him some notes, then turned to him with a smile.

'Hello, I was just off home. I've made a bit of progress on the girl, Amanda Dunn. She was reported missing about five years ago. But social services said they had contacted her mother and there was no need for any further enquiry. Another poor kid that fell through the cracks. They also said they've been recently contacted by a Mrs Thornton at a hostel in Shepherd's Bush, as Amanda was staying there. Mrs Thornton said they had contacted Amanda's mother, who said she could not afford to come to London as Amanda's father was no longer living with her and she was with another man who had never even met her daughter.'

'Christ! She's still only seventeen years old!' Jack exclaimed.

'I thought it was a bit strange, so I did a bit more checking into the family. Mrs Dunn had another child younger than Amanda, who is now deceased. She had two other children: one had been taken into foster care and the other is still living with her. I got on to Social Services in Liverpool again and it seems the Dunn family have quite a history. William Dunn, Amanda's dad, was charged with domestic abuse five years ago, and Mrs Dunn had a restraining order taken out against him. He subsequently breached the order and was arrested . . .'

Jack held up his hand to slow her down as he jotted down some notes.

'Go on . . .'

The officer leaned across to hand him her typed notes. 'It's all here, sarge. Apparently Dunn was also accused of molesting Amanda, by her mother, but it never went through the court as Mrs Dunn failed to turn up for the hearing. I would say that was around the time Amanda ran away. There was at some point a considerable amount of effort by the police and press to trace

Amanda, but Mrs Dunn didn't report her as missing and was uncooperative. She stated that she knew she would be with relatives. It beggars belief really.'

'Thanks, this is just what I needed. I'm sorry, I don't know your name?'

'Sara. I think Tony, the other officer, is still working on getting the probation reports, as well as details from the fire brigade. So much isn't in the files. Tony said it was hard going getting through to all the different departments, but he should have some contacts for you in the morning.'

She started to walk away, then stopped.

'Oh, there's something else. A few names on a notepad that I think you said the clinic passed on to you?'

'How many names were there?' Jack had not even looked at it.

'Three, but one of them – a Brian Henson – is deceased. I think he was second on the list, but I'm not sure.'

'Well, I guess that's one less to try and track down. Thanks again, Sara.'

'Would you like me to bring you a coffee?'

'That would be greatly appreciated – white with two sugars please.'

Jack returned to sifting through the files and copies of more newspaper articles about the fire. One article had photographs of the little girls and one of Karen, their mother. She was very attractive with long blonde hair and was quoted as saying she was 'beyond despair at losing her two little angels and did not know how she would live without them.' There was a small news item with the headline saying Mother of tragic children dies, with the same photograph of Karen. She had died from a heroin overdose ten months after the fire.

He closed the file as Sara returned with his coffee and a KitKat. Jack said it was just what he needed and thanked her again. She hovered for a moment, then said she would leave him to get on with his work.

Jack continued working on his report and did not finish until after 11 p.m. By the time he got home he felt drained and couldn't be bothered to heat up the stew that had been left on the stove. Instead, he got himself a tumbler of whisky and went up to his office.

He looked into the bedroom to see Maggie fast asleep, then continued up the stairs. All was silent, and Penny and Hannah were also sleeping so he moved carefully in order not to disturb them.

He sat at his desk sipping his drink. As tired as he was, he started making more notes for himself. He wanted to check on Amanda Dunn. If her mother seemed not to even want to travel to London, he was concerned about what could happen to her. Would she return to the basement flat? He opened his briefcase and started removing some of the files he had not had time to look over. He was annoyed that they did not include any police reports of Rodney Middleton's previous arrests, but then he found copies of Anthony Middleton's criminal records. He had moved from petty crime to house burglaries, and then there were charges of assault and battery connected to a car theft ring that he had been involved with. He was sentenced to three years. All his criminal activities had resulted in short-term prison sentences, until the last, when he received ten years for armed robbery. That was four years ago.

Jack sighed. The robbery had occurred after the fire, and after the death of his wife Karen. He recalled Anthony saying that there was nothing on the outside for him. And he certainly had no feelings for his son, Rodney.

Jack was about to call it quits for the night when his mobile rang. He made a frantic search for it as he didn't want to wake anyone up, then found it in his jacket pocket. It was Ridley.

'I hope this isn't too late?'

'No, sir, I was just doing some research.'

'I need to talk to you.'

'Do you want to come over?'

'No. Can you meet me tomorrow? Turk's river cruises, just by John Lewis car park entrance. It's closed, but there's a slip road, I'll be outside on their dock, at 7 a.m.'

'Yes, of course. I'll be there.'

'No word to anyone, Jack. It's important and I'm depending on you. Good night.'

Jack leaned back in his chair, puzzled by the call but at the same time pleased that Ridley had at least made contact. He physically jumped when Maggie walked in.

'I heard your phone going . . . it woke me up. Is everything alright?'

'I'm sorry, darling. I was in here working and I should have turned it off.'

'Do you want a hot drink? I think I might make myself one as I'll need to take a sleeping tablet to get back to sleep now.'

'Why don't you go back to bed. I'll bring you up a Horlicks. I might have one myself.'

She hunched her shoulders, smiling. 'Sounds good to me . . . and maybe a biscuit?'

Jack turned off his laptop as she went back into the bedroom. By the time he had heated the milk, searched the cupboard for the Horlicks and found the biscuit tin, it was midnight, and he was suddenly tired out. Maggie was sitting up in bed with a shawl wrapped around her shoulders. She reached out for the tray with both hands.

'Oh, I need this. Soon as I wake up, I can never go back to sleep because I start thinking about everything I need to be doing. I'll have to go to the ATM tomorrow as I had to give Penny cash for the grocery shop.'

'I'll just brush my teeth,' Jack said, watching her place her hot drink on the bedside table.

'I already paid Mum yesterday morning. I gave her fifty quid. I meant to transfer some more money into her bank account, but I had a long day. I'll do it tomorrow.'

Maggie sipped her drink, frowning. 'I gave her forty pounds this morning before I left, and she shouldn't need her bank account topping up until the end of the month. She has her pension, and obviously doesn't pay rent or any of the bills.'

'We would have to cough up a lot more if we hired a live-in nanny to take care of Hannah like Mum does.'

'That's not my point, Jack. She's obviously worth her weight in gold but I'm just a bit concerned about what she's spending all her money on.'

'Bingo!' Jack grinned.

'Oh, be serious! And she doesn't pay for her mobile, you do. The allowance we pay her is really just for extras, as everything else is covered. I know it doesn't amount to that much, but remember, Penny refused to accept any money from us because she said she had her pension and some money from your dad, but we insisted . . . are you listening?'

'Sorry, I was nodding off. I'll have a chat with her in the morning.'

'I think you should. Not that I mind paying her whatever she needs. She is a life-safer for me.'

Maggie took a sleeping pill and drained her Horlicks, placing the empty mug on her bedside table. She just managed to retrieve Jack's half full mug before it toppled onto the duvet as he was fast asleep. She had to reach over him to turn his bedside light off, and then her own, as she snuggled down beside him.

These long days at the hospital were not good for their love life. She started counting how many nights it was since they had actually had sex, and it quickly became like counting sheep because she was soon fast asleep.

CHAPTER FIVE

Maggie was woken by Jack's mobile phone alarm, which he had set for 6 a.m. He almost fell out of bed trying to cancel the alarm, tripping over the tray from the previous night's hot drinks and falling backwards onto the bed.

'My God! What are you doing, Jack?' Maggie sat bolt upright.

'Sorry, I've got a meeting at seven and I really need to get going!'

By the time he had taken a shower and shaved, Maggie was down in the kitchen cooking breakfast. Jack checked his watch as he went downstairs and was pulling on his leather jacket as he went into the kitchen.

'I have to go, I'm sorry. First, I wake you last night, then I fall on top of you this morning! Can you put a coffee in the Thermos for me so that I can have it on the way to work?'

'Where on earth are you going at this hour? It's only six thirty?'

Jack grabbed a piece of toast from the toaster and began to lather butter over it. Maggie poured some freshly made coffee into the flask that was always left on the side of the draining board as he rarely remembered to take it with him.

'It's top secret . . . I promised I wouldn't mention it to anyone, but . . .'

Maggie didn't seem to be listening. 'I was thinking last night . . . I was counting how many nights it's been since we last had sex . . .' Maggie was seductively licking the spoon from the pot of jam.

Jack grinned. 'You just give me the nod tonight . . . I promise you we'll make up for lost time!'

Jack finished his slice of toast, gave her a quick kiss, then dashed upstairs to grab his briefcase and mobile phone. Penny was just carrying Hannah out of her bedroom.

'I love you both, but I have to get going otherwise I'm going to be late . . .'

By the time Jack was back in the hall, Maggie was standing, hand on her hip, holding up the flask. He gave her a crushing hug before he opened the front door.

'I'll call you later . . . and I won't forget my promise about tonight!' Jack closed the front door behind him and ran towards his pea-green monstrosity, then stopped abruptly, realising he had forgotten his car keys. When he turned to go back, Maggie was at the front door in her dressing gown, dangling them from her index finger. He ran back towards her as she tossed them for him to catch, smiling and shaking her head.

'You're always so hopeless early in the morning, Jack. It had better be something important, or are you having an affair with someone on night duty?'

Jack unlocked the driver's door and tossed his briefcase onto the passenger seat, dropping the flask onto the driveway. He just managed to stop it from rolling under the car and was about to respond, but she had already gone back into the house and closed the front door.

Maggie hurried into the kitchen as Penny was heading down the stairs with Hannah.

'Breakfast is ready. Scrambled eggs and crispy bacon for you, Penny, and for Hannah I was going to make some eggy bread.'

'Jack was in a big hurry this morning. I wanted to remind him about my bingo tonight,' Penny said.

Maggie said she would remind him and served out breakfast whilst Penny settled Hannah in her highchair.

'Hopefully there won't be any emergencies, so I should be home by then as well.'

'I have some shopping to do, so I won't have time to make dinner for you both.'

'Don't worry. We can always order in a takeaway. Right, I'm going up to have a soak in preparation for the panic that will no doubt greet me as soon as I walk into work.'

Maggie hesitated, wondering if she should mention the money but decided against it.

By the time Maggie had bathed and dressed for work, Penny had cleaned the kitchen and was getting Hannah changed for nursery. Maggie was able to spend a few minutes with Hannah, who was fighting against wearing a pair of woolly tights and rolling around on her bed. Maggie gave her a goodbye cuddle and Hannah tried to make her stay.

'Mummy no go . . . mummy stay.'

'Mummy will be here later, to make you a special yoghurt and raspberries. Be a good girl for your nana . . . bye, bye.'

Maggie hurried out before Hannah could make any more fuss. She often felt a tinge of guilt that she was so dependent on Penny and wasn't able to spend as much time as she should with Hannah. But the truth was they needed both of their wages to run the house and pay the mortgage. She just hoped she could take some of her long overdue time off soon.

* * *

Jack left the pea-green Micra in the John Lewis car park and walked down the small slip road towards the Turk's boat house. He reached the waterfront and looked out for Ridley. It was just after seven, so he continued walking past the closed ticket office.

Ridley seemed to appear from nowhere.

'Morning. I've got a flask of hot coffee,' Jack said affably.

'Let's just walk for a while,' Ridley said. 'There's a bench further along . . . behind the fences.'

They walked in silence until they reached the bench, which was in shadow and partly hidden from the road above them. Ridley was wearing a heavy grey trench coat, old cord trousers and crepe sole boots with a woollen hat pulled down low. Jack undid the flask and poured a coffee into the Thermos cup as Ridley removed his fur-lined leather gloves. He took a sip and grimaced.

'My God, this is sweet!'

'Yeah, sorry about that, it's my sweet tooth. I should have remembered you don't take sugar in your coffee.'

Ridley nodded but continued to sip the hot coffee. Jack watched three swans glide past, along with a couple of rowers.

Jack nodded towards them. 'They're shifting fast.'

Ridley finished his coffee and handed the cup back to Jack as he pulled on his gloves. He sighed, then turned to look at him.

'Trying to think where to begin, but thanks for coming to meet me.'

'Well, as you always advise, why not start at the beginning?'

Ridley nodded. 'OK. This isn't easy, though. You know after the cancer diagnosis when I got the all-clear and started looking after myself . . . I'd lost weight and began eating better and was going to the gym. Anyway, to cut to the chase, a while back I contacted a dating agency. I obviously didn't use my own name, but it was a reputable organisation with solid recommendations, aiming at the middle-age bracket. I had a couple of dates with very nice women, but they were a few years older than their photographs.' He gave a soft, mirthless laugh.

'Not that I'm a big catch! They were very pleasant, but it was only a glass of wine in a pub. Then, a few months ago, I met Sandra.'

Jack had filled the same Thermos cup to drink his own coffee, try-ing not to reveal that he was taken aback. He could hardly believe what Ridley was telling him.

'She was in her mid-forties, a very attractive blonde, well dressed and charming. We had a couple of drinks and then a couple of dinners.

It was all very straightforward, and like I said, she was very attractive and intelligent. As we got to know each other a bit more, I told her I was with the Met. Sandra found it amusing, especially the fact that I was using a different name. She was single, had never been married but had been in a long-term relationship that had ended badly. She said she was a junior accountant in a top-level accountancy company. I never checked it out, and by then we had become intimate and she was visiting me at home.'

Jack nodded and finished his coffee, still hardly able to believe that this was the Ridley he had known for so long, though his private life had always been a mystery.

'Four weeks ago, I had a date with Sandra. We were due to meet in a pub in Farnham. I had never been to it before – she had chosen it because it had a good restaurant. I arrived at about eight as agreed, but she didn't show. I called her mobile but got no answer. I had a couple of drinks at the bar whilst I waited, but as I was driving, I didn't have any more.'

Ridley pulled at the fingers of his gloves, then leant forwards, and almost whispered.

'That's all I remember. I have no recollection of anything after that, of how I got home, but I had one hell of a headache when I woke up the next morning. My car was missing, so I had to have been brought home. I called the pub and they said that my car wasn't there. It was all very confusing. I called Sandra's mobile several times, then I called the company she said she worked for. They told me that there was nobody of that name working there. I was getting ready to go into work and was going to report that my car had been stolen when I had a visit from Essex CID.'

Jack could feel the tension as Ridley drew in a deep breath.

'No easy way to explain the next bit. My car was found abandoned, and Sandra's body was in the boot. She had been strangled. Obviously the shit hit the fan, and I was interviewed by the Professional

Standards Directorate. They took my mobile and I was immediately suspended and given leave of absence. The mobile phone she used was a burner, and there was no known address for her. And, as I said, she had lied about her employment.'

'Bloody hell!' Jack didn't try to disguise his shock.

'I can only assume I was drugged at the pub, but I have no idea by whom. I also have to assume that Sandra set me up, or someone else used her to get to me, and then killed her. They have been try-ing to discover her real identity, and meanwhile I am the prime suspect; not only is my career about to go down the toilet, but I could be charged with murder.'

Jack swallowed, not knowing what to say.

'I am not allowed access to any of my files, or to even enter the station. I am virtually under house arrest, and they have been searching my home for weeks. But as far as finding out who she really was and who might have killed her, they've got nowhere.'

He sighed and plucked at the fingers of his gloves. 'I'm not that impressed with them, to be honest. They're very slow – my car has been with their forensic team since her body was found in it, for instance. We have to assume it must be connected to something in my past, but I can't think what it could be or who would want to do this to me.'

He opened his coat, taking out a plastic bag. 'I had a short time to gather as much evidence about the whole nightmare before they took everything. I've also made some notes. The main problem will be the fact that the Essex team will be monitoring everything, so you cannot on any account use the computers at the station, as they'll uncover the link to you. You need to use a new laptop and burner phone that can't be traced. There is one person I trust that can help you, and his contact details are in here, but I obviously can't reach out to him; just getting out of the house with this bag was difficult enough.'

Ridley hesitated before passing the bag to Jack; then Jack took it from him. 'I really don't want you taking any risks, so be careful. The last thing I want is for you to jeopardise your career.'

Jack nodded. 'Just tell me what you want me to do.'

Ridley bowed his head, his voice barely audible. 'Help me, Jack.'

CHAPTER SIX

Jack did not get to the station until after eleven that morning. He was still in a state of complete shock about what Ridley had told him, but he had given his word that he would not repeat anything to anyone. It was a heavy burden, but Jack was determined to do whatever he could. He just had to determine how he could do that, and where to start.

Laura had left a note on his desk to remind him that Penny was out that evening and he was supposed to look after Hannah. Maggie had also called to tell him that she might be late home that night. He had just sat down at his desk when Clarke appeared at his office door signalling that he wanted a word. Jack hurried into his office, expecting to be reprimanded for being late into the station.

'We are not psychic, Sergeant Warr; if it's not in the CRIS, no one knows where you are. In future, please make sure the teams are able to track you down if they need to. Now, I have been informed today that Rodney Middleton's trial has been put back several weeks due to the backlog of cases. His lawyer has been on to me to ask for a bail hearing. I denied the request, this being a second violent attack, and because of concerns for his state of mind, but he didn't like it and will no doubt be pestering me again. I'm aware you've been putting our probationary officers to good use and I want you to continue to do so. The sooner we get this cleared up, the better. I've given a lot of thought to your request for a search warrant for Middleton's flat, but we still have no evidence of any crime other than the one he was arrested for. I need something solid, Jack, and I'll need it sharpish.'

'Yes, sir.'

Jack returned to his desk, where Sara was waiting to talk to him.

'You said to focus on young runaways who may have travelled to London from the North.'

'Yes, you got anything?'

Sara passed him a neatly typed report.

'I ran a mispers search through the National Crime Agency Missing Persons Unit. There is one that's a strong possible: Jamail Brown, aged fourteen. She disappeared from her home in the Wirral over eighteen months ago. There has been no sighting of her since, and I'm waiting on photographs and further details. The other girl is from Solihull: Diandra Fuller, aged fifteen. She was in foster care but disappeared a year ago. She seemed to have been in trouble with the police and was sent to a young offender institute. Again, I'm waiting to get more details and a photograph sent through.'

Jack nodded as he skimmed through the report. 'OK, thanks, Sara. Can you ask the others to see me in the boardroom in fifteen minutes? I need to know how they're doing on the probation lists, and everything else. I'll be assigning some new work that I need done.'

'Yes, sir. Shall I bring you a coffee in there?'

'That would be greatly appreciated, thank you.'

Jack opened his briefcase, took out the large plastic bag Ridley had given him and put it in the top drawer of his desk, which he then locked. Next, he checked his notes on the Middleton case and sorted out what leg work he would assign to the probationary officers so that he would have more time to work on the Ridley situation.

Anik looked over at Jack as he rocked back in his chair.

'You seem to be monopolising all the young probationers, Jack. You know there's a suspicious death that's just been called in, and . . .'

Jack collected his papers and pushed back his chair.

'Anik, do I have to use this ruddy CRIS to say I'm going into the boardroom?' he asked, paying no attention to what Anik had been saying.

'You do. DCI Clarke likes to know exactly where everyone is.'

'Shit. It was so easy just marking it up on the bloody board.' Jack returned to his desk and logged in to show that he was due in the boardroom at 3.30 p.m.

'You heard any update on Ridley?' Anik asked as Jack headed to the boardroom.

'No. See you later.'

Jack was in the boardroom sifting through his notes when Sara carried in a tray of coffee and sandwiches. She handed the coffee around and put the plate and some paper napkins in the centre of the table, so they could be easily reached if anyone wanted one.

'OK, let's start by seeing what you've got for me.' Jack reached for a sandwich. 'Who's on the fire brigade situation?'

'I am, sarge.'

Jack nodded, speaking with his mouth full.

'You are Hendricks . . . James, right?'

The officer nodded. He looked very young, with a short haircut and ruddy cheeks. He had a wide gap between his front teeth.

'I tracked down one of the firefighters at the scene, Brian Hookam, and he said that if I wanted further information, I needed to talk to a senior fire investigating officer called Vernon Glover, who retired a year ago.'

James handed over his typed report, as Jack ate another sandwich. 'So, did you talk to Hookam?'

'Yes. He was certain that they had found no evidence of accelerants being used but recalled that the fire started in the young girls' bedroom due to something being placed over the Calor gas heater. That's when he suggested contacting Mr Glover who was a senior firefighter at the time.'

'Have you traced Glover?'

'Yes, but I haven't had the opportunity to talk to him yet.'

'OK, anything else from Mr Hookam?'

James had his notebook open and thumbed through pages. 'He said that as far as he could recall, Mr Middleton senior was drunk and hysterical. He had arrived when the blaze was already out of control, and by then the firefighters were using the pumps and hoses. He had tried to go inside, but they had to hold him back; that's when his wife turned up in a taxi – '

Jack held up his hand to interrupt. 'Did Hookam say anything about Rodney Middleton?'

'He said that, as far as he remembered, Rodney Middleton was treated in an ambulance after he had attempted to get into the house.'

'Did he remember if Rodney was inside or outside when the firefighters got there?'

'I did ask, but he couldn't remember. He said that the boy's clothes were on fire, and he was in a very bad state.'

'OK, fine. Right, next up, who's on the criminal records of Rodney Middleton?'

'I am, sarge.'

'You are DC Lions?'

'No, sir, I'm Leon Elba. Lions was assigned to something with traffic, so I took over. I have here the file of information that I've managed to get so far.'

Leon was dark skinned, with delicate features and cropped black hair.

Leon passed the file to Jack, who began reading through it.

'As you can see, sarge, the last serious offence for assault was four years ago when he was twenty-one years old, and is similar to his latest assault for which he is presently awaiting trial. He served six months in a young offender institution and there are a lot of references to his medical issues, plus four other offences for petty crimes and threatening behaviour.'

Jack closed the file.

'He certainly seems to have been a regular visitor to the station. Who's been tracking down his probation officers?'

Sara put up her hand. 'I have. But before I go through that, I now have photographs of the two missing girls. I also have five more girls of similar age, and from different parts of the country.'

Sara passed the photographs to Jack. She had made notes on each of the photographs, with the girl's name, age, location and dates from the mispers reports.

Jack nodded. 'Good. I want to show these to Amanda to see if she recognises any of them. We do have extra time now due to Rodney's trial date being put back. So, next, what about the probation reports?'

'Well, it's quite hard to get to the actual officer, as there have been so many dealing with Middleton. I had to pull a few strings . . . my brother is a probation officer, so he helped me . . . well, as much as he legally could do.'

Sara passed another file to Jack. He took out the typed documents and looked at the first page.

'What's this?'

'There was a report in 2017 regarding someone claiming to be a Metropolitan Police officer. He called the NHS 111 service and stated that he believed Rodney Middleton was very dangerous. He wanted to give a warning about his behaviour but said he was unable to offer help himself as he was from a different district, and it would be an abuse of power.'

Jack continued reading.

'So, this unknown officer was then put through to a clinician who suggested a welfare check on Middleton, but it's not clear whether this took place? I don't effing believe it!' Jack exclaimed angrily.

Sara nodded. 'Yes, it appeared that there was no immediate threat to life, so nothing was done.'

'So, we don't know if this was followed through or not. And next we have an arrest for breaching a public protection notice . . . and his mental state was assessed by a community psychiatric nurse?'

'Yes, sir. And in her report, she wrote that she had observed Middleton staring at young children in a playground, and then discovered him staring at her own children. It was reported that another assessment should take place to decide whether or not he should be detained, and warned that he could be a risk to other children.'

Jack shook his head as he continued to read. 'That evening he was detained and interviewed by two doctors and a mental health practitioner. They were unable to contact the nurse who had submitted the report, and as there had been no signs of Middleton acting strangely while in custody, they released him. Middleton had told them that his two young sisters had died in a fire and he was still suffering from the tragedy. They said he should contact his local GP and passed their details to a probation officer who had been attached to Middleton when he had committed his first assault.'

Sara nodded, then gestured to the file. 'So that's where we have the probationary reports starting. His local GP referred him for psychiatric help through CAMHS, and he was given an appointment with a Dr Angus Seymour. The clinic was to report to his probation officer, a Linda Harvey, and I have her contact details for you . . .'

There was a knock on the door and Jack turned with a look of irritation as Laura walked in.

'Sorry to interrupt, but I did leave a message for you, Jack. Maggie called this morning to remind you about getting home on time. She just called again to make sure you got the message, as she's held up at the hospital. You left your mobile on your desk.'

Jack jumped up. He had completely forgotten Penny was out that evening and he was supposed to look after Hannah.

'Thank you, Laura. I'll have to leave in a few minutes.'

Jack closed the file. 'I'll take this home, Sara, and finish reading it this evening. Thank you all. I want you to check out if Amanda Dunn is still at the hostel, and if not find out where she is. I'll also want to have a meeting with Mr Glover, and see if you can check out the anonymous officer who contacted 111 – as well as the woman who reported seeing Middleton looking at her children. From what I can see, he doesn't seem to stray far from his original home, the one that caught fire. The basement flat is only a few miles away, and . . .'

Jack checked his watch. He needed to be home before Penny left so he gathered up all the files and put them into his briefcase. He hurried into the incident room to collect the information Ridley had passed him, as well as his mobile phone. Unlocking his desk drawer, he took out the plastic bag and shoved it into his bulging briefcase.

He was just heading out when Anik stopped him and asked if he could work on Saturday as he had a friend arriving to stay. Jack snapped that he had not had a weekend off for weeks and it wasn't convenient. He was further irritated when Anik said he had run it by the DCI, and it was on the schedule.

'Fine, I'll come in, but what about Laura?'

'She's off this weekend. It's all on the duty roster.'

Jack was in too much of a hurry to get home so just shrugged and walked out. But he was pissed off, as he had wanted the weekend to focus on Ridley's situation. Somehow he had to help him prove his innocence, but right now, he didn't even know where to start.

CHAPTER SEVEN

Thankfully Jack arrived home in good time. Penny was waiting for him, about to take a bath and get ready for her evening out.

Jack dumped his briefcase in the hall, threw off his leather coat and went straight up to see Hannah. She was in the play area of her bedroom, with a small TV on and so many toys littered around her that it was like an obstacle course just to go and pick her up. He played with her for a while, then when Penny called out that it was free, Jack carried Hannah into the bathroom.

Jack ran the bath as he undressed Hannah. He tested the water before putting her into the bath, piled high with foam as he had overdone the bubble bath. Hannah was quickly covered in bubbles, splashing around and having a wonderful time. He washed her hair, which caused a few tears as she got soap in her eyes. But he was able to calm her down as he used one of the big bath towels to wrap her up and take her back to her bedroom. He rubbed her hair dry, covered her in talcum powder, and found some fresh pyjamas, whilst Hannah wriggled and chattered away. Penny popped her head round the door to let him know that she was leaving. Hannah began screeching that she wanted her nana, and Jack had to promise that he would read three bedtime stories after making a special eggy bread supper.

Maggie arrived home about an hour later. She hurried into the kitchen as she could hear Hannah shouting. Jack had his shirt sleeves rolled up and had managed to get talcum powder in his hair. He was now attempting to whisk another batch of egg and milk together, as he had burnt the eggy bread on his first attempt.

Maggie kissed Hannah, who was trying to escape from her high-chair, and gave Jack some tips on how to make the perfect eggy bread. 'She had it for breakfast, so I'll see if we have some nice cookies or maybe add honey.'

Jack eventually got the hang of it and cut the eggy bread into slices, poured some honey over it, and put it on Hannah's high-chair tray. She ate eagerly, and Maggie left them to it while she had a quick shower. She had been on her feet all day, and was tired out. By the time she came down, Hannah had eaten all of her eggy bread, had downed a glass of milk and was now ready for her promised three stories.

Maggie ordered a Chinese takeaway, set the table and opened a bottle of wine. She went to the bottom of the stairs and listened to Jack reading aloud from Hannah's favourite book, *The Very Hungry Caterpillar*, smiling as she heard him do all the funny voices, then she almost laughed out loud when she heard her daughter demanding, 'Again, again . . .' Jack began to read the story again and Maggie went and poured herself a glass of wine. She fetched her handbag so that she could be ready to pay for the takeaway delivery, but in the end she couldn't resist going back upstairs.

Standing outside the bedroom, she peeked through the partially open door. Hannah saw her and began shouting 'Mama!'

Maggie went in and kissed and cuddled her daughter, then told Hannah that daddy and mummy had to go downstairs to have their dinner. Hannah was having none of it and demanded that Maggie read her a story. Jack told her firmly that she had already had her promised three stories, and it was time for her to go to sleep.

The doorbell rang and Maggie told Jack that her purse was in her bag on the table in the hall. He went downstairs and paid the delivery boy, then went into the kitchen to lay out all of the cartons. By the time he had warmed the plates, Maggie was back.

'She's asleep,' she said with a smile. 'I was worried you wouldn't get home in time. You weren't answering your mobile this morning, so I spoke to Laura.'

'I know, I'm sorry. I switched my mobile off for my meeting this morning and forgot to turn it back on. Then I was in the board-room with the team, and I left it on my desk.'

Maggie sat down at the table and began spooning out noodles and rice onto her plate, then beef, chicken and some crispy duck.

'I think I over-ordered!' she said, pouring herself a glass of wine.

'Well, I'm starving. It's been a busy day. Thank goodness Laura reminded me about getting home this evening.'

'I thought you might be trying to avoid me or had run off with a young beauty,' Maggie said with a pout.

'Ha! Chance would be a fine thing! I've been up to my ears in this Rodney Middleton case. To be honest, I'm beginning to think I'm just creating more work for myself. If I'd just taken it through to the trial, it would be over and done with.'

Maggie watched Jack eat huge mouthfuls of noodles, whilst talking at the same time.

'Well, I had a heavy-duty day, too,' she said. 'We are totally inundated at the moment, and really short of beds. There are patients being left on trolleys in the corridors while we try and find room for them, and we're short staffed as usual, down three nurses and two doctors. We're all completely run off our feet.'

Jack nodded sympathetically.

'This new DCI is a real pain, too. He's obsessed with every little thing being reported back to him, and we have to use this bloody CRIS system so he can monitor where we are at all times. I mean, with Ridley we just used to mark it up on the noticeboard. Anyway, just as I was leaving, I was told that I have to be in tomorrow, having not had a weekend off for weeks.'

'Same for me . . .' Maggie poured herself another glass of wine then topped up Jack's glass.

Jack took a mouthful then continued. 'What if I'm misjudging him?'

'You haven't actually told me all that much about it. We're like ships passing in the night at the moment. What's he like?'

'He's about six feet two, very trim; he obviously works out. He was one of the first black officers to be fast-tracked. He has impressive credentials.'

'No, not your new boss! The boy who's been arrested.'

Jack sighed. 'Well, I haven't actually interviewed him yet.'

Maggie heaped more fried rice onto her plate, as well as some beef noodles. 'So, what's the problem?'

'It's just my gut feeling, Maggie, that something isn't right. He seems to have been able to use mental health issues to avoid a custodial sentence for his previous assaults, but as far as I can see, none of the psychiatrists running around after him can work out what's wrong with him.'

'If you've not interviewed him, how can you be sure there's more to the whole thing than meets the eye?'

'I'm not!' Jack said abruptly.

Maggie had never seen Jack so frazzled. 'So why are you digging around?'

'It's just a gut feeling. I think he's a very dangerous individual.'

Maggie began to clear away the empty cartons, tipping the leftovers into the food waste bucket. Jack remained sitting at the table finishing his wine, then poured the last of the bottle into his glass.

Maggie went over and put her arms around him.

'Why don't I run you a nice hot bath? Then we can have an early night together. I recall you making me a promise this morning . . .'

Jack barely reacted, and Maggie quickly withdrew her arms and went back to clearing the kitchen.

'There's something else . . .' he said, quietly.

'If you want to talk through the case with me, go ahead, I'm all ears,' Maggie said.

'No, it's not that. This morning I left early because I had agreed to meet Ridley.'

Maggie turned expectantly.

'I gave him my word that I wouldn't mention it to anyone, but I think I need to tell you, Mags. I might have agreed to do something that I'm not sure I can.'

Maggie stopped what she was doing with a look of concern. She could see Jack was clearly weighed down by something.

'You know you can always trust me, Jack. It's not as if I would repeat anything to anyone connected to your work. Talk to me. Come on, let's go and sit in the lounge.'

She took him by the hand and led him to the sofa. She turned on a small table lamp, then fetched a bottle of brandy and two glasses. He sat morosely, head bowed.

Maggie poured them both a large brandy, then put the glasses on the coffee table in front of them and sat down beside him. She was exhausted but was determined not to show it. She had never seen Jack so perplexed, almost childlike.

'He called me late last night,' Jack began, 'and asked me to meet him this morning. He chose this odd location by a Kingston steamboat rental place.'

Jack sipped his brandy and leant forwards, as if distancing himself from Maggie.

'Go on, Jack, tell me why Ridley wanted to see you?'

He took his time, slowly repeating everything Ridley had told him, then as he finished, he started to get emotional.

'He bowed his head, Mags, and said, "Help me".'

Maggie took hold of his hand.

'Well, I think you're the best person he could have asked to help him . . . but I have one important question.'

Jack nodded, threading his fingers through hers.

'Do you believe he's innocent?'

Jack didn't hesitate. 'Yes, I do. It *has* to be a set up.'

'Then try, as best as you can, to prove it. If you want my advice, I'd try and find out who the victim is, first. She's at the heart of it.'

Jack kissed her fingers, then cupped her face in his hands.

'Have I told you lately how much I love you?'

Maggie laughed and drew him to his feet. 'You have, but tonight, as promised, you can prove it.'

CHAPTER EIGHT

Maggie and Jack were both deeply asleep. They had experienced what could only be described as very satisfying sex, twice. After checking on Hannah, Jack had returned to get back into bed beside his wife. He had woken again at almost two o'clock and heard Penny arriving home. He thought it was very late but fell back to sleep almost immediately, for the first time not even thinking about work.

The alarm clock woke them both at seven o'clock. Maggie had to get to the hospital, and that gave Jack a good hour before he needed to go into the station. When he went downstairs, Maggie was in the kitchen making scrambled eggs and already had a fresh pot of coffee made. He went up to give her a hug and a kiss, whispering in her ear to ask whether she thought he had kept his promise. She laughed, nudged him away and said that if he played his cards right it could be a regular occurrence.

She ate her breakfast quickly, whilst Jack sat at the table with his eggs and crispy bacon.

'I heard Penny arriving home in the early hours. It was almost 2 a.m. That's pretty late for a bingo session,' he said.

'She'll no doubt be having a lie-in then. I took Hannah a warm bottle of milk and she's watching her TV in her playpen. Check in on her after I leave, then Penny will no doubt get her up and dressed and take her to the park.'

'Listen, thanks again for last night . . .'

'If you are referring to the sex, judging by your prowess it should be me thanking you . . .' Maggie teased, and Jack grinned.

'You know what I mean, Mags, you listening made all the difference, and I don't feel nearly as frazzled.'

'Good, because you shouldn't punish yourself. Just do what you can and stand by that gut feeling of yours; you always have in the past, and it has always proved you right.'

By the time he had finished his breakfast and Maggie had left for the hospital, Jack was eager to have a look at the information Ridley had given to him. He did as Maggie had suggested and looked in on Hannah, just as Penny was coming out of the bathroom.

'Good morning! Did you have a good time last night?'

'I did, yes. Are you going in to work this morning?'

'I am, in about an hour. Maggie's already gone and left you a note to cook a chicken in a bag. I shouldn't be late home this evening. Do you need anything?'

'No, we'll go to the park. I'll have a go with the chicken. I've never cooked one in a bag before. And I'll get some fresh vegetables when I do the food shopping. Thank you for staying at home last night,' she added.

'As if you need to thank me! It's us who are grateful to have you! I got soaked giving her a bath and washing her hair. I got covered in talcum powder too!'

Penny smiled. 'Yes, she can be quite a little minx when she wants to be! You shouldn't use too much talc – and actually it's mine! I had better get her dressed and ready for her porridge. You have a good day, dear. I might be out again the same night next week, if you can organise it with Maggie.'

'Another bingo session?'

She didn't answer, going into Hannah's bedroom and closing the door behind her.

Jack went back down to the kitchen and out via the kitchen door. Their little garden needed a lot of attention and was always on their 'to do' list, but the garden shed was also Jack's safe hiding place. Hidden under the floorboards was a laptop he had used when contacting the women from the train robbery. It could not be traced to him and he had illegally uploaded the Holmes database on it, with a specific code to open it. There were also some bundles of bank notes, and a cardboard roll containing the painting he had been given by Adam Border. Lastly he had two burner phones, both of which would need charging. He replaced the boards, locked up the shed and returned to the house with the phones and laptop.

Jack poured himself a fresh mug of coffee, then went up to his office. He closed the door so as not to be disturbed and opened his briefcase. He plugged in the laptop and burner phones to charge, then took out all the files the probation officers had passed to him, placing them to one side, before easing out the plastic bag that Ridley had given him. He tipped out the contents onto his desk. There were numerous photographs, plus a lot of typed pages, along with a computer stick. In a separate sealed envelope, on which Ridley had written 'CCTV footage', was a second computer stick. On a single sheet of paper was a note to Jack in Ridley's handwriting. He explained that it was highly irregular of him to be passing the contents of the envelope to Jack, and he urged him to take the utmost precaution with it, never allowing anyone else to have access. It was unsigned. In a white envelope, a single folded page of a notebook had the name Sammy Taylor with an address, and the word 'Badger' underlined. Jack presumed that this was the contact that Ridley said would help him.

The burner phones were being charged up, and the laptop already charged on the floor by his chair. He cleared a space on his desk, inadvertently knocking over one of the files. He bent down to pick it up by the flap and more papers spilled out onto the floor. He pushed his chair back and began to pick up the loose pages. They were from Sara, and although he had not intended to work on anything connected to Rodney Middleton, he couldn't help but read the heading: URGENT and in her neat handwriting, To be checked for confirmation.

Sara had written that after his first arrest for the knife attack, Middleton had actually told a psychiatrist at the prison that he felt protective towards young children. It was noted that Middleton had delusional thoughts that he was a saviour, especially of young girls.

The next note had words underlined regarding the fact that Middleton, aged nineteen, had been held in a secure hospital after threatening a neighbour with a knife. Jack sighed, turning a page to continue reading that doctors had assessed whether Middleton should be detained on another five occasions in the years since the fire. Each time it had been decided not to do so. Sara had then written that she was attempting to trace the probation officers who had been allocated to Middleton's case, in order to acquire the reports from Angus Seymour, George Donaldson and Natalie Burrows. Jack placed the pages back into the file and put it to one side. He was about to work on the material from Ridley when he saw the last note, a reference to a Linda Harvey and a probationary report. He checked the time, and decided it was too early to call her, but jotted down her contact details.

After setting the alarm on his mobile to ring at 8.15 a.m., he spread out all of the documents from Ridley. He began by writing down, as clearly as he could recall, everything that Ridley had told him. He then sifted through everything, deciding not to look at the computer sticks until his laptop was fully charged and he had more time. He started to read the first page of Ridley's notes, with an attached flyer headed DATING AGENCY.

The company name was 'RP' which stood for 'Retired Professionals' and they focused on men and women who had been in successful careers and who were looking to find like-minded people with a view to friendship and possible partnership. On their website there was a lengthy form for applicants to fill in, including age, career details, marriage status, property ownership and financial situation, as well as details of any medical issues. All applicants were required to supply two photographs, one full length and one head shot, and a personal interview had to be arranged before they could be accepted. Ridley had also included a printed page from their website, with background information on the two women who ran the agency.

To Jack, the agency at first sight seemed legitimate, but his first priority would be to do background checks on Mrs Eva Shay and her partner, Selina Da Costa, the two women running the agency.

Ridley had included two photographs of the woman he had known as Sandra. She was a very attractive blonde, with wide eyes and full lips, and on the back of the official agency photograph were her details: 'Sandra Raynor, single, 44 years old, 5'9", retired accountant. Enjoys skiing, country walks, visiting art galleries and museums.'

Jack wondered how Ridley had described himself. He had to be in his mid-forties, and, like Sandra, he was single. He could not really be described as good-looking although he was over six feet tall. He wondered if Ridley enjoyed museums and art galleries. But he could certainly see why he would be attracted to Sandra, if that was her real name. In the envelope were photographs of the two other women that Ridley had dated, both middle-aged and pleasant-looking, but not quite as attractive.

The alarm on Jack's mobile went off telling him that he needed to leave for the station. Reluctantly, he gathered all Ridley's documents to take with him, but before leaving he phoned Linda Harvey's contact number at the probationary department. When she eventually came on the line, he explained as quickly as possible the reason for contacting her and gave his station details. She sounded young, with a pleasant voice, first explaining that her interview with Rodney Middleton had not actually taken place. Just as Jack was about to end the call, thanking her for her time, she said that to prepare for the appointment she had spoken to Dr Donaldson asking for his opinion.

'Off the record, Dr Donaldson did say something that concerned me, and it was frustrating that I was never able to follow up on it because my interview with Mr Middleton was cancelled because of his arrest'.

There was a pause, and he heard an intake of breath.

'What I'm going to say must be off the record. I hope you understand that'.

'Of course,' Jack said.

'Right well, Dr Donaldson said that in his opinion Rodney Middleton's ability to play the system was the only reason he had remained out of prison. He was a very dangerous individual and I should be very careful regarding any interaction with him.'

'Thank you,' Jack said. 'I appreciate you passing that on. And you have my word our conversation will remain between us.'

Jack terminated the call, letting out a deep breath. So his gut instinct had been right. There was no way he was going to drop this investigation now. The only problem was that he now had two investigations to pursue, and one of them had to be secret. Hurrying down the stairs, Jack found Penny had Hannah already in her pushchair to take her to the park, and quickly said goodbye to them both before leaving. By the time he arrived at the station it was just after nine. There were only a small team of officers on duty and Jack went up to the CID office and carefully locked the Ridley material away in his desk drawer. He was taking out his case files as Sara came in with a coffee.

'I read the update on Middleton's past records. Good work,' Jack said.

'I was able to get help through my brother, and I'm now sourcing more information regarding the probation reports,' she told him. 'I've located the probation officer that handled Middleton's previous arrest, and also the one that saw him four years ago, but he's retired. He lives in Twickenham and was quite cooperative if a bit guarded.'

Jack sipped the coffee, which needed more sugar for his taste. He studied her neat report, which gave the contact numbers for both officers she had just mentioned.

'The firefighter you asked us to track down? I called him this morning at his home, and he's happy to meet you.'

'That's Brian Hookam, right?'

'Yes, sarge. He lives in Cobham.'

'OK, Sara, can you find out if he'll see me this morning. Also check with the probation officer. I could see him first, then go on to Cobham.'

'I'll make the calls right now.'

Sara went back to her desk and Jack signalled to DC Elba to join him. He took out the laptop he'd brought in from his garden hut. Well aware of Ridley's warning that the Essex CID would be monitoring anything to do with his case, he knew he was taking a risk. But the Middleton enquiry was really taking up too much of his time, and he needed to start making headway as soon as possible.

Leon stood by his desk, notebook at the ready. Jack hesitated a moment, still unsure about what he could get away with.

'Leon, I need you to do some checking for me, and it's very important. I need you to find out anything you can about a Sandra Raynor, aged 44, working as an accountant. Look through the newspaper archives, pull out anything you can find on her.' He passed over the laptop. 'I also want you to use this, not the station's, as this is a covert investigation. You get any kind of alarm bells, you bring it straight back to me, understand?'

'Will do, sarge.' Leon jotted down some notes in his pocketbook, then put the laptop in his briefcase. 'We also contacted the hostel. Amanda Dunn is still there, but a Mrs Thornton said that she was scheduled to be leaving after the weekend.'

Jack nodded, deciding he would do the visits first and then drive over to see Amanda.

Half an hour later he left the station with Sara, after she had entered into CRIS that they would be conducting two interviews that morning. She giggled when she saw Jack's car, saying that she had never known a detective to drive such an outrageously coloured vehicle.

'Beggars can't be choosers, Sara, and my wife has the Porsche. At least you can easily spot this in a car park, plus I doubt anyone would ever want to steal it!'

'You're probably right about that, sarge,' Sara agreed, then paused before continuing. 'There are a few things I didn't put into my written report. Mr Thompson is retired and was actually semi-retired when he was handling Rodney Middleton's case. He's sixty-seven, and apparently has some medical issues. He's an "old school" probationary officer, and to be honest I doubt he would even be employed these days.'

Sydney Thompson lived in a small terraced house in St Margarets, just after Twickenham Bridge, and fortunately Jack was able to park almost outside his front door. There were cones blocking the spaces in front of an adjacent property that was being renovated; however, there didn't appear to be any builders working on it. They both put on their masks, even though it was not obligatory, and headed towards number 32.

Thompson opened the front door before Jack had time to ring the bell. He looked older than sixty-seven and was very overweight, his enormous stomach bulging out through his crumpled collarless shirt.

'There's a big rugby match on this afternoon, so I hope this isn't going to take too long. And don't worry about wearing your masks; nobody round here bothers now. I've had my vaccinations, so has the wife, as she's got asthma. She's been in isolation for so long she's starting to enjoy making me do all the grocery shopping. Not for much longer though!'

He led them into a small sitting room which had a comfortable, if rather worn, sofa and two easy chairs. There was a coffee table with a pot of tea and a plate of biscuits, with sugar and milk and three mugs. Sydney eased himself into one of the two easy chairs as Sara offered to pour the tea, and they removed their masks.

'I don't want to take up too much of your time, Mr Thompson. I'm here to ask you a few questions about a young man called Rodney Middleton. I believe he was with you a few years ago,' Jack began.

Sydney stirred his mug of tea and took a long sip.

'Obviously whatever I tell you is privileged information, but I'll tell you what I can.'

'I appreciate that, Mr Thompson. First off, can you give me your personal impression of Rodney?'

'He was a gentle soul, very troubled, and was concerned that the medication he had been prescribed made him feel very lethargic. There were a few times when he found it hard to have a coherent conversation. I did query it with his psychiatrist, but it was not my position to question what they had prescribed him.'

'Was he ever violent in any way?'

'No, never . . . on the contrary. In my humble estimation, Rodney was a very traumatised young man. His sisters dying in the fire, his mother leaving him . . . I believe his father was abusive to him; it all affected him. He didn't warrant a custodial sentence but would have benefited from appropriate medical care.'

'How old was he at this time?'

'Just eighteen, that was my first encounter with him. Subsequently he was allocated to me when he was twenty-one and had committed an assault. By this time, he had been held at a young offender institute. He was released for medical assessment from another psychiatric department and was fearful about being prescribed even more medication that would make him feel ill. I believe he had been offered hypnosis.'

'During any of your dealings with Rodney, did you have any concerns regarding his over-protective feelings towards young people, especially young girls?'

'I've been asked that before; surely it's understandable that he should feel protective, after what happened to his younger sisters?'

'So, you never felt that it was a sign that he could have paedophilia tendencies?'

Thompson shook his head. 'No, I did not. Not in any way. I know there was some complaint made against him, but Rodney explained to me that he was concerned for the children in the playground. He was frightened they could fall and hurt themselves if their parent wasn't watching them.'

'How do you feel about the fact that Rodney has just committed yet another vicious assault?'

Thompson waved his mug of tea, spilling some over his trousers and the carpet.

'Whatever has occurred since my retirement isn't my business. If you want my honest opinion, Rodney Middleton has been left to fall through the system without ever getting the proper treatment he needed, being passed from one psychiatrist to the other with no concrete or helpful diagnosis.'

Jack paused. 'Mr Thompson, can I ask you what, in your professional experience, is wrong with Rodney Middleton?'

Thompson was wiping the spilt tea off his trousers with a crumpled napkin. He shrugged and leant forwards, his belly drooping between his fat thighs.

'Have you met him?'

Jack looked embarrassed. 'No, not yet.'

'Well, when you do you'll see why I have strong empathy for this young man. He's a lost soul, and nobody has ever had the time to heal him.'

Jack stood up and signalled to Sara that they were leaving.

'Thank you for your time, Mr Thompson, you've been very helpful. I hope you enjoy your rugby match.'

It was clear that Sydney thought he would be questioned further, and he looked surprised as he hauled his bulk out of the chair. Sara walked ahead of Jack, who turned at the door.

'Do you think that Rodney would be capable of murder?'

Sydney was bending down to pick up the tray, and he turned to face Jack.

'I . . . well, in the end God only knows what people are capable of.'

* * *

They drove in silence as Jack followed his satnav directions to Brian Hookam's address, which he had also put into Waze on his mobile.

They headed back towards Kingston, past the old Kingston Crown Court towards the A1, which would then be a straight drive to Cobham.

'Sarge, what did you mean when you asked if Middleton was capable of murder?'

'If you ask me, Middleton should have been sectioned years ago, and the Sydney Thompsons of this world had no idea what they were dealing with. The psychiatrists were treading on eggshells with their reports, passing Middleton from one clinic to another.'

'What makes you feel that Rodney is capable of murder?'

'Intuition, Sara. He's manipulated the system, spending very little time in custodial environments, always being let off on medical grounds. He's twenty-four and has lived off benefits all his adult life. He was protected by men like Sydney Thompson, who even encouraged him not to take his prescribed medication.'

'He didn't actually say that, but you don't seem to rate probation officers very highly.'

'I don't. They're not qualified doctors or psychiatrists . . . and just seem to act as enablers so that prisoners get released. Those prisoners then often end up going straight back into crime. I know your brother is a probation officer, and I don't mean to lump everyone together, so I'm sure he's an exception.'

'He is, and he's very dedicated. However, in defence of men like Thompson, you haven't met Rodney Middleton yet, so you are assuming an awful lot based on your intuition.'

Jack gave her a side-long glance. He rather admired the fact she was feisty and was questioning him, but he didn't have the patience to go into all his reasons for his suspicion that Rodney was a killer. He knew he could be wrong, but he was not about to admit it.

Satnav and Waze eventually directed them to a small mews courtyard off the main Cobham High Street. These were small workmen's cottages, built close together with a small verge in front and a profusion of flowering tubs and hanging baskets around their front doors. They parked outside number 14, behind a Toyota with stickers supporting firefighters and a 'Vote Labour' sign.

Jack and Sara pulled their masks on as they stood and rang the doorbell. There was the sound of a small dog yapping then the door was opened. Brian Hookam stood, holding a bulbous-eyed Pekingese with a red scarf around its neck.

'Don't worry, he's all bark, and anyway not many teeth left for him to bite with!' Hookam said jovially.

Jack introduced himself and Sara as they were ushered into a small but comfortable-looking lounge, with thick-piled carpet and a flowered easy chair and a two-seater sofa. Elegant flowery curtains fell either side of a small, fabric-covered window seat.

Hookam was a huge, fit-looking man, standing at well over six feet. He had broad shoulders and was dressed in jeans and a black collared t-shirt. He seemed totally out of place with the décor of the room. He offered them tea or coffee, but Jack declined, saying he didn't want to take up too much of his time.

Brian had loose false teeth, which made an odd whistling sound when he talked, and he was constantly sucking in air. The Pekingese remained snuggled in his arms as Jack and Sara sat side by side on the sofa. Brian excused himself for a minute, going out into the narrow hall and calling out.

'Avril?'

Jack saw a tiny woman with mauve hair and a wrap-over apron approach, taking the dog from Brian's arms.

'Do you want a pot of tea?'

'No, thanks, my love . . . just keep Judy out. I shouldn't be too long.'

Brian came back in and closed the door. He was breathing heavily and gave a phlegmy cough as he sat down in one of the easy chairs. He took out a rather dirty handkerchief and spat into it.

'Sorry, too much smoke inhalation over twenty-five years, as well as the fags! But I've given them up since I retired. If you ask me, I don't think having that long-haired Peke does me any good, but it's like her child. We have four of them – kids, that is, not dogs – but we haven't been able to see them for over a year.'

Jack smiled. 'Firstly, thank you for agreeing to talk to me, Mr Hookam, I really appreciate it. I'll get straight to the point. It's a bit of a test of your memory, I'm afraid.'

Brian nodded, sucking in a breath between his loose teeth.

'So, there was a fire at Anthony Middleton's property over five years ago. I believe you were the officer in charge of the fire investigation unit and were called to attend?'

'Yes, I was at the scene . . . it was a night that isn't easy to forget. They never are, particularly when there are fatalities . . . and in this case those two little girls.'

'There was an investigation to determine the cause of the fire, as arson was suspected?'

'Yes, that's correct. It was a very thorough enquiry. No chemicals were found . . . by that I mean no accelerants, and the team were eventually in agreement that the fire was accidental. Let me show you.'

Hookam stood up and went over to a small bureau, opening a drawer. He searched around and brought out a thick, worn notebook. He opened another drawer and took out a pen, lowering the felt covered writing shelf. He began to draw on a blank page in his book. Jack sat patiently, listening to Brian's laboured breathing.

'Right, come on over and have a look. I'm no artist but what I've drawn is the house, the ground floor, the staircase and the bedrooms on the landing. Where I've put a cross, that was the first gasoline heater, which was an old model and no longer sold. The girls' bedroom was at the back. The window was barred and was obviously not facing the street where the fire engine had access. There was a second gasoline heater, a more modern one, against the wall by the bedroom door. It was determined that one of the children had put a synthetic duvet over the top of it. This is where the fire was started, and as the door had been left open, once the fire caught it started to spread very quickly onto the landing. Then the second heater caught fire, creating a fire ball. The banisters had been filled in with chip board, so the fireball was channelled down the stairs.'

Jack looked at his drawing. 'So, the children were totally trapped, unable to get out of the window or make it out onto the landing?'

'Correct, and the smoke was incredibly thick . . . by the time we arrived, the blaze was very intense and spreading all over the ground floor.'

'How long before you could get it under control?'

'It would have been fifteen to twenty minutes, with two fire trucks and hoses. It was impossible to gain entry in order to get up the stairs to the children; the girls were eventually brought out, but it was too late.'

Hookam gave a long, deep sigh and sat down in the easy chair again.

'Can you now tell me who was present on the scene when you were called out to the fire?'

'Yes, there was a young teenager. He had tried to get into the house . . . he was hysterical. He had to be held back as his clothes were already burning. He had to be hosed down. Then his – very drunk – father arrived; we thought he would try to calm his son, but instead he began punching and kicking him until he fell down. It was very unpleasant . . . we had to drag them apart. The father was screaming that his son was to blame. He tried to get into the house and had to be held back as well. He suffered some burns but by this time we had an ambulance there and they were attending to the lad, who was sobbing. I think his father had broken his nose. Then a taxi pulls up with the girls' mother inside. She was screaming, and when they brought out the bodies she collapsed and had to be taken into the ambulance.'

Jack held up the drawing. 'Did you know where the son, Rodney, was in the house when the fire started?'

'I found out later, when he was questioned during the investigation. Apparently, he had been in the front room working on his laptop. He maintained that he had only become alarmed when he smelt smoke. He said he'd tried to go up the stairs, but the heat was too intense, and the fireball started moving down the stairs. Then the fire trucks arrived.'

'Who called the fire brigade?'

'A neighbour, I believe.'

'So, Rodney was downstairs and by the time the smoke had alerted him to the fire, it had already taken hold. He tried to move up the stairs, but they were on fire. Was he wearing headphones?'

Hookam looked perplexed.

'It's just that if he was and the girls were screaming, he might not have heard.'

Hookam shook his head. 'I can't recall, I'm afraid.'

'Did you, at any time, think it could have been arson?' Jack asked.

'Well . . . I heard the father accusing the boy, but that could have been the shock at seeing the house ablaze, and because his son was supposed to be taking care of the girls. Mind you, the mother was also telling the police to arrest Rodney, saying that he had set fire to the house. She was in a very hysterical state and had to be sedated. But you know a fatal fire is always thoroughly investigated. Any allegations against the young boy would have been properly evaluated.'

'So, it was judged to be accidental. But were there any questions about how or why the duvet had been placed over the gas heater?'

'I believe it was thought that one or other of the girls could have thrown it off their beds because they were hot. It was a very small room, more like a box room.'

Jack stood up and asked if he could keep the drawing. Hookam nodded, and Jack thanked him for his time. Sara shook his hand and walked behind them to the front door. They didn't see his wife again, but they could hear the dog barking from the kitchen. Brian laughed as he gestured to the small sign on the front door: BEWARE OF THE DOG.

Brian remained standing at his front door as they drove off.

He sighed, remembering that clasped in the eldest daughter's little charred hand was a doll, the pink plastic face melted into her skin. Sights like that, he knew, never leave you.

CHAPTER NINE

Jack and Sara did not talk on their way back to the station. Both of them were mulling over what they'd learned during the interviews, and Sara intuitively sensed that Jack did not want to talk.

Eventually Jack spoke. 'I want you to see what you can find out about Karen . . . any relatives I can talk to. I think Anthony Middleton said something about being contacted by an aunt?'

'I'm sorry, but I'm not sure who Karen is?'

'Middleton's second wife, who died of a heroin overdose. She was Rodney's stepmother.'

'Oh, right, sorry.'

'I'll make out a report on today's interviews, just so that our anally retentive DCI knows what we were doing and where . . . and I need to grab a bite to eat in the canteen.'

By the time they had parked and gone up to the CID office it was almost two o'clock. Jack decided to miss lunch in order to make out a report, and then go out to talk to Amanda Dunn.

There were a few messages on his desk from Clarke regarding other cases, which Jack had to deal with before he did anything else. Leon came over to his desk, carrying Jack's laptop. 'I just spoke to Sara. She said you were planning to visit Amanda Dunn at the hostel this afternoon. I called to make sure she was available and was told that she checked out before lunch.'

'Shit . . . did she leave a forwarding address?'

'No. Mrs Thornton said that they had no reason to hold her there and it was her decision to leave. She thought she might have gone to Liverpool to see her parents.'

'Go back to Mrs Thornton, see if you can get a phone number for them. If not, call Mrs Delaney, the landlady at Middleton's basement flat, to see if she's turned up there.'

'Yes, sarge. Also, I've had no luck in tracing anyone by the name of Sandra Raynor just on her age and description. I added a few years just in case, but can't find any relevant births or deaths registered in that name. I also checked with the DVLA and there's no licence in her name. I earmarked some women with that name in the London area, but they don't fit the description. I've listed them here anyway.'

Leon handed Jack a single sheet of typed paper. He glanced down at it. Several were married with children and two were over sixty years old.

'OK, these don't fit so I think we can assume she was using a false name. I'll take this back, but thanks anyway.' Jack took his laptop and placed it on his desk.

'Is this connected to the Rodney Middleton enquiry?' Leon asked.

Jack briefly nodded just as Sara walked up. 'Thought you might be hungry ... and I've put extra sugars in your coffee. I noticed how many you heaped in your tea.'

'Very observant of you, Sara, thank you.'

'Do you want me to accompany you to talk to Amanda Dunn?'

'I would if she were there, but she checked out of the hostel. Leon is trying to track her down.'

Jack waited until Sara had gone back to her desk before he took a bite of his ham sandwich.

He then unlocked his desk drawer and took out the small envelope, and the note. He removed one of his burner phones from his pocket and dialled the mobile number. It rang for at least a minute before it was answered.

'Yes?'

'Is that Sammy Taylor?'

'Who is this?'

Jack took a quick look around the room and lowered his voice.

'I'm Jack Warr. Simon Ridley gave me your contact number. I need to see you urgently.'

'Do you? Did he give you anything else?'

'Well, your address.'

'Nothing else?'

'Your name obviously. Are you Sammy?'

'I could be.'

Jack suddenly remembered. 'Badger.'

There was a short throaty laugh. 'Can you make it in an hour?'

'That might be a bit difficult.'

'You said it was urgent, so make up your mind. I'm not available tomorrow.'

'I'll be there, thank you.'

Jack quickly stuffed the phone in his pocket. He put the old laptop in his briefcase, finished his sandwich, drained the coffee and then stood up with a loud yelp. Everyone looked over as he rubbed at his cheek.

'I've just broken a crown . . . shit, that hurts.'

He gave a good performance, saying he was going to the emergency dental practice and asking Sara to give the details if anyone wanted to know where he was. Then he was out and running into the car park, carrying his briefcase.

Sara went over to Leon who was still trying to track down Amanda Dunn.

'Funny . . . he was only eating a cheese and ham sandwich. Any update on Amanda?'

'Not yet, that hostel lets the phone ring for bloody ages. And then when it does connect you get a shed-load of messages about their opening and closing times, and it still has all the checks you have to do for Covid. I'm trying to get Mrs Delaney on the line, but she never picks up.'

Sara rolled her eyes. Sometimes you could ask Leon a simple question and you got a lengthy diatribe, so she returned to her desk to continue the search for missing girls that might be connected to the Middleton case. Jack clearly thought Rodney could have committed arson, and then murder, which had unsettled her. She was intelligent enough to realise that Jack was holding something important back, and decided that when he returned from the dentist, she would ask him to explain.

Jack was held up in traffic, and Waze seemed to be taking him on a very circuitous route to NW3, but he eventually found himself on Platts Lane. 87B was a ground floor flat in a semi-detached, four-storey building. A sign with an arrow pointed to Flat B down a path beside the main front entrance. There was a slight slope, and there was a handrail along the entire length of the path.

Outside the brown-painted front door was an electric mobility scooter with a weatherproof cover partly draped over it, and a thick plastic covered chain and padlock. Jack noticed the CCTV cameras positioned around and above the entrance with a floodlight above the door. There was a spy hole at his level and one lower down, indicating not only a concern with security, but that the occupant could be physically challenged. Jack pressed a discreet doorbell and waited. He heard numerous locks being drawn back before the door opened.

He heard a voice say, 'Come in, first door on your right.'

The door closed automatically behind him. He walked down a dark, rather narrow hallway to the first door on the right. It was partly open.

'Hello, it's Jack Warr,' he said.

The room was dimly lit, the blinds on the window drawn. Sitting in a wing-backed chair with a footrest up, was a figure wearing a padded red velvet dressing gown with satin cuffs and collar. Beneath a bouffant blonde wig he was made up like a drag queen.

'I'm Sammy. Excuse the costume but I do a podcast a couple of days a week . . . a bit unsure about the wig, though. As you can see, I have quite a collection.'

She gestured with long red false nails to an array of wigs on stands, next to a rack of sequinned gowns and feather boas. There was also a mirror with light bulbs surrounding the frame above a small table with pots of makeup. Jack couldn't help being taken aback, wondering if this was really the contact Ridley thought could help him in his present predicament.

'So, Jack is it, darling? You said it was urgent . . . so talk to me.'

'I'm not sure where to begin . . .' Jack faltered.

'Listen, dear, if you were sent to me by the only person in this world I would lie down and die for, just talk to me, and don't leave anything out.'

With difficulty, Sammy drew the footrest closer to the chair by a button, then slowly got to his feet. He shuffled to the chair in front of the mirror, grimacing in pain when he sat down. He placed paper tissues around his satin collar before opening a large pot of cleansing cream.

Jack did his best to explain everything as Sammy removed his false eyelashes and then spread the cream over his face before wiping off the thick makeup.

By the time he had dabbed his face with cologne, it was clear he had a slight six o'clock shadow. The last thing he removed was the wig, holding it up in one hand to inspect the weave before placing it onto the wood-based dummy head.

Jack kept going, as Sammy revealed his almost completely shaved head. The velvet dressing gown was removed and beneath it was a collarless man's shirt and grey tracksuit trousers.

'. . . and I can't use the station's computers because, as I said, the Essex team's investigation will pick up on anyone trying to get information and trace it,' Jack was saying.

'Yes, dear, I picked that up. I think we need a bit more information about dating agency, RP . . . so I'd like you to make me a nice cup of tea, with a Blue Riband biscuit, whilst I have a little troll around for you.'

Sammy picked up a walking frame, and instructed Jack to follow, pointing out the kitchen at the far end of the hall. The door next to the kitchen had a coded entry and Sammy pressed various buttons before it opened inwards.

Jack stood in the small but well-equipped kitchen as he filled an electric kettle. He couldn't quite believe he was searching for teabags in this person's kitchen; having recounted the entire Ridley situation, it felt as if he had walked into some sort of weird dream. He doubted anyone would believe him; even Maggie would find it hard to accept that he was making tea in a transvestite's flat, not knowing a thing about who they were.

Having found a tray, Jack arranged two mugs of tea, a sugar bowl and a chocolate biscuit that he found in the fridge when he got the milk. He carried the tray out into the hall, and gently tapped on the door with the toe of his shoe. When it opened, he almost dropped the tray.

The room was like some kind of high-tech security bubble. There were banks of screens scrolling out data at a blinding rate. Printing machines lined one wall, and the desk – which had to have been specially made – ran the entire length of the room.

There were three keyboards, with the keys lit up in red, green and orange.

Sammy was sitting in a large office chair which had big, rubber-rimmed wheels. There was a wide strip of plastic over the fitted carpet to make it easy to scoot along the length of desk.

Jack placed the tray down, taking a deep breath.

'Two sugars for me, dear, then go and sit in my dressing room and wait.'

'But . . .'

'No buts, dear . . . the less you see and know, the better. I have to work fast to avoid any detection or connection . . . in out, in out, shake it all about.'

Jack left one mug of tea and the biscuit with Sammy, taking the tray and his own mug back into the kitchen. He finished his tea and washed his mug, placing it on the draining board, shaken from what he had just seen – because in the few seconds he'd been looking at one of the screens, he knew Sammy was using the Holmes database. Feeling the ground unsteady beneath his feet, he walked back to the dressing room, where Sammy had first greeted him.

Not knowing what else to do, he had a look through all the glamorous evening gowns, the numerous pairs of gold and silver strappy high heels and the dazzling array of different-styled wigs. He physically jumped when a cat slithered into the room. It was some kind of Persian, with huge blue-grey eyes, long silky fur and a bushy tail. The cat kept its distance as it weaved in and out of the sequinned gowns before jumping onto the big armchair. It had a tiny gold bell hanging from a black ribbon round its neck.

Jack hesitated before he tentatively approached the cat, sitting comfortably in the centre of the chair. He reached out to stroke it, pulling his hand away as it snarled and clawed at him. He stepped back quickly and knocked over one of the wig stands.

As he put the wig back on the stand, and the cat glowered at him, he muttered to himself, 'What the hell am I doing here?'

* * *

Leon Elba was once more calling Mrs Thornton at the hostel. He had been put on hold yet again and looked over to Sara with a pained expression.

'I get through and I'm told that someone will try and find her. How hard can it be? I've been on hold for five minutes.'

'Probably teatime?' Sara said, pulling out her chair and opening her laptop. 'I'm not having much luck tracing any relatives of Karen Middleton, either. I'm hoping to get something from a rehab clinic.'

'Who's she?'

'Rodney Middleton's stepmother, deceased, but Jack wants to find anyone who knew the family.'

'It's Jack now, is it?' he said with a grin.

'Oh shut up!'

'Well, I didn't have any luck tracing Sandra Raynor . . .'

Sara frowned. 'Who's she? I've not heard her name before'

'I have no idea, just that she's connected to the enquiry. But it's as though she doesn't exist.' Just then the phone was answered. 'Mrs Thornton? This is DC Leon Elba. I called earlier to enquire about Amanda Dunn. You mentioned that she'd left the hostel . . . yes . . . yes . . .'

Sara turned back to her desk and dialled the rehab centre.

While Mrs Thornton went to find the contact details for Amanda's parents, Sara was put through to two different departments. She remained calm and polite, saying she understood Karen Middleton's stay at the clinic had been some years ago . . . and was transferred yet again.

'I hope Jack is alright,' she said to herself. 'He's been gone a long time. God, I hate dentists.'

* * *

Jack was just about to call it quits when Sammy walked in, using a walking frame.

'Right, my dear, got a few things for you. I see we've been favoured with Edie's presence. Very good pedigree but a very nasty temperament.'

'I gathered that,' Jack said.

Sammy swiped at the armchair with the walking frame and Edie leapt off and ran out. As he sat down in the big chair, Jack took the walking frame, placing it to one side.

'Right, here we go, dear. Your dating agency. They've been operating for five years. It's jointly owned by Selina Da Costa and Eva Shay. Mrs Da Costa is fifty-five years old, previously married to a wealthy estate agent who agreed to a substantial divorce settlement. She has one son, aged thirty-two, living in California. Eva Shay is sixty and is quite a different kind of woman . . . married and divorced three times but reverted to her maiden name when she started the dating agency.'

Sammy gave Jack a coy look, as he continued.

'I have naughty access to the Police National Computer and found one criminal report, dating back twelve years. She was sentenced to four years in Holloway for fraud, under her first married name of Eva Barras. She was released after two years. Her husband was an Italian importer and as far as I can tell he returned to live in Brazil. Ms Shay qualified as an accountant after being released from Holloway, although I haven't been able to trace any of the companies she said she's worked for. I only went through all the legitimate avenues, you see.'

'What exactly do you mean by the legitimate avenues?' Jack asked.

'Well, most things are easily accessible from the Holmes database, and RP have quite a presence on the internet. However, to gain more details about their company I would need to . . .'

Jack was already shocked that Sammy had been able to use the database never mind access the PNC, the Police National Computer. 'Need to what?'

'Well, go a slightly more irregular route.'

'By irregular, do you mean illegal?'

Sammy smiled. 'Yes, it would mean hacking their computers and gaining access to their clients' details.'

'Can you do that without it being traced back here to you?'

'Oh, yes. You know, dear, lots of students go into one of those internet cafes and pay for a period of time, then disconnect. I used to do it at my local library – not for anything illegal, mind you – but now I'm all set up here. It'll take a bit of time which I don't have right now.'

Jack rubbed his temples nervously. 'You do understand how crucial it is that this remains just between us? Anything you find, contact me directly or I can come back.'

Sammy frowned. 'Who do you think I would impart any of this to, dear? You're making me a tad pissed off. I don't allow anyone into my inner sanctum. You're very privileged. I'm not doing this for you, anyway. Sometimes one gets to repay a favour one owes big time.'

'I'm sorry, but I don't know anything about you, or how much risk you're taking, if anything is traced back to you.'

'Trust me, dear, it can't. Like I said, I'm doing this to repay a favour, and the situation is not as simple as perhaps you have been led to believe. The outcome will eventually provide the answers. Now run along, I'm tired.'

Jack made an apologetic exit, still confused and still with no further insight into Sammy Taylor. Heading up the path to the gate, he looked back down to where the electric mobility scooter was parked. He glanced upwards and could see an array of satellite dishes, and the further he walked the more he counted, high up on the roof of the house.

'Ridley, what have you got me into?' he said, shaking his head.

* * *

It was coming up to six by the time Jack arrived back at the station. Sara greeted him with a sympathetic expression.

'How are you? Was it agony?'

'Erm, no . . . not as bad as I thought.'

'Break a crown, did you?'

'Yep, one at the back. All fixed now, though.'

She shook her head. 'You look really awful. I broke a tooth once. It was excruciating.'

Leon walked up.

'Did you have to have it replaced?'

Jack winced. 'No, but they kept me waiting . . . it's hard to get an appointment these days.'

'But it was an emergency!' Sara said.

'For Christ's sake, it's all fixed!' he burst out. He took a breath and spoke in a quieter tone. 'What's the update here?'

Leon went first. 'Sarge, Mrs Thornton from the hostel gave me Amanda's parents' phone number. I spoke to her mother. She told me Amanda wasn't there and they weren't expecting her home. I then called Mrs Delaney and she was certain that no one had returned to the basement flat.'

'OK, thanks. Let's try again on Monday . . . it's very important we find her. What about you, Sara?'

'Karen Middleton had one regular visitor when she was at the rehab centre, her husband's sister, Joyce Miller. Like I say, she was a regular visitor, but they said she was wheelchair-bound and eventually became too ill to –'

'Where does she live?' Jack asked impatiently.

'Surbiton. I have her phone number but couldn't get through. I reported it and was told there was a fault on the line and had been for some time.'

Jack sighed. 'Let's go and interview her now, then. And I'd like you to come along.'

Sara went to collect her briefcase and mobile phone and hurried to catch Jack, who had already left the incident room.

He was sitting in his car with the engine running. Sara climbed in beside him and gave him the address to enter into the satnav.

'Are you sure you're OK to drive?'

Jack was fiddling with the directions, ignoring her.

'I mean, did they give you Procaine?'

'Sara, I'm fine,' he said firmly, hoping to put an end to the conversation.

Sara pursed her lips and remained silent as they drove to the large housing estate in Surbiton. When the satnav said they had arrived at their destination, she curtly pointed out that the flat numbers were on the side of the building, and they were on the wrong side for flat 324.

Jack did a U-turn and followed the narrow lane round the huge estate to the other side. He was able to park almost in front of the relevant block. Glass double doors led into a reception area and number 324 was conveniently located just inside.

'Now we've got here, she's probably not at home,' Jack said moodily.

Sara rang the bell, waited a minute, then rang it again. They stood side by side, listening.

'The lights are on,' Sara said quietly.

Jack leant forwards and pressed the bell again, keeping his finger on it until the main front door to the building opened. A small, wizened man with a black beret walked in carrying a large box of groceries.

'She can't get to the door, you know. Are you from Social Services?'

Jack showed his ID and introduced himself and Sara. The small man balanced the box on his knee and took out a set of keys to open the flat door.

'I'm her husband. My name's Harold. What are you here for?'

Jack explained that he wanted to talk to Joyce about her nephew. Harold shrugged and Jack quickly took the groceries from his knee as he looked as if he was about to drop them. The door opened and Harold ushered them inside.

'I'll go and see if she can talk to you, but she's not been up for much recently. At weekends the carers only come in twice, to get her dressed and put her to bed, so, I'm at her beck and call.'

They stood in the hallway, which had a hideously garish orange floral carpet. There was no furniture, and Harold took off his coat and beret and hung them on a single hook on the back of the front door.

'Do you need us to wear masks?' Sara asked.

'No, don't bother. We both had all the vacs,' Harold said.

'Go straight ahead into the kitchen while I go and check on her.'

They made their way into a large, tiled kitchen, with a bright lino floor and numerous new-looking appliances. Jack put the box of groceries down on a small table with a plastic tablecloth and two matching chairs. They could hear muffled voices. Sara began to unload the groceries from the box. There was lettuce, tomatoes, bags of different vegetables, a sliced seeded loaf, and a sealed bag containing fresh salmon.

'They certainly eat very healthily.' She placed everything out on the table, not knowing where to store everything.

Jack moved closer to the door and could hear Harold saying that she 'should sit up'. There was a soft moaning sound before Harold came out of the bedroom. He was sweating.

'Sorry, I had to use the hydraulics to get the bed moving for her to sit up. It's a new machine and cost a fortune, but it can be problematic. Give her ten minutes to settle herself, then you can go in.'

'I'm sorry for any inconvenience,' Jack said. 'We tried to call, but your phone's out of order.'

'Tell me about it. We've had one problem after another ever since we got an extension put into the bedroom. BT have been back and forth trying to fix it. Now, can I get you a cup of tea?'

'No, thank you.'

Harold noticed the groceries laid out on the table and thanked Sara. He began putting them into the large fridge.

'Did you order my dinner?' a loud voice called out.

Harold sighed and went to the kitchen door. 'Yes, I did, they're delivering in about half an hour. Do you want a cup of tea?'

'No, I don't. They can come in now.'

Jack and Sara walked past Harold and into the bedroom. As soon as they saw her, they struggled to hide their reactions. Joyce was enormous, swathed in a satin kimono that ballooned around her vast bulk. She was propped up against the padded headboard of a huge bed that took up most of the space in the room. There were various levers and wires attached to it, and the mattress was about four feet off the ground. Positioned next to the bed was a table on wheels, as well as a cabinet on wheels holding an array of pills, medicines, and cosmetics, along with a makeup mirror. The wall opposite Joyce had numerous framed photographs on it, and a very impressive flat screen TV. There was a DVD player and stacks of DVDs on a small bookstand underneath it.

'Good afternoon, Joyce,' said Jack. 'I'm Detective Sergeant Jack Warr and this is DC Sara Norton.'

'I hope he gave you a cup of tea. I'm sorry to have kept you wait- ing. You wasn't expected and I always have to have time to get this contraption working. It helps me sit up, and it can also get me onto my feet, but to be honest it's too painful. Did he tell you I've not left this room for over two years?'

'I am very sorry to hear that. Thank you for agreeing to talk to us.'

'You're a nice-looking young man!' she said, giving him a coy smile.

Joyce had so many chins that her features seemed to be tiny compared with the size of her head. Her arms were enormous rolls of fat hung from her shoulders, with tiny little hands and painted fingernails. Jack guessed she must have weighed at least thirty stone. There was nowhere for either of them to sit, so they just stood beside the gigantic bed.

'We just want to ask a few questions about your nephew, Rodney.'

'How did you find me?' she asked, patting her chest.

'Sara contacted the rehab centre where your sister-in-law, Karen, stayed. They kindly gave us your address.'

'Which one? She went to so many, and none of them did her any good. She'd go in and clean herself up, then come out and go straight back on the drugs. Tragic, she was, absolutely tragic . . . but I got so bad I just couldn't get in to see her. Anyway, she topped herself in the end . . . everyone expected it. She never recovered after her girls died . . . it broke her and broke my heart too. Those little girls were adorable, that's them behind you on the wall . . . first thing I see in the morning . . . and the last thing at night.'

Jack turned to look at the framed photographs of the two pretty girls, at various ages from toddler to around the age they were when they died.

'I have a young daughter, so I can understand how terrible it must have been,' Jack said.

'It was terrible. They used to come for weekends with me sometimes, and I took them to the park. I had an electric wheelchair then and they would sit on my knee and have such a laugh. They were cheeky little devils as well, just like any youngster, and Karen spoiled them. They both had iPads and would be on them whenever they could, playing games; the beeping and pinging used to drive Harold mad. Did he not give you a cup of tea?'

'He offered, but we declined. Thank you. I don't want to take up too much of your time, Joyce, but I just need to ask you about Rodney.'

Joyce's body shuddered as she shook her head.

'He had it hard, with his mother walking out on him. My brother never married his mum. She was from Ghana and was a really rough woman. I always thought she got herself pregnant just to move in with Anthony, but nobody could ever tell him what to do. I think Rodney got a lot of racial abuse at school. He also got it from Anthony as he was such a trouble-maker.'

Sara interrupted, asking if she could use the bathroom.

'It's the big wide door in the hallway, dear. Had it widened so I could get my wheelchair through, but I can't use that anymore.'

Sara left the bedroom, closing the door behind her.

'What was his relationship with Karen like?'

'Whose?'

'Your brother.'

'Oh, he worshipped her. She was a looker, and a lovely girl as well. She was only sixteen and they got married when she had her first baby girl, then it started to get too much for her and she started using. I looked after the baby here, but then she got herself back together. I think she had that depression you get after having a baby. Then she goes and has another one, and it was much worse the next time, but I couldn't have them both here as my health wasn't good. I only had them over when they got a bit bigger.'

Joyce shifted her bulk and winced with the pain.

'I don't use the toilet in there no more. My carers have a commode for me. It's a sad life, isn't it? They are such good women, having to wash me privates. I get very painful sores in the creases, and bedsores as well. They have very good ointments for it all. Then there's a girl who comes in to wash and dry my hair, and gives me a manicure, and . . .'

Jack interrupted. 'How did Rodney react to the girls?'

'How do you mean?'

'Well, he was that much older.'

'He was very good with them, especially when Karen was having her bad times, but she never liked having him at home. I think it was very difficult, him not being her own child. And Anthony was handy with his fists when things blew up. Rodney was getting into trouble and my brother didn't like having the coppers turning up. Could you give me some water? There's a plastic beaker on the table, and I need a straw.'

Jack passed her the green plastic mug, along with a thick straw to insert in the lid.

'Thank you, dear.' Joyce took several sips before holding it up for him to take it back. He replaced it on the table just as Sara returned and came to stand beside him again.

'Was your brother abusive to Rodney?'

'I don't want to speak bad of him. He was doing his best, working a few jobs at once and with Karen having trouble with drugs. I know he did knock Rodney around. There had been a big row and I think Karen told Rodney he had to leave, then my brother got involved and it was him that put his foot down and told him he had to go and not come back.'

'Would you have taken him in?' Jack asked.

'No, he couldn't come here; Harold wouldn't allow it.'

'The night of the fire, Rodney was babysitting the girls, wasn't he?'

Joyce nodded. For the first time she appeared to be uneasy, fiddling with her painted fingernails.

'Your brother accused Rodney of having something to do with it.'

'Bad things were said. It was all down to grief; nothing was ever proved and my brother, like poor Karen, never really recovered. He got into bad stuff, and now he's banged up again, but what could I do?'

'Has Rodney tried to contact you?'

'No, he's a loner. I read he got arrested again. What happened the night of the fire ruined everyone's lives.' She paused. 'I'm feeling very tired now, and I need to have my dinner. I hope what I've said is helpful, but can you go now please?'

Jack had no legitimate reason to continue questioning her, and just then the doorbell rang.

'That'll be my dinner,' she said. 'It was nice meeting you.'

Jack and Sara made their way out as Harold was taking pizza boxes and other takeaway cartons from the delivery boy. He almost dropped one box as he fished in his pocket to pay for it all. Jack helped him with the pizza boxes and carried them back into the kitchen, with Sara following.

Harold hurried in to take out the warm plates from the oven.

'I bet she never said a bad word about that brother of hers, but he's a no-good thug. She thinks the sun shines out of his mean arse. She wouldn't listen to anything I had to say about him – that poor girl Karen was sometimes black and blue, just like Rodney. And that poor lad didn't stand a chance, trying to protect those girls. I told her that something bad was happening in their house. I would have called Social Services on him because those two little ones weren't right. They had bruises on them, and sometimes they were filthy. But Joyce would get into a frenzy if I interfered.'

A bell rang and he pursed his lips. 'I've said too much. It's all over now anyway. But if it had carried on, I would have had to do something.'

Jack watched as Harold heaped a hamburger and chips onto one plate, then put garlic bread and a huge pizza onto a second plate. He took some tomato ketchup from the fridge and a large bottle of Coke, placing them all onto a tray with cutlery and a paper napkin.

Jack moved closer to him and spoke quietly. 'Harold, did you think the children were being sexually abused?'

Harold could not look him in the face, turning away as he fussed with salt and pepper shakers.

'I've spoken out of turn. You can show yourselves out. I need to give Joyce her dinner as it's past her usual time, and she won't like it if it gets cold.'

Sara held the door open as Harold carried the tray through, almost bow-legged from the weight of the food. She then opened the bedroom door for him.

As they closed the front door behind them, they heard Harold's voice.

'I have everything you ordered, Joyce dearest.'

* * *

Jack started the car as Sara pulled on her safety belt.

'Was all that food really for her?' she asked.

Jack shrugged. 'There was only one knife and fork. I think Harold eats the healthy food, poor sod. What a life, with that beached whale of a wife.'

'When I passed his room earlier, he was sitting in what I presume was his bedroom,' Sara said. 'It had a single bed and a desk with a computer and a laptop. He was eating a salad. I said I was on my way to the bathroom and he told me he was working on all the documentation to get the carers in for his wife, complaining that it was a full-time job sorting out the benefits she was entitled to. He had to give up work due to a back injury, apparently.'

'No doubt from shifting his wife around,' Jack said.

'Why do you think she protects her brother?' Sara asked.

'Shame, guilt, who knows. But somebody certainly takes care of her very well. The house is spick and span, gets her nails and hair done every week, and all those carers . . . She didn't provide much insight into Rodney, though. Harold gave us more just as we were leaving.'

Jack dropped Sara off at a Tube station as he was eager to get home. He offered to drive her, but she declined. He was relieved as he sometimes found her rather irritating, but more importantly, after the day's interviews, he had a lot to think about.

CHAPTER TEN

Jack arrived home feeling worn out and went straight up to his office to dump his briefcase. He came downstairs where Maggie was reading Hannah a story whilst she sat in her highchair eating a banana, waving it around gleefully. Maggie caught his arm and whispered to him that he should say something about his mother's hair. Jack gave her a puzzled look, as Hannah threw the banana skin at him and giggled.

Penny was bending down and looking into the oven, checking the chicken.

'Hi, Mum, I'm just going to do some work in my office.'

'It's a chicken in the bag, with stuffing. It's really wonderful, cooks inside the bag and you just take it off and its ready to serve.'

Penny turned around to face him and Jack was glad that he had been warned. Her hair was not only quite short, but very blonde.

'Good Heaven's, Ma! You look wonderful. It really suits you. Turn around for me.'

Penny giggled and did a twirl, then fluffed the curls. 'I decided I was looking too frumpy and old fashioned. Do you like it?'

'I most certainly do. It makes you look much younger. Good for you! Give me a shout when dinner's ready.'

Jack hurried up the stairs, thinking that perhaps he should pay more attention, not only to his mother, but to Maggie as well.

Eager to get back to the Ridley investigation, Jack unloaded his briefcase. He stacked the pages into a neat pile to sort through and prioritise, then picked up the first memory stick which had a typed note taped to it, indicating that this was the post-mortem report. Jack wondered how the hell Ridley had gained access to it. He plugged it into the laptop he had taken back from Leon, still fully charged, and was just about to open it when Maggie popped her head around the door.

'What did you think of the new hairstyle?'

'A bit of a surprise, but she seems very happy with it,' he smiled.

Maggie shut the door behind her and came over to his desk. Jack shut the laptop, not wanting Maggie to see what he was working on.

'I was emptying the bedroom waste bin,' Maggie said, 'and there were loads of Marks & Spencer clothing bags in there. Penny's been buying a new wardrobe by the look of it.'

Jack shrugged. 'OK, so maybe that's where the extra money went. But I don't think she's bought anything new since our wedding. You know, if you ever want to have a new hairstyle, or new clothes, or whatever . . .'

Maggie looked at him quizzically. 'What do you mean?'

'Well, I was just thinking . . . I mean, you look perfect to me, but I know I'm not very good at complimenting you. Maybe you need to take some time out to pamper yourself.'

'What's the matter with my hair?'

'Nothing, I just meant that we've both been working flat out – you in particular – and sometimes it's good to do something for yourself.'

Maggie put her arms around him, but he shrugged her away. 'I'm being serious, but now I need you to leave me alone as I have some work to do.'

'Want to talk about it?' she asked.

'No, it's the Ridley situation. I've not had the time to go over all the material he gave me, so I want to catch up. I can't focus on it at the station as I'm still getting nowhere fast with this Middleton case. His girlfriend has disappeared and I need some information from her.' He raked his hand through his hair. 'I met Rodney's aunt today. She was enormous, like a big wobbling waterbed and . . .' He sighed.

'See, you've got me started. Just leave me to sort out Ridley's stuff. I don't want to even think about bloody Rodney Middleton.'

Maggie held up her hands in mock surrender. 'I'm going, I'm going. I can't wait for dinner: it's chicken in a bag that cooks itself!'

Maggie shut the door behind her and Jack opened his laptop again. A voice-over on the video gave the date, time and the location of the mortuary, then the screen filled with the shot of the body on the mortuary table, covered in a green plastic sheet. Two figures in white suits with hoods and masks were mopping the floor, and the pathologist, a man Jack didn't recognise, stood holding a clipboard. He was also dressed in a white protective suit and had a white hat pulled down over his hair. Jack knew that the post-mortem had already been completed. He saw two other masked men standing to one side, neither of whom were known to him.

'Right, gentlemen, let me take you through the findings,' the pathologist began. 'The victim has deep strangulation marks on her neck, made by some kind of cord, perhaps from an electrical appliance. I would say that the assailant was standing behind her. There are no defensive wounds on her hands, so I estimate it was looped over her head and tightened quickly so that she lost consciousness within a very short time. The stomach contents revealed that her last meal was a steak and salad with fruit. Obviously, we will await the toxicology report to ascertain if there were any drugs or alcohol in her system, but she appeared to be in good health, with good muscle tone. Consequently, I initially estimated her age to be late thirties. However, I was wrong.'

Jack was only half paying attention. The victim's head remained covered, and he was eager to see her face, but then his attention was alerted again.

'I would like my assistant, Nidal, to explain her findings and the reason I may have miscalculated the victim's age.'

Moving into the camera shot was a petite, dark-skinned woman wearing a white coat, mask, and with her hair under a cap. She slowly lifted the plastic sheet away from the victim's head and lowered it to just above her shoulders. Jack craned forwards but she was standing in front of the victim and blocking his view.

'It is clear from her hairline that she has had a lot of plastic surgery: her forehead has been lifted and her neck has been tightened. She also has chin and cheek implants, and her nose has been very carefully reconstructed. Whoever did this surgery was an expert. Examining the victim's rib cage there are a number of small scars, which underscores this, as it is usual, when reshaping a nose, to take small slithers of bone from the rib cage. She does not have any breast implants but has had silicone injections. She has faded white lines from being suntanned some months prior to her death, and her hair has been professionally coloured and highlighted recently, as there is no natural new growth showing.'

At last Jack got a close-up view of the woman on the slab. Even devoid of any makeup her skin looked flawless. The assistant covered the victim's head again and took out a hand from beneath the cover.

'No defensive wounds, and very well-manicured nails. Again, I found slight scars which can be found when surgery is used to tighten the skin and remove age spots.'

She replaced the victim's hand under the plastic sheet and moved to the end of the slab to lift the cover from her feet.

'The victim clearly took care of her feet with regular pedicures and there is no hard skin. The same colour varnish used on her fingernails is also on her toes, but a tell-tale sign of her real age is the fact that on both feet she has quite advanced bunions, which may have been quite painful.'

The pathologist now moved into shot, gesturing to the victim. 'So, we know she is five foot eight, and we know her weight was almost ten stone, but we had some difficulty estimating her exact age; from Nidal's experienced inspection, we both now think that she may in fact be in her late fifties to mid-sixties, rather than her late thirties. I believe that her killer was forensically experienced as we found no fibres of any description, other than from the vehicle carpet. It is possible her naked body had been taped to remove any clues, and with no clothes there was no further examination by a forensic fibre expert. We are still waiting for the toxicology reports.'

Jack leaned back in his chair. 'Bloody hell.'

The video ended and Jack removed the memory stick from his laptop. He then found the biographical details Ridley had been sent by the dating agency. A note attached from Ridley said that the investigation had attempted to trace her identity via the national accountancy register but they found no one of her name, going back 15 years.

Given her real age, Jack wondered if they should have gone even further back. But perhaps they would have done, as the post-mortem had taken place some time ago. He made a note to check. He recalled Ridley saying to him in the past, 'Never presume, Jack, always make sure'.

Jack was just about to insert the second memory stick into his laptop, which the note attached said was the CCTV surveillance footage. Again, Jack wondered how the hell Ridley had got access to it, unless a lawyer was representing him, and they would have been granted access to the evidence. But surely things hadn't got that far. While he was pondering, his burner phone rang. He physically jumped up from the chair, searching his jacket pockets, then delving into his briefcase.

'Hello?'

'Hello, dear, mission accomplished. It will be with you this evening.'

Before Jack could say anything else, the call was cut off. He ran his fingers through his hair feeling a certain amount of panic. He had obviously given Sammy the burner phone number but not his address. How was Sammy going to deliver whatever it was? He would just have to wait.

'Concentrate, concentrate, for fuck's sake,' he muttered to himself as he put the burner phone back into his briefcase and inserted the memory stick with the CCTV footage.

The video was poor quality and grainy. He could clearly see Ridley parking his Volvo car in the pub car park at precisely 7.52 p.m. according to the timer code at the top of the screen, and then, on another camera, he could see him entering the pub. It appeared to be quite an upmarket establishment, with a separate entrance for the restaurant. There was a fuzzy delay as the footage cut to Ridley exiting the pub at 8.45 p.m., indicating that he had been waiting for his date for just under an hour. He paused in the well-lit exit, perhaps searching for his car keys, before putting on his thick leather gloves and walking out into the car park. He did not appear to be inebriated, walking quite briskly, and then there was another delay as the footage picked Ridley up next to his Volvo, getting into the driver's side and then pulling out of the car park. The video then jumped back to the coverage of his car in the car park, from the time he left it to the time he returned. Numerous other vehicles were seen entering and parking during the time Ridley was inside the pub. Although the whole of Ridley's car wasn't visible, it appeared that no one moved close to it or tampered with it.

The footage ended, leaving Jack none the wiser. He ran the footage again to double check that there had been no altering of the timer code. Ridley had claimed that he had no recollection of anything after he had left the pub, no memory of returning home, or where he had left his car. He had woken up in bed, still fully clothed, with a severe headache, feeling nauseous and confused. As it was a Saturday night and Ridley was off-duty he had vomited and returned to bed, sleeping for most of the following day. He woke numerous times on the Sunday feeling very sick and feverish and had not checked whether his car was in the garage or parked outside the house. Late that evening he had received a call to say that his vehicle had been found, and he was instructed to remain at home until Essex CID arrived. His vehicle had been impounded and was undergoing forensic testing.

Jack thumbed through the notes Ridley had made. He had asked to have a medical check as he was certain he had been given drugs. However, this was not done for a further forty-eight hours and therefore whatever he may have been given would not have shown up, as by this time he had eaten and digested two meals.

The doorbell rang and Jack almost jumped again. He hurried out of his office and down the stairs as Maggie came out to answer the door.

'It's OK; it's a delivery for me,' Jack said hastily, and Maggie turned back to the kitchen.

Sammy Taylor was wearing a pinstriped suit, and an immaculate white shirt and tie, and his face showed no trace of makeup. Jack had to catch his breath, as Sammy proffered a brown manila envelope.

'Er, do you want to come in?' Jack said falteringly.

'No, dear, I don't. I have a dinner engagement. I will make this fast as I hate to be late. There was quite a lot of data to record, so I had to use seven sticks, but it's all there. They might not be in the right order, but once I'd opened their files I just kept going.'

'Thank you.'

'My pleasure. Good night.'

Sammy picked up a silver-topped walking cane he had propped up against the porch, turned and slowly walked down the path before disappearing behind the hedge. Jack waited a few moments, then slowly eased around the hedge, trying to keep out of sight. He saw Sammy bleep open a Bentley saloon, but it was too far away for him to get a look at the licence plate before it drove off.

Jack hurried back into the house and up the stairs to his office, closing the door behind him. He had just tipped out the contents of the envelope when Maggie called up the stairs to say that dinner was ready. Jack closed his laptop and put everything back into the envelope before heading downstairs.

Penny was sitting at the table, a bottle of wine open in front of her. Maggie was eulogising about the chicken in the bag.

'It came out perfectly cooked, Jack. You just cut open the bag! Will you carve while I get the vegetables?'

Jack agreed that it looked very tasty, dishing it out before pouring them all a glass of wine.

'Who was that at the door?' Maggie asked as they tucked in.

'Just someone from the station delivering something for me. I might have to work for a while tonight.'

Penny turned to the baby monitor, hearing a noise. She smiled, as it was just Hannah turning in her sleep and giving a little grunt.

'Can I ask you something, Mum? You know when you have your hair coloured, how long does it last before the old colour starts showing?'

'Well, I'm not sure . . . it depends on how fast your hair grows, I think. It could be three or four weeks. But they have this new stuff that you just put along the roots where the grey starts to show, so you don't have to have a complete re-colour.'

Maggie raised an eyebrow, wondering why on earth Jack wanted to know, and if perhaps he didn't like his mother's new blonde look. Maggie became even more bemused when Jack asked Penny which salon she had used. She replied that it was just a local hairdresser, and they had only recently reopened for customers after the Covid restrictions. She went on to say they were very good and not too expensive.

Maggie looked quizzically at Jack, but he was picking up his plate and pushing back his chair.

'I hope you'll excuse me, but I want to crack on with something that might take a while.'

Jack put his plate into the dishwasher, opened the fridge and took out a bottle of water, carrying it out of the kitchen. Penny shook her head, telling Maggie she had lost count of how many times she had told Jack to rinse off the dirty plates before putting them in the dishwasher.

'Listen, at least he's now putting them into the dishwasher,' Maggie laughed. 'He used to just leave everything in the sink, only inches away from the dishwasher. I'll take him up a coffee when I've cleared the kitchen. That chicken was really good – thank you. We should get one again.'

* * *

Jack was glued to his laptop screen, as one photograph after another came up from the agency files, along with the applicants' particulars. He had only been looking at female applicants so far, and there seemed to be hundreds of them. The majority appeared to be middle-aged retired women, widows or divorcees.

As Sammy had warned, they were not in any kind of order and Jack fast-forwarded through the entire file for the past four years. He was eager to talk to Ridley to find out the names of the two women he had dated before Sandra, but he was concerned about contacting him at his home. Ridley had told him that he would call when he could have a safe conversation with him.

He eventually found the photograph of Sandra Raynor, and could see all her details. He had to admit she did look very attractive, but Jack now knew her youthful appearance was as fake as her CV.

He inserted the second stick, hoping it would be the male applicants. Instead, it contained details of the company finances, client charges, rates, rent and tax documents along with VAT. It all appeared to be properly organised and straightforward, but Jack was taken aback by the amount the agency charged, as well as the finance details their clients agreed to submit. Most of them were reasonably well off, but some were very wealthy. He ploughed on, searching for anything that looked illegal, but it all seemed to be very much above board; Eva Shay had been an accountant, after all. When he looked into the agency's bank details, there were three separate accounts. One assigned to the company, then separate accounts for Eva Shay and Mrs Da Costa.

The two women paid themselves a reasonable salary, but, again, there did not seem to be anything that stood out as suspicious, until he looked through Eva Shay's personal account with Barclays. Two large cash sums had been paid in, one for just over £20,000 and a second deposit for over £25,000. Both deposits were then transferred to a bank in Monaco. The dates of the deposits matched the time Ridley told him he had joined the agency. He double-checked Mrs Da Costa's account and saw that both women had savings amounting to £30,000 in their UK accounts, while the agency had £22,000. He wondered if Eva Shay was transferring cash without Mrs Da Costa's knowledge.

Maggie knocked on the door and entered with a mug of coffee. Jack spun round in his chair.

'I always know when you don't want me to see what you're working on! It must be something interesting because you almost jumped when I walked in.'

Jack laughed.

'Is it about Rodney Middleton?'

'No, it's for Ridley. How I've got this information is a bit dodgy, so I'm a little paranoid.'

'I hope you're taking precautions. You're working on this outside the station, aren't you?'

'Yes, and I'm being as careful as I can. I'm just checking out the dating agency Ridley joined at the moment.'

'I'm still amazed that he did that, but then you never really know people the way you think you know them.'

Jack sipped his coffee and rocked back and forth in his desk chair.

'I'm sure he was set up. But I have no idea how or why. Without being able to discuss anything with him, I feel as though I am sort of working blind.'

'I bet you any money it will be connected to some old case, somebody with a big grudge against him; perhaps someone just out of prison, or something like that.'

'Yeah, that's possible. But it's hard to see how anyone like that could have known about the dating agency.'

'That's what makes me worried: because it doesn't quite make sense,' Maggie said.

She put her arms around him and kissed his neck.

'You should quit for tonight. You have Sunday to work. Is this your laptop?'

'Yes, er, it's an old one, I'm just using it to work on Ridley's situation. It's not connected to the internet. I don't want to use the station's; that's under my desk.'

'Oh, well, good for you; keep it private, right?'

'Yes, I'll be along in a few minutes, and thanks for the coffee.'

As soon as Maggie had left, Jack started making notes about what he needed to ask Ridley. It would be difficult for him to dig up old cases Ridley had been involved with, as it would draw attention, and he was certain that the detectives working on the murder would have already gone down that route. But right now Maggie was right: he was tired. His eyes were burning from staring at the small laptop screen.

He decided he would call it a night and continue in the morning. He tidied up all the documents and computer sticks, putting them safely into a drawer. Then he sat for a few minutes, letting everything he'd learned settle in his mind. Nothing stood out as significant: unless it was the fact that the woman calling herself Sandra Raynor and Eva Shay had both been accountants, but he couldn't see how that connected with Ridley. He quickly decided he was too tired to carry on thinking about it.

By the time Jack went to their bedroom it was after 1 a.m. He was in the bathroom cleaning his teeth when his mobile pinged. He pulled it out of his jacket, which he had hung on the back of the door. There was a message from an unknown caller, but as he listened to it, he knew it was Ridley: *Same place, same time, tomorrow. If you can't be there, I'll re-contact.*

CHAPTER ELEVEN

Jack arrived at the John Lewis car park to find that it didn't open until 8 a.m. He drove around the back and parked close to the Turk's boat yard. Maggie had been still in bed when he had left so he had stopped en route to buy two takeaway coffees. Ridley was waiting for him, and it seemed to Jack as though he had aged since their last meeting. He was wearing a heavy coat, a woollen beany hat and fur-lined gloves, as well as his usual corduroy trousers. Jack was wishing he'd put on a warmer coat as it was freezing cold.

A mist was coming off the river as Ridley took the coffee from him. They walked a short distance before sitting on the same bench as before. It was clear that he was depressed with the slow pace of the investigation, with the dead woman still remaining unidentified.

Jack told him that he had watched the video footage of the post-mortem, but without saying anything about her real age. He remarked that it was a very professional murder and Ridley agreed, saying they had found no fibres on her naked body apart from the small amount that matched the carpet in the boot of his Volvo.

'I would say that whoever killed her used sticky tape to make sure nothing was found forensically, wiping her body of anything that might have helped identify her,' Ridley said.

Jack sipped his coffee and nodded. He was feeling the cold, wrapping his hands around the warm cardboard takeaway coffee beaker. 'First up, never mind being unable to trace Sandra Raynor for a minute. Give me the lowdown on Sammy Taylor – dressed up like a drag queen in the afternoon, then came round to my home – which I didn't like, by the way – looking like a conservative MP, driving a Bentley.'

Ridley hesitated before replying. 'He was a top agent for MI5, got caught in a blackmail scam twenty years ago which I sorted out – no press, no scandal. He's a computer genius and until recently used to do covert work for the government and secret service.'

Jack was astonished. 'You are joking! If he was blackmailed before, how come he's now getting away with making a podcast dressed as a drag queen?'

'There's no need to be crass.'

'Crass? Is that what you think I'm being? He fucking freaked me out of my head – he takes me into a room with more equipment and monitors than we've got at the station and is able to hack into private bank accounts and criminal records. My electric bill would come in at almost double if I had that amount of equipment. Are you telling me it won't create suspicion?'

Ridley stood up, moving towards the waste bin.

'Fine. I understand your concerns, and I'm sorry to have dragged you into this. So perhaps we should call it quits.'

Ridley tossed the empty coffee beaker into the bin. Jack sighed, but when it looked as if Ridley was going to walk away, he jumped up. 'No wait, please, I'm sorry, but I needed to sound off, and it's not as if I could let it rip with anyone else.'

Ridley turned. 'I don't want to put any more pressure on you. If it makes you feel better, the debt is repaid. There will be no further contact with Sammy – and he's on his way to New York now.'

Ridley gave a small shrug of his shoulders.

'I won't ask you for another meeting, but if you have found out anything helpful, I'd appreciate you telling me before I go.'

'Let's sit down,' Jack said. 'Come on, you're not going anywhere.'

Ridley came and sat back down beside Jack. Jack took his notebook out of his pocket, tapping it with his forefinger.

'I have made some progress but not a lot. I'm still gathering as much information as I can on the agency, but I need to know the names of the first two women you had dates with. Can you recall if you mentioned anything to either of them about your job?'

Ridley frowned.

'The first woman was called Jessica Phillips. The other was Daniella Foster. As I said, they were very nice women ... just not my type. I certainly never discussed my real work. As you know, I used a different name and occupation ... until I met Sandra.'

Jack nodded. 'On the first two dates, you only had drinks?'

'Yes, apparently on the first date it's normal to just "meet and greet". If you get along, the agency organises a second date, usually meeting for dinner at a restaurant agreeable to both parties.'

'Did either of the first two women ask about your work?'

'Yes, Daniella, did. But I said I was retired.'

'Did either of them get into your car?'

'Jessie had her own transport.'

'What about Daniella?'

Ridley thought for a moment. 'After we left the bar the first time we met, I drove her to her flat in Pimlico. But she realised she had left her gloves on the table, so we drove back to the bar. I went in to retrieve them. I was only gone a few moments.'

'Was there anything in your car that could have given Daniella knowledge of your true identity?'

Ridley frowned, shaking his head. 'I suppose there might have been something in the glove compartment, but I kept it locked.'

Jack nodded. 'Can you recall any case, past or present, which might be connected?'

Ridley sighed. 'I've been over this again and again. And we discussed it the last time we met as well. There's nothing that I was recently working on that gives me cause to think that someone would want to fit me up with a murder rap.'

'How far back did you go?'

'Christ, Jack! I have been racking my brains over it ever since I was arrested! There is nothing I can think of that would make someone want to fucking screw my life up like this.'

'What about anything that came in after you joined the dating agency?'

'Bloody hell, Jack, I had three dates and had only been signed with the agency for a few months. I don't think that route is going to be productive.'

'OK . . . then what about Sandra? Is there any possibility that you might have crossed paths with her under her real name at some point before?'

Ridley sighed. 'I've been over that, too, over and over. I cannot recall anyone that resembled Sandra, whatever bloody age she was when I had the dates. I simply have no recollection of anyone like her. But then God knows what the hell she used to look like before the surgery.'

Jack could understand Ridley's frustration, but he was starting to feel annoyed at having his anger directed towards him. He was doing the best he bloody could.

'OK, let me go down a different route,' he said. 'The agency contacted you to arrange a date with Sandra. Which of the two women at the agency organised it?'

'It was Eva Shay. I only had one brief meeting with Mrs Da Costa.'

'So, you saw Sandra's photograph and you agreed to meet her for a drink?'

'Yes!' Ridley snapped.

'Did you choose the venue, or did Eva Shay?'

'I did, and this is all in my notes, Jack. Then Sandra chose the restaurant for the dinner.'

'Then, after this dinner you . . .'

Ridley answered tetchily. 'I took her home to my house, for more drinks and mutual sex. I put all this in my notes, Jack. But if you want me to spell it out, obviously it was a big mistake for me to have taken her home; she could have found out exactly who I was. She had time to poke around when I took a shower, and when I went out to buy another bottle of champagne. I left her in my bed, for God's sake! There's no fucking idiot like an old sexually frustrated one, right?'

Jack felt bad about making Ridley go through it all again, but the truth was that he had not had the time to go through all of Ridley's meticulous notes. Now he wished that he had.

'I'm working on a possible lead connected to Eva Shay,' he said. 'She was an accountant and so was Sandra – or she claimed to have been one.'

'It's a waste of time, Jack. The company Sandra claimed to work for never employed her, and Eva Shay hasn't worked as an accountant for many years. I'm sorry, I don't want to sound ungrateful.'

Ridley turned, reaching for Jack's hand to shake.

'Anything, Jack, anything you can do. I am so indebted to you, but time is running out.'

Jack didn't take his hand. 'To be totally honest with you, I'm finding it very difficult to understand how you're being investigated for Sandra's murder but you haven't been arrested. If the evidence is so overwhelming, how come you're not in a cell – or at least out on bail? It just doesn't add up, and it feels as if you're not being entirely honest with me. I mean, why get Sammy Taylor to do all that illegal digging around when the investigating team could have done the same thing themselves?'

Ridley sighed. 'You're right, I haven't been entirely honest.' He took a deep breath. 'The truth is, because of my high profile in the Met, I *am* under a form of house arrest until the investigation is concluded, so they can keep it from being made public. I need you to know how desperate I am. So far they've come up with nothing – not even Sandra Raynor's real identity – let alone any connection with me or any motivation to frame me. I am no nearer to being exonerated than when they found her body in the boot of my car. I need you, Jack!'

Ridley lifted his right trouser leg to show Jack he was wearing an electronic tag on his ankle. Jack could tell how humiliating it was for him, and quickly put an arm around his shoulders.

'Let's just walk and talk for a while,' Jack said. 'I'll fill you in on some other stuff that I've been working on that may be of interest.'

'Let's do that. But please hurry, Jack. I don't know how much longer I'll be allowed out of the house, and I wouldn't be surprised if they had someone tailing me right now.'

* * *

Jack did not get back home until after 11 a.m. Penny had taken Hannah to Sunday School at the local church, and Maggie was still dozing in bed, so he made himself a bacon sandwich and went up to work in his office. He re-inserted the memory stick he had accessed before to search through the dating agency's female clients. Eventually he found Jessica Phillips and Daniella Foster. He printed out their CVs and photographs and took a good look at them both. They were not very flattering images. Jessica looked very homely and Daniella had an equally ordinary presence, but it was Daniella's CV that caught Jack's attention. She had trained as a nurse and described herself as a widow and a retired consultant for a prominent plastic surgeon. It was a long shot, but he put Jessica and Daniella's papers to one side, with a view to questioning them both.

Jack finished his bacon sandwich, dropping tomato ketchup onto his note pad. He then inserted the next memory stick into his laptop and trawled through the agency's male clients. It was a lengthy and tedious process, looking for any face that he recognised or who might have a criminal background, but nothing stood out from the catalogue of well-off middle-aged men looking for a relationship, many of whom were widowers.

Then Jack came across Ridley's photograph, with his fake name, Arnold Radley. He had listed his profession as a retired surveyor, stating that he was single, had never been married, slim build, fit and 6ft tall. In addition, he enjoyed sports and would like to meet someone with similar interests, with a view to a serious relationship. Finally he had £30,000 in savings and investments. Jack printed all of Ridley's information out, putting it with the other clients of interest.

He inserted the final memory stick, unsure what Sammy – or whatever his name was – had been able to hack into. What he found was newspaper coverage and advertising for the dating agency, and various related women's magazine articles. Mrs Da Costa seemed to have less coverage than Eva Shay who was featured as a successful career woman promoting a special agency for an older clientele, stating that privacy and security were the company's top priorities. In the article she also said that it was important that anyone applying was given an in-depth interview ensuring that they would be matched with the right partner. This reduced the risks sometimes associated with online dating.

Jack noticed that Eva Shay was very well preserved for her age, perhaps as a result of plastic surgery. She appeared to be quite glamorous, despite a rather old-fashioned hairstyle which was heavily lacquered. She also wore too much makeup. Pictured wearing evening gowns and velvet suits with frilly white shirts, most of the magazine articles about her said the same thing about the discreetness of the agency, which claimed to have an impressive success rate, with a number of matches ending in marriage.

The landline on his desk rang and he left Maggie to answer it. She called out to him from downstairs.

Jack went onto the landing and looked over the banister. 'Is it for me?'

'No, it was for Penny. They're back from church. I'm just taking Hannah to the park. You'll notice that I'm wearing my running kit, as I'm going to jog with the buggy. I don't suppose you fancy joining me for some exercise?'

'Sorry, sweetheart, I'm still working. But I promise to finish so we can have dinner together this evening.'

'OK, see you later.'

Jack returned to his office and looked out of the window to see Maggie running down the path pushing the buggy. She looked so young, with her curly hair tied up in a ponytail. He felt a rush of emotion as he watched his wife and his little girl. He loved them both so much, and it pained him that he couldn't join them as he went back to his desk. Just as he resumed scrolling through more footage his mobile rang. He scrambled around trying to find it amongst all the papers, and eventually located it underneath one of the files. He didn't recognise the number but answered anyway.

'Hello?' The voice was very faint and nervous-sounding.

'Hello, who is this?' Jack replied.

'Can I speak to Mr Warr please.'

'Yes, this is him speaking. Who is this?'

'It's Amanda Dunn. You gave me your number when I was at the hostel.'

*   *   *

Jack pulled on his leather jacket as he ran down the stairs, carrying a large manila envelope. Penny was speaking to someone on the phone in the hall and laughing. She quickly covered the mouthpiece when he stopped in front of her.

'Please tell Maggie I had to go out, but it won't take too long. I'll call her when I know what time I'll be home, but I'll be back in time for dinner.'

'Alright, dear.'

Penny waited until Jack had closed the front door behind him before continuing her call. Her cheeks were flushed pink as she said that her son had just left and that she was having a nice restful Sunday as her daughter-in-law had taken her granddaughter out to the park. She gave a rather embarrassed laugh in response to the other person's next comment, saying that she was flattered, but she was definitely old enough to be a grandmother.

Jack drove to Euston Station, and as it was Sunday, the traffic was fairly light. He parked on a meter before heading into the station via the side entrance, looking around for the Café Nero coffee bar. He spotted it across the virtually empty station forecourt and headed for the three small tables outside. Amanda was sitting at one of them, with a cappuccino in a large white cup with two biscuits in the saucer. Jack waved and she started to stand but then sat down again.

'Looks like you don't need another coffee yet?' he said.

'No, thank you. I don't really like this frothy stuff, but the biscuits come free with it. I've been here for quite a while and wasn't sure if you would come. I just wanted to let you know that I'm going home to Liverpool . . . at least that's what I want to do, but like I said on the phone, I'm a bit short on the train fare. I didn't know who else I could call, so I hope you don't mind.'

Jack pulled out a chair and sat down opposite her. He was unsure if she was telling the truth about going to Liverpool. Sara had spoken to her parents on Friday, and they had said she wasn't expected.

'They were very nice at the hostel, but they kept on asking what my intentions were and whether I was going to see my mother. So eventually I just said that I was, and I left.'

Amanda looked down beside her chair at a small worn holdall.

'So where have you been since then?' Jack asked.

'Oh, mostly just walking around, trying to think what I should do about the money.'

She looked very dishevelled. Her hair was lank, her face was dirty, and she had badly bitten fingernails. She quickly tucked them into her worn coat sleeves when she noticed Jack looking at them.

'You've been sleeping rough, haven't you?'

'Yes, but not here – it's too dangerous. I went into the West End and slept in a shop doorway. A lot of them are still all shuttered after Covid, and there was a van serving hot soup to the homeless, so I was alright. But I kept my eyes open, just in case.'

'You're very brave, but you should have stayed at the hostel until it was time to catch the train. They've been very concerned about you.'

'I needed to get away. Can you lend me the money?'

Jack took out his wallet. He then placed the manila envelope down on the table.

'I need you to do something for me in return, Amanda. The money for your train fare won't be a loan. I am just relieved you are going to go home.'

She grimaced, then looked around the station.

'What do you want me to do? I mean, it's very public here.'

Jack shook his head, realising that she was thinking he was suggesting sexual favours. He opened the envelope.

'I want you to look at some photographs, and all you have to do is tell me if you've seen any of these girls at Rodney's basement flat. That's all I want you to do, Amanda, nothing else.'

'Oh . . . alright. Do you have any cigarettes?'

Jack shook his head. 'I don't smoke. But I'll buy you a pack as well as helping you out with the train fare. So, I am going to lay out the photographs and I just want you to tell me if you recognise any of them.'

Jack pulled out the photographs that Sara had brought up from missing persons and laid them out side by side on the table in front of Amanda.

'Take your time and look at them carefully. Don't worry if you can't recognise any of them – you'll still get your cigarettes and your money. I need you to be very sure.'

Amanda chewed at her bottom lip, and Jack noticed a nasty cold sore at the corner of her mouth. She pulled her filthy hands out from her coat sleeves and leant forwards, scrutinising each photograph as Jack waited patiently.

'I'm ready,' she said quietly.

'Point to any ones you recognise,' Jack said.

Amanda pointed to the missing Jamaican girl, pushing the photograph forwards slightly. She then tapped the photograph of another missing girl, and a third.

'None of the others,' she said nervously.

Jack quickly gathered up the photographs of the ones she had not chosen. He then put the three girls side by side and asked if she could recall their names.

'It was quite a long time ago, but that black girl was called Jamail. The second one I think was Trudie and the third was something like Nadine or Naomi?'

'These girls all stayed at the basement flat when you were there with Rodney?'

'Yes, he picked them up from here, from Euston Station, and brought them back to the flat.'

'How long did they stay with you there?'

Amanda shrugged. 'Sometimes a couple of days, sometimes longer. I never liked them being there, and we had big fights about it. Then he would lock me up and tell me to mind my own business, said he was just being friendly to them.'

'How friendly?'

'I dunno. When they was there I was locked into the other room. They would stay with him in his bedroom. In fact, funnily enough, I was thinking about the one I said was called Jamail, although that might not be her real name; anyway, reason I was thinking about her was because . . .'

Amanda bent down and picked up her small overnight bag. She unzipped it and began searching through the contents, then took out a dirty plastic makeup bag and rooted through it, eventually pulling out a silver bracelet. She kept it in her hand as she replaced everything and then zipped the bag up again.

'I thought it was maybe one of them Pandora charm bracelets, but I don't think so, cos they're quite expensive, aren't they?'

She uncurled her hand to show Jack the bracelet. It was a silver chain with a few small silver charms on it.

'You can have it if you like. It was Jamail's. I found it in the bedsheets after she'd gone. The clasp is broken so it's not much use to me.'

Jack could feel his heart thumping as he smiled and took the bracelet from her. 'Thank you, Amanda. I appreciate it.' He placed it inside the envelope along with the photographs.

'Can I have the money now, so I can get the next train?' she asked.

Jack was just in time to stop her reaching out to take his wallet. 'How much did you say you needed?'

'A standard ticket is nearly seventy quid and I've only got thirty-two. You said you'd buy me some fags and I smoke the Silk Cut purple, and . . .'

Jack opened his wallet and took out three twenty-pound notes and a five-pound note.

'Thank you ever so much,' she said, grabbing them. 'I really appreciate it. I'll get right over to the ticket kiosk.'

Jack stood up as Amanda bent down to pick up her holdall. He was about to follow her when the waiter came out of the Café Nero and asked if he wanted to pay the bill. Jack smiled when he discovered that not only had she had two large cappuccinos but a toasted ham sandwich and two chocolate brownies! He gave the waiter a twenty-pound note and told him to keep the change. Walking back across the station forecourt towards the side entrance he caught sight of Amanda at the ticket kiosk leaning in to talk to the ticket seller.

Jack was just driving away from his parking bay when he saw Amanda crossing back over to the other side of the station to get into a taxi. He knew she had lied about needing the money for a train fare home to her parents, but he had gained so much information from her that he didn't care.

When he got home Maggie was upstairs playing with Hannah. He went straight into his office and tossed the envelope down on the desk. He was certain that with this new information he could get a search warrant, and he would do it first thing in the morning. At least he was getting somewhere with the Rodney Middleton investigation at last, which was more than he could say about Ridley's. He would have to conduct a lot more interviews, which would need to be very carefully planned in order to avoid alerting the Essex team. If it became known that he was involved, Jack would be in serious trouble.

CHAPTER TWELVE

Jack had been held up in traffic due to an accident. An ambulance had crashed through a barrier as a cyclist had veered out of the bike lane into the main road, and Jack had witnessed it, so had to stop at the scene to give his details.

When he finally got to the station, eager to talk to DCI Clarke about the warrant, he found out from the CRIS Centre that Clarke and Anik were both in court that morning and would not be back until lunch time. Swearing under his breath, he sat down at his desk and wrote up his meeting with Amanda Dunn at Euston Station. He had already placed the bracelet in an evidence bag and wanted to show it to Sara before it went into the lockup. Laura walked in, carrying a takeaway coffee. She leaned against the side of his desk.

'Did you read the memo that came in for the DCI yesterday morning? Apparently, he was really pissed off and was going to have a go at the know-it-all legal aid who's in court this morning.'

Jack frowned. 'What are you talking about?'

'Rodney Middleton is going to get bail, and . . .'

Jack pushed his chair back angrily. 'You are bloody joking?'

'No, that's why Anik is in court; he's got a similar situation with his case. There's a massive backlog and they're putting trials back weeks.'

'Has he got bail or is it under review?'

'I don't know. I've only just read the memo myself.'

'Shit! Which court are they in?'

'Kingston, I think, but double-check on CRIS.'

Jack spotted Sara and called out to her to join him.

'Morning, sarge, hope you had a nice restful Sunday off.'

'I need you to do something for me urgently.,' Jack said, 'I met up with Amanda Dunn yesterday.'

Sara followed Jack back to his desk as he quickly explained what Amanda had told him, and then held up the plastic evidence bag.

'I need you to contact Jamail's family and check if she ever owned this bracelet. Then I want you to look into the other two girls she identified to see if they were using the Christian names Trudie, Nadine or Naomi. You'll need to go back to the missing persons reports.'

Sara took the evidence bag and the three photographs, then hurried to her desk whilst Jack grabbed his leather jacket and briefcase, before leaving the incident room together.

Kingston Crown Court was in the new annex. The old court-house was rarely used so Jack parked up there. The old car park had been used for Covid testing and there were still lots of old signs indicating where cars and pedestrians needed to wait. Jack showed his ID to the parking attendant, saying he was due to give evidence.

Jack went in through the court's side entrance and made his way along one corridor after another before he came out into the large reception area. There were numerous lawyers, clerics, proba-tion officers and uniformed officers standing around in different groups, as the court was not yet in session. Any defendant being brought to trial would not have been brought up to the court yet. He looked around, searching for his DCI, but could not see him anywhere. He spotted Anik having a heated discussion with a female barrister and made his way towards them. He tapped Anik on the shoulder.

'Where's DCI Clarke? I need to talk to him urgently.'

Anik looked at Jack, then back to the woman he'd been talking to. 'This is Detective Sergeant Jack Warr, Miss Georgina Bamford. I think the DCI is in one of the consultation rooms, but I don't know which one.'

'Is he with Rodney Middleton's lawyer? I really need to speak to him. That fucker cannot make bail.'

'Detective Sergeant Warr, please mind your language,' Miss Bamford said in an offended tone. 'I am representing Mr Middleton, as his lawyer isn't available. Mr Middleton isn't appearing here today and is still at Brixton. His trial will not take place for another month, perhaps even longer.'

Jack ignored her and went off to try and track down Clarke. He headed towards the area where there were small interview rooms for lawyers and their clients, knocking and then peering into one room after another.

He was just turning back when Anik came down the corridor towards him.

'That was well out of order, Jack. You were very rude to Miss Bamford, not to mention the fact that you interrupted our conversation. If you'd had the manners to wait until she had finished speaking, she would have told you that Middleton has been granted bail, pending a court appearance and probationary appointments. He'll be released either later today or tomorrow morning'.

Jack wanted to hurl his briefcase at him he was so angry, but Anik stepped aside as DCI Clarke approached.

'Morning, sir,' Anik said. 'I'm due in Court any minute. I did have words with Miss Bamford who's a barrister in the same chambers as Colin Marshall. He's a junior legal aid lawyer and she's acting for him whilst he's off sick.'

Jack was leaning against the wall gripping his briefcase with both hands. DCI Clarke listened, tight lipped, and glanced at his watch. He then looked at Jack.

'What are you doing here?'

'I really need to talk to you. It's urgent.'

Clarke turned as two people walked out of one of the interview rooms. He gestured to Jack.

'Right, we have ten minutes before I have to go into court.'

Clarke shut the door behind them, as Jack stood by the small interview table. He took a deep breath and outlined, as briefly as he could, his suspicions regarding Rodney Middleton. He explained about his meeting with Amanda Dunn and her identification of three missing girls. Clarke remained expressionless, glancing at his watch. He waited until Jack had finished telling him about his meetings with the firefighter and probation officer, then he pinched his nose and frowned.

'You have been very diligent, Jack. I agree that this new development, alongside your misgivings about Middleton being granted bail, is serious. However, that is now out of our hands. The harsh reality is that you have found no real evidence to back up your theory that something criminal happened in Middleton's flat.' He held his hand up before Jack could protest. 'But before you interrupt, I agree to a search warrant relating to the missing girls. Get over to the magistrates' court and they'll sign it this morning for you.'

'Thank you, sir.'

Clarke turned to the door, then paused. 'In future, detective, please dress appropriately when you attend court, whether or not you're making an appearance. Your tie is halfway round your neck. And you need a shave and a haircut!'

Jack sighed as Clarke walked out. He had been so eager to make an early start that he had not shaved or combed his hair. He adjusted his tie and hurried out to the car park.

By the time he returned to the station, having been granted a search warrant at the magistrates' court, Sara had contacted Jamail's family. She hadn't been able to speak to Mrs Brown, and Mr Brown was in prison, but his brother had finally agreed to talk to her.

'All he could recall was that Jamail's father used to bring her gifts from abroad. A beaded necklace and some earrings, but he could not recall any silver bracelet. On the off chance, I looked into one of the other missing girls, Trudie, possible surname Hudson, and managed to get through to her mother. Trudie has been reported missing for over two years. I described the bracelet in detail and wanted to send her an email with a picture of it, but she said she had no laptop, computer or mobile, just a landline.

'But she did recall that her daughter had a silver charm bracelet. This is where it gets to be really interesting . . .'

Jack swore and told her to get to the point.

'She could only remember one charm in particular – a small silver St Christopher. I asked the size and she said it was no bigger than her little fingernail, and. . .'

Sara held up the plastic evidence bag containing the bracelet.

'There it is, it's a small St Christopher just by the broken clasp.'

Jack clapped his hands. It was a major breakthrough. Jack told her they needed to double-check with missing persons regarding Trudie, but they now had a surname, as well as more detail on Jamail Brown.

'I think I did a thorough check already,' Sara said.

'Do it again. I want a DNA swab taken on the bracelet. We have a search warrant, but I need as much evidence as possible.'

Jack went off to the gents to use his electric shaver. He could also have done with some deodorant but didn't have any, so he settled for a basin wash, using paper towels under his armpits.

When he returned to his office, Jack updated his report, ready for DCI Clarke, then went to the canteen to get some lunch before returning to his desk. Laura approached and stood in front of him.

'Do you think I should accompany you with the search warrant,' she said. 'After all, Sara is just a probationary officer. As I told you earlier, I've cleared the case I was working on.'

From her desk at the back of the room Sara was clearly listening in, but then became distracted by her phone. Jack shrugged his shoulders, not wanting to get into any pecking order issues, but agreed that Laura could accompany him, asking her to check when

Rodney Middleton was being released. Sara finished her call and approached his desk.

'I'm on my third call and not having much success, I'm afraid. In Jamail's case this is due to the length of time she's been missing. Trudie's files are more recent, but the person dealing with her report in Liverpool isn't in the office. I've reprinted everything off for you, anyway, as well as the photographs.'

'Thanks.'

'You haven't actually met Rodney Middleton, have you?'

'No, not yet.'

'Did you get the time he would be released on bail from Brixton?'

'I'm waiting on it . . . and Laura will be accompanying me.'

'Oh, I would have liked to be there, considering I was with you at his aunt's house.'

Jack did not have time to reply as Clarke had walked into the incident room, gesturing for Jack to join him in his office. He left the door ajar. 'Did you get the search warrant for Rodney Middleton's flat?'

'Yes, sir, I've only just got back.'

Clarke asked if Jack wanted any back up uniforms to accompany him. Jack told him that Laura was going to be with him and he felt they could do a thorough search between them.

'Well, you got what you wanted, so let's see what you come up with.'

*   *   *

Laura had confirmation that Rodney Middleton's bail had been granted. His aunt had agreed to act as surety, which meant that she would be responsible for ensuring that he followed his bail conditions and attended court for the trial. If he didn't, she'd be liable for a substantial sum of money or risk having her property forfeited.

'When's he due to be released?' Jack asked.

'Probably late afternoon or early evening.'

'Let's get on our way then.'

Jack and Laura left the incident room, whilst Sara sat with her arms folded, feeling thoroughly pissed off. She had found Laura quite friendly at first, but she never failed to pull rank.

Leon gave her an understanding raise of an eyebrow, before returning to his pursuit of Sandra Raynor.

'I'm still not having much luck either,' he said.

'Actually, as it happens, I've got a good result on the bracelet,' she told him. 'What are you working on?'

'Trying to track down this woman called Sandra Raynor for the sarge.'

'Is she a missing person?'

'No, well, I've not had any bites from them. I've been through births marriages and criminal records and not got anything, or from the Holmes database'

'Jack's never mentioned her name to me,' she said. 'Do you want me to have a go? Could be in deaths?'

'No, it's OK. I'm going back a few more years next and maybe I'll get lucky.'

*   *   *

Jack spoke briefly about his suspicions whilst Laura listened, silently. They had not worked together for a while, and she had missed being with him. She no longer fancied him, though, and had concluded that dating fellow officers was not a good idea anyway.

'Do you ever hear from that guy with the DEA in New York?' Jack asked.

'No, we e-mailed and had a couple of calls but then I moved on. I don't seem to be able to find Mr Right. I've been thinking about joining a dating agency or going to one of those speed-dating sessions, you know, where you sit opposite a guy and talk to them and a bell rings, and you move on to the next one. But it costs a hundred quid, so I think I'll try online dating first.'

Jack laughed but told her that she had to be careful, especially being a Met officer.

'Well, I know that! I'd use an assumed name. As soon as you mention you're a policewoman you get the same old jokes about wearing your uniform and your police hat.'

'Ah, so you've tried it?'

Laura laughed. 'Yeah, did a phone-in date app, bloody boring. What can you tell from a voice at the other end of the phone? They could be any age, really fat, or even a criminal.'

'I'm sure you'll find someone when you least expect it; you're very attractive. And the best thing about you, Laura, you make me laugh.'

'Thanks for the compliment.'

'OK, Laura, we're here. It's the basement flat. I'll call Mrs Delaney, the caretaker, to give me the keys. No one has been occupying it for quite a while, and I'd like to have a good nose around before Middleton's released.'

Jack parked the car and took out his briefcase and mobile phone. Laura went to the railings of the basement.

'Jack, there's someone there. The lights are on.'

'Shit, he couldn't be out yet, surely?'

Jack led the way down the steps, past the array of over-flowing bins. The same empty milk bottles were still there. He rang the doorbell, waited and then knocked. After a while he loudly said that it was the Police and please could the door be opened. He sighed, not wanting to have to carry out any theatrics by kicking open the door. Instead, he went back up the steps to the main entrance of the building. Laura remained waiting in the basement courtyard, wrinkling her nose at the foul smell of rotting food waste and rubbish spewing out of bins.

Above her, Jack kept his finger on the front doorbell. Eventually he heard footsteps and the door was inched open.

'Mrs Delaney, its Detective Sergeant Jack Warr. I spoke to you recently. I want access to the basement flat.'

'He's not there, and I can't let you in,' she said firmly.

'Yes, you can. I have a warrant.'

Jack showed her the warrant and she peered at it.

'Well, ring the basement doorbell then.'

'I have done, but no one answered. If Mr Middleton isn't home, who's living there?'

Jack suddenly knew without her telling him. 'Is it his girlfriend, Amanda?'

'Yes, she's expecting him home. He called me to say she could go in and wait for him. I need him here as my husband's back is worse and I can't get the bins up the steps. We missed the collection this week.'

Jack had stopped listening and hurried back down to the basement courtyard to join Laura.

'His bloody girlfriend is in there.' He banged on the door.

'Open the door, Amanda. OPEN THE DOOR!'

He heard the chain lock being removed, and then the Yale lock clicked. Very slowly, the door opened and Amanda peered out. She was still dirty and was wearing the same old coat. Her face looked grey and the cold sore on her lip seemed to have spread almost to her nostril.

Jack held the warrant out as he pushed his foot inside the door frame to wedge it open.

'Stand away from the door, Amanda. This warrant gives me the right to enter and search the flat, so you need to move.'

She inched back, and he pushed the door open wider. She was wearing socks, but no shoes, and the smell of damp was overpowering. It was also freezing cold.

'It's cold in here, Amanda. Is there no heating?'

'I don't know how to switch it on. It's a meter thing with dials. I know it does the hot water but it's not on.'

'Right, let me put some more lights on. It's very dark in here.'

They were standing in a narrow hallway, with a rubber-backed strip of carpet over stone flooring. The walls were painted in a faded cream colour and there was a small wooden cabinet close to the door. There was no other furniture or pictures. It felt empty.

Jack looked over to Laura, and then back to Amanda. He asked her to show him the bedrooms and the rest of the flat, suggesting that she should go and put on some more clothes as she was shivering. Amanda hesitated and then said that the first door was the main bedroom, but she was sleeping in the back room. Laura took her by the arm and asked her to show her where she was sleeping.

Jack checked the drawers in the wooden cabinet. There was a directory, a lot of pizza delivery leaflets, Check-a-Trade advertising leaflets, and a central heating instruction book. There were also various warranties regarding a microwave, a cooker, and washing machine. The other drawers were empty.

Jack went into the main bedroom. There was a large double bed with four pillows, and a stained duvet with a fake fur rug slung halfway across it. The wooden floor was bare, apart from a cheap rug on one side of the bed. There was a pine chest of drawers with one drawer partly open. Jack methodically searched each of the drawers, finding a neat stack of t-shirts, underpants, vests and socks, as well as old worn jeans, folded neatly but unwashed. He checked the pockets and felt around the base of the drawers, but there was nothing of interest.

A narrow wardrobe had a lopsided door on one side. It contained a denim jacket, a raincoat and a duffle coat with plastic shoulder pads, as well as two pairs of black trousers folded over a wooden coat hanger.

At the bottom of the cupboard there were four pairs of worn trainers, a pair of heavy boots and some thick-soled canvas boots. It smelt of moth balls. Jack bent down to look beneath the bed. There was an old newspaper, along with a lot of dust. He then carefully stripped the bed, searching every inch of it. He found nothing, not even a tissue. The bedroom, like the hall, had no photographs or pictures. The walls were the same cream colour, and the curtains were drawn over the barred window, which looked out into the yard.

Jack had never searched a room that was so devoid of anything personal, apart from the clothing. It felt like a prison cell. He went back out into the hall as Laura was coming out of the room that Amanda was using.

'There's just a sleeping bag, a cupboard, a hard-backed chair, and a rope-handled chest containing tools. Amanda has her hold-all with a few dirty items in it. The other clothes are folded on the floor next to the sleeping bag. There are some dirty ashtrays, a bottle of water, and an empty bottle of vodka.'

'Does she have a mobile?' Jack asked.

Laura passed it to him. It was an old flip-style model and had a low battery signal. Jack told Laura to ask Amanda for a charger so that they could see what was on it. He then went into the kitchen which was situated at the rear of the basement. The window in there was barred, but the surfaces appeared to be clean. The lino flooring was a dark red with numerous indentations, as if from high-heeled shoes. A Formica-topped folding table was leaning against a wall with two pine chairs with plastic seat cushions. Together they searched through the cupboards. One contained china, with plates and mugs neatly lined up, and another cupboard was filled with tinned food, mostly soups, tuna, and baked beans. There was also an open packet of crackers.

Beneath the sink were various pots and pans and there was cutlery in the drawer next to it, as well as on the draining board. Jack examined the sharp-looking carving knives that were being stored in a wooden knife-holder.

Laura grimaced when she opened the fridge. It was full of rotting food, including some lettuce and tomatoes that had gone watery and mouldy, as well as a bottle of curdled milk and some very out-of-date yogurts.

'Amanda obviously doesn't cook for herself,' Jack observed. 'What's she doing now?'

'She just put on an old pair of joggers and got back into the sleeping bag,' Laura said.

'This place gives me the creeps; it's like nobody's living here, even though he's been renting it for years. Right, we do a clean sweep first then look for secret hiding places.'

Laura nodded. 'The bathroom, apart from needing a good clean, has only a few toiletries in it: shampoo, deodorant and some cologne. Amanda's washbag is in there, very nasty. The towels look dirty as well, but there's nothing else. I even looked to see if the bath panel came away, but the nails are rusted, so it doesn't appear to have ever been taken out. I also ran a test over a few tiles in case there was any blood . . .'

Jack was about to walk away when Laura took his elbow.

'But I want you to see something.' She led him back to the bathroom and pointed to a modern shower unit with new tile surrounds. 'That must have cost a fair bit!'

Jack nodded. She bent down to what looked like an old electrical box attached to the wall. She eased the small door open as Jack watched over her shoulder. On the small shelves were rows of plastic containers filled with pills, as well as bottles with cork stoppers, all labelled.

'I've photographed everything on my mobile; he's got a virtual pharmacy in there.'

Jack nodded, unimpressed. He went into the sitting room which contained a worn sofa, two covered armchairs, and a frayed rug over the threadbare fitted carpet. There was a reasonably modern gas fire, and a small coffee table with an ashtray full of cigarette stubs as well as numerous candles with pools of wax around them. There were two dirty glasses and some well-thumbed magazines next to an old-fashioned computer. On the wall was a very large plasma TV with a DVD player and a stack of DVDs and CDs. There was also a fancy-looking stereo system with enormous speakers either side of the room.

Jack bent down to look through the CDs, which were a mixture of heavy metal, rock and new age music. Many of them looked new, and they were arranged in alphabetical order.

'I think he must have an obsessive streak, these all look new, maybe nicked,' he said. 'And this equipment must have cost a bundle, especially for someone living on benefits. He certainly likes his comforts, and this is a top-of-the-range computer. Right, we're going to take this in. There are plenty of mobile charging cables, but I haven't seen a mobile other than Amanda's, have you?'

'No, just hers. It's just like all the other rooms in here, with no pictures or photographs. Doesn't feel as if a young guy was living here, never mind his girlfriend.'

Laura was sifting through a waste bin that was filled to the brim with old takeaway food cartons and McDonald's containers.

Jack removed the cushions from the sofa but found nothing. He then did the same with the two armchairs, only finding a couple of cigarette stubs and a few coins.

'OK, let's step back and think about this. He has to have some mail or documentation regarding his benefits. I'm going to talk to Amanda because this doesn't feel right.'

'A lot is done online nowadays to save on paper,' Laura said. 'But I'll go back through every room and move all the furniture around to double-check for any hidden storage.'

Jack was feeling very frustrated at not finding anything that could confirm his gut feelings about Rodney Middleton. But oddly the fact he had uncovered nothing incriminating, combined with the strange living arrangements in the basement, only fuelled his suspicions. He could not believe that someone would not have any memorabilia, photographs, or anything personal like letters or bills. The equipment in the sitting room proved that Middleton had spent a considerable amount of money, and Jack was hoping that Rodney's computer would yield something useful.

As Laura re-visited the main bedroom, Jack went and knocked on the door of the back room that Amanda was using as a bedroom. He didn't wait for her to answer and walked in, closing the door behind him. Amanda was huddled in the sleeping bag with her coat on, smoking.

'We need to talk, and you had better be straight with me this time,' he said brusquely 'You lied about going to Liverpool; you never intended to catch the train with the money you got from me, did you?'

Amanda dragged on the cigarette and shrugged her shoulders. Jack fetched the hard backed-chair and placed it near the sleeping bag.

'I am never going back there,' she said. 'Why do you think I ran off in the first place? She don't want me . . . her so-called husband is a bastard . . . tried it on with me and she never believed it, jealous, that's why.'

'Did Rodney get in touch with you?'

'Yeah, I went to Brixton to see him. He told me he'd tell Mrs Delaney to let me in. But I had no money, so . . .' She shrugged and stubbed out the cigarette in a saucer full of fag ends.

Jack leant towards her. 'You had better give me some straight answers now, Amanda, or I could take you in for questioning at the station, do you understand? Look at me when I'm talking to you, please. Look at me.'

Amanda leaned back slightly and looked up at him, chewing her swollen lip.

'Right, the silver bracelet – did you do a trade with your friend Trudie?' He was making a guess that she was her friend.

'I never stole it; I gave her a ring in return.'

'So Trudie was a friend of yours?'

'Sort of, but the clasp was broken so I only wore it a few times.'

'You also picked out Trudie's photograph when I showed you the pictures of the girls.'

'Yeah, and I gave you the bracelet. I wasn't lying.'

'So, when did Trudie come here to the flat?'

Amanda looked down and chewed at her fingernail.

'Look at me, Amanda. When did Trudie come here?' Jack snapped.

'Long time ago. I can't remember. Maybe a year or more.'

'How did she contact you?'

'She was at the station. We saw her there. She'd done a runner like me.'

'So, you and Rodney used to go to the station together?'

'Sometimes. They got shops open at night, and a food stand.'

'Tell me about the time you met Trudie.'

Amanda sighed, shrugging deeper into her coat.

'Like I said, we was there and she was hanging out, had no place to go, so he said she could come back and stay with us.'

'How long did she stay here with you?'

'Maybe a couple of weeks, but she was starting to piss me off. She was after Rodney all the time and we had big rows about it. He locked me up in here.'

'Was Trudie sleeping with him?'

'Yeah, why do you think I was pissed off? She was a right slag and never give me my ring back. I swapped it with her for the bracelet. It had a little ruby, a real one, but the clasp on her bracelet was broken.'

'How long were you locked up in here?'

'A few days and nights. He said it was my punishment, but then he said he'd kicked her out and she wouldn't be back, so we were alright again.'

'Did the same thing happen when Jamail was here?'

She nodded. 'I got no right to argue with him. I mean, he looks after me. I got no job or nothin'. I was always scared I'd be found and taken back to Liverpool.'

'Were you with him when he met Jamail?'

'No, he just brung her back one night. She was alright to start with, but she'd never clean the kitchen the way he liked it, and she messed up his CDs, so . . .'

'Wait a second. Did you get locked up in here again?'

'She said it was me that left the grease in the frying pan, but I never done that. We had a fight and so he promised to get rid of her, like Trudie.'

'You didn't answer my question, Amanda, did you get locked in here when he said he would get rid of Jamail?'

'Yeah, but I got a box of Krispy Kreme donuts.'

Jack leaned back as she lit another cigarette. 'On the nights both Trudie and Jamail were told to leave, did you hear anything? Maybe an argument, or shouting, or even screaming?'

'No, just his music. He always had it on loud and then it was back to normal, just the two of us.'

'So, they just left? What about their belongings? Did they leave anything behind?'

'Not really, and anything they did we tossed into the bins or into the clothes and shoes recycling bins in the Sainsbury's car park. Oh, apart from her socks; Jamail left a pair of thick socks, and I got them on now. My bed socks.'

Jack picked up the chair and placed it against the wall. He went over to the rope-handled chest and bent to open it. It contained coils of rope, reels of duct tape, screwdrivers, hammers and paint strippers. There were also some oil-stained rags, two sets of head-phones, and a tape player. He examined the hammer, which was very clean. The screwdriver had been sharpened and had a lethal razor-sharp edge.

'Whose tools are these?'

'They belonged to Rodney's dad; he used them to repair things.'

Jack decided that they should have the tools checked for any bloodstains, although he doubted they would find any. They looked very clean, as though they had never been used. He decided he had questioned Amanda for long enough. He walked out of the room, leaving the door ajar.

Laura was searching behind the cabinet in the hall.

'Find anything?'

'Nope, nothing – and I've shifted anything that could be moved.'

'Did you search the sleeping bag?'

'Yes, the entire room. I even took out all the pans and tins from the kitchen cupboards, and searched them thoroughly, but there's nothing. One odd thing I found, which I've photographed, though: two gallon containers of bleach, and some wire-cleaning brushes. Did you get anything out of Amanda?'

'Yeah. I want us to take the tools that are in the chest in her room back with us, to get forensics to check them over.'

Laura pushed the cabinet back into place as Jack made a final search, lifting what carpets he could, testing floorboards and look-ing up to the ceiling to see if there were any access points to some sort of storage space.

Laura filled two large evidence bags with bedlinen and all the tools, as Jack carried out the computer. He then instructed Laura to fetch the sleeping bag as it might have evidence of the other girls inside it. There was a loud screech from Amanda as Laura got her out of the sleeping bag and rolled it up before walking out, with Amanda yelling abuse behind her. Jack almost dropped the computer as he heard footsteps descending the basement steps, followed by voices. He hurried into the hall to join Laura.

The front door opened, and Harold Miller looked shocked to see them. He then explained that he had just collected Rodney. He held up a small holdall bag as if by way of an explanation. 'Joyce sorted out his bail for him, and . . .'

Before Jack could say anything, Rodney Middleton walked in, all smiles. Even though he had seen photographs of him, Jack was still taken aback.

Rodney was slender but muscular, wearing a denim jacket, white t-shirt and jeans. He was also good-looking, with his thick, curly hair cropped close to his head. He had an angular face with amber brown eyes and perfect teeth and seemed both youthful and yet mature at the same time.

Rodney was carrying two bags of food shopping and carefully put them down on the floor.

'I am Detective Sergeant Jack Warr, and I am here with a search warrant,' Jack told him.

Middleton nodded affably. 'Yes, Mrs Delaney said you were down here, and Amanda . . .'

There was a screech as Amanda came running down the hall and did a flying jump into Rodney's arms, curling her skinny legs around him. She kissed him, clinging to him like a little monkey, showing off the dirty pink bed socks.

Middleton gently pushed her away. 'That's enough now . . . go and put the groceries in the kitchen for me, sweetie, there's a good girl.'

Amanda picked up the two bags and hurried down the hallway into the kitchen. Harold was still hovering by the front door.

'If it's alright I should be off. Joyce will be needing me. It was nice to see you again detective, and . . .'

He nodded towards Laura who was standing pressed against the wall holding the evidence bags. Harold handed Middleton the holdall, clearly eager to leave.

'Can you just wait one second, Harold?' Middleton said. 'We should have a look over the search warrant. Is that alright with you, Detective Warr?'

Jack felt very uneasy as he took out the warrant and handed it over. Middleton smiled again and suggested they go and sit down in comfort. They trouped into the lounge, Harold sitting next to Middleton, as they looked over the search warrant.

'I will need to take in your computer, Mr Middleton, and we have also removed some tools.'

'What do you want them for?'

'We're just investigating a possible connection to some missing girls.'

Rodney frowned and looked puzzled.

'Girls, plural? I mean, I know Amanda was reported missing, but she's here of her own free will and she's almost eighteen years old. Is that your problem?'

To Jack, Middleton seemed almost over-confident, appearing to be very relaxed and completely at ease with the situation.

'You can search wherever you want,' Middleton said breezily. 'I have nothing to hide. I've been held awaiting trial for some time, but I am sure you must be aware of that, so I've not been home since I was arrested.'

'I appreciate your cooperation, Mr Middleton, but we were just about to leave.'

'Why are you taking my computer? I mean, what do you expect to find? Is it legal, Harold?'

Harold frowned. 'Yes, it is.'

'What have I done that gives them the right to take it?'

Jack responded. 'I just explained to you, Mr Middleton, I am investigating the whereabouts of certain missing girls and I believe that you may be implicated in their disappearance.'

'What missing girls?'

'I am not prepared to discuss it any further with you right now, but l may require you to come to the station to answer some questions.'

'Why don't you ask me now?'

Jack glanced at Laura, who stepped forwards.

'Thank you for your time, Mr Middleton. This is an ongoing enquiry that may not actually involve you, and we need to continue our investigations before we ask you any questions.'

Middleton shrugged and smiled again. 'OK, just take whatever you need. Do you want my computer password? It'll save you wasting time trying to get into it. It's my date of birth. All you'll find on there are games, and my internet search history is mostly for Amazon purchases and looking up some further education courses. Oh, and there'll be some medical searches, plus I think my probation diary dates are on there.'

Jack jotted down the password in his notebook whilst Middleton thanked Harold for collecting him. He asked him to make sure his aunty Joyce got a big thank you from him for signing the surety.

Middleton stood up and took off his denim jacket, tossing it over the arm of the sofa. He was taller than Jack and reached out to shake his hand.

'I best get cracking in the kitchen. Amanda's not a very good cook. If it's not in a tin, she isn't sure what to do with it.' He gave a boyish laugh but Jack sensed he was now eager for them to leave.

'I'll help you carry the computer out,' he said. 'I'd like to get a laptop, but my finances don't run to that yet.'

Jack led Laura down the hallway and opened the front door. He stopped and turned, smiling at Middleton.

'Just one more thing before we leave. I want to take a look inside the coal hole. It's just outside in the basement yard, isn't it?'

He caught the look in Middleton's eyes. It was just a flicker, but the friendly demeanour had briefly vanished.

'It has a padlock on it,' Jack continued. 'Mrs Delaney said you helped her out with a rat infestation. If you have the key, we can have a look in there before we leave.'

'I'm sorry, but I can't help you. I don't have the key, and it's not part of my property. That's right, isn't it, Harold; they can't open it, can they?'

Harold looked flustered as he scrutinised the search warrant. 'He's right, detective, this search warrant is for a search of Mr Middleton's basement flat, but not any external buildings.'

Harold, explained, almost apologetically, that in his previous job he'd gained some knowledge about search warrants and citizens' rights.

'Never mind,' Jack said, managing to disguise his fury. 'It was just a thought and I doubt it will be necessary anyway. Thank you again for your time, you have been very cooperative, and we really appreciate it. I'll leave you with a copy of the search warrant.'

Laura and Jack headed out, carrying the bulging plastic bags, with Harold carrying the computer nervously and looking as though he was afraid he was going to drop it. Jack opened the boot.

'So, your wife came to her nephew's assistance. That was very kind of her.' Jack took the computer from him and placed it in the boot, closing it afterwards.

'Yes, well, blood is thicker than water, isn't it?' Harold said. 'Rodney was frantic to get home, as he worries about that anorexic girlfriend of his.'

Jack got in the car and watched Harold walk off. He sat for a minute, gripping the steering wheel hard.

'Christ almighty! We were had, Laura. There was nothing in his fucking basement, because – I would put any money – he has all his personal stuff stashed in the coal hole. He was all sweetness and light until I mentioned that. I want to organise surveillance ASAP to monitor what goes on until I can get another warrant to go in there. I'm pissed off at myself – all the time we spent searching inside and we should have just kicked the door down and gone into the coal hole.'

'I don't know, we could have got into a lot of trouble,' Laura said. 'If Middleton is as devious as I think he is, he had to know we were there, but he didn't care. He probably got his uncle to stay just to confirm the fact that we couldn't get access. Is he that clever, do you think?'

Jack nodded as they drove towards the station. 'He lives on benefits and uses his mental health issues and sympathetic probation officers to get what he wants. And that stick insect of a girlfriend is totally under his control, or at least she was until she brought up the bracelet.'

Laura leaned back in the passenger seat, tugging at her safety belt. 'You know, Jack, you haven't actually told me why you have been pushing this investigation. I think I have some idea, but please tell me.'

'OK,' he said. 'I think Rodney Middleton picks up young runaway girls from mainline train stations. He acts the friendly, helpful, guy then takes them back to that basement flat, with his supposedly innocent girlfriend. They move in and after a time he gets rid of them – and I mean permanently.'

'My God, do you think Amanda's directly involved?'

'She is definitely compliant and accompanies him to the station,' Jack said. 'But when he's getting rid of them, he locks her in that back room. We need to find out what happened on the night he was arrested. He walked out of that basement flat, gave himself up, and passed over the offending weapon. We need to find out if a girl went missing in that time frame.'

'Do you think Amanda is in danger?' Laura asked. 'She's identified three girls, and we don't know if he's aware of that, or about her giving you the bracelet.'

Jack pulled into the station and parked in his allocated space. He instructed Laura to get surveillance set up on Middleton's flat and to organise a search warrant for the coal bunker. He said that he would take the computer and the tools into forensics and the tech officers.

'I'll be in after I get a result from the labs.'

'OK, will do. I'll get cracking straight away and I'll write a report on what went down this afternoon. And I'll print off the photographs and call you with an update.'

Jack smiled at her as he backed out of the car park to take the items to the labs. He was feeling worn out but at least now Laura understood what was driving him.

CHAPTER THIRTEEN

Jack arrived at the labs the following morning just after eight thirty. The battery had died on his mobile phone, which he'd forgotten to charge overnight. When it had enough juice to be turned on again, he found he had missed three calls from Laura. He decided to wait until he got the results from the IT team about Middleton's computer and Amanda's mobile phone. The forensic department had also said they would test the tools, alongside bedding from Middleton's bedroom.

Christopher Deacon, the young scientist who was working on Middleton's computer hard drive, was eating a bacon roll when Jack found him. He had on thick, Harry Potter-style glasses and his head was shaved on both sides with a tuft on the top slicked up with gel.

Deacon had printed out a pile of material for Jack, and was still producing further data. He had an unfortunate manner of eating whilst he was talking, spitting out breadcrumbs everywhere and wiping his mouth with the back of his hand.

'My God, there's more stuff on here about mental illness than in a bloody medical journal,' he said. 'He's concentrated on manic depression, schizophrenia, multiple personalities, the mental states of serial killers and their trials. There are lists of prescription medications, stuff about psychoanalysis, hypnosis and suicides . . . I could carry on . . . it's obsessive.'

Jack pulled up a chair and sat beside him. Deacon then talked about all the computer games that Middleton had accessed, but there was no pornography, or accessing of paedophile sites; Middleton had just downloaded cartoons and Disney films.

'Anything personal? Any family snaps?' Jack asked.

Deacon shook his head. 'No. He's done a lot of research about arson, though, and bizarrely, documentaries about seriously obese people weighing over forty stone ... but nothing personal, not even e-mails. But I'm going to do some more digging as they could be carefully buried. This is not a very up-to-date computer, but your user is pretty savvy.'

Jack sat with Deacon for over half an hour, reading the printed material. He then went to get a coffee and to see if there was any development on the content of Amanda's mobile phone. The phone department was a very small area and they only worked on mobiles. There were two young specialists who, like Deacon, looked like teenagers to Jack. They had laid out in front of them about thirty different mobile phones taken from drug dealers and other criminals. Amanda's mobile was relatively old and they had easily retrieved the numbers that had been called and received. The most recent calls were to a café close to Brixton prison, the basement flat and the hostel. There were also two other mobile numbers and a Liverpool number.

By the time Jack had finished, he was armed with a thick dossier of printed material. It was after 11 a.m. when he parked at the station and headed towards the incident room, carrying a takeaway coffee and a bulging briefcase. Pushing open the double doors he stopped in his tracks. Every desk was occupied and standing by the newly placed white crime board were DCI Clarke, Laura and Anik. Photographs of the missing girls were pinned up on the board, along with Rodney Middleton's mug shots and information about the search of the flat. Jack could also see that two teams of officers had been allocated for 24/7 surveillance of the basement flat.

Jack felt as if the ground was opening up beneath his feet and he had to take a deep breath as he walked over to his desk and put his briefcase down. His hand shook as he eased the lid off his coffee.

DCI Clarke gestured to Laura and pointed at Jack.

'Give Sergeant Warr an update in my office, Laura, and then get back as soon as you can for a meeting in the boardroom. Also, we'd like the information from the IT team following your visit this morning, and as soon as possible.'

Jack knew he was flushing, not from embarrassment but anger as he struggled to take it all in. What the hell had Laura been doing in the twenty-four hours since he had last seen her?

Laura shut the office door and before Jack could say a word, she rounded on him.

'I've been trying to contact you since last night, Jack! Why the hell haven't you called me? I even spoke to your mother this morning and told her it was urgent . . . and you just breeze in with a bloody takeaway coffee. I've been up half the night and . . .'

'Shut up, Laura,' Jack interrupted, 'and just tell me what the fuck is happening out there.'

Laura pursed her lips and took a deep breath. 'Right, I did exactly as you asked me to do last night. But when I got back here, DCI Clarke was still here and asked me how it had gone on the search. I told him, and he just took over. We worked most of the night creating the crime scene board and collating all the information to date. He called in six more officers and delegated the surveillance team, and he's expecting more officers to arrive for the board meeting. He has just taken over, Jack, and there was nothing I could do or say. He's pressuring missing persons for results and updates, and he has a search warrant for the outside cellar coal hole. The officers who arrested Middleton are being brought in for a debrief, and an interview has been arranged with the man Middleton assaulted. The DCI is having meetings with Middleton's probation officer, also his psychiatrist – Angus Seymour – but someone you tried to interview, George Donaldson, is away on holiday, and . . .'

Laura had to stop to draw breath. 'I think he's gearing up to bring Rodney Middleton in for questioning this afternoon.'

Jack drained his coffee cup and tossed it into the waste bin.

'I might as well fucking go home,' he muttered bitterly.

'Jack, listen to me. I don't want you thinking I did anything behind your back. To the contrary, I told the chief exactly what you suspected and that you had been determined to find the evidence. I explained the frustration regarding not being able to trace the missing girls. The DCI said he believed you were right, and this was a much bigger and more urgent situation than he had realised. I was here until God knows what hour. He called Anik in to help get all the info onto the board. I don't think he even went home.'

'I bet Anik is loving it. He can't wait to take over.'

Laura glared at him. 'Just stop it, Jack. This has all come from your intuitions and gut feelings and nobody is going to take away any credit from you now that it's become a whopper of a case. Now, we need to get into the boardroom, alright?'

Jack took a deep breath. 'Yeah, sure. I'm sorry for not returning your calls. My battery died and then I had to get out early to the labs.'

'I hear you.'

'Sorry to sound off at you like that; it was uncalled for.'

Laura nodded before walking out.

The incident room was almost empty. Jack went to his desk to collect his briefcase. Hendricks walked by, carrying a loaded tray of empty coffee mugs and stale sandwiches from earlier and asked Jack to open the door for him. As he passed through, Hendricks paused.

'A quick question: the trace Leon has been working on, Sandra Raynor . . . do you want her name on the crime board too?'

'No, drop it,' Jack said quickly. 'We'll talk about it later.'

Hendricks hurried away down the corridor as Jack made his way to the boardroom. When he walked in, he was taken aback at how many officers were now gathered, some in uniform but also numerous plain-clothed detectives who had been brought in from other stations. DCI Clarke was at the head of the table, stacking papers in front of him. He indicated the empty chair beside him.

'Good timing, Jack. Come on in, I was just about to start.'

Jack sat down and placed his briefcase on the table in front of him, nodding to everyone as DCI Clarke cleared his throat then sipped from a bottle of water.

'Right, everyone, I'm going to make this as brief as possible. Firstly, I want everyone to know that Detective Sergeant Jack Warr was originally given the Rodney Middleton case in preparation for his forthcoming trial on an assault charge, with Middleton being held at Brixton prison. At the time he had not been granted bail due to a previous similar assault charge using a knife. Middleton was arrested at his flat and admitted the assault. He went quietly and handed over the knife he had used in the attack at his local corner shop. He was taken before a magistrate and pleaded guilty.'

He took a sip of water before continuing.

'To all intents and purposes this was a straightforward arrest. Detective Warr had to prepare for the trial but as an extremely dedicated officer he wanted to eliminate any possible loopholes. I think I am correct in saying that he subsequently became suspicious about Middleton's ability to use his mental health history to secure lenient punishments and to avoid a prison sentence. Detective Warr then became aware of the disappearances of a number of underage females. He has been able to establish that some of these girls lived with Middleton and his girlfriend, Amanda Dunn, who went missing at the age of twelve. She's lived with Middleton for the past five years and was at times being held as a virtual prisoner. It will be our priority to remove her from the premises as she could be in danger, but we also have to consider the likelihood of her aiding and abetting Middleton to entice the girls to his flat.'

DCI Clarke paused and took another sip of water.

'So far we have been unable to trace any of the missing girls, who were all picked up from Euston Station before being taken to the basement flat. In each case, Middleton subsequently told his girlfriend that he had "got rid of them". I believe that Middleton is a very dangerous individual and we need to consider the possibility that these girls are murder victims, and there may possibly be more. Middleton was released on bail yesterday so there is obviously an urgent need to find the evidence to justify an arrest.'

Clarke then asked Laura to describe the search of the basement flat. She explained, concisely, what they had discovered, including the bleach, the large amount of prescription drugs, and the fact that the flat was devoid of any personal items. Laura explained that the search warrant did not cover the basement's large bunker-like space which had previously been used as a coal hole. They had been able to obtain the dimensions and it was surprisingly big, extending halfway beneath the road outside the flat. The delay in gaining a search warrant for the coal hole was because the original warrant had only been for the flat Middleton was renting.

It was then Anik's turn to confirm that they had allocated a surveillance team to monitor Middleton, and see whether or not he would access the bunker. This had proved difficult as it was hard to see any movement on the basement level from the road, so the surveillance team had asked the landlady, Mrs Delaney, if they could use one of the front rooms above the basement yard, to enable them to look down onto it. Surveillance had reported that there had been no movement during the night, but they were continuing to observe.

Sara then took over from Anik to talk about the missing girls, also summarising the results of their meetings with the firefighter and the probation officer, and the visit to Joyce Miller and her husband Harold.

At last, it was Jack's turn to stand up. He suggested that everyone read the printouts regarding the contents of Middleton's computer, as well as the details of the calls from Amanda Dunn's mobile phone. He told them about the bracelet Amanda had given him, claiming she had found it in Middleton's bed, and that they had verified it had belonged to Trudie.

'I think we need to be wary of Amanda. She may well be involved in drawing in other runaways, even if she claims she was locked in a bedroom when other girls were there. We need to consider that Rodney has groomed her over the years she has lived with him, and I think she is very much under his control.'

The printed material was passed around the boardroom table as Jack continued.

'I do not think we should arrest Rodney Middleton prematurely, certainly not before we get access to the coal hole. I'm hoping that, at the moment, he believes we don't have any incriminating evidence so he may think he's in the clear, so long as the surveillance team haven't tipped him off. Mrs Delaney is not to be trusted and she might well have told our suspect that he's being monitored. But if he thinks he's being watched, it means he can't remove anything from the bunker, which could work in our favour.'

DCI Clarke raised his hand. 'I have given the green light for us to begin the search in an hour's time. I am concerned about the safety of Amanda Dunn, but I am prepared to go with DS Warr's delaying tactic since we have a surveillance team in place. Right, we are open to questions but let's keep it short as I want to move on this as fast as possible.'

A young detective raised his hand. 'Sergeant Warr, if you believe that Middleton is a killer, what evidence do we have, apart from the fact that the girls are missing?'

'Well, no direct evidence. But there's a new shower unit, gallons of bleach, and he's locked up his girlfriend for hours, sometimes days at crucial times. I'm certain we'll find the clues inside that bunker. It's possible that he dismembers his victims, and puts the parts in the refuse containers in the courtyard of the basement. His landlady told me that they were sometimes very heavy, and she often needed her husband to help carry them to the pavement to be collected.'

The meeting continued for another half hour as questions were asked and answered. DCI Clarke then called for everyone to begin their assignments. He turned to Jack as he was about to get up and walk out along with everyone else.

'One second, Jack. I received a warning shot over the bows before the meeting. I took a very curt phone call from Georgina Bamford, the barrister you met in court. She complained about harassment of Middleton, who she's representing while Colin Marshall is off sick. Middleton said he was being targeted by officers searching his flat because he had been granted bail.'

'That's bullshit!' Jack burst out. 'She can't have any idea why we were searching his flat and it has nothing to do with his bail. I even left a copy of the search warrant.'

'Yes, I know that,' Clarke said, making a placating gesture, 'but we need to be careful. Let's just hope we get a result today.'

CHAPTER FOURTEEN

Jack felt frustrated at not being present during the search of the bunker, but it made sense to leave it to the professional teams. He began to sift through the paperwork relating to Middleton's two recent arrests, feeling that they did not quite make sense. Middleton had not attempted a robbery or asked for money in either case. The shopkeepers knew him, as he was a regular customer, and he had not hidden the fact that he was carrying a weapon – a stiletto knife on the first occasion and a carving knife on the second. And in both cases, there were other customers in the shop, all of whom gave similar statements. They described how Middleton had suddenly become very aggressive for no reason and had just lunged at the shop owner, shouting. The first victim was Indian and the second was Greek.

Jack matched the assault dates to around the time he estimated two of the missing girls were at Middleton's flat, first Jamail, and then possibly Trudie.

Jack was standing by the crime board looking at the photographs of the missing girls when Leon joined him with a sheet of typed paper.

'I think I just traced your Sandra Raynor. I could be wrong, but I've spent hours cross-referencing and going through all the records, you know births and marriages, etc.'

Jack nodded impatiently.

'I found literally hundreds of them, aged between thirty and sixty, but they came up blank as they didn't fit the description, and in some cases had remarried or emigrated. That's when Sara suggested going through the deceased. I had already done some checks, but I went back to earlier dates.'

'For Christ's sake, Leon, get to the point.'

'OK, I've got a Sandra Raynor, aged six years, buried in Brighton in 1961. Both parents deceased in 1975. The grave isn't tended to and is very overgrown. I checked on the parents, a Norma and William Raynor, who both died of natural causes. If someone wanted to use a false name, the child is a perfect example as no relative is going to come forward and no passport was ever issued in the little girl's name or to either parent.'

Jack frowned. It was possible, but at the same time it didn't really help him discover who she really was. Leon hovered.

'Is she a missing person to do with the Middleton investigation?' Leon asked.

'No, I thought she might be, but too old. Forget it, but thanks anyway; we'll need everyone on this case, so ignore the Sandra Raynor request as it's a bit of a time-waster.' He took the sheet of typed notes, folded it and put it into his pocket.

Jack went over to Sara's desk and asked her to see if she could check the exact dates Jamail and Trudie had been reported missing. He returned to his desk and took out the single sheet Leon had given him. The little girl was buried in Brighton and Preston Cemetery. Perhaps it might be a lead after all. Maybe the dead woman came from that area, and perhaps she had been seen in or around the cemetery. Jack would do some more checking at home as the search team at the basement flat were calling in, and he wanted to go and see for himself whatever they had uncovered. He also wanted to drop by the corner shop where Middleton had assaulted the owner.

The shop was only two streets away from the basement flat. It sold everything you could think of and also did newspaper delivery. The shelves were crammed with toilet paper, tins, bread, soft drinks and cleaning products, and behind a grille was alcohol and tobacco. A large freezer was filled with frozen meals, and there were racks of confectionery and crisps at the counter. An attractive girl, who looked about fifteen, was serving. She had dark eyes and thick, dark silky hair.

Jack went up to the counter. 'Hi. I wondered if I could talk to the owner, Mr Andrios? I'm from the Met Police. It's nothing of concern, I just need to have a quick chat with him.'

'Dad, someone for you,' she shouted, then turned back to Jack. 'He's at the back, stacking the baked goods.'

Jack squeezed through the packed shelves to the back of the shop. Andrios was reaching up on a step to stack sliced bread on a shelf. Jack showed him his ID and waited for him to step down from the small stool.

'You want to see me?'

'Yes, I just need to ask you a couple of questions. You were assaulted by a young man named Rodney Middleton.'

Andrios nodded and took out a handkerchief. 'Yes. I tell you, it was a shock. He came at me with this big knife, sliced my arm quite badly. It scared the life out of me. I saw him. Look behind you.'

Jack turned to see a curved mirror reflecting the counter. He looked back at Andrios.

'Was he stealing something?'

'No. He was regular, so I knew him. He often bought cigarettes, and I saw him in the mirror.'

'What made him attack you?'

'I saw him looking at my daughter. She was behind the counter. I had seen the way he looked at her before. I didn't want to make a big thing of it, so I just said to him that I wouldn't serve him in here again. Then he came at me with a knife. My daughter called the police after he'd run off.'

Jack asked Andrios if he had mentioned this to the arresting officers and he shrugged, saying that at the time he was more concerned that Middleton might return and kill him.

* * *

When Jack arrived at the basement flat, he had to park some distance away due to all the police vehicles blocking the road. The steps down to the basement were piled with large forensic bags and SOCO were going up and down, carrying items to their vans. The small basement courtyard was filled with officers taking a break, some sitting on the steps with takeaway coffees and sandwiches.

Jack showed his ID as he passed by everyone to gain access to the bunker. Stepping inside he was amazed at the size of it, the whole space illuminated by large forensic lamps. Anik was there, wearing a paper suit and examining a large plastic container. He turned as Jack walked in and gestured to the papers and documents that were neatly stacked in the container.

'I think this is where he kept all his photographs and data, but I've not had time to sift through it all. I think it'll be best to get it straight to the incident room. There's a mound of stuff.'

Jack remained standing at the open door, still stunned by the size of the bunker. The walls had been whitewashed, so the glare from the high-powered lamps was even stronger. Anik explained that a large selection of tools, including saws, drills and a work bench, had been removed. They had also found two vats of chemicals with the lids tightly closed. The contents hadn't been examined yet. Their intention was to clear the entire area in order to examine the stone floor and walls using spray luminol to detect any blood splattering.

Anik replaced the lid on the plastic container. 'The original coal chute is at the far end – there's just a few bits of coal left – but apart from that the place has been cleaned and painted with numerous coats of whitewash. I think the consensus is that this is where any dismemberment would have occurred. It stinks of mildew and the damp is making it hard to work for long periods. There are some rat traps, with a few dead ones at the far end, and two canisters of rat poison. The canisters look old and that make is no longer sold.'

Jack looked around and asked if there had been any movement inside the basement flat. Anik replied that no one had been in or out, but there had been two food deliveries – one from a Chinese restaurant and one from McDonald's. Amanda had come to the door on both occasions, and no one had seen Rodney Middleton.

Jack made his way back to street level. A forensic van pulled away, taking the items they had removed to the labs. He knew from experience how long it would take for everything to be item-ised and examined. The only item he was interested in looking at closely was the plastic container of personal items, but he would have to wait until it was returned to the incident room.

Jack decided that it might be helpful to interview the first man who had been attacked by Middleton. He called the incident room to check his address and Leon answered, keeping Jack on hold for several minutes. He eventually located the address in the case file.

Sara came on the line to say she was collating the information from mispers, but was finding it difficult to ascertain how long the girls had actually been missing before an official police report had been recorded.

'The girls were all from troubled backgrounds,' she explained. 'We know that Amanda was the first, and then the timeline seems to be Trudie Hudson then Jamail Brown, then possibly Nadine O'Reilly – she's the girl Amanda was uncertain of.'

Jack interrupted to say that he really needed more specifics and especially exact dates. In addition, the parents needed to be con-tacted to check their DNA, in case they uncovered any evidence from the coal hole. Leon then came back on the line with the address for the corner shop. It was not as close to the basement flat as the first shop, located just off the main road next to an Indian restaurant. The owner was Mr Devi Kumar.

The shop was almost as packed to the roof as Andrios' shop with the same huge quantities of toilet paper, but outside were crates of fresh fruit and veg. The smell of curry inside was quite intense as they also had a counter with takeaway curry meals. Jack asked a young Indian woman if it was possible to speak with Mr Kumar and she said that he was in their restaurant next door.

The restaurant was closed, but Jack knocked on the door and waited. Eventually a small, rather dapper Indian man came to the door. He moved the blind aside and eased open the door saying that they were still only doing takeaways. Jack explained who he was, showing his ID. When he was let into the restaurant it was clear that it was being refurbished, with the tables stacked on top of each other, alongside piles of gilt chairs.

Mr Kumar was very gentlemanly and exceedingly polite. He took down a gilt chair for Jack, and one for himself, as he explained they were re-carpeting and building a new kitchen. He said that he recalled the assault very clearly, even though it was four years ago. At the time he had been very busy as he was working in the shop whilst his brother managed the restaurant. His brother needed him to close the shop as they had customers waiting and were short-staffed, and he was just shutting the till when Middleton had suddenly appeared from behind one of the shelving units. Mr Kumar had explained that he could not serve him as he was closing the shop.

'He came towards me. I said that if he had selected some goods already, I would let him pay for them, but if not then he had to leave. I didn't see anything in his hands, so I became very nervous as the till was still open. I thought he was going to rob me. I told him that he had better leave as I didn't want any trouble. He came closer and took out this flick knife and started jabbing it at me. He slashed my arm, so I cried out for help, and he ran out.'

'That must have been very shocking,' Jack said.

'Yes, very . . . and I recognised him. He had been in many times, I had even delivered to his flat, so I knew his address. I gave it to the police and he was arrested.'

'When you told him to leave, how did he react?'

'He stood still, then moved closer. That's what frightened me. He was so quiet. It was shocking when he pulled out this knife and clicked it open, then started waving it around.'

'What was his expression like? I mean, did he look threatening?'

'No, he was calm – very calm – and that's all I can remember. I know he was charged with assault with a deadly weapon, but to be honest the way he acted was very confusing, like he didn't know what he had done, like he was mentally ill.'

Jack thanked Mr Kumar and left to drive back to the basement flat. It was now very dark but there was still a lot of movement in and around the basement. Anik had left, but the surveillance team were still there. The white and blue-suited forensic team were examining the interior of the coal hole and Jack stopped one of the team to ask if there had been any developments. He was given a brief rundown of the items that had been removed for testing, but the huge wheelie bins were still waiting to be taken in as they needed replacements to be delivered before they could remove them. Behind his hooded protective suit, the scientist looked tired, his eyes red-rimmed.

'The chemicals in that place are giving us all headaches; we're going to have to call it quits for today and return in the morning.'

'Have you found any blood traces?' Jack asked.

'Not to my knowledge, but tomorrow we'll be spraying the entire area. In my opinion that place has been chemically cleaned, and the walls have clearly been whitewashed numerous times. There's also a heavy-duty spray washer and two drums of what could be acid. We had to get the specials in to remove them because in that confined space we didn't want to prise them open. If there's been any dis-memberment in there the luminol will show it up. No matter how hard criminals try to hide blood stains, there is always something they miss. We might have to dig up the concrete floor as well.'

On his way back to the car Jack called in to the station to say that he was leaving for home unless there was anything urgent. He was put through to DCI Clarke, who was also just heading home. He instructed Jack to be in first thing in the morning to go through the personal items taken from the coal hole. 'I hope to God we got some evidence today. But we just have to wait for the scientists to do their stuff.'

When Jack got home, he was unsure exactly how he felt. It seemed as though he had been moved aside and that DCI Clarke had taken over the running of the show. But the reality was that whenever an investigation team suddenly expanded, it always felt as if things were being taken over. The thing that was beginning to really bother him, however, was that despite all the items they had removed, they still had no evidence of any murders. Without something new, and most importantly bodies, they had nothing.

CHAPTER FIFTEEN

Maggie was on late call and said that she might even have to sleep over at the hospital as they had so many staff off sick. After having dinner with Penny and Hannah, Jack went into his office to focus on the Ridley situation, as all the activity on the Middleton case had prevented him from dedicating any time to it. He googled the Brighton and Preston Cemetery, which turned out to be an eerie, old-fashioned graveyard – it was even suggested that it would make a good place for a ghost hunt, which Jack thought was ironic, given that it felt as if that was exactly what he was doing as he searched for the real Sandra Raynor.

Jack couldn't decide whether it was necessary for him to physically go and see the grave of the child. He was on early call at the station and knew he couldn't get out of that. It was now almost 8.30 p.m., so driving to Brighton was unlikely to achieve anything.

Next on his list was interviewing both of the women who owned the dating agency. He thumbed through all the data that Sammy had given him and decided that he would try to contact Eva Shay first. He hesitated about calling her, and instead decided that he would pay her a visit. He popped his head round Hannah's bedroom door to let Penny know that he would be out for an hour or so, then put Eva's address into his mobile phone.

By the time Jack had arrived at Chelsea Wharf it was after 9.30 p.m. The apartments in the riverside complex looked very upmarket, and he wished he'd at least changed his shirt. He parked in a visitors' space and walked to the reception area. It was manned by a uniformed doorman and the elegant interior matched his pristine grey tailored suit and peaked cap. He opened the tall glass-fronted door for Jack, who made his way down a thickly carpeted corridor to the elevators. A male receptionist sat behind a small desk, wearing a red waistcoat and bow tie. His hair had such a deep parting that it looked as if it had been cut into his scalp.

'Good evening. I'm here to see Ms Eva Shay in Apartment 43A. She's expecting me.'

The receptionist squinted at Jack and reached for the telephone. Jack hastily showed his ID and leant forwards.

'No need. As I said, she is expecting me.'

'It's the fourth-floor apartment, at the end of the corridor, sir.'

Jack stepped into the elevator and checked his reflection in the polished chrome wall, using a comb to tidy himself up. There was nothing he could do about his six o'clock shadow but he straightened his tie and tightened up the collar on his leather jacket anyway. On the fourth floor the same thick carpet ran the length of the corridor. All of the apartment doors had cream frames with brass doorbells and numbers. At the end of the corridor there was a large floor-length window and a massive floral display on a plinth.

Jack rang the bell and waited. He heard the sound of a yapping dog, so he rang the bell again. The yapping got a bit louder.

The door opened and a frowning Eva Shay, holding a very small Chihuahua, peered out.

'I am so sorry to disturb you, Ms Shay, but I'm investigating the Sandra Raynor case.'

'It's very late,' she frowned. 'You should have made an appointment.'

'I know, I apologise, but I just need a few moments of your time. It is very important.'

Eva hesitated, then opened the door wider. She was wearing a pale-blue quilted robe with satin slippers, and her hair and makeup were immaculate. Still carrying the tiny dog, she ushered Jack along the corridor, lined with large gilt mirrors. She stood back to allow Jack to walk ahead of her into the living room, which made up for its lack of size by having long windows with views of the river.

The furnishings were rather dated, with cream-covered and fringed oval chairs, as well as a settee with stacks of satin cushions. There were flimsy curtains, gathered with a satin bow, and the coffee table had a selection of illustrated books along with a pile of *Vogue* magazines. On every space possible there were ornaments, and on a side table next to the settee was a large glass of wine, a bowl of crisps and an open laptop.

Eva gestured for Jack to sit down, but she remained standing as she shifted her dog from one arm to the other.

'Do you have a card?'

'I don't. We're all so used to seeing TV cops handing out cards, but actually we usually just show our ID. My name is Angus Seymour.' It was the first name that came into Jack's head as he took out his leather ID wallet, flipped it open quickly, then put it back into his pocket.

'So, what do you want to ask me? I've lost count of the number of times I've been questioned, and I've told each officer everything I know. I have to say that this whole thing is very distressing, especially in my line of work as we go to such lengths to protect our clients.'

Jack knew that Eva was in her late fifties, but she definitely looked younger. Her makeup was expertly done; she wore false eyelashes with shadowed cheek bones, and a deep red lipstick that matched her long fingernails. Her curly, shoulder length reddish-brown hair gleamed so perfectly, Jack wondered if it was a wig. She put the dog down on the settee and sat down beside it, reaching for the glass of wine as Jack spoke.

'I'll try not to make you repeat everything over again,' Jack said. 'I am aware that you're very protective of your business, and rightly so. To have a client found dead in such horrendous circumstances could be very damaging. Luckily there has been no publicity about the case so far.'

She frowned. 'So far.'

'Well, let's hope that can continue. Right, first I need you to tell me how the woman known as Sandra Raynor first approached your agency.'

'By the usual means. She had seen an advert and requested an interview, which we arranged.'

'This was all done by phone?'

Shay sighed with impatience. 'Yes, but we explained that, when she came to see us, we would need her CV and some personal data before we could agree to take her onto our books.'

'So, tell me about when she came to see you.'

'I have described this over and over . . .'

'One more time please. Perhaps you could start with how she was dressed?'

'Very smartly, wearing a fitted suit, a white bow-tied blouse, high-heeled Jimmy Choo shoes, and an elegant handbag. She had some nice pearl earrings, with a large signet ring on the pinkie finger of her left hand. She was very well made up and her blonde hair was nicely styled.'

'So, she gave you her age, her previous employment, and bank statements?'

'Yes, it all seemed legitimate, and both my partner and I felt she was suitable to be put on our books.'

'Are you aware she was lying about her age?'

Shay frowned, and Jack wondered if she had been told about the post-mortem report. He sensed that she probably hadn't as she turned away and picked up her wine glass.

'The woman you knew as Sandra Raynor was estimated to be nearer sixty than the age she gave you.'

Shay sipped her wine, then carefully placed the glass down.

'Well, I'd like to know who her plastic surgeon is.' She gave a brittle laugh.

'So, she lied to you and your partner,' Jack continued. 'But I'm sure that's not the first time that has happened. On the other hand, you obviously need to be extremely careful about taking on someone with criminal intentions.'

Shay's lips tightened. 'Excuse me? I'm not sure what you're insinuating.'

'I am not "insinuating" anything, Ms Shay. But the fact is that Sandra Raynor was using a false name, and you arranged a meeting, a date, and a dinner for her with a person now accused of her murder.'

'We went through the same strict procedures we go through with every one of our clients,' she protested.

'Did you do a criminal check on Sandra Raynor?'

'No, but we do if we think it's necessary. In this instance there was nothing to make us suspicious.'

Jack nodded. 'How do you select a match? Show them photographs and do it a bit like an identity parade? We show someone six faces and ask them to pick out the criminal.'

Shay licked her lips and took another long sip of wine. Jack could see she was becoming anxious.

'We have our clients' photographs with their ages, previous work experience and hobbies. And if they are retired professionals then we also include a bit of a CV.'

'So, Sandra came in to go through your client photographs in order to pick out the one she wanted?'

'Yes, that is it exactly what happened. We then submitted her photograph to the person she had chosen, and when it was accepted, we arranged for them to meet in a location suitable to both parties.'

'How long did this take?'

'How do you mean?'

'How long was it from when Sandra came to see you before you got her a date with the man she had chosen?'

'It was unusually quick, just under a week.'

'A week, and during this time did she return to your office? How did you contact her?'

'She did come back into the office, but we also had her mobile number. I gave this to the officers, straightaway.'

Jack knew that the phone in question had turned out to be a burner that was no help in tracing who she really was.

'How well did you know the gentleman she chose?'

She shrugged. 'As much as we know any of our clients. We had already organised two dates for him that proved to be unsuitable.'

'Did Sandra Raynor know the identities of the unsuitable clients?'

'Oh no, we never disclose anything like that.'

'OK. So, just let me go back to the beginning. In Sandra walks, looking very presentable and glamorous, with an impressive CV and a healthy bank balance. She pays the fee, chooses her date and they appear to get along well. They then go on a second date for drinks and dinner, and before you know it . . .' Jack frowned. 'Something about it doesn't sit quite right with me.'

Shay pursed her lips. 'We have a number of clients who have become more than just friends very quickly, and in many cases have got married. I don't know what you are referring to.'

Jack smiled. 'You, Ms Shay. You are a very intelligent woman, running a very successful business, and yet you are completely taken in by this woman. I think she may have made a mistake, and I think you caught on to it.'

Shay looked flustered. 'I don't know what you're talking about. I've answered all your questions to the best of my recall and, repetitive as they've been, I've been very patient.'

'Did you not question her about her previous employment as an accountant?' Jack persisted.

Her false eyelashes fluttered, and she took a large gulp of her wine, draining the glass.

'You were also an accountant, so surely it would have been natural to question her.'

'I think I have spent enough time talking to you. I'd like you to leave, please.'

Jack didn't move. 'I know about your bank account in Monaco, Ms Shay, and I know that recently there were two large sums deposited there.'

She pursed her lips. 'My ex-husband has property there. And yes, I also have an account, but . . .'

'I just need some answers,' Jack continued, 'because it looks to me as though you might be creaming off money from your agency, and I don't think Mrs Da Costa is aware of it. Of course, I'm not about to share that information unless I have to do so.'

Jack watched her get up and cross over to a silver tissue holder. She pulled out a tissue and returned to sit beside her dog.

'Alright. She did come back to the office. It was early evening, and I was there alone. We take it in turns to stay late. I didn't like the fact she just walked in without an appointment. We take a lot of precautions for our own safety, but she was very insistent and wanted to find out when the date she had requested would be organised. I told her that we had to wait for her selected man to get back to us to confirm if he wanted to go ahead. We don't like to put pressure on anyone.'

'Get to the point please, Ms Shay,' Jack said.

Shay licked her lips. 'She went to wait in the small reception area whilst I made the call to the client, as I obviously didn't want her to overhear me. There was no response. I glanced at her CV again, as I was becoming slightly irritated by her manner. I knew the accounting firm she had listed – to be honest anyone in the accountancy world knows them. I was attached to a very small firm but hers was top of the range. I knew someone who worked there, who'd previously been a colleague of mine.'

Eva got up again, opened a small fridge and took out the bottle of wine to pour herself another full glass without offering one to Jack. She was very tense, almost sitting on her dog when she went back to the settee.

'My contact, Debra, said she would run a check but that it would take a while. So, I went into the reception area and told Sandra that I was just waiting for him to call me back. I offered her a drink, and just out of curiosity I asked about what it was like working with such a high-powered company. She said it had been a big learning curve as they were very competitive and rather discriminating. My desk phone rang so I went back into the office and Debra told me that there was no present or past employee of that name working with the company.'

Jack leant his elbows on his knees, waiting whilst she drank more wine. Her hand was shaking.

'I went back and faced her, telling her that I had discovered she was lying and that for us this was unacceptable, and . . .'

She blew her nose, her eyes brimming with tears.

'I couldn't admit this to Mrs Da Costa as she's been a lifeline for me, but that woman wasn't fazed by what I'd found out. She just dismissed it as over-eagerness to find a man who would respect her. She then offered me the money. Two cash payments: one when I organised the date for the first drink and the second when they went out for dinner.'

Jack leant back as Shay blew her nose again, becoming more tearful. He decided he had heard enough and stood to leave.

'One last thing . . . it may mean something, I don't know . . . she was very keen to have that date, but it was the way she organised the money transaction. If she wasn't an accountant, then she certainly knew her way around banking, telling me how long I could keep it in my account to avoid tax. It made me think that perhaps at some time she had worked with an accountancy company.'

'When previously questioned, did you disclose that you knew she had been lying?'

'No, I did not. I assumed they would look into it themselves.'

When he returned to his car, Jack jotted down the name of the woman who had checked out Sandra Raynor. He wondered if Debra Smith might be able to give them an insight into her real identity. Jack found it strange that such a seemingly intelligent woman would have taken the risk of lying on the CV she submitted to the dating agency. He was also certain that it was no coincidence that she had chosen Ridley, and that there had to be some kind of link between them in the past.

That link was what Jack now needed to find.

CHAPTER SIXTEEN

It was not yet 8 a.m. but the incident room was a hive of activity. Laura and Anik had taken over the boardroom to empty the large plastic container full of Rodney Middleton's effects. When Jack joined them, the tables were lined with neat rows of receipts, outstanding bills, documents relating to benefits, and medical data. There was a stack of personal letters to him from his aunt and his father, as well as some worn letters from his biological mother, posted from Ghana.

There was also a photo album containing pictures of Rodney as a child and as a teenager, with numerous photographs of the two little girls who had died in the fire. Some loose photographs had also been piled up beside the plastic-covered photo album, including several of his stepmother, Karen, their wedding and a few of Rodney and his father fishing and roller skating.

'You've been busy,' Jack said, taking off his coat. Laura turned to him and smiled. She was wearing latex gloves and pointed to a box for him to put on a pair.

'Yeah, we both came in at six to get cracking, but we're still just sorting everything out to get it into some kind of order. The reports from Middleton's probation officers and the various psychiatrists are in one pile, though I'm not sure how he came to be in possession of them as they were all internal reports. It might be due to him or his lawyers being given access to them the last time he went on trial, and there's a couple of letters from the legal firm that represented him.'

Anik was emptying the last of the contents, including a few small, dirty boxes that contained bits of jewellery. He placed them in a row and then picked up a clipboard.

'Right, I'll have a look through these and take photographs, then they can be sent to the lab for DNA testing. I've made a list

of everything as, you never know, they could be sick tokens that
he's kept from his victims. That's often what happens, isn't it?'

'You talking about serial killers?' Laura asked, reading the back
of a photograph.

'Yeah, that's the thought process, isn't it? I mean, we're looking
at the possibility of three missing girls, but there could be more.'

Jack made no comment and pulled up a hard-backed chair to
begin sifting through the stack of letters.

'Take a look at this, Jack; I think it's a photograph of his mother,
but read what's written on the back of it,' Laura said.

She passed him the black and white photograph. It showed a
very young Ghanaian girl wearing a school uniform, dated 1981.
Written on the back in a childish print were the words, *Mama, I
miss you. You should have taken me with you.*

Jack turned it over in his mind, trying to think if she could
have given birth to Rodney. He knew that Middleton was seventeen when the fire happened. He estimated from the photograph
that the girl looked no more than about ten or eleven years old.
He took out his notebook to remind him to check the dates,
recalling that Joyce Miller had remarked that his mother had
been very young.

The three of them worked together, tracing the large number of
benefits paid to Rodney over the years. It appeared that he handled
his own admin very efficiently, copying forms and applications,
submitting doctors' letters and psychiatric reports, and managing
a Post Office savings account. They found warranties for the TV
and stereo equipment, as well as an estimate for a new shower and
a receipt for a power-jet cleaner. Jack read the various personal
letters, some sent to Rodney when he was detained in the young
offender institute. The correspondence was mostly from his aunt,
but there were a couple from his father, one saying he was enclos-
ing five pounds. Jack suddenly sat bolt upright.

'Hey, listen to this. Written from Wandsworth prison: "Rodney, I have tried my very best for you under difficult circumstances, but this is the last time I am writing to you. I blame you for my beautiful girls' deaths. Now Karen's gone, so I went off the rails and I got into trouble. I can't blame you for what I done, I was stupid and needed some ready cash for your aunt; she's in a bad way and I am still paying Harold to look after her. They don't want to see you, same as me. I hope you rot in hell for what you done."'

'You interviewed him, didn't you?' Anik said.

'Yes, he was even hoping Rodney would be sent to the same prison as him so Anthony could beat the shit out of him.'

'And you interviewed the firefighter who attended the scene of the fire, so do his accusations have any credence?' Laura asked.

'They investigated the possibility of arson, but no accelerants were found,' Jack told her. 'The fire started in the kids' bedroom, from a duvet that was left hanging over one of the gas heaters.'

Laura reached across the table to a folder that was full of newspaper cuttings. She cleared a space in front of her and took out the cuttings, all neatly held together with a paper clip.

There was a loud rapping on the boardroom door. All three of them stopped what they were doing as Sara opened the door and stepped in.

'The guv wants you to get over to the basement flat, sarge. The forensic team have called in to say they're ready to do the luminol testing. He's outside waiting in a squad car.'

Jack sprang to his feet, as Sara asked if she could stay with Anik and Laura to help them out.

'I think I'd like to accompany Jack,' Laura said sharply.

'DCI Clarke stipulated that only Jack should accompany him and the fewer people there, the better. He's waiting for results to come in from the lab and . . .'

Laura waved her hand to show she'd heard enough and sat back down, then held the latex glove box out towards Sara.

'Put a pair of these on. We need to itemise everything on the table. Anik, have you sorted out what's in all the small boxes yet?'

'Sorry, no, I got side-tracked by the letters. You can do that, Sara.'

Jack left quickly, finding their competitiveness irritating. Nevertheless, he was pleased that Clarke had requested his presence and he was keen to get to the flat. He ran out to the squad car, which was waiting with the engine running.

Clarke was sitting in the front. 'Let's hope we get a result, Jack. There's nothing confirmed from the tests on the tools that were taken, and the lab is now checking out the contents of the two drums they removed. There's oil in one and it appears the entire house had an oil central heating system which was changed seven years ago, but there was a waste section containing the stuff used in fertilisers. Superphosphate of lime is non-flammable but phosphorous sulphur when heated can produce toxic gases.'

Jack nodded. 'We've found a lot of interesting material amongst Middleton's personal belongings, including photographs and letters.' Jack was about to continue when the DCI's phone rang. He listened to the caller before checking his watch to say they would be there in fifteen minutes, and then said that he had it with him so was ready for any eventuality. Clarke ended the call and turned to Jack.

'I've decided to arrest Middleton on suspicion of murder and abduction, but we need to be prepared for that bloody woman Georgina Bamford to stick her oar in. The surveillance team are still on standby, but as yet Middleton has made no move to leave the property. He had a delivery of hamburgers and chips last night.'

Jack said nothing but his heartbeat quickened as they approached the turning leading to the flat. They got out of the squad car and crossed over to the large van parked outside, to put on protective suits and shoe covers.

Uniformed officers had cordoned off the street and were standing by to direct traffic towards a diversion, due to the discovery of possible toxic fumes. Clarke and Jack moved down the basement steps as two suited forensic officers were removing their lamps from the coal hole and placing them in the courtyard area outside the basement flat's front door.

Jack and DCI Clarke stood to one side as the large luminol pump was prepared to spray the now empty interior of the coal hole. Jack had never seen anything like it, as usually they just used a small hand-held spray. There was a faint hissing sound as the forensic scientist moved around the dank coal hole and then began to slowly back out to join them. He had sprayed all the walls, the ceiling and the concrete floor and now handed the pump back to his assistant. He then picked up a high- powered torch and went back in, followed by Jack and DCI Clarke. The luminol would take a few minutes to take effect, so they got everything ready to photograph the glow when it appeared.

'Oh my God,' Clarke exclaimed in a shocked voice.

Florescent green marks covered the walls, ceiling and floor. There were splatters, drag marks and handprints, as well as dense pools over the concrete floor. No explanation was needed: the horror of what must have occurred there was obvious.

They were all so focused on the scene that surrounded them that the sudden sound of Beethoven being played at ear-splitting volume was startling. The music stopped as suddenly as it had begun as the basement door opened. Rodney Middleton stood there smiling. A uniformed officer had been positioned at the door and stepped to one side.

'I suppose you want to arrest me? I've been waiting.' He seemed to be enjoying the moment.

DCI Clarke gestured to the two uniformed officers to come down to the basement courtyard. He cautioned Middleton and explained that he was being arrested on suspicion of murder and abduction.

Middleton didn't seem to be paying much attention. He turned to Jack and calmly said, 'Can you go in and see Amanda? She's very upset.' Clarke nodded to Jack as Middleton was handcuffed and led up the stone steps to the street level.

Jack was badly shaken, and took a breath before going into the flat. He stood in the hallway and he called out for Amanda, but there was no answer and he suddenly felt afraid at what he might find. He called out again, more loudly, then pushed open the main bedroom door. The room was strewn with takeaway cartons, littering the bed and the floor. Most of the containers looked half-eaten and there were also empty bottles of Coke.

Jack hurried down the hallway, pushed open the bathroom door, then opened the door to the back room where he had last seen her. Amanda was sitting propped up on the bed, wearing a set of headphones connected to her phone. He quickly went to her side.

'Amanda ...' He gently removed the headphones, and she instinctively shrank back. He could tell by her eyes that she was high. He pulled the duvet away. She was fully dressed, wearing the same pink bed socks.

Jack called for an ambulance before gently easing Amanda out of bed and walking her to the open front door. He walked her up and down the courtyard, trying to keep her awake and asking her what she had taken. She was completely incoherent and it was a huge relief when the two paramedics arrived to take over.

Jack stayed with Amanda until the ambulance left to take her to the nearest hospital. A young female officer accompanied her, and Jack called the station to ask Sara to meet them at the hospital and to keep him updated about Amanda's condition. She was a key witness, and they would need to take further statements from her at some point.

Rodney Middleton was placed in one of the station's cells. As DCI Clarke had anticipated, he soon received a belligerent call from Georgina Bamford declaring that her client was being harassed and demanding to see him, though she instantly calmed down when it was explained that her client was being questioned about at least three murders and that she would be allowed to speak to him at the appropriate time.

'You know perfectly well, DCI Clarke, that I have every right to talk to my client before you interview him,' she said, regaining some of her poise.

'Obviously and, as I said, that will be permitted, but not at the present time,' Clarke insisted firmly.

Jack was relieved that Middleton was finally in a police cell. He also knew that the hard work of building the evidence against Middleton to convict him was only just beginning. The most urgent task was to identify the victims they believed had been murdered in the coal hole. It would be a marathon task, but the forensic team were busy collecting blood samples to be tested for DNA. Tests on a wire brush, a saw and the contents of the rubbish bins also came up positive for blood stains. The subsequent search of the basement flat after Rodney's arrest had also revealed matted human hair in the drains, from the plugs in the bathroom sink and shower, and the missing girls' families had been contacted, asking for any personal items that might contain DNA for matching.

In all there were now fifteen officers who would be working 24/7, all assigned to different groups by DCI Clarke. Rodney Middleton had lived in the basement flat for five years, so efforts were being concentrated on the missing girls who were known to have been staying with him during that time, but Jack couldn't help wondering how many more victims there could be.

Jack eventually returned home after 10 p.m., having called Penny earlier to let her know that he would be late and would have dinner at the station. DCI Clarke's schedule had been divided up and Jack had agreed to take his fair share of day and night duties. There were officers who would be travelling to the homes of the missing girls in order to obtain as much information and evidence as possible to enable identification. Family liaison officers had to approach the families ahead of the officers' arrival, and the detailed co-ordination of all this was very time-consuming.

The forensic teams were working round the clock to process the vast number of items that had been brought in for testing, while another team were still at the basement flat, taking up floorboards and carpets and removing the entire shower unit and bath pipes in order to look for further evidence.

Jack made himself a cup of coffee and laced it with brandy. He expected to find Maggie asleep, but she was sitting up in bed waiting for him. She knew just by looking at him that he was exhausted. He had a shower and scrubbed his body. He switched off the bathroom light and climbed into bed beside her.

'Do you want to talk, or just crash out?' she asked softly.

'Dear God, Maggie ... my brain feels as though I have a tight steel ring wrapped around it ... I don't honestly know where to begin. It was hell today.'

Maggie said nothing and didn't complain that his hair was soaking wet as his head flopped back onto the pillow. Instead, she turned towards him and gently stroked his shoulder as he began to recount his day to her. He spoke quietly and unemotionally. Maggie just listened without interruption, sensing him gradually starting to relax.

'Then he was just standing there, Mags, waiting at the front door. He was obviously expecting to be arrested, smiling and calmly asking me to check on his girlfriend. Amanda was out of it; I don't know what she had taken, or maybe he had given her something in the hope of killing her. She's going to be a vital witness. They pumped her stomach and she's been sedated. There's an officer protecting her, but we'll need to find a safe place for her to go, if she isn't arrested and charged as an accomplice. My gut tells me she's a liar and a devious little bitch.'

Jack sighed deeply, then turned to face her.

'I'm not sure if I can keep going, Mags. I feel completely worn out. I don't know if I'm right for this job anymore. Sometimes I wish I could just keep toeing the line and not get so involved in cases. I feel as though I've lost my way. I still haven't told you about what Ridley has got me into, because I could get right in the shit if it ever came out that I was digging into his case. As it is, I stupidly used one of the probationers to try and track down Sandra Raynor, the woman found murdered in the boot of his car; it was dumb, and he got no result, but it could come back and bite me on the arse.' Maggie could feel him getting tense again.

'So what did Ridley want you to do?'

'I had to meet the contact he said would help me, because I'm stuck, Mags, and I can't use the station's computers.'

'Yes, yes, you said that before.'

'So I get there, a flat over in Fulham, and his contact turns out to be this drag queen, in full slap with a wig, false eyelashes and a velvet dressing gown, I mean, I dunno if it's a he or she, or what the fuck I am doing there.'

'Oh, come on, Jack, trans issues aren't that complicated. Basically, we should all have one simple rule. If you were born male and want to live as a woman, go for it; same applies if you are woman and want to live as a man. But this person doesn't actually sound like a trans woman; more like a male transvestite.'

Jack propped himself up on his elbow.

'Jesus Christ, Maggie, what the hell are you talking about?'

'It sounded as if you were being derogatory about this person just because of their lifestyle.'

He lay back closing his eyes.

'Right, just forget it. I'm sorry I even brought it up. Now I feel even worse about what I'm getting into.'

It was Maggie's turn to prop herself up on her elbow so she could look down at him.

'You might feel that way tonight, Jack, but once you've had a good night's sleep things will seem better. Just remember that if it wasn't for you, they would never have uncovered these poor innocent girls' monstrous murders.'

She looked at him and cupped his face in her hands. 'Would you like me to give you something to help you sleep?'

'Yeah, that would be good. I'm not due at the station until late tomorrow afternoon.'

Maggie got out of bed and went into the bathroom. She took out a packet of sleeping tablets from the cabinet and tipped two out into her hand. She then emptied the toothbrush mug and filled it with water, carrying it back into the bedroom. Jack was fast asleep, so she swallowed the two tablets herself and set the alarm for 6 a.m. as she was on duty the next morning.

She lay beside Jack, knowing how awful it must have been to see what he had seen today. But she also couldn't help resenting his complete obliviousness to the horrors she had been dealing with on a daily basis. She had become reliant on sleeping tablets to knock herself out in order to be able to get up and face yet another horrific day. She also needed to discuss her concerns about Penny with him. Twice she had found the kettle boiling dry as well as the iron left on. Penny had also heated up some ready meals that were long past their use-by dates. Maggie was worried about Penny not checking that the freezer door was closed properly and concerned about how fresh the food was that she was giving Hannah.

Maggie sighed, turning on her side and tucking her shoulder under her pillow. She felt like having a good cry. She was carrying so much responsibility and Jack seemed to be losing his confidence just at the moment she needed him to be strong for her and their daughter. She decided that tomorrow she would have a long talk with him; if he felt as if it was all too much, he should try stepping into her shoes for a while.

CHAPTER SEVENTEEN

Maggie had left for work and Penny was getting ready to take Hannah to nursery, having been instructed not to wake Jack.

Penny was preparing Hannah's orange juice and packing a little ham sandwich and a biscuit for her mid-morning break. The smoke alarm suddenly went off and she ran to the toaster. She had forgotten that she had put a slice of bread in it earlier and hadn't checked to see if it had got stuck, which it often did. The toast was now blackened, and smoke was billowing out into the kitchen. She opened the back door and swung it back and forth, then took a tea towel and wafted it around the smoke alarm. The alarm eventually stopped and she sighed with relief. Penny decided after she had dropped Hannah at school she would go and buy a new toaster. She listened for any movement upstairs, and was relieved that the alarm didn't seem to have woken Jack.

Jack eventually woke feeling totally disorientated, then looked at the bedside clock. It was 10.30 a.m. and he was about to jump out of bed when he remembered that he was on a night shift at the station. He rarely, if ever, slept late and assumed it was down to the sleeping tablets Maggie had offered him, although he had no recollection of having taken them. He shaved and got dressed, then went down to the kitchen to make himself some breakfast. He was concerned to find the back door wide open, so closed and locked it. He made himself some fresh coffee and scrambled eggs and was about to put a slice of toast into the toaster when he saw the blackened piece left inside.

It was almost 11.30 a.m. when he went up to his home office, feeling energised. As he had some time, he thought he would do a bit of work on the Ridley investigation. He googled the top accountancy firms and scrolled through the results until he found the one Sandra Raynor had put on her CV. It was a big firm with an annual turnover of over a billion pounds. Their London head-quarters were Cannon Street, but they also had offices in Brussels, Madrid, Paris and New York, employing over a thousand staff.

Jack was about to put in a call to the London office, but then changed his mind. Instead, he removed his t-shirt and joggers, putting on a fresh shirt and tie, and his good suit.

* * *

If Jack had been impressed by the company website, he was even more impressed as he approached the building after parking his car. The towering glass office block rose up between two older, less impressive, buildings, dwarfing them. The vast reception doors had polished gold handles and opened automatically as he approached. The reception was almost the size of an airport check-in area, with marble floors and huge sculptures. Three women sat behind a long, glass-topped reception desk and a gleaming corridor lead to polished steel elevators.

'Good morning,' Jack said pleasantly.

The receptionist he spoke to looked Chinese, her gleaming hair brushed back from her face and caught in an elegant comb.

'I'm here to meet Ms Debra Smith.'

'Which company does she work for?'

'I'm not exactly sure, but I do know she's employed here. It's rather an urgent matter. Do you want to see my ID?'

Jack put his briefcase down and took out his ID, flipping it open and closed very quickly.

'Detective Mathews,' he said.

Her face expressionless, she tapped on her keyboard with long pink varnished fingernails then reached for her phone.

'Ms Smith is on the executive floor. Please wait one moment.' She spoke into the handset.

'I have a Detective Mathews here for Ms Smith. It seems to be an urgent matter.'

After listening for a moment, she replaced the handset.

'If you go up to the sixth floor, someone will be waiting for you.'

Jack gave her a wide smile before walking towards the mirror-like elevators.

The elevator moved so fast that it made Jack gasp. He then stepped out into a vast carpeted corridor with floor-to-ceiling glass windows at one end. An office with double doors opened and a young man in an immaculate suit looked towards him.

'Detective Mathews?'

Jack nodded as the young man eased one of the doors wider with an outstretched arm. Jack walked past him into another wide corridor and paused for him to overtake.

'Ms Smith is taking a call but will be with you shortly. This way please.'

Jack was ushered into an enormous boardroom with a highly polished oak table with gilt legs that was twice the size of the station's boardroom table. Placed around the table were expensive-looking chrome and leather chairs and in the centre of the table were leather pots of pencils, a pile of note pads, and a state-of-the-art conference call set.

Against one wall was a long cabinet with trays of white china mugs, silver flasks, and trays of biscuits, as well as a small glass-fronted fridge that was filled with milk, fruit juice and cans of soft drinks.

'Please help yourself. Ms Smith will be with you directly.'

As the door was closed Jack pulled out a chair, laying his brief-case on the table and taking out a file. He leaned across and took a few pencils and a notebook. After five minutes he stood up and helped himself to a coffee and two biscuits. A further five minutes later, as he was finishing the coffee, the door opened.

Debra Smith looked to be in her mid-fifties. She wore a grey suit over a white blouse and her well-cut wavy hair was iron -grey. With very little makeup, she had a very steely presence.

'Thank you for seeing me, Ms Smith. I'll try not to take up too much of your time.'

She moved closer and nodded.

'You say you are a detective; can I see your credentials please?'

Jack smiled and took out his ID, holding it up for a moment. Debra Smith was about to take it from him when he quickly put it back into his pocket.

'I'm hoping you'll be able to help me with a sensitive situation.'

Smith frowned and sat down on the opposite side of the table.

'I was advised to talk to you by Eva Shay, whom I believe you have recently spoken with.'

'That is correct.'

'She asked you a question regarding a woman called Sandra Raynor, about whether or not she was employed here.'

'Yes, that's correct. As I told Ms Shay, to my knowledge we have never employed anyone by that name. Coincidentally, my assistant also received a query regarding the same woman from an officer in the Essex police, I believe. I've been here for more than 30 years and Sandra Raynor wasn't an employee during that time, so if you are here to ask me the same question, it is a waste of your time, as well as mine.'

Jack nodded affably. 'I would like you to look at this photograph please.'

Jack opened his file and pulled out the photograph that Sandra Raynor had given to the dating agency. He pushed it across the table and Debra picked it up with her well-manicured fingernails. She took her time, examining it closely.

'No, I have never seen or met this woman,' she said eventually.

Jack asked her to look again.

'How old would you say that woman is?'

'I wouldn't know.'

'Have a guess. It's rather important.'

Smith sighed, pursing her lips.

'Perhaps in her late thirties or early forties, I couldn't really say.'

'What if I was to tell you she was in her sixties?'

For the first time Smith almost smiled, then shrugged her shoulders. Jack continued.

'Extensive plastic surgery, possibly done in the US. She is almost five foot nine, quite athletic, or she was.' He let the statement hang in the air for a moment.

'Well, I have no idea who she is or was. I'm sorry I can't help you.'

Jack smiled. 'I think perhaps you can. I want you to think back, not just a few years but maybe 20 years or more. Think of anyone in that age category who perhaps was plainer looking then, but the same height, someone exceptionally clever whom you can recall working here, who maybe left under strange circumstances?'

'I'm sorry but you are asking me the impossible. The company moved into this new location fifteen years ago and there have been hundreds of employees during the time I've been here.'

'What if I was to say that there might be a link with Brighton? Perhaps going even further back?'

Jack waited as Smith held the photograph up and looked closely at it. She then leaned across the table and picked up a pencil. She started scribbling on the photograph, then looked up.

'I'm sorry, is it alright if I do this?'

Jack nodded. 'Yes, it's only a copy.'

She made a few more pencil strokes, then chewed at the end of the pencil. She reached for a notebook, tearing a page out and placing it across the photograph. Jack pushed his chair back and walked around to sit beside her.

'This is a bit of a long shot, but it could be her. I've not heard from her or seen her in decades – I'm going back to the late 70s, early 80s. Brighton rings a bell and I think her name could be Leonie or Lorna, but I really can't be sure. She was tall and she was a very good tennis player. She was rather plain looking and had very bad teeth, but I'm afraid I can't recall her surname.'

'Would you be able to find her name in the company records?'

She shook her head. 'No, not that far back. When we moved here a lot of the historical files were shredded. If it is the girl I'm think-ing of, then she was very clever. I think she had a First from Oxford before she became an accountant, so that would mean that when she joined the company she would have been in her early twenties. She was a workaholic and not very sociable, a bit of a loner with not many friends. Hang on, I've just remembered; it wasn't Leonie, it was Lorna, and her surname was Elliot.'

Jack was buzzing as Debra Smith went quiet.

'Do you know if she has any family?' Jack asked.

'My goodness, it was all so long ago. She may have had a sister because I do remember that she often used to stay in Brighton, so perhaps it was with a sister. I really can't be certain, but I just remem-ber how clever she was; actually she was quite brilliant. She quickly started moving up the ladder and was then head-hunted by another firm. As far as I can recall nothing unpleasant occurred when she left us, but by that time she was in a position way above mine.'

Jack was surprised when Smith suddenly pushed back her chair.

'There is someone here who might know more than me, and you're in luck because although he's semi-retired he happens to be here today. Can you wait for one minute?'

Jack nodded enthusiastically. After nearly fifteen minutes Debra Smith returned, opening the double doors wide to allow a wheelchair to enter. The occupier was an elderly gentleman who appeared to have some kind of throat problem as there was a microphone taped to his neck above his immaculate shirt and tie. A cashmere rug was folded over his knees and his shock of white hair and neat moustache made him look as if he had walked off a film set.

Smith introduced them. 'Mr Quentin Henderson, this is Detective Mathews.'

She pushed his wheelchair towards the table as Jack eased back one of the leather chairs. She explained that Quentin Henderson was one of the original CEOs of the company, and had been there for as long as she had.

'Thank you so much for your time, Mr Henderson,' Jack began. 'I'm investigating a woman who called herself Sandra Raynor, but may have been employed by this company under the name Lorna Elliot.'

Henderson remained expressionless as Smith pushed the photograph across the table.

'It was many years ago,' she said, 'but with extensive plastic surgery, this could be the girl I remembered.'

Jack wished she would stop talking so Henderson could focus on the photograph. Suddenly he heard a distorted guttural voice.

'Nothing-like-her.' Each word had a gasp between it.

'Do you remember a girl called Lorna Elliot?' Jack asked.

'One-that-got-away,' the distorted voice gasped.

It was clearly a huge effort for him to talk, so Jack waited patiently for him to explain what he meant.

'She-was-head-hunted-by-a-com-petitor,' Quentin gasped. He adjusted the contraption around his neck. 'But-did-not-remain-went-on-to-another-company-then-with-Anton-Lord.' He was now really struggling to breathe.

'Do you know who that is, Ms Smith?' Jack asked.

'I'm sorry, I don't. Quentin, who is Anton Lord?'

'Partner . . .' he stuttered.

'Ah, I see, so this Anton Lord was her partner; you mean business or personal?'

'Both-they-opened-their-own-company-sale-of-leases. Lot-of-money. Russia.'

Jack had been making notes in one of the company logo notebooks. He was concerned that Quentin was quickly becoming exhausted.

Smith shrugged. 'I'm afraid I don't know anyone called Anton Lord, detective.'

With a trembling hand Quentin tried to pull a handkerchief from his pocket to wipe the spittle from his lips. Smith quickly assisted, gently wiping his mouth.

'No-good-crook!' He spat out the words and waved his handkerchief to indicate that he wanted to leave.

As much as Jack would have liked to try and glean more information, he recognised that the old man was completely drained by the effort of talking. But at least he now had two names to work with. Smith turned the wheelchair round as Jack opened the double doors to help them leave. He was taken aback when the hoarse distorted voice box suddenly cackled: 'Never-trust-an-ugly-woman!'

As the boardroom doors closed, Jack gathered up his papers. He had just closed his briefcase when Ms Smith returned.

'Quentin is an amazing man with an incredibly retentive memory. I hope you found it useful talking to him.'

'I did, Ms Smith, and I'll forward the information onto the Essex team right away. Thank you so much for your time. And please pass my thanks on to Mr Henderson, especially as he's clearly not in good health.'

'He's ninety-three but still likes to come in once in a while. He's actually the reason I'm still here and not retired.'

Jack nodded. 'Just one more thing, Ms Smith, what do you think he meant by that last comment – "never trust an ugly woman"?'

She considered for a moment. 'I would imagine that's connected to his first comment about "the one that got away". He would have been grooming her for a senior role in the company, but she left to join a competitor. As I said, she was a rather unattractive woman, with buck teeth. That she could have transformed herself into the very glamorous woman in the photograph is amazing, but these days who knows what the surgeons can do. I hope we have been helpful to you, detective.'

Jack shook her hand and thanked her again as Smith ushered him into the corridor. She waited with him for the elevator doors to open and Jack descended to the ground floor.

He got back home at 1 p.m., running up the stairs two at a time to get into his home office. He opened his old laptop and began transcribing the conversations with Ms Smith and her old boss, Quentin Henderson. He then accessed the Holmes database and put in the names Anton Lord and Lorna Elliot. Although it was illegal for him to have this database at home, he knew that many officers did the same. As with so many things, Jack mused, you just had to be careful not to get caught.

CHAPTER EIGHTEEN

Jack was concentrating so hard that he didn't hear Penny returning home with Hannah, and he started when there was a knock on his door. Penny popped her head in and asked if he would like a toasted cheese sandwich as she was making one for herself. She told him that Hannah was having an afternoon nap, then said with a smile, 'I bought a toaster. I burnt my toast this morning as it was always getting stuck . . . this new one does four slices at the same time!'

'That's terrific,' Jack said. He paused. 'Listen, Mum, you left the back door wide open, so I locked it when I came down. You need to be a bit more careful.'

Penny put a hand to her mouth. 'Oh, my goodness me, yes . . . I opened it to let the smoke out when the alarm went off. I'm so sorry, Jack, please don't tell Maggie, she's very nervous about things at the moment . . . it's down to stress, I think. Anyway, toasted sandwich coming up with a fresh mug of coffee.'

Penny shut the door, then opened it again straightaway.

'*What?*' Jack snapped.

He hadn't meant to sound so cross but using the Holmes database at home was making him tense.

'Sorry,' Penny said quietly. 'Just asking whether you're working today?'

'No, Mum, I'm going in for night duty later. We're all switching to half weekdays, half nights as we have so much work on.'

Penny closed the door and Jack turned back to the screen. He had managed to pull up the details for Lorna Elliot, including a twenty-year-old black and white photograph. Debra Smith had been very uncomplimentary about her looks, and he could now see why. She had slightly buck teeth, a sharply pointed nose and thick eyebrows that accentuated her wide-set eyes, but Jack was certain this was the woman who had called herself Sandra Raynor. There was also a newspaper article dated March 1991 about the mystery disappearance of a wealthy businessman, Anton Lord. His partner in life and business, Ms Lorna Elliot, claimed that he had gone to spend the weekend at their country cottage in Kent. When he had not answered any of her calls she had driven to see if he had perhaps fallen, and found the cottage unlocked. Their Spaniel had been locked in the garage and it appeared that Mr Lord had been in the middle of having breakfast as there was food left uneaten on the table. It also seemed that he had still been wearing his dressing gown and slippers.

Jack sat back in his chair, looking at the photograph of Anton Lord. He was handsome, with dark eyes and thick hair. He had a chiselled face with a wide smiling mouth and was considerably younger than Lorna. He was described as a 'millionaire businessman' and they were planning to get married.

Jack continued reading one press cutting after another, all covering the same story. The police were still searching for him and there were fears for his safety, which seemed to be related to his various business deals with Russia. There were suggestions that he was owed a considerable amount of money and had recently put pressure on a billionaire businessman in Moscow for payment, threatening to reveal details of their business dealings. It was hinted that illegal transfers of large amounts of money were involved.

This was all extremely interesting, but the reality was that although he was now convinced Sandra Raynor was Lorna Elliot, he still had no proof. He needed to get in touch with Ridley. As usual there was no reply on his mobile, so he left two messages asking him to call back urgently. For a moment he considered contacting the Essex team, but then decided against it until he had confirmation that he was on the right track.

After some more digging around, Jack managed to trace Lorna Elliot's family. She was born in Brighton in 1967, which made her current age fifty-five. She had one older sister, Norma, who was deceased. Both parents were also deceased but there was an aunt still living, Barbara Elliot, aged 88, living in Hove. Jack looked up her address and phone number and was just contemplating calling her when Penny knocked on the door with his toasted sandwich and coffee.

'Sorry it took so long,' she said. 'Hannah woke up, so I had to see to her. I think I'm going to make fried chicken with rice for dinner. Maggie will be due home early today. And I think we need a new coffee machine as something seems to be wrong with it; I had to make you instant.'

Penny put the tray down on his desk, and the next minute Hannah tottered in with a sippy cup in her hand. She swung it around and juice sprayed out from the spout. Penny quickly picked her up and Hannah started howling that she wanted to be with daddy. Jack stood up and took her in his arms.

'Daddy's working but if you wait for a little bit then I can come and play with you. Daddy has important work which he has to finish before he can play.'

Hannah wasn't happy and started kicking and wriggling in his arms. In the end the only thing that quietened her down was half of his toasted cheese sandwich. Penny then took her firmly by the hand and led her out of the room to leave Jack in peace.

He focused on collating all of the new information for Ridley to look at. He had not been that successful with Anton Lord and was about to do some further checks when his mobile phone rang. It was Ridley who, as usual, said that he was unable to talk. He asked if they could meet in their usual place at the same time. Jack started explaining that he was going to be on nights and would leave a message if he was unable to see him, but Ridley ended the call before he could finish.

Jack was now really pissed off. 'Ungrateful sod. He's got no bloody idea what I've got on my plate,' he muttered to himself.

He took a mouthful of the cheese toastie and was gulping down half a mug of the now-cold instant coffee when there was yet another knock on the door.

'I *said* I'd be there in a little while!' he snapped.

Maggie opened the door, carrying a full laundry basket.

'Well, excuse me for living! I've only just got home. I'm gathering all the dirty laundry to do a wash. Why aren't you at the station?'

'I told you I was going to be on a mixture of nights and day shifts with all the work on with the Middleton case. And you won't believe what I've dug up this afternoon; it's mind-blowing. I think I've found out who that woman Sandra Raynor really is . . .'

Maggie dumped the laundry basket down and stood with her hands on her hips.

'If you're going to be working all night, why are you working on that Ridley business as well? You need to get your priorities straight, Jack; you'll get into the station and after a couple of hours you'll be knackered. Remember how you felt last night?'

Jack shook his head. 'I feel great. I'm really buzzing, and the leg-work I've been doing is paying off. I know who Sandra Raynor is. Her real name is Lorna Elliot.'

Maggie sighed. 'You know what, Jack: I don't really care if her name's Jemima Puddle-Duck. We need to talk about some important stuff that you keep pushing to one side.'

Maggie closed the door so that they couldn't be overheard.

'Penny has bought a new toaster which is very kind of her, but the old one was perfectly adequate. And to be honest, if we had needed a new one then I would like to have chosen it. I'm really not that keen on a toaster with bright yellow sides! And now the coffee percolator is burnt out, although it was in perfect working order this morning. The iron has been left on twice; she's boiled the kettle black, and I am not going to get a new electric one because she'll probably blow that up. I really think you need to sit down with her and have a talk, Jack.'

'Listen, Mags, I'll do whatever you want me to do, but I have to move my butt now or I'll be late for work. I agree that I need to have a chat with Mum, and I promise you that I will as soon as I have a minute. We'll sit down and have a proper heart to heart.'

'When?'

'What?'

'*When will that be, Jack?*'

'Christ, as soon as I get a break, alright?'

'You had a break today. You had a lie-in. Why didn't you have that chat with her today?'

'Because I had things to do. Like I said, I've traced this woman's identity and I had to go into the city to meet a contact who helped. It gave me a big energy boost, making some real progress.'

'Well, bully for you,' she said dismissively. 'When do you think I might get to have an energy boost, whatever the hell that is? Doesn't it ever occur to you that I also have a lot of work pressures? I'm worn to a frazzle, but I never get so much as a pat on the back from you. The whole family has to focus on Jack Warr, and it's about time you started to think about somebody else for a change – starting with me!'

'Come on, Mags, don't be like this, please,' Jack said in a placating tone. 'I'm very sorry for whatever I've done or haven't done.'

'That's just it, Jack. You don't do anything that is important for us as a family. It's all work, work, work, and then you moan about how you can't deal with the pressure.'

'I never said that.'

Maggie threw her hands up in the air.

'Fine! Look, now is not the time to have an argument. I'm too tired, and you have to go, so let's just leave it at that for now. When you do "have a minute" we need to have a serious talk about things.'

Maggie picked up the laundry basket and opened the door, slamming it behind her.

Jack sat in his chair, rocking from side to side. He and Maggie rarely argued – he had certainly never seen her as angry as this – and he was unsure how to handle it. He cursed himself for being such a selfish prat.

Last night he had needed her so much, and she had given him solace. He reflected on the quiet and gentle way she had tended to him, listening to the horrors he relayed without making any response or judgement. He knew he needed to be a better and more caring person for her.

He wanted to apologise to Maggie before he left for the station, for not treating her the way she deserved. He straightened his tie and ran his hands through his hair, deciding to stay in his suit. He shoved all the files and papers into his briefcase, then hurried down the stairs and into the kitchen, stopping in his tracks at the sight of the gleaming chrome and yellow plastic toaster. He called out for Maggie as Penny came into the kitchen.

'You just missed her,' Penny said. 'She's gone for a run, pushing Hannah in her stroller. I don't want to talk out of turn, but you know she's under so much pressure at work, and with you working all hours too, you need to spend some quality time together, go out for a nice meal. I can always babysit. You need to look after her, Jack.'

Jack smoothed his hair and smiled at Penny. 'That's a very impressive toaster, Mum. Tell Maggie I'll see her in the morning. I'm on nights now so I won't be back until then. Please just tell her that I love her, and I'll organise a dinner for just the two of us.'

He left quickly, not wanting to get into any further conversation.

CHAPTER NINETEEN

Jack was surprised to see how many officers were on duty. The incident room was a hive of activity and the crime board had now got two additional sections listing the officers assigned to various duties. Jack checked which department was dealing with contacting the missing girls' families, but nothing new had been added, so he went to his desk, which was piled with files and other paperwork for him to deal with. He sat down and opened his notebook.

Laura came in, wearing a bright yellow quilted coat that made her resemble a Michelin Man and carrying a McDonald's takeaway bag.

'Good evening, Jack.'

He waved in her direction as she hung up the outrageous coat. It reminded him of his new toaster.

'I've just been out to get a burger.'

Jack had started sifting through all the files on his desk and didn't reply.

'I must say, you're looking very dapper, all suited up.'

She approached his desk.

'You want a few fries? They always give you too many. I even asked for a child's portion.'

'I wouldn't say no, thanks,' Jack said.

Laura tipped some of the fries into a paper napkin and passed them over.

'What are you working on? I wouldn't mind you popping into the boardroom to have a look at what I've been doing. Anik was working on it during the day but was called out to do something else, so I took over. Why are you looking so smart?'

'I felt I needed to be ready for the long night ahead. I have a theory, which may be a waste of time.' Jack ate a handful of the fries.

'What about?'

'Well, Middleton's been able to use his medical history to get away with claiming mental incapacity, and that's obviously the last thing we want now.'

Jack finished the fries and threw the napkin into the waste bin.

'You know Middleton's very manipulative. Well, what I found odd were the two assaults. They didn't make sense because he was known at both of the shops and could be recognised by the owners. He also gave up his weapons, admitted the offences in interview and told them he would plead guilty. Now, at the last arrest, he came out of the flat with his hands up.'

'Yes, I know that, so what are saying? He's stupid?'

'No, to the contrary. I believe he's a psychopath, as well as being a narcissistic shit. I think he plans it out and is almost wanting punishment. Or perhaps he wanted to be removed from the flat to give himself an alibi of sorts. So, I reckon he did these assaults after he had murdered and dismembered the missing girls.'

'We obviously don't know he did that yet,' Laura countered.

'I know. But I was there when they uncovered the blood bath in the coal hole. I now just need to match the dates the girls went missing with his arrests.'

'Right now, Jack, we don't have confirmation that it was all human blood. And we are assuming there were more than two girls, aren't we?' Laura said, still playing devil's advocate.

'Yes, we are,' Jack insisted. 'He may have dismembered them and put the body parts into bin bags. Forensics found bloodstains in the bins – not confirmed as human yet – but if Jamail was the first victim, Mrs Delaney's husband saw her at the flat, so that gives us a time frame. Mrs Delaney also spoke about a stench from the basement, which Middleton claimed was rat-infested.'

Laura nodded as she munched on her burger. Jack ruffled his hair.

'Middleton needed help to carry the bins up to the pavement because they were very heavy, right? Are you still with me?'

'Yes, but if Jamail was the first, didn't he get arrested after she disappeared?'

'I thought of that. She would have gone missing around the time of the stench. I've looked back at all the refuse collections and the bins were all collected as usual, until the last one after his second arrest. That may have been around the time of Nadine O'Reilly; there was a strike in that area and the rubbish was mounting up on pavements.'

'At the moment it's still all supposition, Jack, and until we get an ID on the victims you might be wasting your time. So far, the most damning evidence we have is the bracelet that we know belonged to Trudie. The girlfriend told you she found it in the bed sheets, right?'

'Yeah, but she also said it belonged to Jamail, so she lied about that.'

Jack leaned back in his chair, frowning. Laura went back to her desk and picked up a flask.

'Come into the boardroom and I'll give you a proper cup of coffee.'

He pushed his chair back and followed her out of the incident room into the boardroom. The table was covered with photographs of the items of jewellery that had been taken out of the boxes found in Middleton's plastic container. The boxes were lined up in a row, and above them were photographs of the items taken from them.

'Anik made sure they weren't all jumbled together. The team going up to visit the missing girls' parents have photographs. We placed them in separate clear bags beside each box. As you can see, we have five small boxes, indicating that we could possibly have five victims. But in a couple of the boxes there are just small items, broken chains, a crucifix and a silver necklace . . .'

Jack moved around the table and picked up one of the photographs. He stared hard at it for a while.

'Let me see the contents of this one.'

Laura picked up the bag and placed a sheet of white paper down on the table, to tip the items onto. Jack pulled on surgical gloves. There was a beaded friendship bracelet, a string of cheap pearls and red beads, one earring, a hair grip and three painted false nails. Jack peered closer, using a pencil to divide and separate the items. He separated out a small gold ring with a ruby stone.

'This belonged to Amanda Dunn; she traded this for the bracelet she said Trudie gave her.'

'How do you know?'

'Because she told me it was not a fair trade; the bracelet clasp broke shortly after they had swapped. She said that Trudie refused to give the ring back to her. She described it as gold, with a real ruby.'

Laura leaned forward. 'Shit, this would mean that Trudie . . .'

Jack straightened up, still staring at the ring. 'Any news on Amanda?'

'We know she's recovered, but she's on suicide watch whilst we determine what to do with her. I think the guv wants her in a safe house for her own protection; they refer to it now as "special measures" because obviously she's going to be a valuable witness, unless it's proven that she was an accessory. What do you think?'

'She's naive, but at the same time she's cunning and a very good liar. She told me that she was always locked away in the back room when Middleton was with one or other of the runaways, but who knows what the truth is. She also, as I just said, initially lied about the bracelet belonging to Jamail. I did put this all in a report. If we're to believe that Amanda was with Middleton from the age of twelve, he could have manipulated her into being an accessory, helping to pick up the runaway kids from the station. If it was up to me, I would arrest her and put the frighteners on her. She could be a mine of information.'

'But she's still a juvenile, Jack. I think we should take good care of her; maybe out of his grasp, she will come to her senses.' Laura replaced the items Jack had looked at as they all still needed to be taken to the labs for testing. She then indicated a large evidence bag at the end of the table. 'We had this taken to the forensics and they've done some tests, but as yet nothing conclusive. However, when it came back to us, I took a good look.'

Laura carefully withdrew a rolled-up sleeping bag from the evidence bag.

'Is that the sleeping bag Amanda was using?' Jack asked, moving closer.

'Yes, and it's pretty disgusting. Anyway, when I was checking it over I pulled up the flap at the end of the bag. It's probably used to cover the sleeper's face if you're outdoors. It's very faint, and easily missed as it's in the folds.'

'What?' Jack leaned forwards.

'It's a name, faded but written in felt tip pen. Heather 4B.'

'No surname?'

'No, maybe the 4B could be a class when she went camping with her school.'

'Shit, she could also be another victim,' Jack said.

Laura nodded. 'Yes, that's what I thought. So we need to find out from Amanda how long she'd been using this sleeping bag and obviously ask her about a girl called Heather. I'll start running her name through mispers, but with so little to go on, we might not get a result.'

Jack smiled. 'Good work, Laura, even if it does mean more legwork for everyone.'

Jack returned to the incident room. The evidence board was filling up, with new information coming in minute by minute. After being shown photographs, Trudie Hudson's mother had identified the jewellery as belonging to her daughter and this new development was being written up on the notice board. Trudie had gone missing four years earlier and there had been no sighting of her since she left Liverpool. Jack made a note, underlining the timing. It tied in with the date of the first assault case carried out by Rodney Middleton.

At 10.30 p.m. another piece of information came through, this time regarding Nadine O'Reilly. Her stepfather had identified the photograph of the silver crucifix as belonging to his fifteen-year-old stepdaughter. Nadine had last been seen eighteen months ago before she ran away from Leeds. She was reported missing a week later as her parents had initially believed she had gone to see family in Dublin. The officers visiting both families had taken DNA swabs to compare to the crime scene blood, and also brought back photographs, which would be added to the board as soon as they returned to the station.

All of this new information served to validate Jack's suspicions. They were still waiting on the information from Jamail Brown's family, but if Jack was correct, she was Middleton's first victim, although they now had to add another name to the board, the one from the sleeping bag. And it would take forensics a while to match the blood samples they had acquired from the basement to the new DNA evidence that had just been brought in.

The team that had been working on collecting the evidence from the basement flat were now ready to finish up. They had taken further blood and hair samples from the drains, and various items of clothing belonging to Middleton, including a pair of underpants found under the sink, that had been used for cleaning. They had also bagged up shoes and stained garments and bedding, including the sleeping bag Amanda had used. Her small collection of clothing and personal items had also been bagged and taken for evidence.

The night was dragging on. The team on duty prepared the files ready for interviewing Middleton. Laura was back in the incident room to detail the items of jewellery that had been identified, and was feeling despondent: although it had been confirmed that some of the jewellery belonged to two of the missing girls, there were four more boxes to go through. Sara had put forward a list of several missing girls who might turn up to be the additional victims. They were all young runaway teenagers who had not been sighted for years.

'There could be more girls, Jack,' she said, looking over at him.

He nodded grimly. 'I know that. I expect the forensic team will eventually confirm just how many blood groups we're dealing with.'

He swung back in his chair. 'You know Amanda said she remembered a girl called Nadine or Naomi, and we know we have some items from Nadine, so see if there's a missing girl called Naomi, and the latest one, Heather.'

'It's heartbreaking that these kids could just go missing for all these years,' Laura said sadly.

'He had five years in that basement flat, so Christ knows how many girls became his victims.'

DCI Clarke's office door opened. He looked exhausted.

'We've just had verification from Ishmail Brown that his daughter, Jamail, owned the pearl and bead necklace; he brought it back from Jamaica for her eleventh birthday. He also identified a silver bangle and a fake pearl and amber earring.'

'How old was she when she went missing?' Laura asked.

'She was thirteen. Mr Brown is currently serving time in Strangeways for domestic violence and sexual harassment of Jamail's mother. She continued contacting mispers to try and get information about Jamail, but it's been such a long time, and with her husband in prison she returned to the Bahamas six months ago. We're trying to contact her.'

'So, we've done Liverpool, Manchester and Huddersfield to date. Do you think the girls knew each other?' Laura asked as the DCI stood in front of the board.

'Predators are able to spot the runaways at the train stations, especially the young ones, then they pick them up like lost puppies,' he said quietly.

'And if you have another young runaway in tow with you, like Amanda Dunn, that will give any new girls the confidence to go with him. She admitted to me that's what she did,' Jack added.

Clarke walked over to Jack's desk. 'We know that, but we need her on the prosecution side. So I want her wrapped in fucking cotton wool until I'm ready to question her. In the meantime, we keep working round the clock.'

He turned and walked back to his office, closing the door behind him. Laura waited a moment before speaking.

'He's run ragged. I think this is the biggest case he's ever had. If you ask me, he needs to take a break. He's been here 24/7 and did an all-nighter as well. You know, I really miss old Ridley . . . He was much calmer. We have so many officers assigned to this case now; Ridley would be in his element.' She sighed and stepped closer, lowering her voice.

'I did hear a whisper that he was in some kind of legal trouble, and not actually ill as we assumed. Have you heard anything?'

Jack shook his head. 'No.'

'Well, if you ask me, something is very wrong. What do you think's going on, Jack?'

He shrugged. 'I really don't know. With so much going down right now, I've not really given him much thought.'

Laura went back to her desk, as Jack yawned loudly. He was already feeling tired. He revisited the notes he had taken after the meeting with Joyce Miller, as well as the later interaction at the basement flat when Mr Miller had brought Middleton back from

Brixton. Jack then re-read the letter from Rodney's father, saying that he wanted nothing to do with him, and that he was financing Joyce and paying her husband to care for her. Jack speculated that he was more likely to be feeding her to death and wondered if there might be a reason for that.

The long shift continued, and Jack spent it cross-referencing and putting the accumulated evidence into chronological order, ready for Rodney Middleton's interview.

At 2 a.m. refreshments were brought in for the team, including pizza, hot dogs and flasks of tea and coffee. It was a 'down tools' break for everyone, and Jack didn't recognise some of the officers who trooped in to partake of the food and drink.

Two overweight male officers circled the refreshments, with an equally rotund short woman who had a wonderful head of snow-white hair. She was loudly complaining about cold hot dogs and no mustard. 'Considering we've been here since 7 p.m., I'd have thought a decent hot meal could have been provided. When I worked in Wimbledon, we used to get Krispy Kreme donuts. It's a bloody liberty. I wouldn't feed my poodle this rubbish.'

Jack hid a smile but straightened up when she marched over to his desk.

'Detective Sergeant Warr, they said you were good-looking, but they didn't say you were a savvy dresser . . . very nice suit. I'm Glenda Bagshot, leading the CCTV footage investigation. I think you should come up to our dank hole on the top floor . . . we've come up with a few things of interest.'

Jack immediately stood up, eager to see what they had unearthed. Glenda waddled ahead of him, still complaining about the refreshments, as he followed her up the stairs. They eventually went into a room at the far end of the top floor corridor. Because the team had to focus on monitors for lengthy periods the blinds were down and there was only a low light overhead. Three Perspex screens separated the areas, and it appeared that Glenda was working on two screens at the same time.

'Pull up a pew. Have you got a mask? If not, there's a box of them on the side of my desk if you can be bothered. But I'm not worried. Lot of people don't bother now. I took my wee poodle in for a groom and they wouldn't let me in without a mask. I said it's my dog that wants a wash not me! I'm wearing one, but only as it limits the smell of BO. Right, I'm working on footage from the security cameras positioned across from the basement flat, and next to the house. There are also two further cameras up the street. It's a relief that they're all up to modern digital standards as having to work on old tapes is a nightmare. This makes my life a lot easier.'

Jack pulled forward a small office stool on wheels to sit close to Glenda. She pointed to the two other monitors.

'They're taking a bathroom break. The bloke at the end is concentrating on the rubbish collections, and the unfortunate gent beside me with nasty BO is focusing on a large charity clothes bin used for second-hand shoes and clothes, outside a food store. The shop has good CCTV. I think the shop owner made complaints about people dumping old push chairs and baby seats which weren't getting collected, so he installed a good quality security surveillance camera, which is handy for us.'

Glenda hardly drew breath as she went on to say that DCI Clarke had instructed them to go back some considerable time. She squinted at a thick notebook, then flicked through the pages.

'We were told to begin from the time this SOB was arrested after his first assault. We immediately faced one big problem: with it being a basement flat there's no footage of the basement courtyard, only the few steps at the top and the pavement outside. We had instructions to keep going further back for as long as we needed to in the hope of finding something useful. I've been editing clips together to avoid wasting time scrolling through hours of footage, and I mean hours. We've been at this all night and will probably still be working on it tomorrow.'

Glenda was constantly pushing her face mask up over her round face, pinching it across her nose to try to keep it in place.

'Right, handsome, let me show you what I have so far.'

Jack smiled, then turned to watch the footage. A lot of it was very grainy, and Glenda gave a running commentary to explain what he was looking at. He could see Rodney Middleton being escorted to a waiting patrol car between two uniformed officers, dated and timed as the evening of his first arrest for assault. Middleton seemed totally unfazed and at ease, and at one point he turned to face the camera. One officer carried an evidence bag which presumably contained the weapon.

The footage continued, showing Amanda Dunn leaving the basement flat carrying what looked like a bulging pillowcase. This was timed and dated as the day after the arrest. There were then numerous clips of her going in and out of the flat with what may have been the same pillowcase. She also went in on various occasions with food shopping bags, then finally left with a small holdall. Jack noted that one of the dates tied in with when she had called him from Euston Station.

On the same night she told Jack she was catching a train to Liverpool, Amanda was seen carrying a brown paper bag, a bottle and boxes of biscuits. Then there was coverage of Jack and Laura parking outside and entering the basement, fast-forwarding to see Harold Miller pulling up in a car and Rodney Middleton stepping out of the passenger side. Miller opened the boot and took out a bag. He held it out to Rodney, but he ignored him, so Miller shut the boot, locked the car, and stopped on the pavement to talk to Rodney. He put the bag down and opened a wallet, handing Rodney some cash. It was obvious that Rodney didn't think it was enough as he shoved it back at him. Harold reopened his wallet and took out some more notes, before putting his hand in his coat pocket. They then went down the steps to the basement.

'Can you freeze on that last interaction?' Jack asked.

Glenda moved her mouse and rewound, then pressed pause. Jack peered closer to the screen.

'Do you know, he has no bank account, or cards, with just a Post Office savings account for his benefits to be paid into. No driving licence, no car and so far, no mobile phone. The handset we have taken in is his girlfriend's, which is very outdated, with no apps and just a few contact numbers. Middleton is very tech-savvy and has lots of the latest gadgets in TV and stereo equipment, so it doesn't make any sense that he wouldn't have a mobile. Can you enlarge that section where it looks like he's being handed money, then passes it back and then Miller opens his wallet?'

Glenda zoomed in as requested and Jack peered at the screen. He then sat back.

'I think Middleton passed Harold a mobile, underneath the bank notes that he handed back. Harold opens his wallet and hands him more cash, then puts his hand into his coat pocket. I'll get the team onto it because I think Harold Miller took away Rodney's mobile because Middleton knew we were in the flat.'

Glenda tapped her notebook, turning to Jack. 'Well, you're now up to speed with the coverage so far, from the original time frame we were given. To my mind it doesn't add anything concrete, so now we go further back. These new CCTV cameras don't wipe over anything, so everything is stored digitally – unless they're switched off.'

Jack stifled a yawn, and she glared at him. 'Keeping you up, are we?'

'Sorry . . .'

Glenda turned as two officers came back into the room. She was certainly right about the bad BO. She rolled her eyes at Jack and pinched her nose over the mask.

'Right, so this is me clipping a lot of footage together, but it gives you a really good look at the SOB and what he does. It's not a lot, I'll grant you, but keep watching,' she said.

Jack leaned forward as he watched Rodney go in and out of the basement. He was seen carrying food shopping and stopping to talk to Mrs Delaney, then helping her husband carry the bins up to the pavement. He staggered as he carried what must have been an especially heavy bin up the steps.

Next there was footage of Rodney carrying what looked like large rolls of bubble wrap. Jack was finding it difficult to keep his eyes open, but then Glenda barked out that this next section was interesting and he should pay attention.

He leaned closer, watching Rodney heaving a bin on his own, bouncing the wheels up the stone steps as he became visible at the pavement level. As he reached the top step, the lid opened, and a package fell out. Rodney bent down to pick up the tightly wrapped black plastic parcel and quickly stuffed it right down into the bin. He positioned the bin on the pavement and ran back down the stone steps, returning with a black bin bag with a yellow drawstring tie, which he placed on top of the rubbish already inside the bin, pushing it down. He shut the lid and leant heavily on top of it to press everything tightly down.

Jack took a deep breath as Glenda instructed him to join the odorous officer beside her. He sat watching footage of the charity bin. Amanda was seen with the pillowcase, taking out clothes and shoes and pushing them into the open lid of the big container. The officer had so far been able to show three different trips over a period of many months, and on each occasion, Amanda carried a full pillowcase and emptied the contents into the container. She looked very unwell, with lank hair, and was always wearing the same old coat.

Glenda leaned on the back of the officer's chair. 'As this footage was some time ago, it's highly unlikely we'll be able to track any of the items she's getting rid of. But you can probably cross-reference the dates of the missing girls with the clothes drop-offs, as they could belong to the victims.'

The other officer had been focused on bin collections, dates and times, and reported that there were three different collections. The green bin was for glass and plastic, the blue for cardboard and paper, and the black bin was for general non-recyclable waste and food. There was also a brown bin for garden waste, but that was only collected once a month. Each bin had to be positioned on the pavement on the appropriate collection day.

Glenda said that it appeared that the black bin was always the heaviest, and therefore the most likely to be used for dismembered body parts. They watched Mr Delaney assisting Rodney, heaving the bin up the basement steps. There was also footage of the other tenants heading down to the basement with their respective kitchen bin liners or black dustbin bags. They never stayed any length of time in the basement courtyard.

Glenda said that it was a *very* long shot, but they could begin searching the local landfill sites for any human remains.

Jack remained with the CCTV investigators for another hour, and by the time he returned to the incident room he was feeling nauseous. This was partly caused by the intoxicating BO, but also from viewing the footage for over three hours.

Some of the night duty officers had already left and Laura was just gathering her things together as it was almost 6 a.m. The thought of now having to go and meet Ridley made Jack's head throb, but he hung back to mark up his findings on the board.

'Bit over-eager, aren't we?' Laura said, putting on her Michelin Man coat.

'Just finishing up a few things,' Jack said, checking his watch. He was about to call home to talk to Maggie, but then Anik arrived, annoyingly bright-eyed and bushy-tailed.

'Morning all. How did it go last night?' he asked breezily.

Jack smiled wanly and suggested that he take a look at the CCTV footage upstairs, then went over to knock on the DCI's office. He waited, then eased the door open. DCI Clarke was lying on the floor next to his desk, using his overcoat as a pillow, with his mouth wide open. Jack quietly closed the door and packed up his briefcase.

A very bouncy Sara suddenly launched herself through the door.

'Morning, everyone. Can I get a round of coffee or tea?'

There were a few orders shouted out, and requests for bacon butties. Jack was ready to leave when she stopped to ask if he wanted anything. He shook his head.

'Just my bed. It's been a very long night.'

'I've got some good news from mispers about two of the girls,' Sara said, looking at a report on her desk.

Jack waited.

'They've been traced.'

'Good, that's really good . . .' he said quietly.

CHAPTER TWENTY

Ridley looked in even worse shape than the last time they had met. Jack handed him a coffee and sipped at his own double macchiato in the hope that it would give him some energy. They sat on their usual bench, and it was soon clear that depression was weighing heavily on Ridley.

'It's over, Jack; we have nothing. Apart from it appearing that someone was attempting to trace Sandra. Of course, they ran it by me, but they'd got nowhere so they weren't really concerned.'

'Maybe we should sit in my car so that I can tell you what I've discovered, and you can tell me what a fucking genius I am. I think I may have discovered Sandra's identity, but I need you to look at everything I've got. I didn't park too far away, so come on.'

Ridley actually smiled as they approached the pea-green Nissan Micra, asking Jack if he had ever considered driving something a little less obvious. He climbed into the passenger seat while Jack sat in the driving seat beside him. Jack reached over to the back seat for his briefcase.

'Did you know a woman called Lorna Elliot?'

Ridley frowned and shook his head. Jack took out the newspaper photograph and showed it to him. He stared at the cutting and simply shook his head again.

'OK, what about someone called Anton Lord?'

Jack was taken aback at Ridley's lack of response. He had been so certain that he had made a breakthrough. He told Ridley about the gravestones for the Raynor family, that their dead child had been called Sandra, and that the mother's maiden name had been Norma Elliot.

Ridley continued to stare at the photograph. Frustrated, Jack told him to think back twenty years, to any case involved with accountancy, perhaps a big fraud.

'She is the right age, sir. She looks like a dog's dinner in these photos, but if she had a lot of work on her face . . . she's the same height and build. And this Anton Lord may have been a bad sort as well; take a look at his photo and see if it jogs your memory.'

Ridley closed his eyes and Jack felt his frustration mounting.

'Russia, they could have been working on something in Russia. Have they tested your car for any of that fucking Russian poison? Are there any results back from your blood and urine tests?'

'Wait a minute,' Ridley spoke quietly. 'Is there something about a farmhouse?'

Jack found the notes he had made from the newspaper cuttings. He passed them to Ridley. It was only a moment or two, but it felt like an age before Ridley's head snapped up and he looked at Jack.

'I don't believe this. It's got to be more than twenty years ago. I can't remember her, but something is starting to click. Jesus Christ, it was so long ago that I think I was still in uniform for fuck's sake. But how does it connect to the present day? I just don't understand?'

'What do you remember?'

Ridley took a deep breath.

'There was an investigation into the disappearance of a young guy, a banker or something like that. He disappeared from his country farmhouse, maybe in Essex, just disappeared off the face of the earth. I wasn't on the case originally but was brought in years later as there had been a development in tracing a suspect.'

'Go on . . .'

'Well, like I said, I was just part of a team, but the suspect involved in this bloke's abduction and possible murder had been traced to Moscow. It dragged on for eighteen months or so, while they were trying to bring him back to the UK to stand trial, but there's no extradition treaty; they were going to be sending some-one over to confront him. But before they could question him, he committed suicide. As far as I can remember there was a lot of money involved, all connected to illegal currency dealing. The poor bastard that disappeared was apparently very skilled at hiding money in complicated business webs and offshore trusts.'

'This was Anton Lord?'

'I honestly can't recall, but the name rings a bell. I never met him, or his partner.'

'That would be Lorna Elliot?'

'I don't know . . . but I can get the team working on it. They can start to dig up everything there is on the case. Right now, they're still attempting to find all the CCTV footage where my car might have been driven. It's still with forensics officers; they're even test-ing soil particles from the tyres in an attempt to match a location. They've interviewed everyone in the bar the night it happened. But there's no one suspicious . . . It's a nightmare.'

'Did they test for anything like Novichok, the nerve agent used by the Russians on the Skripals? This was a few years ago, but I remember a woman died because she had found a bottle the killers had discarded in a trash bin. I did a bit of research a while back: the symptoms are intense breathlessness, muscle pain, vomiting and it can also result in permanent nerve damage, but if you were given a minuscule dose, it could be why you lost consciousness.'

Ridley was clearly becoming very anxious, but Jack picked up a slight hesitation before he answered.

'Jesus Christ, they're testing every inch of my car, and all the clothing I wore that night; I've had urine and blood tests. But the problem is that I was violently sick, so it all went down the toilet.'

'If you had so much as a molecule it can stay in the system for up to two weeks,' Jack said.

'Well, as I said, they took blood samples, skin, hair, you name it. It could have been one of the date-rape drugs. Victims don't recall anything for long periods.'

'And you have complete memory loss for the entire night after leaving that pub?'

'Yes, I've already told you that. Now can we go back to the woman? You say her real name is Lorna Elliot, correct?'

Jack intuitively knew Ridley was changing the subject, but couldn't fathom out why.

'Yes, I believe that's right.'

'So why me? Why did she want to see me? How did she know me? I honestly can't ever recall meeting this Lorna Elliot in connection with the Anton Lord investigation. I was a young, uniformed officer at the time. How would she have found out I was ever part of it?'

'There has to be a link,' Jack said. 'You taught me that. Maybe the team looking into all this can find it. I'd start with what Anton Lord was up to in Russia.'

Ridley nodded. 'Yes, you're right. They've done fuck all to date. But at least it's something new for them to start working on. And Jack...' Ridley turned to him. Jack had his head down and his eyes closed.

'Jack!' he said loudly, and he jerked awake.

'Sorry, sir, I'm totally wiped out. I've been on duty all night. But I've only just skimmed the surface. I can keep digging...'

Ridley shook his head. 'Let me start working on it. I'll just say that I'm trolling through old cases. You've done enough. I don't want your name getting mixed up in it all.'

Jack was relieved, as juggling two cases was exhausting him.

'What about this relative who lives in Sussex... an aunt?' Ridley asked.

'Her name is Barbara Elliot, but I've not had time to do a check on her.'

'Can you just do that for me? If I go, wearing this damned tracer on my ankle will tip them off. It's against the law as I'm a bloody Met officer, but I suggested it.'

'How come you can get out to meet with me?' Jack asked.

Jack sensed the hesitation, before Ridley answered. 'I use a burner phone, and they have a change-over at 8 a.m. every day, which gives me just enough time to walk along the river and get back. I *am* allowed out for some fresh air. They will obviously be able to track how far I am from the house, but I doubt this is going to last as they can't keep this situation under wraps for much longer. That said, I still want you to be very careful, so don't take any risks. Just see what you can do. Right now, you've proved to me that I was right about you: you're the only person I can trust.'

Jack couldn't really say no, despite his exhaustion, so he agreed to find time the following day to track down Barbara Elliot. He watched as Ridley got out of the car and headed back towards the river. He didn't know why he felt so uneasy. Had Ridley lied to him? Was there more to his situation than he was admitting? He couldn't help feeling that Ridley was using him somehow – but to what end?

By the time Jack arrived home the house was empty. Maggie had left for work, and Penny had taken Hannah to nursery. He drank a glass of milk and ate some biscuits, then he crashed out in bed, after setting his alarm for the night shift.

* * *

The team were waiting for more forensic results. They had DNA from the three missing girls' families – taken from toothbrushes, hair slides, hairbrushes as well as blood samples from family members. The scientists were working in shifts as there was so much evidence from the coal hole and basement flat to work through, examining a saw blade, a wire brush, a shovel and a fifteen-inch sharpened screwdriver, along with four long, sharp-bladed knives.

They had their first match by 10.30 a.m., with Nadine O'Reilly's DNA.

At eleven o'clock the second match came in. This time it was for Trudie Hudson, and the match had come from the wire brush as well as a section of the stone flooring in the coal hole. No one celebrated.

Sara had pinned up four other possible runaways who were still missing – two of them now had the word 'traced' stamped across their faces. But even with the horrific evidence, they still did not have any bodies or body parts, and that could be a problem.

Local officers now had the sad and difficult job of visiting the families and telling them about the positive DNA matches. Meanwhile, Sara was keeping a watchful eye on Amanda Dunn's progress. She had been diagnosed with severe anaemia and was dangerously underweight. She had been put on a glucose drip and appeared to be gaining strength. She had been asking when she could go to see Rodney, and when she could have her mobile phone back. The officers had been given strict instructions not to allow Amanda to make any calls on the landline, unless they were recorded, and her mobile was not to be returned to her. She did not have any money and had to remain in hospital until the doctors discharged her into a hostel or protective custody. Interviewing Amanda was obviously urgent but according to the doctor caring for her, he felt she was not yet fit to be interviewed as she had a high temperature.

Sara put down the phone after speaking to the female officer who was monitoring Amanda. She looked over to Anik. 'The officer said Amanda was very childlike, like she's a bit backward, although she's getting a bit tetchy apparently because she's not allowed to smoke. What do you think?'

Anik pursed his lips and shrugged.

'I've never met her, but from what we have on her sick boyfriend I would say she is likely to be a co-conspirator. She picked up the girls with the bastard; she had to know what was happening in that fucking shithole of a basement flat, just like Rosemary West. I think she should be arrested.'

'For heaven's sake, she's only seventeen years old!' Sara protested.

'So were the dead girls, some even younger. Laura told me Amanda Dunn was an accomplished liar and even pulled the wool over super-sleuth Jack Warr's eyes. He gave her cash for a train fare back to her parents, but she never went. Oh, and by the way, he left a memo for us to check into the possibility that Rodney's aunt or her husband may have provided him with a mobile.'

They were interrupted by Leon, passing on a message from the desk sergeant.

'There's a Mrs O'Reilly in reception, waiting to talk to someone about her daughter.'

'Oh my God, we sent a liaison officer to her home. Does she know about the DNA match?' Sara asked.

'I don't know, I'm just bringing the message. What do you say, sarge?' He looked at Anik.

'Listen, I'm not good at this stuff. You go and talk to her, Sara. If you're not up for it go and talk to the DCI, because by rights he should be the one talking to her; but he's got his hands full with that fat little woman Glenda Bagshot, and the Chief Super is in with them.'

Sara hesitated, then agreed to go and talk to Mrs O'Reilly. She had never had to break bad news to the relative of a deceased person, whether it was accidental or murder. She told Leon to take Mrs O'Reilly into the small interview room and to organise a cup of tea for her. She then took out her makeup bag and opened a compact to check her hair and freshen her lipstick.

'What on earth are you checking yourself for?' Anik snapped. 'Just go and do it and get back as fast as you can. We have a big backlog of statements to check through.'

The small interview room contained a table and two chairs. It smelt stale, and the only window was high up on the back wall. The strip lighting was blinking as if the bulb was loose or needed changing.

Mrs O'Reilly was sitting with her back to the door. Her dark, rather greasy hair was tied with a black rubber band, and she wore a heavy tweed coat and fur-lined ankle boots.

On her lap was a large worn leather bag. She turned expectantly when Sara entered the room.

'Thank you for the tea,' she said in a soft Irish accent.

Sara introduced herself and sat down opposite.

'I got the train, straight after they'd come around to the house for some of Nadine's things. They told me that they were officers working for the Metropolitan Police here in London and gave me the address. I knew that it must be important – my husband said to me that they asked for certain things and he said he had seen programmes on the TV, you know, real crime ones, and they always asked for things like toothbrushes and hair accessories. He said that it was for identification purposes. That's right, isn't it?'

'Yes, Mrs O'Reilly, that is correct.'

'Then we got another woman come round and she told us that they was doing a murder investigation, that Nadine might have been killed at a house in London. She was very nice, trying to be helpful. She said it wasn't confirmed yet, and so now I'm here to find out if they have found her.'

'Mrs O'Reilly, I am very sorry to tell you, but we have found items that belonged to your daughter.'

'Does it mean that you've found her? Maybe I've wasted the train fare, I was just eager to help . . . at least to speak to her because

I never meant to get into such a row with her . . . I've been wanting to slap myself for being so nasty to her, but she can be a right little madam sometimes, and . . .'

Sara was desperate to stop the flow, but just as she was about to try and explain that they had found evidence that her daughter was no longer alive, Mrs O'Reilly dug in her worn handbag and pulled out a postcard.

'This is what I wanted to bring here, because when we got it . . . well, it was a while back, but it made me feel not so worried. Here, dear, you read it.'

The postcard was a photograph of Buckingham Palace and had been posted almost eight months ago. Sara turned it over and read the message on the back:

Dear Ma – Just to let you know I've met some friends from Snapchat, and they let me move in with them. I'm going to try and get a job in a hair salon and I'm not coming home. Love Nadine.

'Thank you for bringing this in,' Sara said. The date on the postcard would be helpful in constructing their timelines. As she was about to give Mrs O'Reilly the sad news, she dived into her bag again and this time brought out a mobile phone.

'This is what caused the big row. She was never off it, and we had to pay the bills. So my husband took it away from her and it made her go crazy. She attacked me. She was that angry. Next morning she'd gone. We thought she was just messing, so we didn't report her missing for a couple of days. Then we got that postcard saying she wasn't coming home. The phone's dead and it's been in a drawer all this time.'

'Is the handwriting on the postcard Nadine's, Mrs O'Reilly?'

'Yes, that's her handwriting . . . she was very clever at school.'

'When you reported Nadine missing, did they ask you whether she had a mobile phone?'

'No, I don't think so, but it wasn't turned on or charged up, just in the drawer.'

Sara reached over and touched Mrs O'Reilly's hand. She took a deep breath.

'Mrs O'Reilly, I am very sorry to tell you that Nadine may not be coming home.'

She looked bewildered. 'I don't understand. Has she got herself into trouble? I knew it when the coppers came round asking for her things, showing me photographs of her things; I just knew it.'

Sara quietly explained to Mrs O'Reilly that they had DNA and other evidence indicating Nadine was probably dead.

Mrs O'Reilly repeatedly shook her head, then suddenly broke into tormented sobs. Sara felt terrible for being the bearer of such devastating news. She offered her another cup of tea, then got up and walked around the table to put her arms around the distraught mother. Sara spent another half an hour with Mrs O'Reilly, then ordered a taxi to the train station for her.

Sara returned to the incident room, feeling emotionally overwhelmed. As she slumped into her seat, Anik came over to ask how it had gone. She shrugged her shoulders.

'It was horrible. I couldn't give her any details, like Nadine's body not being found; it was just so hard . . . totally heartbreaking.'

Anik looked at the mobile phone and the postcard she had placed on the desk in front of her.

'What's this?'

Sara told him that Nadine's parents had received the postcard and that they thought she had run away because they had taken her mobile phone away. He picked up the card, read it, then studied the mobile.

'This is a major breakthrough! This means that little two-faced bitch Amanda Dunn could have been in contact with Nadine on Snapchat. The guv is going to love this.'

Sara watched him scoot across the incident room and go into DCI Clarke's office. All she could think of was the expression on Mrs O'Reilly's face when she had told her that Nadine was possibly never coming home. Anik came back to his desk after a short while. 'I'm going to go and interview Middleton's aunt and her husband about giving him a mobile phone.'

'Do you need a search warrant?' Sara asked.

'No, just going to put the frighteners on them. As you met them both, you can come along with me if you like.'

After they had left the station, new information came in from forensics. They had now identified a DNA match with the missing girl, Jamail. The positive result came from blood splattering in the coal hole and the hairs recovered from the drain inside the basement flat, indicating that Jamail had probably been dismembered in the bathroom.

The incriminating evidence was mounting by the hour. However, no relevant clothing had been found from the charity drop cabinet yet, but they were still searching the vast warehouse where the clothes were being sorted, ready for distribution. Twenty officers had been assigned to the landfill sites, but as yet, they hadn't unearthed any evidence connected to the murders. Leon had been compiling the missing girls' dates of birth which had been passed to them by the victims' respective families. He knocked on DCI Clarke's office door.

Clarke looked up at Leon with an irritated expression, as he was busy trying to collate all the new evidence.

Leon was hesitant.

'Sir, I just wanted you to know that I've been double-checking all the birth dates of the missing victims and matching them with the missing persons reports.'

'Yes, and. . .?'

'It's Amanda Dunn, sir. She was born on 15th March 2006 and is therefore a bit older than we thought. It means she's now eighteen years old as her birthday was last week. She's no longer a juvenile.'

DCI Clarke sat back in his swivel chair.

'Good lad. That could be a great help when we question her, or if we go as far as arresting her. The more we uncover, the more it appears she was an accessory to the murders.'

Leon went to record the new information on the notice board. There was now a fourth section to accommodate the new developments. In the light of Leon's discovery, Clarke contacted the hospital to check on Amanda's wellbeing. He was told that she was no longer on a drip feed and had recovered enough to be moved from the hospital to a different facility. Clarke started the process of arranging a safe house with local authorities plus 24/7 surveillance.

* * *

Sara and Anik rang the bell at the Millers' flat and waited. There was no sign of anyone coming, but they knew it was occupied and continued to ring. Eventually Harold Miller opened the front door. Anik held up his ID and asked to speak to Joyce Miller.

'She can't see anyone right now. She's with her carers, being washed,' Harold told them.

'That's alright,' Anik said. 'I can talk to you whilst my DC goes into the bedroom.'

Reluctantly Harold let them in.

Sara knocked on the wide bedroom door. The folded wheelchair was leaning against the wall in the hallway and Sara doubted that Joyce had left the room for some considerable time.

A care worker in a navy blue overall opened the door. Sara explained that it was important she speak to Joyce on an urgent matter.

'Well, we're almost finished,' the carer explained. 'We just turned her, but her bed sores are very painful. She's in a lot of discomfort.'

Sara walked into the bedroom. The second care worker was attempting to put a vast kimono-style garment over Joyce's head and Sara could see her bloated stomach falling in rolls down to her massive thighs. Her legs were also bloated, making her feet look as if they belonged to a tiny doll in comparison to the bulky body above them. Joyce gave Sara an angry look as she struggled to put her arms through the sleeves.

'You should have waited. I was being washed.'

'I do apologise. I urgently need to ask you a question with regard to your nephew, Rodney Middleton.'

The two carers packed up their equipment and, after pulling a sheet up over Joyce's body, they left the room. Joyce proceeded to clean her teeth, using a mug and a bowl for her to spit into. Sara moved closer and stood beside Joyce's bed. She watched as Joyce began to comb her thick dark hair. Joyce then balanced a plastic makeup bag on her breasts and dug around in it until she found some moisturiser and foundation.

'Did you supply your nephew with a mobile phone?' Sara asked bluntly.

'No, I did not,' Joyce said indignantly. 'I haven't seen him for a very long time. Why would I purchase a mobile phone for him? I have one, but I only use it for my carers and the hospital and for ordering in food deliveries.'

'Could I see it, please?' Sara asked.

Joyce waved her tiny hand at the bedside table, then went back to applying her makeup. Sara went across to the table and picked

up an old-fashioned flip-top mobile, almost hidden by piles chocolate bars and biscuits.

'Can you give me the PIN, please?'

'3-2-4-5, but you won't find anything on there, apart from what
I just told you.'

Sara leaned against the bed as she opened the phone. She scrolled
through the list of recent calls, jotting down the numbers so she
could verify that they were the ones Joyce had mentioned: carers,
hospital and food deliveries. Joyce was now applying eye shadow
and mascara.

'You probably think this is a waste of time,' she said. 'But I
always wear makeup just in case I have to be seen by a doctor, or
a nurse. I always try to look my best. I have a woman come in to
do my hair once a week: she dry washes it, and then once a month
I have it properly washed. We've got a plastic thing for me to rest
my head against and she has a basin propped up behind me with
a hose from the bathroom, I'm very particular about the way my
hair is set.'

Sara finished checking through the phone. There were no text
messages, no apps and there was no contact stored on it for
Rodney Middleton.

'Do you have Wi-Fi here?' she asked.

'My husband has it in his office, but I don't use it. I just watch the
TV and DVDs. Why do you want to see my phone?'

'Just confirming some details regarding the investigation, Mrs
Miller. Thank you for your time.'

Joyce pointed to the photographs adorning the wall. 'That was
me, that photo next to my little nieces; one of them looked a bit like
me. I was quite the looker when I was younger.'

Sara glanced over at the large photos of Joyce's two dead nieces –
two adorable-looking little girls dressed in pretty clothes, smiling. The
smaller photograph beside them was of Joyce as a young woman. She

was slim and attractive, and it was shocking to see how much she had changed.

Sara thanked her again and put the phone back down on her bedside table. She declined the offer of a Mars bar as Joyce unwrapped one, sucking at it as she switched on the TV.

Anik was sitting with Harold Miller in his office. He turned to Sara as she walked in giving him a little shake of her head to indicate she had found nothing. Anik stood up and carried the small hard-backed chair back to its place against the wall.

'Mr Miller says that he has never supplied his nephew with a mobile phone. We were just searching for the receipt for his wife's mobile, but he seems to be having difficulty tracing it.'

'Mrs Miller has an old flip top mobile, with only a few numbers and no apps,' Sara explained. 'There's no contact for Rodney and the numbers are mostly medical or for food delivery companies. I didn't think we need to take it in, but I can double-check with her service provider. She said she doesn't use Wi-Fi, but we found Netflix and Prime on the TV in her bedroom.'

Anik moved closer to Miller, and Miller reacted nervously.

'I don't think we need to take Mrs Miller's phone,' Anik said in his most officious voice, 'but I think we need to escort Mr Miller in to the station for questioning. We have video footage of Mr Miller passing money and a mobile phone to his nephew. I don't think he realised the seriousness of him withholding evidence in a murder enquiry, and how it could have serious consequences for him.'

'What do you mean?' Harold asked in a high-pitched voice.

'You have been lying, Mr Miller. Perhaps you can start telling us the truth or we'll have to take you in. Your nephew has been arrested and will be charged with three murders . . .'

Anik leant very close and kept his voice low.

'You are obstructing this investigation, Mr Miller, and I'm losing my patience.'

Miller swallowed hard. He had begun to sweat. He retrieved a set of keys from his pocket and unlocked one of the drawers on his desk.

'You have to understand that I was pressured by Rodney to do this. He said it was because he couldn't get one for himself and he needed one whilst he was in prison. He smuggled it in, but I didn't help him to do that. I was forced to pay the bills because it was in my name. You have to understand, I didn't want to get in any trouble with his father; he has threatened not to give me money for Joyce.'

'Why would his father threaten you? He hates his son?' Sara said.

Harold shook his head. 'They know something, him and Joyce. I just get paid to look after her, and now it's going to get me into trouble. I've got a mobile for myself, but in Joyce's name. I pay her bills as well and . . .'

Harold took two mobile phones out from the drawer and held one up.

'This is mine, you can check it. They're all my own calls.'

Harold then handed Anik an expensive-looking smart phone and pulled out an envelope from the drawer.

'These are all the bills I've paid. Rodney upgraded the original phone with this one, which I had to pay for. But he gave it back to me when he came out of Brixton, and then when I wanted to give it back, he told me to just keep it for him.'

Anik looked at the phone as Sara passed him an evidence bag. Harold said he had no idea what the password was, but Anik knew the tech team would be able to open it within seconds.

'You said that Rodney's father and Joyce know something; what do you think they know?'

Harold was now sweating profusely as he shook his skinny shoulders.

'I don't know their secrets. You tell me what makes a woman eat herself to death? That's what she's doing, and I'm trapped here looking after her and am too scared to walk out. That bastard is in prison at the moment, but he'll get out and I've got to look out for myself. Now you're telling me that Rodney is being charged with something terrible, but I'm not involved. I swear before God. You can take all the receipts and bills. Take everything.'

Sara collected the stack of phone bills and receipts, placing them in another evidence bag. Anik stopped Harold from closing the drawer and held out his hand.

'What's that?'

'Family photo album. It belongs to Joyce. She doesn't like to look at them.'

Sara looked at Anik, who nodded for her to take it.

'Thank you for your cooperation, Mr Miller; I'll see that it goes in your favour, just in case this information you have given us implicates you in any way.'

Harold ushered them out of the flat and stood by the open front door looking relieved at their departure.

'I can't leave. I have to stay here. I'm as much a prisoner as she is,' he muttered.

Harold closed the front door as the internal bell rang from Joyce's bedroom. It was time to feed her.

CHAPTER TWENTY-ONE

Jack woke just after 1 p.m., after at least a few hours deep sleep. He showered and dressed and went into the kitchen. Penny was setting up the ironing board.

'Heavens, Jack, you sleep like the dead. I don't know how Maggie does these night shifts; she's amazing. She was already gone when you got home this morning, and probably won't be back until late tonight.'

'I know, the night shifts really do your head in; next week I'm back on days, so that'll be a relief. Tell her I had to go and that I'll make it up to her.'

'Well, this Friday I need one of you to look after Hannah as I have another bingo session and then dinner with my friends.'

'I'll sort it . . . and I'll grab some lunch in the canteen.' He kissed his mother on the cheek and left the house. He had already googled the village of Pyecombe where Lorna Elliot's aunt supposedly lived, which was about ten miles outside Brighton. He thought he would call on her first and then try to find the headstones in the Brighton and Preston graveyard. Jack felt hungry and picked up a coffee and a sandwich at a petrol station on the way. He headed onto the A23 and after almost forty-five minutes he turned onto the A273, eventually arriving in the small, picturesque village. He pulled up in front of an attractive old-fashioned pub called The Plough to double check the address, turning off Waze and looking up the address on Google maps.

Jack eventually found the narrow lane which led to the little cottages which had probably at one time been farm labourers' accommodation. They had white picket fences and neat gardens with a profusion of flowers surrounded by manicured hedges. He parked near the end of the lane and then walked back to number 12. The curtains were drawn over the latticed windows, and Jack wondered if anyone was at home.

He walked up the path, noticing a lot of dry, unswept leaves. He rang the bell, cursing that he had driven all the way there for nothing.

He pressed the doorbell again and suddenly the dark-blue door was opened. A middle-aged woman appeared, wearing a pink knitted cardigan and matching pink and grey pleated skirt, looking rather like a school mistress.

'You're earlier than I expected, but I'm almost finished,' she said.

'I'm sorry, I'm Detective Sergeant Mathews.' Jack flashed her his ID.

'Oh, I'm so sorry, I thought you were from the Red Cross. We've just finished labelling everything to go to their charity shop. Do come in.'

Jack stepped into a small, dark hallway. The woman led him into an old-fashioned but tasteful drawing room, with a settee and matching chairs and large Persian rugs over polished wood floors. There were numerous glass-fronted cabinets filled with china dinner services, and a tiled fireplace with a three-bar electric fire in it.

'I wanted to talk to Ms Barbara Elliot.'

'Oh goodness me, are you here officially, or as a friend?'

'Officially . . . and you are?'

'Mrs Foster . . . well . . . I'm sorry to inform you but Barbara died three days ago.'

Jack closed his eyes with frustration as Mrs Foster gestured towards the cabinets.

'I'm putting red dots on all the things to be sold and green dots on the ones for the Red Cross and Macmillan's. I've been cleaning and getting everything ready. Please, do sit down. Would you like a cup of tea?'

'No, thank you. Can you tell me how Miss Elliot passed away?'

'She'd been suffering from dementia for a few years but was in good health otherwise. As old as she was, she still took care of herself. She cooked and gardened but was becoming increasingly frail. I'm an old family friend. I live on the outskirts of the village, so I was a sort of carer for her, checking in on her almost every day. They think she went into the garden and fell, but she hadn't taken her panic button with her. She usually wore it around her neck. The next door-neighbour found her and called an ambulance. She was in her nightdress and freezing cold. So very sad. She was a really lovely lady.'

Jack sat down on one of the big comfortable cushioned seats.

'You say you were a family friend?'

'Yes, for many years. Are you sure you won't have a cup of tea?'

'No, thank you. I just wanted to ask Ms Elliot a few questions regarding an enquiry I'm working on, but sadly it's too late. Do you know if she had any visitors recently?'

'Yes, a surprise one, actually, I don't think she'd seen her for many years. Her niece came, quite a few months ago now. I've been unable to contact her, as I am sure she would want to know.'

'Lorna Elliot?'

Mrs Foster looked surprised.

'Yes, Lorna, she had arrived from LA, but said she didn't want to stay too long as she had to get to her hotel. I offered to let her stay with me, but she declined.'

'How well did you know Lorna?' Jack asked.

'I used to know her very well a few years ago, but ...' She hesitated.

'It is important to my investigation, Mrs Foster.'

'Oh, is it about that terrible thing that happened? Her fiancé disappeared ... it must be almost thirty years ago now. It was so shocking, and she never really got over it.'

'Did she say anything about it when she came here?'

'I think she said that she had found something out, but she didn't elaborate. After it happened, she sold everything, including the flat in Mayfair and the country house they had bought together. There were too many memories. She was very well off, but she was bereft. He had been the love of her life, and to never find out what happened to him ... I think that made it even worse, it broke her heart. Are you sure you wouldn't like a cup of tea, or perhaps a sherry?'

Jack was so eager to keep her talking that he accepted the sherry. Mrs Foster left the room, and returned a minute later with a bottle of sherry and two small glasses. She poured a liberal amount in both glasses and passed one to Jack.

'I am someone who knows what it feels like to be bereft. One morning, and in very few words, my husband told me he wanted a divorce. He also said he had asked our two sons, twin boys aged thirteen, which of us they wanted to live with, and he said they had chosen him. He was leaving for a new life in Los Angeles, along with his bimbo who was twenty years younger than him. I had been working for him and built up his practice until the boys were born. I had a terrible time getting over it, suffered from depression, but life does go on. I had alimony and a little studio flat in London, but my parents owned the cottage here. So, when they passed, I came to live here. Sad to admit it, but I am still heartbroken, same as poor Lorna.'

Jack sensed that she was eager to talk, perhaps from loneliness. But he was keen to get her back onto the subject of Lorna.

'Did Lorna know your husband?'

'Yes, she did; in fact, it was me that persuaded her to see him.'

'Was he in finance?'

'Good heavens, no! I was his medical nurse. He was a plastic surgeon and had a Harley Street practice. He opened up in LA and made a fortune. Married her, this so-called nurse! Brought up my boys, and they had another child, not that I ever met them again.'

Jack was becoming confused.

'I don't understand. You said you persuaded Lorna to see him. Did they go to LA together?'

'No, no, that was quite a while later. It was me that suggested she made an appointment to see him. Lorna was rather a plain-looking young woman, with a very prominent nose. I said she should try to make herself feel better as she was so depressed and heartbroken. She was almost obsessed with trying to find out what happened to her lovely fiancé, Anton. She was calling the police every day, waiting for news. At that time, she lived here with Barbara, and in the end even poor Barbara was feeling the strain because Lorna wouldn't leave it alone, accusing the police of begin inept. Anyway . . .'

She sipped her sherry, then took out a tissue from the sleeve of her cardigan and folded it into a square to dab beneath her eyes.

'Please go on, this is all very helpful to me,' Jack encouraged her.

'Well, after a few years with no news and no hope of ever finding his body, she left to move to Los Angeles. I believe she contacted my husband, or some other surgeon, because when she came back, I honestly didn't recognise her. She looked wonderful . . . quite beautiful.' Mrs Foster gave a sad laugh. 'Made me wish I'd done the same thing, but after being a nurse and seeing what was involved – unlike that other woman, I was qualified – I just couldn't have it done myself. Maybe I should have . . . silly really . . . I've been on my own ever since my divorce.'

She poured herself another sherry and topped up Jack's glass. He could feel his heart rate going up, as he now had the positive link between Lorna Elliot and plastic surgery.

'I can understand your loss,' Jack said. 'My mother is a widow and I do worry about her being lonely. Perhaps if she could find someone . . .'

Mrs Foster lightly laughed again.

'Yes, I have to say it creeps up on you. Now that my boys have grown up, they e-mail me. But I lost them when they chose to live with my husband and that woman.'

'Do you think Lorna was lonely?'

She nodded as she sipped her sherry. 'Yes, but she was always a loner. She was never that friendly, always very private. When she last visited, I felt that she was also very nervous. Her aunt didn't really recognise her, and I felt she had not actually come all this way to see Barbara. There was something else . . .'

She took another sip of her sherry and gave a girlish laugh. 'You know, young man, you do have a way of making me talk a lot about myself! You are very easy to talk to, but I don't want to bore you with my life, and you're here about Lorna.'

'You are being exceptionally helpful, and the more I know about Lorna the better as we're trying to trace her,' Jack said.

'Well, I keep calling her mobile but she never answers. I'm a bit worried about her, to be honest. As I said earlier, she was very nervous . . . even a little frightened . . . as if she needed protection. But she never told me what was bothering her. I suggested that she contact the police, but she became very tetchy and said that she didn't trust them as they had done nothing about finding out what had happened to her beloved Anton. They've never found his body, you know . . .' She paused. 'But I've said too much.'

Jack was concerned that perhaps the sherry was not helping her to concentrate, but then she gave that girlish giggle again.

'I told her what I had done, hoping that it might help her. I told her I had got myself onto the books of a dating agency. It was expensive and only had clients from good backgrounds in London. I still have my small flat in Pimlico which I use when I want to do a bit of shopping, so I applied using that address.'

Jack smiled, trying to sound calm. 'A dating agency?'

'Yes! Anyway, I told her about the date I had with a nice man whom I met for a drink. He was very kind and thoughtful. I was a bit naughty because I found out he was actually a police officer. I looked in the glove compartment in his car and saw that he was a detective, so I told Lorna that she should contact the agency and pick him out as he had not asked me for a second date, and he could protect her.'

'Did she tell you she was concerned about her safety?'

'Not in so many words, but you know, in the short time she was here it was obvious to me she was very anxious: if the phone rang, she'd physically freeze, checking at the window, and she was constantly on her mobile.'

Jack swallowed hard. Another link. He had not recognised Mrs Foster as one of the women Ridley had gone on a date with via the agency. He could hardly believe it! He was now eager to get back to London, and to talk to Ridley.

'So, did Lorna contact the dating agency?'

'I don't know. She left here and I haven't heard from her since.'

'I am very grateful to you for all your information, Mrs Foster. Did Lorna give you any indication about where she was staying? Which hotel? Or anything else you can remember?'

Mrs Foster frowned and chewed at her bottom lip.

'She said something about living in Monaco for a while, doing some investments. But she would always become very quiet if I asked anything too personal. She was quite a difficult woman, and as I said before, she was a loner.'

'She never told you where she was staying when she was not here at her aunt's?'

'No, I offered her my flat in Pimlico as I was here looking after Barbara. I called the landline there just in case but got no answer, so I presume she didn't take up my offer. Oh yes, I remember now, she actually had a copy of my flat keys made. She was a very methodical woman. She said she didn't want to put me out in any way and didn't want to take my keys in case I needed them . . . I didn't have a spare set, you see.'

'So it's possible she did use your flat?'

'I suppose so . . . as I just said, I called there but there was no answer. And I must have rung her mobile numerous times, and then it just went dead. I haven't been to the flat in London since she was here. Poor Barbara needed me, and to be honest I expected Lorna to return. She might not even know that Barbara has died. I'm executor of her will. Barbara was rather like Lorna . . . meticulous and methodical and she left detailed instructions about everything . . . including which charities should benefit.'

'Did she have much luggage when she came here?'

'No, not really. Just a couple of rather nice matching suitcases and her laptop.'

Jack now had another urgent priority: checking out the Pimlico address. He stood up to indicate that he was leaving, and Mrs Foster jumped up and crossed over to the desk.

'I don't know if you have any of her family details. It's very sad as there is no one but Lorna now. She had a sister called Norma who was tiny and very different from her. Norma married a rather tedious young man. I think his surname was Raynor. They lived in Hove and had a gorgeous little girl called Sandra. She tragically died very young, poor little soul; had what they thought was a bad cold, but it was tuberculosis. Norma never recovered and had a nervous breakdown. I think she died about ten years ago, and her husband died shortly afterwards of bronchial pneumonia. There was a little album somewhere, unless Lorna took it. You can tell how long I've known the family though.'

She started hunting through all the drawers and Jack explained that he should really be going, thanking her for her time.

'Well, perhaps Lorna took it. I'm sure it was here, so you may want to come back. I hope I haven't put a green sticker on it!'

'Thank you. I really appreciate your time, Mrs Foster, and you've been very helpful. If you could just give me the address in Pimlico, I can check if Lorna is there and get back to you.'

Mrs Foster jotted down the address in a notebook and tore the page out as the doorbell rang.

'Oh, that'll be the Red Cross people coming to collect everything.'

As Jack left, two young women entered the cottage, carrying boxes, bubble wrap and large bags for the Red Cross charity donations.

Jack almost ran to his car, adrenaline coursing through him. He made a quick stop at the pub to use the restroom and have half a pint of beer, then bought a takeaway ham sandwich which he ate on the drive back to London. He would just have enough time to stop at the Pimlico flat before going on duty.

CHAPTER TWENTY-TWO

As Jack was heading towards the A3 he received a call on his mobile from Laura, which he switched to speaker phone. She was talking very fast and was obviously excited.

'I came in a bit earlier for my shift because so much has been happening. You were right about Joyce's husband having supplied Rodney with a mobile. It was in Harold Miller's name. He paid the bills, but it was only used by Rodney. We also have another phone, brought in by Nadine O'Reilly's mother; you won't believe it, but Amanda Dunn used Snapchat, so they knew each other from that. One other thing that just cropped up. Amanda is actually now eighteen years old! I have a feeling that DCI Clarke is going to put her into protection with 24/7 monitoring before he brings her in to interview her. It's all happening, Jack. Maybe you should come in a bit earlier so that we can catch up. Anik is very much the DCI's sidekick and loving it.'

Jack said he would be heading in from home straightaway and ended the call. He drove onto the A3 and put his foot down as he still wanted to visit the Pimlico flat before going to the station. He pulled over into the slow lane as a police patrol car with lights flashing passed him, but they signalled for him to pull over onto the hard shoulder. Two uniformed officers got out and signalled to Jack to get out of the car. Jack lowered his driving side window.

'What is it?'

'Do you know the speed limit, sir?'

'Yes, I do, but I am . . .'

Before he could finish, the officer opened the driver's door and told him to step out. Jack got out, then put his right hand into his jacket breast pocket to take out his ID.

'Both hands on the bonnet please, sir.'

Jack could hardly believe it. 'I'm a police officer. DS Jack Warr,' he snapped as he complied with the instruction.

'Is this your car?'

'Yes, it is my car.'

One of the officers returned to the patrol car to run the number plate while Jack stood with his hands on the bonnet.

The second officer returned to say that the car was registered to a Doctor Janakan Narajan.

Jack sighed with impatience.

'My wife, Doctor Margaret Warr, bought it from him. If you look in the glove compartment, you'll find the insurance certificates. This is bloody ridiculous! I told you I'm a detective. . .'

'He stinks of booze,' one of the officers said.

It was a further ten minutes whilst the officers checked the insurance and ascertained that the car had been sold, but somewhere along the line the vehicle registration papers had not been filed. To Jack's fury he was then asked to take a breathalyser test. He swore as he snatched it, but then he tried to slow things down. He had consumed two sherries and half a pint of beer and had only eaten one bite out of the sandwich.

'You do know you were doing over seventy in a fifty-mile zone?'

Jack reached into his pocket for his ID.

'I am a detective sergeant with the Metropolitan Police on an urgent call out to get to my station. DCI Clarke will verify this.'

One officer checked his ID while his partner gestured for Jack to breathe into the bag. He did as he was requested making sure he held his breath in his chest for a moment before blowing into the tube. He was just over the limit.

The two officers conferred, then one of them returned to the patrol car and called in. He spoke for a few moments before he returned to the now very irate Jack.

'I'm going to let you go, sir, but take my advice and keep your speed down. And please stop at the next service station to get a black coffee. We'll have to report this as it's protocol.'

Jack had to take a few deep breaths when he got back into his car. He had now lost valuable time, and there was no way he could get to the Pimlico flat before going to the station. He knew the patrol car was following him so, as requested, he stopped at the next service station and bought a black coffee, then continued on to the A3.

Laura was at her desk checking through statements. They had brought in Mrs Delaney's husband, and he had identified Jamail as the girl he had seen at the basement flat on a couple of occasions. He also confirmed that he helped Rodney carry the bins up the stairs. He described them as often being very heavy, so it required two of them to manoeuvre them up the steps. He said the bins were used by all the tenants so he never queried why they weighed so much, and as he had a bad back, he could not cope lifting them on his own anyway. He described Rodney as being very strong and always very helpful, but if he was not there then one of the other tenants would assist him. When he was asked if the bins were as heavy on the occasions when Rodney had not been available to help him, he said that as far as he could remember they were much lighter.

There were also statements from various hardware stores describing the purchase of bleach, sacking, bubble wrap and a large amount of sturdy black bin liners by Rodney Middleton, who paid in cash, and CCTV footage from the stores clearly showed that it was him. The rat poison had been acquired from a pest-control company. They described Rodney Middleton and were able to provide the number plate of his vehicle, which was registered to Harold Miller, who they now decided to bring in for questioning.

It was like an enormous jigsaw puzzle slowly being pieced together, but DCI Clarke knew it was getting close to the time they would have to bring Rodney in for interview. He was obsessive about every detail, compiling notes for himself and double-checking everything to build the strongest possible case before they questioned him. He knew the biggest outstanding problem was they had no bodies, only DNA matched to three victims. The forensic department were still working on separating other DNA blood samples and the consensus was that other victims had been killed in the coal hole. Clarke had therefore ordered that the families of the missing persons of a similar age and background to the confirmed victims, Jamail, Trudie and Nadine, should be tracked down and tested.

Jack had only just sat down at his desk when DCI Clarke opened his office door and gestured for him to come in. 'I cannot believe it,' he fumed before Jack had got through the door. 'In the middle of a huge case, one of my leading officers is pulled over for drunk driving. What in God's name were you doing, Warr? And why were you on the A3 when you should have been here at the station?'

'I'm sorry, sir, but I needed to get a breath of fresh air, a walk by the sea. I admit I did have a half pint, but the officers were real assholes about it. I just needed to clear my head, sir. I apologise . . . but we've made great steps forwards. I was right about Harold Miller providing Middleton with a mobile phone, and it seems he was also handy in transporting the acid and the rat poison, so I hope they're being fingerprinted.'

'Yes, Jack, obviously,' Clarke said with a scowl. 'The tech division are working on it right now. Give it another 24 hours and we'll be bringing Middleton and Miller in. But that bloody Georgina Bamford woman has been bending my ear two or three times a day.'

'What about his legal aid lawyer? Has she replaced him?'

'Of course she has. She knows that legal aid wanker Colin Marshall can't handle this. It's going to hit the press any minute and I have to be ready. It's taken a lot of work to keep a lid on it.'

'Good work on that front so far, sir,' Jack said, hoping to mollify him.

'It's not going to be easy, but I have to say the superintendent has been behind us one hundred percent. I'm still hoping we'll find some remains, but it's not looking likely. We need to get that Amanda Dunn talking. Anik is working on collating all the evidence against her ready for interview.'

Jack said nothing. He knew he should be the one to interrogate Amanda, as he had had more dealings with her than any of the others. But after his dressing down about being breathalysed, he wasn't in a good position to argue. Clarke sighed and told Jack to get back to work, opening his office door.

'Disappointed in you, Warr. There isn't an officer on this investigation that wouldn't mind a walk on the beach to get some fresh air, myself included.'

Jack returned to his desk, not exactly with his tail between his legs but certainly not in a very ebullient mood. He had a stack of statements that needed to be checked over and written up on the crime scene board. Laura called over to say that Maggie had rung a few times and that his mobile had been ringing. He checked his mobile and muttered to no one in particular that he was going to get something to eat in the canteen. He was starving hungry, having only had a bite of the ham sandwich in the car. He filled a plate with sausage, mash and baked beans and grabbed a bowl of apple pie with custard, eating quickly as he rang Maggie. She didn't answer so he texted her to say he hoped to be home in time to kiss her goodbye before she left for work in the morning. He then sent a second text to say he loved her.

He finished eating, got a coffee and headed back to the incident room. The next couple of hours were spent making copious notes to be used for the interview. He then looked back at the notes he had taken on his original interviews with the probation officer and the various psychiatrists.

Jack was certain that Georgina Bamford would attempt to use Middleton's spurious mental health issues, just as Middleton had done to hoodwink the judge and jury at every previous court appearance.

Jack was also attempting to match the dates of the previous assault cases with the murders of the three missing girls. It proved an impossible task, because they couldn't be sure exactly when the murders had occurred. But he was convinced that Rodney Middleton was timing the assaults deliberately. He had dismembered the bodies, dumped them in the rubbish bins and then made sure he was incarcerated around that time by way of an alibi.

Jack rocked back in his chair, flipping a pencil up and down on his desktop, as he tried to make his theory fit the facts as they knew them. Then it hit him: Middleton might have been in prison or in mental institutions, but Amanda was at home. He matched the dates of the CCTV footage when she had been seen emptying clothes into the charity clothing bins. He began to believe that Amanda had played a significant role in the crimes.

'Laura, do we know when they're bringing Amanda in?'

She shrugged her shoulders and went back to selecting photographs and gathering them into a folder.

'She's in protective custody, apparently. She's feeling fine, getting bored and wants her mobile returned. They're arranging some clothes for her, so I would say the boss is getting ready to bring her in. Hard to believe, but as all her clothes were removed to be tested, she's just been wearing hospital-issue gowns and dressing gowns this entire time. Apparently she said unless we buy her new clothes and shoes, she won't be questioned!'

'Tomorrow?'

'I don't know, Jack. I just told you, she's in protective custody.'

'I know she is, but she has to be questioned soon, for God's sake,' he said irritably.

'I think the boss is waiting for the tech team to analyse the contents of the mobile phones.'

Laura glanced towards DCI Clarke's office as he came out and clapped his hands.

'OK, everyone, as you know, the forensic teams have been working 24/7, and the tech support officers are coming in tonight to give us an update. I've ordered the canteen to remain open and I suggest everyone gets something to eat. I want a meeting in the boardroom in forty-five minutes. Glenda Bagshot, our CCTV investigator, is setting up a screen so we'll be watching footage from mobile phones, plus any new video footage she thinks might be important to our enquiry. I wanted you all to be the first to see what we've got, and obviously it will also be accessible for the day shift tomorrow.'

Clarke paused to smile.

'It goes without saying that I am very grateful to you all for all your hard work. I know these long night shifts aren't easy, but I believe we're very near to the interview stage with Rodney Middleton, and I feel we have a strong chance of a positive outcome.'

Clarke returned to his office as the team of officers began standing, stretching and leaving their desks to head to the canteen. Laura looked over to Jack who was staring into space.

'You coming?'

He turned and smiled.

'Yeah, but I might wait until the line thins out. I'll see you up there.'

He rubbed his hair making it stand up on end. He had often been reprimanded for not being a team player because he had not shared information with his colleagues. He had always preferred to handle things himself, and time and time again it had proved beneficial to the case they had been working on. The fact was, if he had not persisted in investigating the Rodney Middleton case, none of them would be here working their bollocks off. He felt angry that nobody seemed to give him any kudos.

Fifteen minutes later Laura waltzed in with a tray of shepherd's pie, swimming in gravy with carrots and peas and a custard-covered pudding.

'You should go to the canteen. It's a feast, thanks to Glenda Bagshot. She's ordered everything in herself, and there's fresh coffee, tea and a massive chocolate cake.'

Jack pushed his chair back and walked out, banging the door behind him. He went into the canteen to survey what was left of the spread and managed to grab the last piece of chocolate cake. Standing behind him was Hendricks, who had already had one serving and was back for more. He smelt like stale fish and Jack glared at him.

'I know, I can't get rid of it . . . even wearing protective clothes. It seeps into your skin and hair . . . it's disgusting. I'm not going back to that bloody tip. I never signed up for this, and I've now been on it for two days straight.'

Jack raised his eyebrows, passing by him to get a mug of coffee.

'Found a dead dog yesterday, wrapped in a duvet. But those are the only remains we've found.'

Jack left the canteen and was just about to take a bite of chocolate cake at his desk when there was a shout for everyone to be in the boardroom. He saw DCI Clarke hurrying out with a tray of half-finished fish and chips and a custard sponge.

There had been a lot of activity in the boardroom. The chairs were stacked up and the boardroom table had been pushed back almost to the far wall. A trestle table was in the centre of the room, covered in files, with a large screen at the far end of the room.

There was a high-powered laptop linked to a projector to show the footage.

DCI Clarke took a seat at the end of the trestle table, close to Glenda Bagshot. The front seats were occupied by the team, with a lot of complaints about Hendricks' smell. Everyone seemed in good spirits, possibly due to the decent dinner they had all just consumed.

Clarke waited for the last of the stragglers to fill the room, which by now was standing room only. He stood up and waited for everyone to go quiet.

'Right, everyone, first off, I want to thank Glenda Bagshot for organising the dinner tonight. I know everyone is getting very tired working the split week, so my thanks to all the officers from the different departments who are working flat out to get the results we need. We all know that time is of the essence. I am going to ask Daniel Burkett, Head of Forensics, to start off this meeting.'

Burkett was a short, square-faced man with iron-grey hair. He was wearing a short-sleeved shirt showing off his muscular arms. He took out a pair of half-moon glasses from a leather case and picked up a file.

'Ladies and gentlemen, we have had our work cut out in the lab due to the number of items brought in for examination. As you know, we have already identified three victims by matching DNA samples provided by their families. One sample taken from a wire scrubbing brush had such deep indentations of blood and skin, it was ascertained that this was taken from a cadaver, specifically internal human debris. In layman's terms it means that what had been congealed came from internal lacerations, so the victim was already dead.'

Burkett then nodded to his assistant, an attractive Asian girl, who was preparing to project images onto the large screen from a laptop.

'As you all know, we have been testing the various tools and instruments and have discovered blood from a screwdriver which does not match any of the three victims identified. We also have blood from the various rubbish bins that again wasn't found to be a match. We have managed to raise DNA profiles from these samples to be used for identification comparisons at a later date, if and when you discover other victims. We then began to concentrate on the garments brought in for testing. Regina will now begin to show the footage on the screen.'

Regina tapped the keyboard and the image of a pair of jeans pinned out on white paper appeared on the screen.

'As you can see by the white chalk marks and small flags,' Burkett continued, 'we found three pin-head-sized droplets of blood . . . please continue, Regina'

The film footage continued, showing images of clothing that had belonged to Rodney Middleton, including shirts, underpants, vests, more trousers, and trainers, all with tiny droplets of blood on them.

'We have been able to match more than ten samples to each of your three identified victims, but we also sadly have a number of unidentified samples. Now, the footage will show our work on the bedding.'

Jack nodded to himself. This was good and getting better.

The images of the bedding showed semen, blood, pubic hairs, and three long blonde hairs. The film continued, showing the discovery of the blood and hair clogging the drains. Some of the DNA matched the three identified victims, but, chillingly, there was also blood and hair they could not yet match. Lastly, and shockingly, were images of the pink bed socks Amanda had worn. Matted into the soles and the heels of the thick fabric, there was blood identified as belonging to Nadine O'Reilly.

Jack leaned forwards, listening intently. He knew the socks had belonged to Trudie. He took out his notebook and jotted a few things down, before turning his attention back to Burkett.

The next batch of film showed the interior of the coal hole. It showed the moment the luminol had revealed the blood splatters. The team allocated to this work was led by a tall, blonde woman who took over from Burkett. She explained how they had dug up sections of the coal hole and moved blocks of heavily stained sections to the lab. The footage showed the bloodstains which matched the identified victims. Again, they had also discovered further blood samples they had no match for, and the consensus was that dismemberment of all the bodies had occurred inside the coal hole.

'We'll forward all these details to be checked against the UK missing persons and unidentified bodies DNA database to see if a match can be found,' she concluded.

Burkett nodded to Regina, who had paused the film for a moment. Now the footage showed the removal of the bathtub and the shower, and the discovery of further blood splattering on the plastic shower door.

Glenda Bagshot took over from the forensics team. She had been splicing sections from all the hours of CCTV footage in order to show the teams only the most relevant sections. Jack had already seen most of this footage, so he sat back and closed his eyes, thinking about the monster that was Rodney Middleton. How many women had he murdered over the five years he'd lived in that basement? And in how many of those murders had Amanda been a willing accessory?

It was after 10 p.m. when the meeting finally ended. There was an uneasy silence, not just because everyone was exhausted, but because of the horrors they were now imagining taking place in that basement flat. DCI Clarke thanked the experts for their diligent work, then thanked all the officers again, saying there would be tea and coffee set up for them in the incident room. He looked haggard as he shook hands with Burkett and helped pack up the equipment. When most of the team had filed out, Jack overheard him asking Burkett how many victims he thought there might be. Burkett shrugged his thick-set shoulders, carefully replacing his half-moon glasses in their leather case.

'I wish I could tell you, but it could be perhaps five or six. The place was literally a bloodbath.'

Burkett put on a tweed jacket with a deep sigh.

'As soon as I have any further information I'll be in touch, but now I just need to get some sleep.'

DCI Clarke spotted Jack, who had started jotting down more notes, as Burkett left the room.

'I could do with some of that sleep, too, but I doubt that I'll be able to after what I've just seen. How are you coping, Jack?'

'Me? Oh, I don't think I'll have any problem crashing out for a few hours. This night duty isn't doing any good for my marriage, though. We're like ships passing in the night.'

Clarke nodded. 'You take yourself off home now, then. But I need you in a few hours earlier tomorrow. I'm going to take off in a minute myself. I want to be ready to interview Amanda Dunn.'

Jack looked surprised. 'You're interviewing her?'

'Yes, after what I saw tonight, we have to make it a priority. I have no doubt she knows the answers to a lot of our questions. Anik will be assisting, so please brief him with the latest findings first thing. Right, good work, Jack . . . now go home to your wife.'

Jack was so taken aback he reached out to take Clarke's arm. 'Sorry, sir, but surely it makes sense that I . . .'

Clark gave him a disdainful look as he eased his arm free. 'Anik's been at my side throughout the past few days, working through the night. Whereas you . . . this situation with you taking a break and getting pulled over and breathalysed is very unsatisfactory. Don't get me wrong, Jack, you have done some very good work – '

Jack couldn't contain his anger. 'Done some *good work*? If it wasn't for me, Middleton would have been released to probably kill another innocent runaway, quite apart from the fact that I know more about the bastard than anyone else.'

Clarke frowned. 'Don't query my judgement, Jack. It's obvious you have a personal agenda with this case, and I am not prepared to let that get in the way of things. Goodnight, Jack.'

Jack tried to control his rage as he collected his briefcase and coat.

'Where are you off to?' Laura asked innocently.

'Home,' he snapped.

'You're sure it's not another trip to the seaside?' she said with a grin. 'Well, watch what you drink; you don't want to get stopped again.'

Jack went and stood very close to her. 'Why don't you mind your own fucking business,' he said through gritted teeth.

Laura went pale. 'Bloody hell, Jack, I was only joking . . .'

He walked out, slamming the door behind him. As he reached his hated pea-green Micra he muttered, 'Fuck them all!'

Much as he wanted to go straight home, he still needed to check out the flat in Pimlico. But he decided that after he had done that, he was going to tell Ridley that he could fuck off as well. He was sick and tired of the lot of them.

CHAPTER TWENTY-THREE

When he got to the Dover Court flats in Pimlico, Jack parked in the residents' car park and walked into the reception. A cheerful-looking porter simply smiled as Jack passed him, as if he was one of the residents. Still angry, Jack scowled as he headed for the lift.

When he got to the top floor where the smaller flats and studios were located, he was relieved to find no one was about. He pulled out his set of skeleton keys, a bunch he had pocketed after an arrest a few years years earlier, but he was not that skilled with them and had to try the door of 54B a number of times before he success-fully opened it, even though it was a simple Yale lock. Luckily there was no alarm. He quickly shut the door behind him and took a moment to assess the small, dark hallway before searching for the light switch.

It was a very small apartment. The narrow hallway had doors leading to a sitting room, a bedroom with an en-suite bathroom and a kitchen. It was furnished with rather worn items and felt unlived in and lacking in anything personal.

It also did not look as if anyone had been there for some time. In the kitchen he found a bottle of milk in the fridge that was a week beyond its sell-by date, along with some shrivelled fruit and a bottle of vodka. In the sink there was a glass and a plate. The bedroom contained a small double bed, dressing table and ward-robe. Jack stopped and drew in a deep breath. Beside the bed were two matching Louis Vuitton suitcases, and on it was an expen-sive leather briefcase. He opened the largest case first and checked through the selection of stylish clothes and shoes. There was also a blonde wig, neatly wrapped in a silk bag. Next, he opened the smaller case which contained underwear, nightdresses and a leather makeup bag with cosmetics and bottles of perfume, bath oils and skin-care pots. He felt round the lining, then closed the case and pulled the briefcase towards him.

There was a laptop, a mobile phone, and an envelope containing two memory sticks. Tucked into the pocket of the briefcase was a small photo album. He flicked through it briefly, knowing it was the album he had been told about that morning.

In the same pocket he found a passport belonging to Lorna Elliot with several hundred-dollar bills tucked inside. In the small leather-trimmed business card pockets were numerous bank cards in her name, including Chase Bank, Bank of America and Coutts Bank.

After carefully replacing all the items back in the briefcase, Jack searched the rest of the flat. He was looking for other things that he felt should be with Lorna's belongings: a handbag, keys to the flat, a wallet . . . He went into the drawing room and looked under and around all the furniture, then went back into the kitchen. He hesitated, then went into the ensuite bathroom. There on the side of the washbasin was an elegant leather handbag with YSL on the gold clasp. He opened it and found exactly what he had been looking for: a set of cars keys for a Jaguar with a rental tag in the name of Sandra Raynor, a folder from the dating agency, and a crocodile-skin wallet. The wallet contained a lot of crisp new £50 notes.

Jack's dark mood had lifted by the time he left the flat with the handbag and briefcase covered by his coat. At the car, he opened the passenger door and tossed them inside. He was now keen to get home and take a look at the contents of the laptop.

As soon as he arrived, Jack hurried inside and ran straight up the stairs to his office with the briefcase and the handbag. He had just put everything down on his desk when Maggie walked in. She was wearing a dressing gown, and from her expression it was obvious that she was not in a good mood.

'Well, thank you for letting me know what time you'd be home,' she said. 'I thought you'd still be at the station.'

'Sorry, sweetheart,' Jack said, 'but DCI Clarke let me off a bit earlier in exchange for being at the station early tomorrow morning.'

'Have you eaten dinner?'

'I have actually. This wonderful woman Glenda Bagshot ordered in a decent meal for everyone, as she was sick and tired of the awful canteen food at night.'

'That's alright then,' she said in a sarcastic tone. 'So now can you come to bed. I really want to have a talk.'

He hesitated, gesturing at the briefcase. 'I had to collect this on the way home and I was going to have a look at the contents. It's connected to the Ridley situation.'

'I don't care about him, Jack. We've hardly had a moment together since you've been on nights. I know the case you're work-ing on is pretty tough going, but you're running yourself ragged trying to do two things at the same time.'

'Yes, I know you're right. I had a big breakthrough earlier this evening, though.'

Maggie walked to his desk and picked up the handbag. 'This looks very posh. . . Yves Saint Laurent. Who does it belong to?'

Jack raked his fingers through his hair. 'I believe it belonged to the woman found in Ridley's car. That's her briefcase, with a laptop and mobile phone.'

'So, what do you intend to do tonight?' she asked, frowning.

'I was going to check over it all and then contact Ridley.'

'Tonight?'

'Well, I don't have time to do it when I'm on duty.'

'So instead of spending time with me when we haven't seen each other properly for days, you'd rather be chasing around after Ridley. I think you need to get your priorities sorted, Jack!'

He had never seen her in this aggressive mood before, and he put his hands up in a defensive gesture.

'You're right, and I am so sorry. I feel bad. You don't need this; I know how tough it is for you at work right now.'

'Really, Jack?'

'Of course . . . you're still under incredible pressure day and night.'

She folded her arms. 'You can say that again. We also need to consider the pressure we put on Penny having to look after Hannah virtually all day and night, without either of us being able to take any weight off her shoulders. Jack, we need to talk about this properly; why don't you go and have a shower and come to bed so we can discuss things?'

He nodded. 'OK, I'll be right with you.'

'No, *now*!' she said, raising her voice. 'Come on, out of here! I need to get some sleep, and I know if I leave you here, you'll get distracted and you'll forget about everything else.'

Jack had to walk past her as she turned off the lights in his office. He went straight into the bathroom for a quick shower and when he got into bed Maggie had turned on the electric blanket and was sitting propped up by pillows. He flipped back his side of the duvet and snuggled up, putting his arms around her.

Maggie pushed him away. 'No, Jack, we need to talk. I have virtually had to tape my eyelids open as I am so tired. I don't want any update on your cases, or sex, I just want you to listen to me. I have real concerns about your mum.'

Jack lay back beside her with his eyes closed.

'Are you listening to me?'

'Yes, Maggie, and as you said earlier, she has virtually been running the house whilst we've both been working 24/7. We need to give her a break.'

'Jack, she took Hannah out this evening; they weren't home when I came back and that was after eight. She was very flushed and apologetic when she found me home and said that she had been visiting friends. What friends, Jack? She didn't explain to me where she had been, and it may not seem late to you, but it was way past Hannah's bedtime.'

Jack sat up.

'OK, let me talk to her tomorrow; maybe it's these new people she goes to bingo with.'

'She hasn't been honest, Jack, because I phoned the church and asked about the bingo sessions, and they haven't been happening since before the lockdown. Apparently, they're hoping to resume next month because the man who organised them passed away, so they have been recruiting someone to take over.'

'What?'

'She's lied to us, Jack.'

He frowned. 'Shit, that's unlike Mum.'

'Yes, I know. So tomorrow you need to have it out with her. Will you do that?'

'Yes . . . yes, of course,' he said.

Maggie turned off her bedside light and the electric blanket and snuggled down under the duvet. Jack rested back on his pillow, concerned about his mother's odd behaviour. He switched off his bedside light, rolled onto his side and spooned his body around Maggie's. He loved the way they fitted together. He had a moment's thought about pulling up her nightdress but felt the rhythm of her breathing and knew she was asleep. Even with so much on his mind, just being beside her filled him with peace, and he fell into a deep sleep.

Maggie's alarm went off at five thirty the following morning. As usual she jumped out of bed and hurried into the bathroom. Jack was jolted awake by the noise. He had slept so soundly that he was confused when Maggie wasn't beside him, then he heard the shower running and flopped back on his pillow. He turned to look at the time, and after a few moments decided it would be a good move on his part if he got up and made coffee for her.

He was inserting four slices of bread into the lurid yellow toaster when Maggie came in, dressed and ready to leave for work. He handed her a portable flask of coffee, as he knew she liked to take one to sip on the way to the hospital. She declined his offer to butter her some toast, saying she would grab a bite to eat in the canteen. She gave him a big hug and a kiss, then paused on her way out of the door.

'You will talk to Penny, as you promised last night, won't you?'

'I will. You have a good day. I'll go back to bed for a while, then help with getting Hannah ready for nursery. I also think it's time you and me went out for dinner – just the two of us.'

She smiled. 'That would be nice. Bye, then.'

Jack waited for the front door to close before he buttered two slices of toast for himself and poured a mug of coffee. He was eager to get into his office and look over the things he had brought back from the Pimlico flat. Still wearing his boxer shorts and a dressing gown, he sat down at his desk and opened Lorna Elliot's laptop. It was dead, but fortunately his own laptop charger fitted, so he plugged it in to charge the battery. He then took out the two memory sticks and inserted them into his old laptop.

The first didn't seem to be working, not allowing him access to the contents. He pulled it out and inserted it into a different USB port. A folder then came up with lists of dates and locations. He scrolled through the contents whilst he ate his toast. The name Gazprom featured numerous times with dates beside it. He googled it and discovered that it was one of Russia's biggest energy companies. The dates were also linked to Rossiya Bank, which Jack discovered was based in St Petersburg and heavily associated with the corrupt practices of Putin's regime.

As he continued to scroll, Jack had no notion of exactly what he was looking at. He paused at the mention of a website called Proekt Media, which seemed to be a Russian investigative company specialising in in-depth journalism. The dates listed were associated with huge sums of money, millions and then billions. Jack took out the memory stick and inserted the second one. The name Dmitry Skigin immediately came up, alongside a company called Petersburg Oil Terminal (POT) which was part of the consortium that won a contract to manage the city's seaport. Putin's name also cropped up again, first as head of the FSB, the Russian domestic secret service, and then as president.

Jack sighed. The data was from before the Russian invasion of Ukraine, and it all meant nothing to him. He sat staring at the screen, his attention wavering as he continued to scroll. The name Skigin came up again, with a note that he had been traced to Monaco, but in 2000 he was expelled for money-laundering.

Skigin had died three years later, of cancer. He had left a fortune and a personal estate said to be valued at £560 million.

Jack checked the time. It was already gone 7 a.m. so he removed the memory stick and put it back in the envelope with the other one. He checked to see if the other laptop had charged yet and the home screen came up. He had no idea what the password was. He tried 'Sandra' then 'Lorna', then 'Elliot', then 'Raynor' but none of them worked. He picked up the briefcase and took out the passport in Lorna Elliot's name. Flicking through it he could see stamps reflecting the many trips she had made, to Moscow, St Petersburg and more recently to Monaco, the latter frequently, until two years ago.

He went back to the laptop to try some more passwords. This time he tried 'Russia', then 'Monaco' and as a last attempt 'Anton', the Christian name of her partner. There was a satisfying 'ping' and the home screen opened up. He was about to start looking through the files when his mobile rang. It was Ridley. Before Ridley could give him the details of a new meet, Jack interrupted.

'Listen, I am not coming to the ruddy John Lewis car park, or the river. If you and your ankle bracelet can make it, then you can come to me. I will be at home for another hour, then I have to go to work. It's in your best interests to meet me. I found her for you.'

There was silence on the other end of the phone, then Ridley said he would be there. Jack ended the call and tossed his mobile onto his desk, just as Penny knocked on the door.

'Long time no see . . . you're quite the stranger these days. Do you want some breakfast?' she asked.

'No thanks, Mum . . . er, I have to get dressed quickly as I'm expecting someone. I'll go in and see Hannah first though.'

'She's in the kitchen, in her highchair.'

'Right, let me get dressed and I'll be right down.'

Jack hurried back to his bedroom, had a quick shower, then shaved and dressed. He was heading down the stairs when he saw a figure through the stained-glass window in the front door. He opened the door to find Ridley, wearing a black tracksuit with the hood covering his head and part of his face.

'Go upstairs into my office and wait for me, second-floor landing, door on the right. I just need to go and see my mum and Hannah in the kitchen,' Jack told him.

Ridley nodded and moved towards the stairs as Jack went into the kitchen. He played with Hannah for a few minutes and helped her to eat her cereal as Penny prepared orange juice and biscuits for her morning break.

'Mum, I have to go up to my office on urgent business so please don't come in. I'll be making important calls about my case and don't want to be interrupted.'

'OK, dear. Do you want a coffee?'

'No thanks, I made one earlier. Hope you have a good day. Hannah, you are a very good girl and daddy loves you. This weekend we're going to have some special time together.'

She waved her spoon at his head, then threw it across the room.

'You have remembered that I need you or Maggie to stay at home with Hannah on Friday, for my bingo session?' Penny asked as she selected some biscuits.

Jack paused at the door, wiping a milky cornflake off his jacket. He knew he should say something in the light of what Maggie had told him last night, but he couldn't keep Ridley waiting.

'OK . . . I'll organise it. Is everything alright with you, Mum?'

'Yes, why wouldn't it be?'

'Er, no reason – I've got to go.'

He legged it up the stairs two at a time, went into his office and closed the door. Ridley was standing with his back to him, looking out of the window. He had a woollen hat on.

'You were very terse this morning,' Ridley said quietly.

'Terse? Jesus Christ, do you have any idea how much running around I have been doing on your behalf?' Jack countered.

He sat down at his desk and swivelled around to face Ridley.

'The first thing you should know is that you were not the target; you were for protection. The woman you knew as Sandra Raynor, aka Lorna Elliot, knew who you were and just needed it to look like she was in with the law. I think it was a pure coincidence that as a young, uniformed officer you had been part of the hunt for Anton Lord. I believe she was hunting down the men she felt were responsible for his disappearance, and probably his murder.'

Ridley sighed, perching himself on the edge of his desk. He was unshaven and looked very gaunt, his eyes red-rimmed.

'I know that now. Let me show you something.'

Ridley unzipped his hoodie and took out a manila envelope. He slowly withdrew a photograph and passed it to Jack.

'Recognise her?'

Jack took a few moments, unable to draw his eyes away from the horror.

'Dear God, it's hard to recognise her after what has been done to her face. But, yes, I know who she is.'

'Her name is Daniella Foster.'

'I just bloody said I knew who she was. She also had a date with you, and she also knew who you were; she recommended Lorna joined the dating agency, specifically to get to you, as she wanted protection but didn't trust going to the police. Maybe she felt they had let her down with their poor investigation into her lover's murder. Mrs Foster said she seemed very anxious and scared . . .'

'Her body was found last night. Her cottage had been ransacked and she was presumably beaten to find out where Lorna Elliot had been staying.'

Jack frowned, then held up his hands. 'Wait a minute. You don't think that I had anything to do with her death, for God's sake?'

'Of course, I don't, but I know you were there. I also know you visited Mrs Foster's London flat in Pimlico.'

Jack shook his head. He could hardly believe what he was hearing. It felt as if everything he had been doing was a waste of his time. Ridley pulled out a second photograph and passed it to him.

'This was reported early this morning. As you can see, the flat was ransacked – after you had been there, fortunately.'

Jack looked at the photograph and passed it back. He lifted up the briefcase and the envelope with the two computer sticks.

'I found these, and that's her laptop and her handbag. From her passport you can see she had been travelling back and forth to Moscow and to Monaco. You can take it all, because to be honest, I have had it up to here.'

Ridley held his hands up. 'Jack, please let me try to explain. Because of your diligence you have been able to uncover these connections, whilst I had to be held under house arrest. But now . . .' He took a deep breath.

'But now what?'

'I am truly grateful for everything you have done to date. This is now being handed over to the National Crime Agency because we believe that Lorna had uncovered a massive fraud and laundering facility in Russia, possibly being run by the men who killed Anton Lord. The FBI will also be investigating. Due to what has been going on in Ukraine and the mega-rich henchmen around Putin, it is a very complicated situation.'

'I bet it is. So what about this man she refers to a few times, someone who lived in Monaco? I looked at all the information on the memory sticks, but I have no idea what it all means.'

'I don't know either,' Ridley admitted. 'It is possible she recognised someone living in Monaco and started to investigate. Lorna was clearly a very clever woman, and never gave up the hunt for whoever killed Anton, but at the same time she began to uncover further large-scale fraud and money laundering involving people connected to Putin. So, although she only intended to find Anton Lord's killers, she ended up discovering a lot more.'

Jack swivelled in his desk chair, then pointed to the laptop.

'She obviously never got over him as she used his name as a password.'

Ridley leant over and was about to close the laptop when Jack stopped him.

'I just want to have a proper look at what's on it. What made some bastard beat that poor soul to death? It must be explosive stuff.'

Ridley leant forward again and snapped the laptop shut.

'I am taking this, Jack, and I don't want you to get any more involved. I mean it. I am also going to take your car.'

'What?'

'It's for your protection. I have had a tracker on it; that's how I knew where you'd been.'

'You had a tracker on me? When did you organise that? When I was parked in that bloody John Lewis car park?'

Jack got to his feet, intending to punch Ridley out, he was so angry. He then stepped back and lowered his hands to his sides. 'You've lied to me from day one, used me like a puppet on a string, and I want some explanation. I trusted you, Goddammit. Jesus Christ, I've worked my arse off and now that poor woman is dead because of you, because of me doing your dirty work and you putting a tracker in my car. They must have fucking hacked it – and I led them straight to her!'

'You don't understand,' Ridley said. 'I was looking out for you and now I can take over . . . and that means right now.'

Ridley picked up the open briefcase and began taking everything from Jack's desk and dropping it into the case. He stuffed in the photo album, the envelope with the memory sticks, and lastly the laptop. He then held up the YSL clutch bag, flipping it open using the elegant gold clasp with the designer initials. He then opened a folded black shopping bag and placed everything inside.

'How am I supposed to get around if you take my car?' Jack complained.

Without hesitating, Ridley took out Lorna's wallet, removed a wedge of £50 notes and handed them to him.

'Use this until I can sort out your compensation.'

'Compensation? What's that supposed to mean?'

'Your car will be taken to a wrecker's yard and destroyed. I don't want anything leading back to you – it's just a precaution.'

Ridley had now packed everything into the large shopping bag and started to head towards the door. Jack moved quickly to stand in front of it.

'A precaution? Just you wait one second ... You and your so-called house arrest team have just been using me.'

Ridley took a deep breath. 'Jack, I don't think anyone else could have uncovered the information we have, or identified who Sandra Raynor really was ...'

'*We?* Who's fucking "we", Ridley?'

Jack gripped the front of Ridley's hoodie, drawing him close.

'If you need to get rid of my car as a precaution, are my wife and my family are in danger? If anything happens to them, I swear to God I will ...'

Ridley didn't react. 'Don't threaten me, Jack,' he said calmly. 'Your family is being protected. I swear to you nothing will happen to them. I've always known that you have an intuition and ability far above any other detective I've worked with, and you've proved me right.'

'Well, that's brilliant, that makes me feel so much better,' Jack snapped.

Ridley nodded his head to indicate that he was leaving, and Jack reluctantly moved aside. He stood at the top of the stairs watching as Ridley hurried down and out of the front door. Jack returned to his office and looked out of the window. He watched Ridley hand his car keys to a thick-set man wearing a similar black track suit. Ridley then climbed into a black Mercedes with tinted windows. From behind the window blinds Jack watched his ridiculous little car being driven off. He looked at every parked car he could see on the street. None of them seemed occupied. If his house was being watched, they were certainly being covert. He felt hurt and angry, convinced that Ridley had still not told him the full truth. Ridley had lied to him, something he never would have thought possible.

CHAPTER TWENTY-FOUR

Jack tucked the wedge of £50 notes into his wallet and went downstairs to the kitchen. He paced up and down, unsure what to do. He felt worried sick about Maggie, Penny and Hannah. It was now after 9 a.m. and even though he had told DCI Clarke that he would be in earlier than the start of his night-shift duty, he was reluctant to leave the house. He decided he would order an Uber and go and visit Maggie at the hospital to check that she was alright and to warn her to take precautions. He checked that the back door was locked, then went through the entire house checking all the windows before going back into his office.

Just as he was about to order an Uber, his mobile rang. It was Laura, first apologising in case she had woken him. She had received a call from Anik.

'I didn't get home until the early hours, but the DCI is bringing in the main team to be on standby.'

'Why?'

'It's Amanda Dunn. She's being brought in this afternoon. We've got Social Services on our back saying even though she's eighteen she's mentally vulnerable and needs an adult present for the interviews. I suggested we get one of her parents to be present.'

'She ran away when she was twelve years old and she hasn't been in contact with her parents for six years, so I doubt Amanda would want them.'

'Then we'll get Social Services to send someone. The DCI's had that barrister Georgina Bamford bending his ear about legal representation for Amanda.'

'But she can't represent her if she's Rodney Middleton's brief!' Jack said, trying to remain calm.

'I know that, but she is insisting on a lawyer not attached to her chambers representing Amanda. I don't know who it is, and I'm not at the station yet. As you have had more dealings with Amanda than anyone, I suggested that you should be present to conduct or at least monitor the interview.'

'Well, at least someone respects the work I've done. But I was told that Anik was going to be involved in the interview, which really pissed me off.'

'I know, he's been so far up the DCI's arse it's embarrassing.'

'Have the press got hold of it yet?'

'I don't know, but the DCI is under pressure to issue a press release this morning. Oh, by the way, they brought Harold Miller into the station last night. He came in after you'd left. He was sweating and shaking. He admitted that on occasions he had gone with Rodney to some depot to pick up the cans of acid. He claimed he was told they were for clearing the rats. Anyway, they let him go because he's the main carer for his wife.'

She paused. 'Are you listening, Jack?'

'Yes . . . yes . . . so what time are you going into the station?'

'I'm leaving home in about half an hour. There was something else: the new commander from Scotland Yard was also in with the DCI, and Clarke looked very shaken after he left.'

'Did he say what happened?'

'I think the gist of it was that we need to have a confession as there are so many unidentified victims, and still no remains. I think they hope Amanda will turn prosecution witness. It was quite funny, actually.'

Jack frowned. 'What could possibly be funny?'

'It was Hendricks. He said surely we have enough evidence against Middleton to charge him for all three murders, even without a confession. DCI Clarke rounded on him. He said that they had the Yorkshire Ripper bang to rights but it wasn't until he made a confession that they knew how many he'd actually murdered.'

'Well, well, well, I'd say our DCI is under a lot of pressure,' Jack said.

'So, you coming in early? I didn't think you'd want to miss out on the arrival of Amanda Dunn.'

'I'll be there,' Jack said.

Jack ended the call, then ordered an Uber to take him to Maggie's hospital. Whilst he waited, he stood by the window and lifted the blinds a fraction. The same cars were still parked outside the house, most in the residents' bays. There was also a gas repair van, with a small canopy tent pitched over a section of pavement. Three men in hard helmets and hi-viz jackets with GAS BOARD printed on their backs looked to be hard at work. Jack continued watching them, wondering if they were a surveillance team. He continued watching them for another five minutes, then he saw the Uber taxi drawing up. It was a Toyota Prius with an Egyptian driver Jack recognised from previous trips.

He left the house, glancing over at the gas workers. One of them was using a mobile phone and immediately turned away when he saw Jack looking at him. Jack was now sure they were monitoring his house and he felt a wave of relief wash over him. He kept a careful watch from the back of the Prius but saw no one following him. Arriving at the hospital, he asked the Uber driver to wait but he told Jack he would have to call in and book another journey. Jack got out, put in another call on his account and the driver gave him the thumbs up and indicated that he would wait for him in the pick-up and drop-off section.

The signage in the reception area was still instructing anyone entering to respect social distance, and masks were obligatory. Jack fished a rather crumpled one out of his pocket whilst the receptionist tried to contact Maggie. She was eventually tracked down, but he had to wait another ten minutes until she came into the reception. He could see she was concerned, and he quickly reassured her that it was nothing serious, he had just come to have a quiet word with her.

'Is it about Penny?'

'No, I'm sorry, I didn't get the opportunity to talk to her, but I'm not going to be late tonight as they've just called me in. I wanted to talk to you about something . . .'

'What?'

'Ridley turned up at the house. This case he's been involved with has got pretty serious. He says we need to be very vigilant about locking doors and not letting strangers in.'

'You're kidding?'

'I'm serious, Maggie, but there are people looking out for us, for you and Hannah especially; a surveillance team, 24/7. Ridley wanted me to underline that it's serious, so I came here to tell you personally, but not to alarm you.'

'Oh, thanks very much, Jack! Of course, I'm alarmed! Do you think I should go home?'

'No, just be watchful. Like I said, I'll be home early this evening and hopefully by then I'll have more details. But if anything at all looks suspicious, you need to let me know straightaway.'

'You sure I shouldn't go home?'

'Yes. Like I said, I just came here to make you aware of everything, and to tell you that I love you.'

Jack lowered his mask and kissed her. He hated seeing how concerned she was, but he reassured her again that they would be fine. Maggie watched him leave the hospital, then hurried back to the ward. She spoke to the head of department who was working the schedules for all the staff and explained that there was a family situation and she needed someone to take over her shift after lunch because she had to go home.

As Maggie was a highly respected doctor, and had never asked for personal time off, it was agreed that she could leave after the lunch break. Despite Jack's reassurances that everything was OK, she was not going to take his word for it. He had never come to the hospital before just to tell her to be vigilant, and she wanted to be at home with her daughter and Penny.

Jack arrived at the station and knew that something had been leaked as there were a group of press photographers waiting outside. He side-stepped them and went inside to the main desk. The duty sergeant released the security gate for him to go into the main corridor.

'They've been here all morning, like bloody wasps; it's always a sign that something big is going down, not that I'm likely to be told. But if they try to get in, they'll get short shrift from me.'

Jack headed to the canteen and could feel the anticipation that something big was happening. There were only a few officers in there, and by the time he got his breakfast they had left. He carried his coffee and bagel down one flight of stairs and headed along the main corridor to the incident room. Nobody passed him and when he pushed open one of the double doors and stepped into the incident room it was oddly quiet, even though most of the desks were occupied.

Making his way to his own desk, he passed Anik wearing an Armani suit with a crisp white shirt and tie and looking very pleased with himself. In contrast, Jack still had some of Hannah's breakfast splattered on his jacket and his shirt was very crumpled, with a tie that had already dangled in his coffee mug. But at least he had shaved. He felt loath to bite into his bagel as everyone appeared to be poised and waiting. As if on cue, the door to the incident room opened and Sara put her head in.

'We have Amanda Dunn's mother in interview room one with one of the WPCs. She has asked for a coffee. Can someone organise that from the canteen as I have to be out in the yard?'

Leon stood up and hurried out after Sara. Then Hendricks appeared, to let them know that Amanda Dunn's brief had arrived and was waiting in reception. Anik got up, straightening his tie, saying that he would go and talk to him. He picked up a thick folder of files as he walked out. Laura came in carrying a coffee and said they had received confirmation that Amanda Dunn was arriving via the back entrance. She asked that the officers assigned to meet her be ready to usher her into the interview room with her brief after she had been booked in with the custody officer.

'She has a social worker with her and hasn't been told that her mother's here. I presume she'll be joining her in the interview room.'

Jack looked on with some amusement and decided he might as well tuck into his bagel. At that moment DCI Clarke opened his office door and came out carrying a clipboard.

'Right, can I have everyone's attention please. Before we begin to question Amanda Dunn, have we received confirmation that Miss Margaret Langton is available to attend as the appropriate adult?'

There were glances around the room before Laura put up her hand. She stood up beside her desk and DCI Clarke nodded at her.

'Miss Langton is six months pregnant and not currently fit to attend.'

DCI Clarke gave a tight-lipped nod and closed his eyes.

'Didn't anyone check this out? Let's hope Mrs Dunn will be acceptable as a supervising adult; if not, get someone else on standby. We should be ready to begin the session in fifteen minutes. I have allowed her solicitor to have a private consultation pre-interview.'

He walked back into his office and Jack quickly finished his bagel, screwing up the napkin and tossing it into the waste bin. Laura looked over to him and raised her eyebrows. Like Jack, she felt the whole situation was being over-orchestrated. Everyone was waiting for the arrival of their prized witness, who alternatively could end up being charged as an accessory to murder. There was no window in the incident room to see into the yard, so everyone just waited patiently for information.

DCI Clarke appeared again, saying that Amanda Dunn was now here and would be taken into Interview Room Two to confer with her brief and Anik. He then asked everyone listed on the board to be present in the viewing room, to go directly there and to wait for the interview to begin.

Jack, coffee in hand, sauntered across to the board. It had now been extended so many times that it was covering most of one wall. There was a list of the officers required to be in the viewing room and he noticed that he was at the top of the list, along with Laura, two other officers, and Glenda Bagshot.

Jack knew from past experience that it would take some time before everyone would be ready for the interview to commence. He left the incident room and headed along the corridor and down a flight of stairs, heading towards the interview room. He passed one of the smaller interview rooms, and through the window in the door he could see a small, bleach-blonde woman sitting with a mug of coffee. She was wearing a very loud plaid coat with a wide collar, and knee-high leather boots, and was clutching a bulging leather handbag. There was something about her over made-up face that gave her the appearance of being beaten in some way.

Laura caught Jack looking through the window.

'That's her mother. Sara is trying to sort out her return ticket to Liverpool, and to get some petty cash for a meal for her.'

'Yeah, I thought she must be the mother. What's going on with Anik and our star witness's brief?'

'Well, he has to be given a certain amount of disclosure, but we haven't yet charged her and at the moment she is just "helping police enquiries", so I don't know how long it's going to take. He's very good looking, though, a young Indian man. He must be worth his weight, as he's a pet boy of that Georgina Bamford. He was wearing a very expensive long cashmere overcoat, and gorgeous . . .'

'For Christ's sake, Laura! Where's Amanda?'

'They took her into the private interview room first, then when the cashmere coat is ready, she'll have a meeting with him before it all goes down.'

'Terrific, I'm glad you dragged me in here. I could have had a few hours extra kip.'

Laura walked off as Jack continued along the corridor, heading down the staircase to the lower ground floor where the new high-tech viewing room was located. He went into the 'spectator' section and found Glenda Bagshot overseeing a trolley with an array of takeaway cartons.

'Miss Bagshot, I have to say you are fast becoming everyone's favourite person. I presume this is down to you . . . It looks like a feast.'

'Listen, Sergeant Warr, I have been in this business a very long time and I know just how important it is to feed the workers. But don't think I'm a walking charity; I make them pay for all this. Clarke tried to tell me it wasn't ethical, so I told him to stuff it. Help yourself because it's going to be a long night.'

'Night? Bloody hell, Glenda, it's only three o'clock in the afternoon.'

'We might all be running around the clock to keep to a bloody timetable, but this is a very big investigation, on a par with Fred West. And it's even more newsworthy because we have two young kid kill-ers. God only knows how the press will handle it when some of the facts get out. I have nothing against the DCI but it's his first major murder investigation and in my opinion, he's out of his depth. I heard the commander was here so that must have put a rocket under him.'

Sara knocked and entered, looking flustered. 'I'm sorry to interrupt, but I'm not sure who I should talk to about organising Mrs Dunn's travel arrangements? Also, she's asked for something to eat as she got the early train from Liverpool, and the buffet on the train wasn't open.'

'Sorry, I'm not following? If she got here, we must have arranged a return ticket, so what's the problem?' Jack asked.

'They arranged a single. It wasn't down to me; it was Hendricks. Everyone keeps on directing me to someone else. Do I put her in a taxi?'

Jack shook his head in disbelief. 'Has she had a meeting with her daughter?'

'No, Amanda has refused to see her. She said, and I quote, "I wouldn't see her if she was in spitting distance." We tried, but she was adamant that she didn't want to even speak to her, let alone see her. So now I have to send her back to Liverpool. The canteen isn't open for another ten minutes and they won't let me have so much as a sandwich.'

Jack picked up a paper plate. 'Go and talk to the clerical staff that handle the kitty and organise a taxi to take her to the station and a return fare to Liverpool. In the meantime, if you don't mind Glenda, I will take a selection of these goodies and give them to Mrs Dunn myself.'

'Thank you, sarge, I'll go and sort the transport,' Sara said gratefully. 'Mrs Dunn is downstairs in one of the lower ground floor interview rooms.'

'I know, I saw her when I was coming up here.'

Sara hurried out as Jack piled a paper plate with sausage rolls, some chicken and ham sandwiches and a small container of what looked like curry. Glenda watched him, then handed him a spoon and fork and some paper napkins.

'Well, that should keep her going, and she can take some back on the train. Typical isn't it; they organise a single ticket!'

Jack headed back towards the interview room. He knocked and entered.

'Mrs Dunn, I do apologise for you being left in here on your own. I understand the buffet on the train wasn't open so I hope this will suffice. He placed the food selection down in front of her on the table and took the cutlery out of his pocket, along with the paper napkins.

'She bloody refused to see me!' she said in a strong Liverpool accent. 'Can you believe it? After me coming all this way, but I suppose I expected it in some ways. I've not seen her for four or five years, and there's been no contact or nothing. Believe you me, I've tried. I used to call the missing persons place every other day asking if they had found her.'

Mrs Dunn peered at the contents of the plastic container. 'Is this a curry with noodles?'

'I believe so, and there's some fresh sandwiches with chicken and ham.'

He watched as she jabbed at the noodles with the plastic fork and took a mouthful. She chewed and swallowed, then nodded. 'Very nice.'

'Did your husband accompany you?'

'No, he's her stepfather . . . and to be honest, he's had enough of her. I have been worried all this time . . . and like I said, I kept on calling the Social Services and the missing persons, but eventually I gave up. She's done it before you know.'

Jack waited as she forked in two more mouthfuls of the spicy noodles, then wiped her mouth with the napkin.

'Running away, you mean?'

'Yes, when she was about ten. Disappeared for three weeks. We found her with one of her friends after searching the streets, as well as contacting the police. She made horrible accusations against my husband, all lies; she was a terrible liar. She was always skiving off school; the number of times I had the school calling me to say that she hadn't turned up.'

'These accusations against your husband, were they of a sexual nature?'

She nodded. 'We had the Social Services round to question me and him, and we had two little ones as well. It was all lies, and they said they wanted her assessed by a therapist because they reckoned she was suffering from . . .' She frowned chewing at her bottom lip. Jack waited whilst she bit into a sausage roll.

'Suffering from what?'

'Asperkers, that's what it was.'

'I think you mean Asperger's? What did they suggest you should do about it?'

'She was supposed to go to a therapist and have some extra tuition at school. But she never turned up and then the school would report her not being in class. It was just non-stop with her. She was nothing but trouble. I would always try to stick up for her, but you can only make excuses for someone for so long.'

'She was only twelve years old though.'

'I know how old she was,' she said indignantly. 'And before you say anything, you don't have to remind me how long she's been away from me. I'm her mother, and I got two younger kids to look after. I'm very protective about them, even more so when she was at home because of what happened to Sharon.'

'Sharon?'

'She was Amanda's younger sister, by my first husband. We divorced after it happened; he couldn't deal with it. Mind you, he couldn't deal with much, and with him being in the Navy he was never around. He was at home when it happened, though, and from then on it was always difficult. He was a bad drinker.'

'What happened?'

Mrs Dunn wiped her mouth with a paper napkin, then crumpled it in her hand.

'Amanda was jealous of her, I know that. She was such a pretty little thing. When he was home, he would bring such lovely presents for them, and I suppose it was Sharon he showed more affection to. She was a little angel compared to Amanda.'

Jack waited, aware that she was finally showing some emotion. She used the crumpled napkin to wipe her mouth again then began to twist it in her hands as tears fell down her cheeks. He reached out to touch her arm, but she pulled away from him.

'It's hard for me to talk about it, even now. She was only four and half and Amanda was seven. My husband and I went out to the pub for a drink and Amanda was babysitting. We didn't often leave them on their own, but like I said, he was in the Navy and not home that much. I didn't usually leave them on their own because I'd caught her slapping Sharon a couple of times. She had a nasty, mean streak in her and she would take the presents he bought for Sharon and destroy them.'

Her eyes continued to brim over with tears, as she pulled at the paper napkins, tearing off small strips.

'We got home at about ten, and Amanda was watching TV. When we went upstairs, we found Sharon with the cord from the window blind around her neck. She was still using a cot, you know with sides, and it looked as if she had tried to climb out, got caught up in the cord and choked to death.'

Jack was deeply shocked. Mrs Dunn's tears ran down her cheeks and she wiped them away with the back of her hand. Her face was distorted with anguish and anger.

'It was an accidental death, but one thing always bothered me, the sides of the cot was down, so she could have easily got out. Why did she reach up for the cord? Why?'

'Did you think that Amanda was to blame?'

Mrs Dunn became more composed and reached down next to her chair for her handbag. She placed it on her knee and took out a compact and lipstick. Jack watched as she looked at herself in the compact mirror, took out a worn powder puff and dabbed it over her face. She then opened the lipstick and applied it thickly over her top and bottom lips before rubbing them together. Jack remained silent, and eventually she continued.

'We got divorced and a few years later I re-married and we changed our names. Whatever I thought, I never told no one. After it happened things was never the same between me and Amanda. I never accused her – but it was like always between us – then I got pregnant again, and it put me on edge, especially after having the baby. I was always watching out for her doing something, and that's when she started running away. It sometimes felt a relief not having her home, to be honest, because I could never forget what happened to Sharon. We redecorated her room, moved the cot away from the window, but every so often when I went to check on the little ones, I'd see it again. See my lovely little girl, like a broken doll, just hanging.'

Jack watched as she carefully wrapped the uneaten sandwiches in a spare paper napkin and put them in her handbag.

'I am deeply sorry for your loss, Mrs Dunn, and thank you for coming into the station. I'm sorry that Amanda is refusing to see you. If you'd like, I could talk to her again and see if she changes her mind.'

'No, don't bother, I expected as much. She's eighteen now and at least I know she's alive. Unlike my little Sharon, who never grows old . . . she's always as beautiful, always four and half years old.'

Sara tapped on the door and entered. She explained that she had ordered a taxi and had booked a train ticket for Mrs Dunn, apologising for making her wait.

'That's alright, love, this nice young man's been talking with me. He brought me some food, so I'm ready to go home.'

Sara looked at Jack gratefully, as she ushered Mrs Dunn out.

He sat for a moment, digesting everything he had just been told. It both shocked and saddened him and it gave him a different insight into Amanda's personality. Could she have been responsible for her young sister's death? He considered the fire at Middleton's home, and the death of Rodney's two sisters. Could their similar losses have been some kind of bond between them? Jack was becoming more and more certain that Amanda was not the innocent girl she claimed to be.

CHAPTER TWENTY-FIVE

Jack entered the viewing room, surprised that Amanda was still not being questioned. Laura was sitting with a plate of sandwiches and asked him how it had gone with Mrs Dunn. Jack shrugged and said that it was quite informative, but didn't elaborate. Instead, he helped himself to the curry and some items from the salad bar. Glenda was sitting reading the *Evening Standard*, moaning about the length of time she had been waiting for the 'show' to start. Just then the lights came on in the viewing room as Anik entered, carrying a thick folder of files. He was followed by Amanda, who looked like a different person. Her usually lank, greasy hair was shining and full. She was wearing a fashionable denim jumpsuit and had applied makeup and lipstick.

'My God! She brushes up well,' Jack said as they all looked intently through the large two-way screen. Raj Bukhari was last to enter. He was no longer in his cashmere overcoat but was wearing a very fashionable suit with a white shirt and maroon tie. He carried a folder and sat beside Amanda. Next to enter was a matronly-looking woman, presumably from Social Services. Last to walk in, also with a large folder, was DCI Clarke who sat down beside Anik.

Anik kicked off by explaining that the interview would be both filmed and recorded. He switched on the machine and introduced himself. DCI Clarke gave his own name and rank and the matronly lady said that she was Mrs Hardcastle, acting as the appropriate adult. Raj turned to Amanda who gave her name and then he introduced himself as Raj Bukhari, acting as legal representative for Miss Dunn.

Anik explained that they wanted to question Miss Dunn regarding the disappearance and possible murders of Nadine O'Reilly,

Trudie Hudson and Jamail Brown, saying they believed Amanda might be able to assist the investigation. He then cautioned her.

'You do not have to say anything, but it may harm your defence if you do not mention, when questioned, something which you later rely on in court. Anything you do say may be given in evidence.'

Amanda sat upright in her chair, appearing not to listen, looking at her false pale-pink nails. She was pressing down on them, as if to keep them in place.

Anik opened his bulging file.

'Amanda, could you please tell us how long you have lived in the basement flat in Leighton Avenue that is leased to Rodney Middleton?'

'No comment.'

Anik paused, then continued.

'How well do you know Rodney Middleton?'

'No comment.'

'What age where you when you first met Rodney Middleton?'

'No comment.'

Anik swallowed. He was beginning to look flustered.

'Amanda, if I was to show you a Snapchat photograph of Trudie Hudson, could you tell us about your friendship with her.'

'No comment.'

'Did you exchange a bracelet with Miss Hudson for a gold and ruby ring?'

'No comment.'

Glenda gave a loud yawn in the viewing room, saying that this was going to be a very long night, as she had expected.

'Look at her, Little Miss Confidence. She's not even looking at her brief sitting beside her. He certainly schooled her well. She's loving it, and poor old Anik is starting to sweat.'

Jack looked on in disgust. He could not believe they were not being tougher on her. It felt like a waste of time. The questions continued for over half an hour and Amanda had still not answered a single one. They had upped the game by showing photographs of the coal hole and the accumulated evidence, but nothing moved her. If anything, she appeared to be becoming bored. She asked for a glass of water and was handed a small plastic bottle. She took a long time unscrewing the top because of her false nails, and then took deliberately tiny sips before re-screwing the lid back on.

Anik continued, slowly moving to the evidence showing that they had identified the three girls, but she still maintained her stance of 'no comment'. He raised his voice as he said they had a witness to prove that she had been living at the premises when Jamail was there, but Amanda wasn't remotely fazed, responding yet again with 'no comment'.

Anik changed tactics, explaining that by being uncooperative she was only implicating herself and was more likely to be charged as an accessory to murder. She smiled and shrugged her shoulders.

Jack leaned over to Laura and said he was going home. He knew they had only just started and that this could continue for another couple of hours. He told her that if needed he was contactable on his mobile, but he had heard enough to know they were not going to get anything tonight.

Glenda pulled a face. 'I don't blame you. I'm waiting for them to show some of the CCTV images but, as I told you all, this is going to be a long night and by the sound of it she's not going to crack.'

Jack ordered an Uber to collect him and take him home. He would have liked to have been in on the interview, but by the sound of it the cashmere coat brief was playing hardball. It was looking like they were going to have to charge her with accessory to murder and hope that persuaded her to give evidence against Middleton in return for a reduced sentence. Right now, however, the game was only just beginning.

The Uber dropped him off at home just after 9 p.m. He was about to switch on the hall lights when he saw a bulky grey-haired man coming down the stairs. The man looked shocked to see Jack, and Jack didn't hesitate. He ran up the stairs towards him, grabbed him by the collar of his jacket and they both fell to the bottom of the stairs. The man tried to get to his feet and swung a fist, catching Jack on the nose. Jack head-butted the man in the face, then dragged him to his feet ready to punch him out. Suddenly Maggie came running out of the kitchen screaming.

'Jack ... *Jack!* What the hell are you doing? Stop it. Stop right now, for God's sake!'

Maggie forced her way between them. Jack's nose was bleeding profusely. She put her arms out wide to protect the burly man.

'What are you doing?'

Penny came running down the stairs, looking shocked.

'What on earth is going on? Oh, my goodness, look what you've done to him.' The man was holding his chin and was obviously dazed.

'Who is this for Christ's sake? What is he doing in my house?' Jack demanded.

Penny took the man in her arms, saying she would get an icepack. Maggie held up her arms to Jack and told him to calm down.

'Calm down? He was coming down the fucking stairs in our house!'

'Jack, take a deep breath and listen ... *listen to me*. His name is Marius and he's from Romania. He's the caretaker at Hannah's nursery. Are you listening to me?'

'What was he doing upstairs?'

'He was saying goodnight to Hannah. Penny was with her. Is your nose broken? Let me see ...'

Jack was still in such a fury that he backed off as Maggie reached out to feel his nose.

'Leave it, just leave it, and tell me what the hell is going on.'

'Marius is Penny's boyfriend. She's been seeing him for a while. She didn't want to mention it to us, especially to you, in case you flew off the handle about your dad. You'd better let me see to your nose.'

Jack's anger subsided like a deflated balloon. Maggie led him into the kitchen where Marius was sitting at the table with a pack of frozen peas held to his head. Maggie sat Jack down and felt his nose, then after a moment tweaked it hard. It clicked.

'There you go. Penny, have we got any more frozen peas? Jack's going to have two black eyes tomorrow.'

Nobody said anything for a few moments. Jack held a bag of frozen green beans to his face whilst Marius sat opposite him with the peas.

'I'm sorry, Jack,' Penny said. 'I kept on wanting to tell you, but I was just concerned about how you would feel about it. Marius and I have been seeing each other, as friends, for some time. We enjoy each other's company. I was going to tell you both about us, but lately there never seems to be the right time.'

Jack sighed. 'Look, I am sorry about reacting like that. I'd been warned to take extra precautions lately, so seeing someone I didn't know heading down the stairs just freaked me out.'

Marius removed the frozen peas to speak. 'I understand ... you'd never met me.' He chuckled. 'I have to say you have a very good right hook. I used to be a boxer when I was a kid. Anyway, I work at the church's gym, and at the nursery school, painting and doing odd jobs ... a bit of plumbing or electrical stuff. In fact anything that needs doing. I'm retired now, but I had my own decorating company once.'

Jack listened as the poor man continued telling him about his life, that he was a widower, how he had met Penny, and how much they enjoyed each other's company, taking their long walks in the afternoon with Hannah.

Maggie eventually interrupted with a suggestion they all have a glass of wine, and perhaps order in a pizza.

Jack had a tissue stuffed up each nostril and shook Marius's big, gnarled hand saying that perhaps a whisky would suit them both better.

They spent the evening apologising to each other, eating pizza and even laughing about it in the end. Maggie was keen to see if Marius could do some work around the house, and he said that he would be happy to do whatever she wanted. Penny remained quiet, obviously relieved that it was now out in the open.

After Marius had left, Jack gave Penny a hug and a kiss, reassuring her that he was happy she had a new companion and saying that he thought Marius was a fabulous old boy.

Later on, in bed with Maggie, his nose still stuffed up with tissues, he asked in a whisper if she thought his mum and Marius had consummated their relationship. Maggie nudged him in his sore ribs and told him not to be so nosy. She was more interested in Marius tackling the various things that needed doing around the house.

'I think all this memory loss stuff I've been concerned about is probably due to her keeping her boyfriend a secret. It's obviously been going on for months and must have put a lot of mental strain on her.'

Jack's head was throbbing and Maggie gave him a couple of painkillers. 'Well, ironically it'll be good to have him around the house, given the situation with Ridley,' he said with a wry smile.

Jack briefly told Maggie about Amanda Dunn's interview, then repeated what Mrs Dunn had told him about Amanda's sister, Sharon.

'You know, I think she's a devious little bitch, but they're treating her with kid gloves. She was clearly loving doing the "no comment" show, which means we will probably have the same scenario with Rodney Middleton. This is really going to drag on.'

'How come, when you have so much evidence against him?' Maggie asked.

'No bodies, so it's all circumstantial, apart from the matching DNA that ties him to the horror that went on in the coal hole. But he could easily claim that he never knew what went on in there. Anyone could have had access while he was on remand. He could say that he used the chemicals to get rid of rats, and any blood splattering found on his clothes could have got there from him cleaning up afterwards. The DCI hinted at the pressure on him to get a confession. Any day soon it's going to hit the press big time; they were already hanging around outside the station.'

'You told me you have footage of Amanda getting rid of the missing girls' clothes?'

'We have footage of her shoving items into a charity container, but who's to say they were the victims' clothes? We have to have proof, and with no bodies it's twenty times harder.'

Maggie sighed. 'Dear God! What I find so repulsive is the way they've both got these high-powered briefs working for them. I mean, what kind of man or woman wants to help get a sick killer free? For the publicity? It's just a game for them, isn't it? The kudos of winning. The reality is those two young people are monsters.'

Jack started to nod off, the painkillers taking effect. The tissue stuffed up his nostrils were making him snore, and Maggie leaned over him to switch his bedside light off, then hers. She lay beside him in the darkness, thinking that sometimes he was such an adolescent, impulsively attacking poor Marius. But he had a very lovable side, the way he had hugged Penny, and made it up with her boyfriend.

Maggie was aware that there was another side to him, a darkness that he had to control, that set him apart from the officers he worked alongside and stopped him from being a team player. She knew that was the reason why he had not been promoted after his last successful case. He was a loose cannon, and she knew that if anyone harmed his family, he would fire back with everything he had. But if the anger she had witnessed tonight was unleashed in the wrong direction, it could be devastating.

CHAPTER TWENTY-SIX

The following morning, before leaving for work, Maggie rubbed arnica into the bruises on Jack's face. He still needed to stuff his nose with tissues as when he removed them his nostrils started bleeding again. There was also no way of disguising that he had one black eye, the lid partly closed, with a red bruise above the other. He was not officially on duty until 10 a.m. and was hoping that by continuing with the ice packs until then, his face might look a little less swollen.

Penny came into the bedroom to see him before leaving to take Hannah to nursery. Maggie had suggested that he did not go and see his daughter as she would probably be scared by his appearance. Penny continued to be apologetic about the previous night's situation, but Jack reassured her that it was all water under the bridge. He was happy that she had found a companion.

Jack had just taken a couple of painkillers and lain back on the bed, as his head was still throbbing, when his mobile rang. He had to bend down to pick it up off the floor beside him, which didn't help his headache. Laura was calling to give an update about the interview, which had gone on until almost 11 p.m. Amanda had not been charged and she had not answered one question, maintaining her stance of 'no comment'. By law she now had to be given eight hours of rest before any further interviewing. It was very frustrating. Anik had suggested that she could be charged with accessory to murder and requested for her to be held in custody for further questions the following morning.

A female officer had taken Amanda to the protective house and would remain with her until she was collected the following morning. They were approaching the CPS to discuss the charges she could face.

'How did she react to the possibility of being charged?' Jack asked.

'No reaction, really; by that time, I don't think she really understood what it meant. She just asked for an orange juice. Mr Smooth was tight-lipped and said in passing that he hoped they had some very strong evidence before they charged her with anything. He seemed pretty unruffled.'

'How much did Anik disclose to her?'

'As much as he could do in the time he had, but her continual "no comment" was very wearing . . . It was the DCI who eventually called a halt to the interview.'

'That's very interesting. So what time is she back at the station?'

'I've been told we need to be ready at 12 noon, but we were hoping for a bit longer as everyone is delving into the evidence we've got to see if we can put the frighteners on her.'

'I'd say the ring and the bracelet are good starters,' Jack said. 'As well as the Snapchat messages. And don't forget the bed socks with traces of Trudie's blood.'

'They have already mentioned the bracelet and the ring and got no response. If you want my opinion, she is so dominated by Rodney and now by this brief of hers that she will say whatever she is told to say, or not to say, if you get my meaning. I wish you were interviewing her, Jack; Anik is just going by the book, and you know more about her than anyone else.'

'Tell me something I don't know,' Jack said.

'You sound a bit muffled, are you alright?' Laura asked.

'Actually, I'm not. I tripped over one of my daughter's toys and fell down the stairs. I got a nasty smack in the face from the banister. So, in answer to your question, I'm not feeling that bright.'

'I hope you're up to coming in. Do you want me to warn anyone that you might not feel well enough?'

'No, but I might come in a bit later than ten. Thanks for keeping me up to date, Laura.'

He ended the call and rested back against the pillow. He wondered if he should have relayed the conversation he'd had with Amanda's mother, but then decided it could wait. He was just settling the ice pack back over his face when his mobile rang again. It was Ridley. Jack was about to tell him what had happened the previous evening and how it was all his fault, but he'd only got as far as angrily saying that he had a lot to answer for, when Ridley interrupted him.

'It's over, Jack. The National Crime Agency has already made three arrests at Heathrow Airport, as they boarded a plane on their way to Moscow. We have CCTV footage of them, all identified as the men who not only murdered Mrs Foster but broke into her flat in Pimlico. They were apparently running scared and under heavy-duty orders. They are now being given a grilling at NCA headquarters. This is just the tip of a massive iceberg regarding billions of illegal transactions going right to the top of the Russian government . . .' He paused to draw breath.

'Are they also responsible for the murder of Lorna Elliot?' Jack asked.

'We believe so. It's thanks to Lorna's incredible research that we have the names of some very high-powered crooks, along with links to the top man himself. Her determination to get revenge for the murder of her lover was tireless. We now know that five years ago, she was doing business in Monaco and recognised someone Anton had been doing business with before he disappeared. It took her five years to unravel his part in Anton's abduction and murder. Sadly, the man is now deceased, but they are looking into the vast wealth he left behind after being kicked out of Monaco for money-laundering. He has heirs to his fortune.'

'So, what happens with you now?' Jack asked.

'I won't be returning to work for a couple of months, perhaps even longer, but my own involvement in all of this will be brushed under the carpet.'

Jack hesitated, then asked about his pea-green Micra.

'I want more than bloody compensation . . . and I don't want some second-hand piece of junk, either. I deserve some thanks for what I've had to go through, so you can make it a Mercedes. I'm not joking; I risked my neck, never mind my family, for you.'

'I know that Jack . . .' Ridley said quietly.

'Good. I trusted you and you made me feel like I was being used. Can you give me your word that my family and I are now safe?'

'I give you my word, Jack. Your contribution was very much appreciated, not only by me but everyone connected to this night-mare. You were the only person I knew who could dig deep and not back off. You are a hunter. I had a really hard time watching the footage on Lorna's laptop. She spoke into the camera and piece by piece gave the connections to all the banking frauds. The memory sticks suddenly made sense, providing details of hundreds of accounts. She hardly altered her expression on the film and spoke very quietly, then right at the end . . .'

Jack waited. He could tell by Ridley's voice that he was finding it difficult to continue.

'She was a very special woman, Jack, one of the most attractive and interesting women I have ever met. At the end of the foot-age, she said that she hoped she would be alive to be able to put her beloved Anton to rest. If she was not, and the footage was being viewed by the people who murdered him, she had failed. If it was being watched by someone who would continue her fight for justice, then it had all been worthwhile, then she gave this sweet, tender smile.'

Ridley hesitated before continuing.

'So, there you have it, Jack.'

Jack was tempted to make a joke about it being a lesson to him about joining any dating agency. Instead, he simply thanked him and ended the call.

He replaced the ice pack on his face and lay back on the pillows. Relief that Ridley's case was over washed over him. He wondered where Ridley would be going now, doubting that he would re-join the station. He certainly knew he would not want to work with him again. He had trusted Ridley and in return Ridley had used the very thing that he was constantly being reprimanded about, his dogged persistence and inability to be a team player.

Jack slept for a couple of hours, then had a long shower and dressed in clean jeans and a fresh white shirt with a grandad collar, which was always frowned on at the station. He checked his face in the wardrobe mirror and realised that he looked as if he had gone a couple of rounds with Tyson Fury. His right eye was no longer as swollen, but the left was still puffy. He put a small wad of cotton wool up each nostril to hold back any bleeding, then rooted around in Maggie's makeup drawer for some tinted moisturiser to try and cover up the bruising, and after combing his hair and checking himself in the mirror again, finally felt he was ready to go into the station.

It was after twelve when he got there, and the Uber driver made a joke about hoping that the other fella looked worse. Jack laughed, feeling strangely upbeat. He knew he was about to get a lot more ribbing from his colleagues, but he couldn't give a toss. He went straight to the canteen to get a coffee and then into the incident room. Laura had obviously relayed the story of his accident, and there were some sympathetic glances as he stood looking at the incident board.

Amanda Dunn was on her way in, and her brief was already in the viewing room waiting for her. Anik was with DCI Clarke in his office, and when they walked out together Jack turned towards them.

'Good God! What on earth happened to you?' Clarke exclaimed.

'He fell over his daughter's toy on the stairs,' Anik replied, before Jack could answer.

'Are you alright?' Clarke asked.

'Fine, sir.

'If you don't mind, could I give you and Anik a heads-up about Amanda? After watching the interview yesterday, I have one or two thoughts.'

Anik was clearly irritated, but Clarke glanced at his watch and nodded.

'We're up against the clock today, so whatever you have to impart, make it quick.'

Sara approached with a pink bottle of Bisodol. She apologised for interrupting and handed the bottle to Anik.

'You said you needed this so I went out to the pharmacy for you.'

'Thank you, Sara. If you don't mind, guv, I'll just go to the gents and take it. I've got a bit of a dickie stomach.'

Clarke nodded and turned back to Jack. 'Fire away.'

'Well, sir, Amanda has obviously been told to go the "no comment" route, so I would advise a more indirect method of questioning. She's not the brightest, and I doubt she's really aware of what it would mean if she was charged with being an accessory to murder, or of committing perjury, in terms of actually going to prison. Also, I was going to mention the bed sock.'

Clarke nodded and took another look at his watch, and Jack knew he had to quickly get to the point.

'Amanda admitted to me that the bed socks she was wearing had belonged to Trudie. When they were tested there was matching DNA from blood on the soles, which obviously suggests she was present when Trudie was dismembered. She had insisted that she was always locked in the back bedroom, but no blood samples were discovered in that room apart from those on the bed socks.

Basically, sir, you have to put a lot more pressure on her because she's a very adept liar.'

Clarke turned to move away as Anik appeared and signalled that they needed to leave.

'Thank you for that, Jack, and I believe we do have the evidence bag with the offending socks ready to be shown to her.'

'Sir, if I'm in the viewing room and feel I could help with the direction of the questioning, is there any way that I can relay that to you?'

'If you feel it's important, then yes. But we can't delay things. We have to charge her or release her by this evening.'

Jack watched Clarke stride off with Anik as Laura approached. She looked at his face.

'My God! That was some fall. Are you sure you're alright?'

He nodded. 'I'm fine.'

'Well, Anik isn't. He's got a bad stomach and was very sick earlier. Sara went out for something to settle it, but if you ask me, it's nerves. Little Miss "no comment" kept the car waiting this morning, because she was blow-drying her hair. I tell you, she's something else. I honestly doubt she has any idea how serious her situation is. It's like a game to her, and she's just loving all the attention.'

Jack nodded. 'Yeah, I know. Is the appropriate adult in again?'

'I believe so. Glenda is hoping the CCTV footage is going to be shown today because they didn't get to it last night. Are you going in there? If so, I'll come with you.'

Laura and Jack entered the viewing room to find that Glenda had done her culinary work again. There were bacon sandwiches and flasks of tea and coffee. Glenda was sitting with her feet up on a chair reading the *Daily Mail*. Jack and Laura helped themselves as she put the newspaper aside.

'Did either of you have the Chinese or the curry from yesterday? I have had a complaint from DS Joshi that it has given him food poisoning, which is rubbish as I had some and I'm fine. Did you have any, Jack?'

'Yes, I had the curry and the sausage rolls, but not the Chinese. Mine was delicious,' he added with a smile.

'Well, no one else has complained, but if he came in after they had finished late last night, it could have been out for quite a few hours, I suppose, and there were prawns in the Chinese.'

Laura looked through the viewing room window and could see that they were already interviewing Amanda, but there was no sound. She looked to the others and asked for the microphone to be switched on.

Glenda shrugged. 'Sorry, I turned it off; they were supposed to start at noon and the CPS chap hasn't shown up yet.'

She swung her feet off the chair and folded the newspaper as Laura turned on the intercom microphone so they could hear the interrogation. Jack picked up the newspaper. There was a report on the front page about an arrest of Soviet agents at Heathrow Airport.

'Do you mind if I just nip out for a second . . .' Jack didn't wait for anyone to reply as he walked out carrying the newspaper. He stood in the corridor reading the article, which said very little other than that National Crime Agency officers had boarded the plane to make the arrests. He went up the stairs to the incident room to look on his computer to see if there were any other articles with more information. He was scrolling through an article in *The Times*, when Hendricks hurried from the back of the room, banging through the double doors. Leon looked over to Jack.

'He's got a severe case of the runs . . . I think he should go home.'

'Did he eat anything from the viewing room yesterday? Glenda Bagshot had a feast delivered and apparently Anik isn't feeling too good today either,' Jack said.

Leon shrugged.

'I think Hendricks brought a load back in for the night duty guys.'

Jack returned to scrolling through the newspaper articles. He found three more articles, one in the *Daily Telegraph* and another in the *Sun*. Neither gave too many details, but the *Telegraph* suggested the arrests were connected to an international fraud involving Russian oligarchs and the Soviet government. Jack leant back in his chair. There was no mention of Lorna Elliot, or Ridley, or even the murder of Mrs Foster. He sighed. The duplicity of governments never ceased to amaze him. That the brutal murder of Lorna Elliot could simply be made to disappear made him wonder just how much more never surfaced, and whether he would ever fully understand what Ridley's – and his own – role in it all had been.

Leon approached his desk and asked if he was feeling alright. 'I heard you had an accident?'

'Yeah, I'm fine, but thanks for asking. Just have to keep the cotton wool plugs up my nose to stop the bleeding.'

'You should put some salt in a glass of warm water and snort it up your nostrils; makes your eyes water but it does the trick because the dried blood can get clogged and then you can get an infection in your sinuses.'

Jack stood up. 'Thanks for the advice. How come you know so much about it?'

'First aid sessions. We still have regular refreshers.'

'Right, yes, I remember . . . thanks anyway. Better get back to the viewing room.'

'I was an amateur boxer, so I've had my nose flattened a couple of times,' Leon smiled.

'Really?' Jack said, moving away from his desk. But Leon seemed desperate to have a conversation and trailed after him.

'You know, if you ever want a workout let me know; I've got spare gloves and pads.'

'Thanks, Leon, I appreciate that. I'll let you know.'

Jack went into the gents before heading down to the viewing room. He took out the cotton wool and his nose promptly started dripping blood onto his clean shirt. He swore, then ducked his head under the cold taps. He eventually stemmed the bleeding with wads of twisted toilet paper.

A few more people had been allowed into the viewing room by the time Jack returned. He sat beside Laura who burst out laughing when she saw him.

'It's not funny,' Jack grimaced.

'Have you got a headache?'

'Excuse me, you two, if you want a private conversation, please leave the room. We're here to monitor what's going on,' Glenda snapped.

'Sorry,' Jack said sheepishly.

'Not that you've missed very much. She's still stonewalling. They showed her the bed socks, she just shrugged.'

Jack looked through the viewing window, noting that Amanda was looking tired and was fiddling nervously with her fake nails. She rarely looked up. A small monitor had been placed in front of her, showing the CCTV footage.

'About bloody time . . .' Glenda said.

Anik leaned forward.

'As you can clearly see, Miss Dunn, you are placing clothes into the charity collection bin, shoes in the top level and clothes in the wider slot beneath. Could you please explain why you're doing this?'

'No comment.'

'We have a photograph of Jamail wearing a blue and white striped t-shirt, and you can very clearly be seen placing it in the bin, along with a pair of shoes.'

'No comment.'

'Please continue to look at the monitor; on two further occasions you are seen placing items of clothing into the charity bin. It is quite obvious that you're getting rid of items of clothing that belonged to other girls, specifically Trudie, Nadine and Jamail.'

'No comment.'

'Miss Dunn, you are consistently refusing to answer every question put to you. This leads me to believe that you are deliberately concealing the truth. You were disposing of the victims' clothing so they would not be found in Rodney Middleton's flat, which means you were aware of what had happened to these girls. You have had every opportunity to assist this investigation, but by refusing to cooperate . . .'

Everyone leaned forwards. Suddenly Anik started to heave, unable to control it. He gasped for breath as if to stop the retching, then leant sideways over the arm of his chair and began to vomit.

DCI Clarke immediately halted the interview, while an officer went to assist Anik.

'Bloody hell,' Glenda exclaimed. Led by DCI Clarke the room was cleared and Anik was taken to the sick room. Amanda and her brief were taken into another interview room with a uniformed officer while a maintenance team cleaned and disinfected everything.

Laura turned to ask Jack what was going to happen, but he just shrugged. They were already up against the clock and couldn't keep Amanda in custody for much longer before they had to formally charge her. But they had never had an incident of this kind before so, nobody knew exactly what the next move would be.

Glenda was certain they would have to reconvene the following day. She was unsure about the legalities, but as it was an emergency, perhaps they would be able to extend Amanda's stay in custody. DCI Clarke walked in and gave a signal to Jack that he wished to speak to him.

Jack followed him into his office.

Clarke took a deep breath.

'I have two options, Jack: I take over, or I let you take Anik's place. I can give you some time to get up to speed if you need it.'

Jack didn't need to think about it. 'I can do it, sir. And I'm as familiar with the case files as anyone.'

An hour later the interview room had been fully cleaned and disinfected, then sprayed with air freshener, so it smelt like a bowl of fresh flowers.

Amanda and Raj Bukhari were brought back in and Clarke explained that due to DS Joshi's indisposition, Detective Sergeant Jack Warr would be taking his place. Amanda was read her rights again and to everyone's surprise burst out laughing in Jack's face. She pointed at him, then covered her mouth with her hands, giggling uncontrollably.

Jack just smiled. 'Perhaps you don't recognise me, Amanda. I'm the officer you met at Euston Station. Do you remember that time?'

'Yes,' she said, then quickly looked at her brief, as if she'd done something wrong.

'Good. We had a long chat then, and, as I recall, you persuaded me to cough up £70 for your train ticket to Liverpool. But you actually had no intention of catching a train. Perhaps you were feeling a little bit guilty, and that's why you gave me a bracelet with a broken clasp, which had at one time belonged to your friend Trudie. Do you remember?'

She looked at Bukhari again, then swallowed. 'No comment.'

Jack maintained his friendly expression. 'You know, Amanda, I understand sometimes why people say "no comment" in interviews because they think it will help them avoid getting into trouble. But another way of thinking of an interview like this is as an opportunity to tell us their side of the story. Because if you don't tell us now, and then you find yourself in court, it could harm your defence. Do you understand?'

She nodded, and this time she didn't look at Bukhari. 'Yes.'

'Good. You also described a gold and ruby ring which you had given to Trudie in exchange for the bracelet, but you were a bit peeved because you said the clasp was broken and it wasn't a fair deal.'

'It wasn't . . .'

'I agree. We found the ruby ring and it was gold, not cheap silver like the bracelet.'

'Right.'

'We found it in the coal hole, did you know that?'

He didn't wait for her to reply. It was clear that he had already unnerved her as he opened his file and took out Trudie's photograph.

'She was very pretty, wasn't she?'

He laid out two more photographs of Trudie, given to them by her parents.

'She was very young, but most importantly she was such a pretty girl. Don't you agree?'

Bukhari leaned forwards. 'I don't see the importance of whether my client found her pretty or not.'

'Because you don't like pretty girls, do you, Amanda?' Jack continued. 'You don't like them sleeping in the bed that you sleep in with Rodney; that makes you very upset.'

Before she could repeat her mantra of 'no comment' Jack ploughed on. He pulled out photographs of Jamail and Nadine.

'Prettier than you, aren't they, Amanda?'

'No, they were not,' she said angrily.

Bukhari touched her arm, but she pulled it away.

She scowled. 'He's saying things about me that aren't true.'

'I'm sorry,' Jack said gently. 'It's just that I know pretty little girls have always been a thorn in your side. I'm sorry to be talking to you looking like this; perhaps I should explain what happened. My daughter left a toy on the stairs. I was in a hurry because Sharon is only four and half, and I was worried because she was playing with the cord on her blinds in her bedroom.'

'I don't want to hear any more! Shut up!'

'I'm just trying to explain that I was very concerned that she might get the cord round her tiny little neck . . . It has happened, you know, children accidentally hanging themselves on blind and curtain cords, and . . .'

Amanda shoved the table hard with both of her hands. Her face was distorted with rage.

'Fuckin' shut up! It was not my fault!'

Jack put both hands up in the air.

'I don't think you realise that you could be charged with being an accessory to murder. You could be sentenced to spend the rest of your life in prison . . .'

Now it was Bukhari who interrupted Jack by slapping the table.

'I refuse to allow my client to be subjected to this any longer. If you have any questions to ask Miss Dunn then please do so, but don't introduce some story that has nothing to do with why we are here.'

Jack kept his calm demeanour. 'I'm just trying to explain to Miss Dunn that by refusing to assist in our enquiries she is placing herself in a very dangerous position. Amanda, you were wearing the dead girl Trudie's bed socks, socks with her blood on them. Have you forgotten? You showed them to me; you told me they had belonged to her and that you liked them . . . so you didn't get rid of them like the other girls' clothes, did you?'

Everyone in the viewing room was listening intently. Laura turned to Glenda and whispered, 'His daughter's called Hannah, and she's not four and a half; what is he trying to do?'

'Break her,' Glenda said. 'Look at her, she's biting off her false nails. It's about time someone put the wind up her, and I think Jack knows exactly how to do it. I don't see the DCI interrupting, even though he looks a bit taken aback.'

Jack was looking at his file in a relaxed way, then quietly said, 'You love him, don't you?'

Bukhari looked as if he was about to interrupt but Amanda simply nodded.

'I think you're trying to help him by not answering any questions, but just repeating "no comment" is not going to help you, or him.'

'My client is fully aware of what she's doing,' Bukhari said firmly.

'Do you mean that your client is aware that if she assisted our enquiry, it would be in her best interests?' Jack responded. 'I do not believe that Amanda wants to spend the rest of her life in prison. Time is running out, so I would like to revisit some of the questions that were put to her earlier.'

Jack placed her mobile phone on the table.

'Is this your phone, Amanda?'

'Yes.'

Next Jack pulled out the mobile phone they had taken from Harold Miller.

'What about this one? We know you've been using it, since we have records of your calls, as well as your Snapchat conversations with one of the victims. You were arranging for her to meet you at Euston Station. In addition, we also have a postcard from Nadine O'Reilly, sent to her parents. Please read what she says, Amanda.'

Jack pushed the postcard forward as Amanda bit one of her false nails off, then took it out of her mouth. Jack continued.

'We have evidence that clearly implicates you in meeting these girls and encouraging them to return to the basement flat which you occupied with Rodney Middleton. Can you explain to me, if you had nothing to do with the murders, why you persuaded them to accompany you back to the basement flat?'

Bukhari interjected.

'You do not have any evidence that my client had any part in meeting these girls, or in encouraging Mr Middleton to take them to his flat.'

Jack gave him cool glance 'Amanda, were you forced to make these calls?'

Jack could see she was cracking. Her 'no comment' was almost inaudible.

'"No comment?" Are you really asking me to believe you never heard any screams, any howls of pain? Perhaps what really upset you and made you stay in that back bedroom, was when he was having sex with one or other of these girls. That really got to you. I think that, rather than stop what was happening, you hid out in that back bedroom because you knew when it was over you would be back in the bed beside him.'

Jack leaned over the table facing her. She wouldn't look at him and kept on chewing at her nails.

'Look at me, Amanda . . . *look at me!*' he said, raising his voice. 'Time is running out, but you still have an opportunity to tell the truth. If you do so, we will protect you, do you understand? Because your lover will not protect you. He is never going to be released, whether you try and help him or not, so you may as well stop lying and help yourself.'

Jack sat back and began to put the postcard and mobile phones back into the evidence bags. He then closed the file. He sat calmly, looking at Amanda.

When she spoke, her voice was tearful and childlike. 'What do you want me to tell you?'

Bukhari immediately asked for a break, but his request was refused – not by Jack, but by Amanda herself. Mrs Hardcastle passed Amanda a box of tissues. She plucked one out and blew her nose as Bukhari moved closer to her.

'Amanda, I advise you to adhere to our agreed strategy. I really need a break to talk to you.'

'Shut up,' she said. 'I'm not listening to you no more. I don't want a break. He's right. I hated it when Rodney took them into our bed, I hated it. Now I want to answer the questions properly because I don't want to go to prison.' She looked at Jack. 'So please tell me what I got to do now.'

A spontaneous round of applause burst out in the viewing room. It had taken a long time, but at last they had the result that everyone had hoped for.

Laura went to get a fresh round of tea, coffee and sandwiches. Anik had re-joined them, pale-faced and still not feeling well. He sat down, looking very subdued.

Two forensic experts had joined them, along with the SOC detectives, but there was a limit to the number of people allowed in the room. Glenda deemed it to be a full house and would not allow any more spectators in. The atmosphere was intense, as everyone waited to hear what Amanda would say.

The show was about to begin.

CHAPTER TWENTY-SEVEN

The tension in the viewing room had slowly begun to ease as they watched Jack quietly and gently guide Amanda through his questions. She spoke about her first meeting with Rodney Middleton, as a twelve-year-old runaway. She wanted to explain how she had never met anyone like Rodney, someone so kind and caring.

'He offered to help me find someplace to live and I told him I had no money, so he took me back to his flat.'

'Were there any other girls living there at this time?' Jack asked.

'No, he told me he had split up with his girlfriend. He said the sleeping bag was hers and he said she might come back, so because he had this girlfriend it never worried me about being there with him.'

Jack nodded. 'At what point did Rodney Middleton initiate a sexual relationship with you?'

'Oh, not until about six months after we met. He said he was concerned about doing it cos I was underage, and he could be arrested. That's why he used to keep me at home.'

'Did his girlfriend, the one who owned the sleeping bag, ever return?'

'No, but I was glad. It was like we was a married couple.'

Amanda explained that he would buy the groceries and do the cooking and cleaning, and would buy DVDs for her to watch, and games to play. She got upset when she recalled the time he started to get a bit nasty with her, locking her in the flat. Then, about eighteen months after she'd moved in, he asked her to go to Euston Station with him.

'I met Jamail, and we got talking. I said she could come back to the flat with us, like he told me to do. She was very young and a bit daft, and he was all over her, sending out for curry and takeaway food that she liked. But I didn't like it, and she got right on my nerves. Anyway, he moved her into our bedroom and told me I had to sleep in the little back room. I was really upset and told him I was going to leave. He got very angry and said he was going to get rid of her because she had told him she was pregnant. I didn't believe it cos she was only my age. Anyway, he give me a bottle of cider and a hamburger and told me to stay in the back room. He got a padlock and locked me in.'

Amanda pointed to Jack.

'You was right; I did hear some screaming . . . well, a lot of screaming. She left about a day or two later, then he let me out. He gave me some money, and I had to go and take a bag of Jamail's clothes to the charity dumpster. Then he went and did this attack on the local corner shop owner. It was stupid, cos he was arrested, and it left me on my own. But he called me from prison and told me that I was special. Said he wanted me to stay and wait for him, so I did. Then he was sent to some medical clinic, and I was allowed to go and see him.'

Jack checked through the files. The date Middleton committed his first assault now linked to the murder of Jamail. He'd also underlined the name Heather in connection with the sleeping bag and that they needed to continue to make enquiries about her.

'Did you not worry that perhaps something had happened to Jamail?'

'No, she was a pest, I didn't like her. What she left behind was rubbish, and Rodney told me she was rubbish too. When he come out from the clinic, we had a very nice time together.'

Amanda appeared to be enjoying the fact that she was now the centre of attention. She asked for a fresh bottle of water, flicking her hair from her face. Jack led her back to the next meeting at Euston Station, as she had gone off on a tangent and was telling them about which TV programmes she liked best and how Rodney would record some for her. Amanda spoke about a tall blonde girl they had met, but she hadn't stayed for long because she had tried to steal something. She couldn't remember her name but thought she was Scottish. Then she described another girl. Neither had come up on the police radar, but Jack knew there was a considerable amount of DNA that had not yet been matched.

'Tell me about Trudie,' Jack said.

'Well, I told you that we swapped things, like that bracelet, which was not a good deal as the clasp was broken, and I gave her my gold ring. We met her at the station, and she was all over Rodney. I couldn't believe it; it was like I didn't exist. It was pretty disgusting because he wanted the three of us to have sex in the same bed, but I refused. He put her into the back room, and she was really nasty, shouting and screaming and telling him she was going to the police. He got very angry and took her out, trying to persuade her to be nice, but she was a real bitch, biting and kicking. The next minute he had her in our bedroom.'

She drank some bottled water, then shrugged.

'He got rid of her, but he let me out. Gave me money to go and exchange some DVDs and have my hair cut. When I got back, she had gone. He was really angry because she had tried to steal some of the films he had bought. He said I needed to take the bed sheets to the laundromat cos she had stained them. He was washing down the shower and said that he hated the fact that she had used it, cos she had been on her period.'

'Did she leave her clothes behind?' Jack asked.

'Yeah, they were nasty, dirty. I took them to the charity bins. Rodney got mad when I was going to keep a sweater, and I said to him she had my gold ring, but then we made up the bed again, nice fresh clean sheets, and it was all good.'

'So, didn't any of the things he asked you to do strike you as suspicious?'

Amanda was getting tired. She yawned, sipping more water.

'Please answer the question, Amanda.'

'I had helped wash the shower before, cos it was a new one and he said he wanted to keep it clean, but I didn't think anything about it.'

'When did Nadine come to the flat to stay?'

Amanda shrugged and said she couldn't recall when it was. Rodney was helping her use Snapchat and had bought her the DVD of *Frozen*.

'I loved that film – I really loved it – but then she came back with us to the flat and she kept on playing it and singing that song, you know the one, "Let it Go". I said to her it was my film and she ignored me. Kept on singing that fucking song over and over again. It was driving me mad. Then it happened again, and this time I was really pissed off. I mean, Rodney and I had been really good together, you know, like man and wife. Then he turfs me out of our bedroom into the back room again and she moves in with him.'

'How long did Nadine stay with you in the flat?'

Amanda pursed her lips.

'Was it a lengthy period this time, or just a few days?' Jack asked, trying to keep her on track.

'They was doing drugs, taking some of his medication, and she was singing at the top of her voice. I got my bag and I said I was moving out. Rodney started to get really upset and came and sat with me in the back room, then he got into me sleeping bag with me. He was trying to make it up to me, bringing me hot chocolate, and promised he would send her packing cos he was tired of her and hated her singing, and . . .'

'Go on, Amanda,' Jack said gently.

She lowered her head, and her voice was a hoarse whisper. Jack had to ask her to repeat herself.

'The screaming happened, like an animal.'

'Did you think it was Nadine?'

'No, it was the rats. He had to get rid of the rats in the coal hole and some were caught in traps, and then they scream. I never went in there, cos I was scared of them; some were the size of cats. I got hysterical about them. He give me a sedative from his prescriptions, but they gave me terrible nightmares and sometimes I couldn't get out of bed in the morning cos my legs were so wobbly. Then there was the smell of the chemicals he'd used to get rid of the rats.'

'How did he get rid of the bodies?'

There was a flash of panic in Amanda's eyes, then Jack quickly said. 'Of the rats, I mean?'

'Oh, in the wheelie bins. He wrapped them up in plastic and tied them with string.'

'How big were they?'

Amanda held out her hands about eighteen inches apart. 'Like I said, some of them was the size of cats.'

'But you never actually saw one of the rats?'

'No, I never went in there . . . too creepy.'

'So, Nadine left. Did she also leave behind some of her belongings?'

'Yeah, but they weren't worth keeping.'

'Were you not surprised that she had left without taking her belongings? I mean, there had now been three different occasions when a girl had come to stay, and then when they left, you took their clothes and shoes and put them into the charity bins.'

'No, not all of them I didn't.'

'We have you on CCTV footage, Amanda, making three trips to the same charity collection bin, but you didn't find this in anyway suspicious?'

'No, why should I? I took a lot of his clothes as well, you know, for the poor in Africa.'

'But you mainly took the girls' clothes, and you didn't ever question why they would up and leave without taking their things with them?'

'Well, I did a bit, but I kept Trudie's bed socks cos I liked them. The rest I didn't want, so why not let some poor people have them?'

'What about toothbrushes and hairbrushes and things like that, did they leave those items behind as well?'

'Yes, they left them too . . . I tossed them out eventually, into the bins outside the flat.'

'OK, so you kept Trudie's socks because you liked them. So how do you explain the fact that they had traces of her blood on the soles?'

'I dunno, it could have been from the shower . . . I told you we got a new shower and Rodney liked it kept immaculate, scrubbing it with bleach. I might have trodden in it before she left cos he told me she had been on her period; the sheets was stained with it too.'

In the viewing room, Laura sat back in her chair, shaking her head.

'Can you believe this? She may be on the thick side, but my God she is doing a good job implicating herself. She had to have known what was going on. I think she's got more intelligence than we have given her credit for.'

Anik agreed, but at least they now had enough to charge Rodney Middleton with three murders.

'When is he being brought in?' Laura asked.

'Soon, and after this it's going to be very interesting. I don't think he has a leg to stand on with all the evidence we have against him, and with Amanda Dunn as a prosecution witness he'll get three separate life sentences, I reckon.'

Finally, Jack asked Amanda about the last time she had seen Nadine and what had happened afterwards.

'Well, he did it again. Rodney goes out and attacks the fucking Greek shop owner that knows him. They come round to arrest him, and he walks out with the knife he'd used, telling them he's guilty and he done it.'

'So, while he was in prison, did you live there alone?'

PURE EVIL | 334

'Well, not straightaway. I went and dossed down on the streets for a while, hung out a bit at Euston Station. They got good cafés, and it's warm there.'

'So, during this time did you keep in contact with Rodney?'

'Yeah, every day. He was making calls from the phone at Brixton to keep my spirits up, and he told me that if I needed anything I could call his aunt Joyce.'

'Did you visit Joyce Miller?'

'Yeah, but they wasn't that friendly. Gave me a few quid and told me to go back to Liverpool. But I was never going back there. It got me really angry, that awful big fat woman telling me to get out, that if I knew what was best for me, I would leave. For a while I sort of thought about catching the train; I mean they had been nice to me at that hostel place and I was really angry at him. That's when I called you, because I was fed up with him and I had no money, but he called me. I never said I talked to you cos it would have made him go ballistic. He told me that he had spoken to Mrs Delaney, the caretaker. She had a spare key so she could let me into the flat.'

Jack nodded. 'I remember, that's when you told me about the bracelet, and the ring you gave to Trudie.'

'Yeah, that's right. To be honest, I was still pissed off about being left on the streets, but when you offered to pay for the train ticket . . .'

'Can I just clarify: did you meet me before or after that phone call from Rodney to say that you could collect the spare keys to the flat?'

'Oh, it was before I think, yeah, cos I should never have told you about the bracelet. But I was still mad that when Trudie left, she took my ring. I never told him about telling you about that either.'

Jack tapped his notebook with the pencil and looked up.

'Can I just take you back to the evening when Rodney was arrested for the first assault?'

Amanda pulled a face, sighing.

'Yes, they took him away, arrested him.'

'So, how long were you with Rodney after he had committed the assault, and before the arrest?'

Amanda shifted in her seat, chewing at her bottom lip. Jack repeated the question before she answered.

'Few hours.'

'I see, so in those few hours with Rodney, did he tell you what he had done?'

'Not really, but he had blood on his shirt cuff. He said it was nothing, though.'

'What did he tell you to do?'

She was becoming anxious, squirming in her seat, crossing her legs and then uncrossing them.

'Amanda, you need to answer the question. Rodney had assaulted a man with a knife, someone he knew, as he was a frequent customer in the shop. We know he's already committed a similar offence in the past and served time for it, so he had to know that it would only be a short while before he was arrested. What did he tell you to do?'

Bukhari put up his hand. 'You're coercing my client. She has already made it clear that she was concerned that Mr Middleton had blood on his shirt sleeve.'

'I am asking what Mr Middleton asked Miss Dunn to do once he was arrested, because he had to know it would only be a matter of time before the police would be round.'

'I didn't know what he had done,' Amanda said firmly.

'I am only interested in exactly what Mr Middleton discussed with you, because shortly after his arrest, if we are to believe what you have told us, you left the flat and were living on the streets.'

'I never had a front door key to get back in. But I was hungry so I went out for some food and then I couldn't get back in,' she said.

'So, you left to buy food shortly after Mr Middleton was arrested, taking a holdall with all your belongings? That doesn't make sense, does it, Amanda?'

Amanda looked to Bukhari, then back to Jack. In her hands she was twisting the paper tissue she had used, tearing small strips from it, in exactly the same nervous way her mother had done when she was talking with Jack.

Jack flicked back and forth through his notes, then looked back up at her.

'Did you go to speak to Mrs Delaney?'

'I don't remember.'

'We have a statement from Mrs Delaney saying that she saw the arrests from her window. She claims that you came to her front door to tell her that Rodney could not help her husband carry the bins to the pavement, and that they were due for collection early the following morning.'

'Oh right, yes, he told me to do that. Sorry, I forgot.'

Jack looked over his notes. This was the time when the bins were not collected due to a strike. It must have freaked Rodney out as he obviously expected they would have been collected as usual.

'What else were you told to do?'

She gave a long sigh and shrugged. 'Clean up the kitchen and the bathroom.'

'What about the shower?'

'Well, yes, as it's in the bathroom.'

'So, after his arrests you remained at the flat until the following morning, waiting until one of the tenants helped to carry the bins to the pavement.'

'I wasn't waiting just for that. I had to get my head round being on my own.'

'Then what did you do?'

'Well, the bins wasn't picked up. I told him and he went funny, got really angry. But they was only out a couple of extra days before they were collected.'

'That would mean you stayed at the flat longer than you previously claimed.'

'Yeah, suppose so. I just forgot.'

'So what was the next thing you were instructed to do?'

'I used the hose pipe to clean out the bins after they'd been emptied; that was Rodney's job, he always did that.'

'So, he told you to do it for him?'

'Yes, and I hosed down the courtyard as well.'

'That was quite a big task, and you just complied with his wishes?'

'Yes, I did, because sometimes the bins smelt bad. I had helped him before, using bleach.'

Jack glanced at DCI Clarke, then back at Amanda.

'After the other girls left, was it usual that the bins were very heavy and often had a bad smell?'

Bukhari interrupted again, accusing Jack of trying to bully his client into admitting that she was involved in the disposal of bodies. Jack cut him off.

'I am simply asking her to describe the contents of the bins. She has admitted to cleaning them with a hose pipe. Bodies decompose quickly, and there would have been residue in the bins. We believe the bodies were dismembered in the coal hole, and the remains possibly washed in the basement flat's shower, before being deposited in the bins. The reason I'm pressing for Miss Dunn to answer my questions is the fact we know that on this specific date, contrary to expectations, the bins weren't collected in that area due to a strike. This delay would have resulted in quite a stench.'

Jack glanced at DCI Clarke and tapped the table with his pencil.

'Have you anything further to say, Miss Dunn, regarding my previous question?'

'No, I don't. And for your information, he never told me to leave. I just did that on my own.'

'When did you last speak to Mr Middleton?'

'I'm not going to answer that because I don't want to get any-one in trouble.'

Jack knew she must have been in contact with him recently, probably via one of the carers at the safe house where she had been held after leaving the hospital.

Jack looked at DCI Clarke again, who nodded.

'Miss Dunn, I believe you haven't answered all my questions honestly. You will, therefore, be charged as an accessory to the murders of Jamail Brown, Trudie Hudson and Nadine O'Reilly.'

Amanda gave a loud screech and hurled the empty bottle of water at Jack.

*   *   *

There was a short delay whilst Amanda Dunn was given her arrest details and told that she would be held in a secure place for pro-tective custody until she was re-questioned prior to her trial. She appeared confused, believing that after the interview she was going to be walking out, then started sobbing loudly.

Jack made his escape and left it to DCI Clarke and Bukhari to explain the proceedings to her. Jack was exhausted. His head throbbed as he hurried to the incident room to collect his brief-case. Anik was also getting ready to leave and looked over at Jack.

'Well done, very impressive. You made the first big crack in her defences when you brought up that story about you falling over your kid's toy and the curtain cord. What was that all about?'

'Oh that, I just made it up. I hope you're feeling better?'

'Yeah, a bit. Stomach's still churning, though, so I might take the day off tomorrow.'

'Well, you started the ball rolling for me. Good work.'

Jack watched Anik walk out. He was still irritating, but at least he'd made the effort to thank him. He picked up his briefcase as DCI Clarke opened his office door.

'Jack, a moment. That was impressive, if at times a bit unethical. I have made the decision that you'll lead the interview with Rodney Middleton on Monday. We all need a break, you more than anyone. It will give us the time to assess Amanda Dunn's statements and see how we can use them. So, I'm holding back until Monday, which will give you two days off. We can reconvene on Sunday to discuss the Middleton interview. It will also give you the time you need to be ready for him and the formidable Georgina Bamford. You made mincemeat of her prodigy, Mr Bukhari, but she's far tougher.'

'Thank you, sir.'

Clarke shook his head. I've got to say, Amanda Dunn even had me for a while, believing she was an unwitting pawn in the murders.'

'Almost had me too, sir. But I always had a gut feeling she was a devious liar.'

'Well, you get some rest and get ready for Monday. Good work, very impressive.'

Jack walked out and once he was alone in the corridor, all the tension of the last twenty-four hours was suddenly released. He pumped a fist in the air and let out a muted 'Yes!'

Tired as he was, he couldn't wait for Monday.

CHAPTER TWENTY-EIGHT

That Friday evening, Maggie prepared a dinner for Penny and Marius, laying the table in the dining room, not the kitchen.

Jack had spent most of the day in his office checking through files and making notes in preparation for the Monday interview, but after the elation of the Amanda Dunn interview, he had crashed back down to earth and now felt utterly exhausted. Maggie had to nudge him at the table a couple of times when he nodded off, but at least when he was conscious, and he seemed to enjoy the evening, amused to see his mother being so flirtatious and happy. He also found it a relief not to talk about, or even think about, the case. Maggie made him rinse his nose well with salt water before finally sending him to bed with an ice-pack mask on. Despite feeling a bit uncomfortable, he dropped into a deep, dreamless sleep almost immediately.

Saturday was a lovely crisp, sunny day and Maggie and Jack decided to take Hannah out to Richmond Park. She was so excited at seeing the ducks that she almost fell into the big pond. Penny cooked a roast lamb for lunch, with all the trimmings, and it was only after she had served the sticky toffee pudding that Maggie asked Jack where the car was.

'Oh, yes, been meaning to tell you,' he said. 'Had a big engine fault, so I'm waiting to see about exchanging it for something else, perhaps in a less conspicuous colour than pea green.'

If he'd thought Maggie would be pleased, he was wrong. 'We paid a decent price for it. Maybe I should go back to the man we bought it from and complain,' she suggested.

'I wouldn't bother,' he said. 'The insurance will cover the difference.'

'What do you mean? Did you have a prang or something?'

He shrugged. 'Kind of, don't worry, I'm sorting it.'

Maggie decided not to push it, but she was very suspicious. Penny changed the subject by saying that Marius had suggested that she take driving lessons. Jack and Maggie were open mouthed.

'Driving lessons?'

'Yes, I could then do a lot more for us, like taking trips out with Hannah. I've got to get a provisional licence first, but I want to try. I don't like the thought of getting stuck in a tedious routine; you only live once, don't you?'

After their initial surprise, Maggie and Jack nodded enthusiastically. Since she had met Marius, Penny had definitely become more outgoing, and they put her forgetfulness down to her anxiety about how Jack would react to her having a 'gentleman friend'.

When Penny had left them alone in the kitchen, they instantly looked at each other. Maggie burst out laughing.

'Your face, Jack, when she said she wanted to have driving lessons!'

'You looked gobsmacked too,' Jack protested. 'I mean, you're the one who's been thinking she had dementia, not me. And now, on the contrary, it turns out she's got a new lease of life.'

'Yeah, I know. And thanks to Marius we'll have the hall redecorated and a new coat cupboard, too.'

She leaned in close to him and whispered.

'Talking of a new lease of life, what would you think about taking me upstairs and ravishing me?'

Jack grinned. He scooped her up in his arms and carried her out of the kitchen but had to put her back down on her feet to go up the stairs. They walked up arm in arm and as they reached their landing they heard the high-pitched voice of the character from the *Frozen* movie singing, 'Let it go' Hannah was trying to join in. Jack stopped in his tracks, listening.

Maggie frowned. 'What is it? Don't you try and back out of ravishing me. I'm all geared up now and . . .'

'That song is from the film *Frozen*, isn't it?' Jack said, remembering Amanda telling them about the way Nadine had kept singing it.

'Yes, it's Hannah's favourite. We got the DVD for her last Christmas, remember. She loves it. There's now a sequel we need to buy her, actually. And when she's a bit older we could maybe take her to see the musical.' Maggie put her arms around him. 'What is it, Jack?'

'Nothing, nothing,' he said, his thoughtful expression replaced by a lascivious grin as he pushed open the bedroom door. 'Now, just be careful you don't bash my nose . . .'

* * *

They were woken by the sound of the doorbell. Maggie sat up quickly, looked at the bedside clock, then flopped back onto the pillow. She dug Jack in the ribs and he leaned up on his elbow.

'What time is it?' he asked blearily.

'Seven thirty on a Saturday evening! I thought it was an emergency call for me or something. Maybe Penny's expecting the boyfriend.'

The doorbell rang again, and Jack got out of the bed and put on his boxer shorts. Maggie snuggled down and pulled the duvet closer. 'I'm not getting up, whoever it is.'

Jack dragged on his dressing gown and hurried down the stairs, stopping midway as he could see through one of the stained-glass windows in the front door. It was Ridley.

Opening the door, Jack took a step back as he was presented with a large bouquet of red roses.

'For Maggie,' Ridley said with a broad smile. 'My apologies for calling unannounced but I wanted to get a few things sorted before my departure.'

'Where are you going?' Jack asked.

'The Caribbean for three weeks, leaving first thing Monday. Are you going to invite me in?'

Jack opened the door wider for Ridley, then closed it behind him. He started up the stairs. 'Give me a moment to put some clothes on.'

Halfway up the stairs he paused.

'Actually, why don't you follow me up and go into my office. I'll be right with you. Maggie's sleeping.'

Ridley left the bouquet of roses on the hall table and followed Jack up the stairs. He moved slowly, stopping once to take a deep breath before he continued. Maggie sat up when Jack entered the bedroom.

'Who was it?'

'Ridley,' Jack whispered. 'He bought you a huge bouquet of roses. I told him you were sleeping. He's in my office so that we won't disturb Penny if she goes into the kitchen for a cuppa.'

'Bit odd, isn't it? What does he want?'

Jack shrugged as he pulled on a pair of jeans.

'He's going on holiday for three weeks in the effing Caribbean. I dunno what he wants, but I'll get rid of him as soon as I can.'

Maggie sat up, watching him search for a t-shirt, and then almost losing his balance as he tried to put on a trainer.

'Do you want me to go and make coffee?'

'No. Listen, if you make an appearance, which I don't think you should, you didn't know anything about the situation he was in, right?'

'Right, "I know nuffink, guv – I'm just 'is wife, he never tells me nuffink."'

Jack laughed. 'You just stay put and I'll get rid of him as soon as I can.'

'How's your nose? You only yelped once when you were kissing me.'

Jack tapped his nose. 'I think I can go another round with you later tonight, so don't move.'

She grinned. 'I'll be waiting.'

Jack went down to the kitchen to fetch a bottle of whisky, some glasses and the ice tray, then hurried back up the stairs to his office. Ridley still wearing his coat and woollen hat was sitting in Jack's swivel chair, looking at the stacks of files and notebooks on his desk. He stood up as Jack came in.

'What have you done to your face, Jack?' Ridley asked.

'Oh, had a run-in with the banister, almost broke my nose. It's a lot better than it was . . .'

'You've certainly got a lovely shiner there!'

'Yeah, I'm keeping an ice pack on it whenever I can . . . I've got a big day coming up.'

Ridley drew up a hard-backed chair, leaving Jack to sit at his desk. He had folded his overcoat neatly placing it on the floor.

'Here, let me get the ice out while you pour – and not too much for me.'

Ridley expertly squeezed the ice out, plopping a couple of cubes into each glass and Jack poured a double measure. They clinked them together but neither of them said 'cheers'. They sat in silence for a moment as they drank. Ridley still looked very drawn; he had obviously lost a considerable amount of weight.

'It's over with the investigation, Jack . . . well, my part, anyway. The rest will be ongoing for some time, years probably; it's a hell of a fraud they're uncovering, quite apart from the murders. But for me, it's "Take a holiday and keep your mouth shut."' He sipped at his drink.

Jack noticed that Ridley's hand was shaking slightly. Sounding more affable than he felt, he asked, 'So, after your sunshine break, do you know what's going to happen?'

'Not yet. I'll be given details on my return, apparently. But I wanted you to know that your part in it did not go unnoticed. I'm obviously personally grateful – that goes without saying – but you won't regret assisting with the investigation. Your involvement can never be made public, but, as I just said, it has been noted and not just by me.'

Jack shrugged. 'I didn't do it for that; I just wanted to help. It's already forgotten, and you or whoever they are should have no concerns about me discussing it with anyone, if you're worried about that. That said, personally, I do have a few questions I'd like answered, because the whole thing still doesn't make sense to me. You put me at risk and, God help you, my wife, my daughter and my mother. Then you turn up with a bunch of roses and tell me you're off on holiday and everything's back to normal. But it isn't, especially not between you and me because I don't think I can trust you anymore.'

Ridley took another swallow of the whisky, before he carefully placed the glass back on the desk. 'Firstly, I want you to know that when I found out the dangerous situation I had inadvertently drawn you into, my priority was the immediate protection of you and your family. Your safety was the investigation's top priority, even before you traced Sandra's – I mean Lorna's – identity.'

Jack looked unimpressed. 'So at what point did you put a tracker on my car?'

Ridley sighed. 'OK, almost day one. I also lied about the ankle bracelet; that was also for my safety, so they always knew exactly where I was. Look, I apologise for the lies. I was not staying at the house because of the murder enquiry; it was really for medical reasons. I have been very sick. I needed treatment round the clock. The truth is, I still do.'

Jack could hardly believe it. He drained his glass and poured another one straight away, stopping himself from lashing out at Ridley. There was a long pause before Ridley continued his story.

'The night Lorna had arranged dinner with me, she said that it was time she told me the truth, that she had used me from day one as a form of protection. But, she said that she was meeting someone important before our dinner, someone who could provide a crucial piece of evidence. I didn't know evidence of what and she wouldn't tell me. I believe now that her obsession with finding Anton's killers turned into something else as she began to uncover evidence of fraud and money-laundering on a global scale. But she couldn't stop, even though she knew the more she uncovered, the more her life was at risk.'

'Well, she got that right,' Jack said brutally, 'seeing as she ended up dead in the boot of your car.'

'Yes, yes she did,' Ridley said.

'Did you find out where she was murdered?' Jack asked.

'No, but whoever she was meeting had to be the killer, or killers. From what you found in the Pimlico flat, it was obvious that she was careful not to take any of the evidence she had gathered with her, or any personal items: handbag, passport etc. As soon as you identified her, we checked the CCTV footage in the area of the flat, but it was spotty. There's footage of Lorna leaving the building and heading towards the main road. She was wearing a camel-hair coat, a headscarf and dark glasses but carried no briefcase, purse or anything. That was the last sighting of her alive.'

'So, all that bullshit you fed me, about being suspected of her murder was . . . what? More lies?'

'No, not to begin with; it was what else they eventually found inside my car that changed things.'

'You mean beside her naked strangled body?' Jack snapped.

Ridley sighed. 'I understand why you're angry. But I am trying to explain.'

'OK, so, tell me, what did they find in your fucking car?'

Ridley slowly pulled off his woollen hat, revealing his bare scalp with just a few tufts of hair. The skin looked raw and scabbed.

'Jesus Christ!' Jack exclaimed.

As Ridley drank the rest of his whisky, Jack could see how drawn and drained his face was with dark shadows beneath his red-rimmed eyes.

'I was barely alive when they found me, Jack. I'd had convulsions for two days, hardly being able to breathe, pissing and shitting myself, constantly vomiting. The only reason they reckoned I'd survived was because of my chemotherapy sessions, and the fact I'd spent so long in the shower, trying to get to my feet. By the time they got to me they had already found Lorna's body, and my car had been towed for examination by the forensic team.'

'You keep on referring to "they". Who exactly are "they"?'

'Well, at first it was just the Essex officers, as they were first to find my abandoned car, but they were replaced very quickly by the special agents.'

'So, they were the ones at your house when I called round to see you?'

'Yes, and more came later. Let me explain. You remember the poisoning of the Skripals using a nerve agent. The Government accused Russia of attempted murder, announcing punitive measures that included the expulsion of numerous Russian diplomats.'

'What the hell's that got to do with your situation?' Jack demanded curtly.

'I just need to explain that because Novichok is a binary chemical, which means it uses two or more ingredients that are either non-toxic or less toxic on their own, and only become active when mixed, it makes it easier to store and transport. It also makes it harder to detect. However, careless preparation can produce a non-optimal agent, with less deadly effects, and that's what happened in my situation. It's also the reason certain other assassination attempts have failed over the years.'

Jack was finding it hard to keep his anger under control. Early on he had suggested that perhaps Ridley had been poisoned. He had even mentioned the Skripals' case and the use of Novichok, and Ridley had denied it. Before he could confront him about it, Ridley continued.

'They had failed, using it on Lorna, so then they strangled her. The reason the PM didn't discover any obvious signs of substance, or injection sites, is because it's odourless, and can be deadly when inhaled, ingested, or simply by coming into contact with the skin. No more than one and a half minutes to kill you.'

'Jesus Christ, I don't know whether I can believe what you're telling me.'

'Please, let me explain. On the night we were to meet, it was bitterly cold, and I was wearing gloves. Thankfully when the forensic team eventually got to work on the car, they were all wearing forensic suits and masks, so they were protected.

'They discovered a minuscule residue of Novichok on my steering wheel. When that was confirmed, as you can imagine, all hell broke loose. By this time I had already got you involved, but they assured me that because the mixture that had been used was non-lethal, you were in no danger. At the same time, they began to monitor you. I had been medically protected inside a bubble supplying me with oxygen and heart monitors as they stripped down my house for any other substance. They didn't find anything, and I also had good security cameras, so anyone seen entering my house would have been caught. However, if what had happened to me had gone public, there would have been mass hysteria, hence the covert nature of the operation.'

Jack sat in total shock, shaking his head at the level of danger Ridley had exposed him to, as well as his wife and child.

'Jack, please believe me, before you met with me, I knew nothing about the Novichok. But we were getting nowhere on identifying Lorna Elliot, so I took a gamble and brought you in. I meant it when I said I have never known another detective with your abilities. And my faith in you proved justified. As soon as we knew who she was, and with what you found in the Pimlico flat, everything moved very fast.'

Jack shook his head wearily, then proffered the bottle of whisky to Ridley. Again, Ridley's hand shook as he held out his empty glass for a refill.

'Did you ever suspect that Lorna was lying to you?' Jack asked.

Ridley shook his head. 'No, and even if she was just using me at the start, I believe at the end she did have genuine feelings for me. But that last phone call was probably the only time I really heard her being honest. I had a gut feeling something was wrong: everything was different, the tone of her voice, her anxiety level. She must have suspected they were onto her, but I just thought she wanted to end the relationship. I loved her, Jack.' He sighed deeply. 'I'm glad I have been able to spend this time with you and tell you the truth. At times you've felt like a son to me, Jack, and I've hated deceiving you.'

Jack decided that it was time for Ridley to leave. He had heard enough and he just wanted him out of his sight. He was just about to encourage him to do so when Ridley nodded to the stack of files and, after a brief hesitation, Jack told him about the Rodney Middleton case. He kept it as brief as he could, though he deliberately didn't play down his own part in bringing it all to a head. Ridley was a good listener, never interrupting, as Jack explained how the case had turned into a real horror story with an as yet unknown number of young girls murdered. Once he had started, he found he couldn't stop, showing Ridley the photographs, explaining the forensic evidence and detailing the incredible lengths to which the teams had gone to accumulate all the evidence, finishing up with his account of Amanda Dunn's interview.

Ridley nodded thoughtfully. 'Very impressive, Jack. But the question is: will it be enough?'

*　*　*

Maggie had dressed and gone in to see Hannah and Penny. They had all crept down the stairs so as not to disturb Jack in his office. They had some tea and sandwiches and as it was now Hannah's bedtime, they went back upstairs to bathe her and read stories.

It was now almost 9.30 p.m. and Maggie was standing outside Jack's office door. She could hear Jack talking, so she went back downstairs to put the bouquet of roses into a vase.

She thought about offering them coffee and sandwiches but decided against it. Instead, she went and washed her hair, put some rollers in, and ran a bath with some perfumed oils. She lay in the warm scented water, thinking of their afternoon of lovemaking and smiling contentedly. But after a while she started to worry about why Ridley was still there and what they were talking about. After she'd got out of the bath, they still seemed to be at it, so she got into bed and picked up a novel she had been attempting to read for months, but after a few pages she fell asleep.

*　*　*

Jack was listening intently to Ridley's advice on how to handle Rodney Middleton.

Ridley impressed on Jack that he was dealing with a very intelligent psychopath, and it was going to be up to Jack to find a crack in his egotistical, narcissistic defences.

Ridley glanced through a file, then tapped it with his index finger.

'Use this; come out of left field with it. He won't be expecting it. He is being questioned about the three victims you have identified through their DNA; bring this up when he is least expecting it and then use his reaction. I believe this is the key.'

Ridley paused and went back to Jack's notebook. He took a pen and underlined some of Jack's handwritten notes.

Jack waited until he was finished. 'Going back to the beginning, can I ask you why you wanted me to double check the Rodney Middleton case in the first place. That's what started the whole ball rolling.'

Ridley nodded. 'I had an off the record talk with a probation officer that I'd been told was handling Middleton. I'd been on good terms with her on another couple of cases, and she suggested I talk to a psychiatrist who had treated him. He was very helpful and thankfully not too worried about patient confidentiality. He told me he was going away for a lengthy well-earned break and would be uncontactable. Perhaps that's why he opened up.'

'Dr Donaldson? Is that who you're talking about?' Jack asked.

'Yes, but, as I said, it was off the record and so I didn't write it up, but I would have mentioned it to you, given the opportunity.'

Ridley hesitated a moment before he continuing.

'Donaldson said that in his estimation, there was a real darkness deep inside Rodney Middleton, buried beneath a carefully constructed outer layer. Whatever had caused it, had to have occurred at a very young age. The little child, found hanging: you used that in the interview with Amanda. I'd use the same tactic with Rodney. It's possible that both of them are child killers and that's what unites them. They have killed and got away with it.'

Maggie woke up and saw that it was after midnight. She could still hear voices, but it sounded as though they were going downstairs. She sat up and was relieved to hear Jack laughing.

Ridley had waited until he was being shown out before pausing to use his mobile to order an Uber. Jack looked surprised and said that he had assumed Ridley was driving. Ridley smiled.

'I did drive here, Jack, but I need to get a cab to take me home because these are yours.' He held up a set of car keys.

'It's not a Mercedes, I'm afraid, but hopefully you won't be disappointed. It's the new electric four-door Tesla saloon, insured and in your name. You don't need to know how I got it for you; just call it a thank you from an old friend.'

Jack took the keys and went outside to inspect it whilst they waited for the Uber to arrive. He knew it would take a bit of explaining to Maggie, but as he sat at the steering wheel, he couldn't help grinning like a schoolboy. The interior even smelt amazing. Ridley sat in the passenger seat and looked on with an almost fatherly expression.

Jack turned to him. 'Tell me one thing, sir. You know you said you had the house under surveillance. Did they use gas works vehicles as their cover?'

Ridley laughed. 'Hell, no. We had officers in the house opposite, and one in a house at the rear. You have very accommodating neighbours. They thought it was something to do with the council. By the way, we also knew about your mother's friend; we had him checked out, seems to be a very decent, hardworking chap.'

Jack was still speechless when Ridley's Uber drew up. Ridley got out and walked to the car, moving slowly like an old man, and then bending painfully to get into the back. Ridley waved briefly, and then they were gone. Jack knew then that he might never see Ridley again, suspecting that his mention of going to the Caribbean was yet another lie. He was obviously a very sick man.

Maggie had been standing at the window, watching them. By the time Jack came back to the bedroom she was sitting up in bed.

'I have something to tell you,' he said, smiling.

'I know, it's that amazing car outside! Ridley let you have it as he's going abroad, right?'

Jack laughed, pulling off his t-shirt.

'You, my beloved, are always right. It's fully insured and it's ours; well, until he wants it back.'

Jack went into the bathroom to clean his teeth.

'He made one major proviso about the car – no learner drivers. So Penny will have to learn in yours, I'm afraid.' He closed the bathroom door and sighed, relieved that he wouldn't have to tell any lies about the car. He then stared at his reflection in the wash basin mirror.

He felt a deep sadness, thinking that he'd perhaps seen the last of Ridley. Ridley was the only person he had respected and loved as much as his adopted father, and in his own way he had become a father substitute. He had been best man at his wedding, godfather to their daughter. But Ridley had told him so many lies that even when the truth had emerged, the trust had gone for good. Jack knew their relationship was over and a hard lesson had been learned: never to put so much trust in another person again.

Tears started trickling down his cheeks and he quickly splashed cold water over his face and patted it dry. He needed to stop thinking about Ridley and focus on what he had to do. Jack had all of tomorrow to prepare for Monday. Then he would be ready to take on the devil and attempt to get inside Rodney Middleton's twisted psyche.

Jack switched off the bathroom light and went to get in bed beside Maggie. He lay next to her warm, beautiful body, which moved closer into the curve of his own. Just by being with her the sadness about Ridley lifted, and with her love entwined with his own, he was no longer alone.

He shut his eyes and fell into a deep, peaceful sleep.

CHAPTER TWENTY-NINE

Waking early, Jack quickly dressed and collected the things he needed to work on from his home office. He was just getting ready to leave, standing in the hall writing a note for Maggie, when Penny came down the stairs in her dressing gown.

'You're up early,' she said.

'I know. I'm going into the station. I didn't want to wake Maggie so she can have a Sunday lie-in. Will you tell her I should be home around noon? I just have to get a few things sorted for Monday.'

'Have you had breakfast?'

'No, I'll grab something from the canteen.'

'Did you do what you said you were going to do?' she asked.

He looked puzzled. 'What?'

'Book a table for you two to have a dinner together.'

'Not yet, but I'm on it. I'll maybe get it together when I get back today.'

'Do you want me to do it for you?'

'No, no, I've not thought where she'd like to go yet.'

Jack was gone before Penny could ask anything else, eager to drive the Tesla, and then get what he needed done quickly so he could return home.

He sat in the car with the manual beside him and started the engine. It was so quiet that for a minute he didn't think it was turned on. He then drove very slowly and nervously down the road. Gradually he gained confidence and picked up speed, enjoying his luxurious new wheels. It was certainly a big improvement on the pea-green Micra.

Carefully parking in one of the allocated bays at the station, he got out and then stood back to admire the car. Hendricks wheeled his motorbike past him and stopped.

'Wow, that is some car, Jack. It's a Tesla, isn't it? It's beautiful, but I always wonder if there are enough recharging points. Is it yours?'

'No, belongs to the wife; she's a surgeon. But I'm allowed to drive it at the weekends.'

Hendricks moved off as Jack took another admiring glance at the car before heading into the station. The canteen was half empty and he was able to get a fry-up and coffee with two rounds of toast. As he was eating it at one of the empty tables, Laura stopped by with an armful of Sunday newspapers.

'Have you read these?'

'No, I left before the papers were delivered.'

'Well, the cat is well and truly out of the bag. The DCI was throwing a fit a minute ago. The headline is "Teenage Killers" and they've already got interviews with Mrs Delaney, the bloody caretaker, and . . .'

'Just give me the papers, Laura.'

'Here you are. The *Sun* and the *Mail on Sunday*, plus the *Sunday Times* and the *Sunday Telegraph* . . .'

Jack took the papers from her as she went to the counter to order her breakfast. He quickly skimmed through the articles. It was the usual sensational, speculative stuff.

He tossed the papers aside. He felt an added pressure on him to get a result with Rodney Middleton, knowing that DCI Clarke would not be able to hold out on giving a press conference for much longer. Laura came back with a coffee and a toasted bacon sandwich.

'Hendricks said you're driving an amazing car.'

'Yep, it's the wife's, a brand-new Tesla.'

'Gosh, they cost a fortune. Hendricks said they're about seventy grand.'

'It's just on lease for her to try out. But it's definitely a step up from the green goblin car I was driving around in.'

He was unsure why he was lying about the car being Maggie's, but as Hendricks was already gossiping about it, he thought it best to try and shut them up.

Jack finished his breakfast, then went to his desk in the incident room with all the newspapers. He made a list of priorities for the team, then wrote on the incident crime board who he wanted in the boardroom. By 9 a.m. he was sitting waiting as Laura, Sara and Leon came in, then lastly Hendricks, carrying a coffee and toasted sandwich.

'Right, I'm going to be asking you to help me prepare for Monday. First, which one of you was asked to check out the mobile that Amanda Dunn got hold of in the supposed safe house?'

Sara held up her hand, taking out her notebook.

'I was there yesterday. Everyone denied they had allowed her to use their mobiles but eventually it came down to two possible people. One was the night staff nurse who said that her phone was always locked in her locker and Amanda could not have had access to it.'

Jack pointedly looked at his watch, and Sara flushed as she continued.

'Sorry, it's just that I wanted you to know that I had a bit of a run-around. Anyway, the day nurse wasn't on duty, so I had to go to her home in Surbiton. She denied it but was very nervous, and eventually told me that she had been preparing to leave, and had her coat and bag with her, when Amanda asked about her family. She told me that she opened her bag and showed Amanda photographs of her two toddlers on her phone. She said that she was certain that she had put the phone back in her bag but had been distracted for a few moments as the replacement officer was late . . .'

'For Christ's sake, get to the point, Sara.'

'Well, when she got home, she realised that she didn't have her phone and she immediately called the safe house. They told her they searched Amanda's room and found the phone beneath her bed. This was the evening before she came into the station for her interview.'

'I hope there's a point to this story,' he said through gritted teeth.

'It does, sir. I retrieved the phone and checked the outgoing calls. The one call made that evening was to another mobile. It was fifteen minutes long and it was to Georgina Bamford.'

'What?' That was not what Jack had been expecting.

'Yes, sir, I didn't say anything to anyone as I felt it might be important that Ms Bamford was not aware that we knew she had been contacted.'

'Well, that is very interesting, and good not to tip her off. OK, next on the agenda, I want all the photographs of the victims, as well as the photographs taken from Middleton's aunt Joyce, the ones from her bedroom wall. We have them all, yes?'

'Yes, we also have the family album taken from the same property,' Laura said.

'Good. I want those photographs grouped together. Please select any photographs from the album that have Middleton as a child, or any with his aunt, father and mother; these all need to be stacked together in the same folder.'

Jack checked his notes before continuing.

'Next, I want to get our forensics ducks in a row. Contact Daniel Burkett to compare the amount of DNA evidence from inside the basement flat with the DNA evidence from the coal hole. I also need to know which items of Middleton's clothing had blood on them. I want photographs of the items in a second file. Laura, can you handle that?'

'Yes. What about the tools?'

'Photographs of any of them that had Middleton's DNA on them, and any of the victims'. I think there is a wire brush and also the sharpened screwdriver, along with the saw. Plus, details of the company that sold the chemicals and rat poison in a third file, along with Glenda Bagshot's CCTV footage. That has to be ready to be shown on the small monitor screen inside the main viewing room.'

Jack glanced up from his notes and nodded to Leon.

'I need all the medical notes that I recorded and statements from Dr Seymour, Dr Donaldson and Dr Burrows. I also need the statement from Mavis Thornton at the hostel, from the probation officer, and from the firefighter we interviewed . . . What was his name, Sara?'

'Er, Brian Hookam.'

'Good, yes. These are to be added to file number three. OK, now last but not least, I want a trace on Middleton's birth mother. She left the UK when he was seven years old and returned to Ghana; see if there is anything in passport control that far back.'

'Sir, I think we did try a trace weeks ago, but it was unsuccessful,' Sara said.

'I know, but I want you to have another go. There's a photograph in the plastic container we removed from the coal hole, so use it to see if anyone remembers her. Also, double-check the previous address for Rodney Middleton, the one before the fire. I also want that photograph to be in file one – it's very important.'

'We don't have much to go on as we never established her correct name,' Sara said, 'and they never married . . .'

'Well, if you look at the photograph from the coal hole, it's a young girl in school uniform. The team on the ground bagged it without examining it, but we've since discovered that Middleton wrote a message on it which makes me think it's his mother. It's in pencil and very faded, but the name looks like Abena Mensah. I did try to trace her but gave up when I found that Mensah is a very common Ghanaian surname. It might be wrong but try your best. Leon, you're the IT super sleuth, so you take that on as well as the other things I've asked you to check out. Start with births, OK?'

Jack repeated everything again to make sure they knew exactly what they were all doing, emphasising that it was important they delivered everything by the end of the day, so he was ready for Monday morning. He left them sitting in rather subdued silence as they each checked over their notes.

Laura pushed her chair back and suggested they get cracking. She had found the meeting rather unnerving as Jack seemed to be on speed. He had been impatient and abrupt and a couple of times she felt that he had deliberately undermined her. When Sara asked her if the files should be in different colours, she had snapped at her: 'How the hell would I know? Do whatever you want.'

Jack had gone in DCI Clarke's office to discuss the press coverage. Clarke was fuming, as the phones were ringing non-stop and the press were now gathered outside the station questioning anyone who was entering. Jack smiled and suggested they all say 'no comment' but Clarke didn't find it amusing.

'I'm about to go to Scotland Yard for a meeting with the superintendent and I need every bit of ammunition you can give me, Jack,' he said.

'Well, we have Amanda Dunn arrested and charged, so that's a plus. By the way, as a matter of interest, sir, we have proof that she called Georgina Bamford on a mobile she swiped from one of the nurses at the safe house. She had a fifteen-minute call with her the night before she came in for her interview.'

'You're kidding me.'

'Interesting, isn't it? And as yet she doesn't know that we know. It confirms that they're in cahoots and is further proof that Miss Dunn is a devious bitch.'

Clarke nodded, but he clearly wasn't sharing Jack's confident mood.

'I see you had the team in a conference this morning?'

'Yes, sir. Preparing for tomorrow. I don't want anything falling through the cracks.'

Clarke grunted. 'Well, I need to get myself over to Scotland Yard. I'll see you here first thing tomorrow. I'll have Middleton brought in a van, and make sure his face and head are covered. He will travel with two outriders and drive straight through the back gates. And I want to vet anyone in the viewing area . . . there were too many in there during the Amanda Dunn interview.'

As they walked out of his office, Jack could feel the DCI's tension and hoped he would be calmer in the morning. It was another reminder of how much Ridley's calm presence was missed, making everyone around him feel relaxed.

While the team worked flat out on acquiring all the material he had requested, preparing the files and putting them in the order he wanted, Jack remained available for them until after lunch. He was impressed with the way Laura was overseeing their work with calm efficiency. If she had been disgruntled at the start of the day, she was now working at full steam. She had only one query for Jack and that was about Leon as, due to it being a Sunday, he was having problems making any headway with tracing Abena Mensah. Immigration had not been at all helpful.

'Yeah, I had the same problem,' Jack acknowledged. 'I think the people who have the answers are Joyce Miller and her husband.'

'If I manage to get everything done here, would you mind if I paid them a call, just to see if I can get anything more from them?' she suggested.

He gave Laura one of his warmest smiles.

'If anyone can get them to talk, Laura, you can. Go for it and just let me know the outcome.'

'There is something else,' Laura said. 'Anik is due in this afternoon, and his nose is pretty out of joint, so could we maybe do the interview together? I think he would appreciate it if you suggested it.'

'Yeah, why not. I'll leave a memo on his desk, asking if he could give us a hand.'

She was about to walk off when he caught her hand.

'Thank you, Laura, I really appreciate yours and the team's efforts. I need it, and I'm grateful.'

She flushed, and he could see how much it had meant to her. Her support meant a great deal to him as he felt confident he could leave the station in her hands. He needed space to make himself completely ready for the ensuing combat with Rodney Middleton.

He also couldn't wait to get back into the Tesla and to give Maggie a spin in it when he got home.

*   *   *

Laura and Anik had to exit the station through a throng of flashing cameras, before arriving at the Millers' council estate just before 7 p.m. Laura pressed the bell and after a few minutes Harold Miller eased open the front door.

'Sorry for the intrusion,' Laura said pleasantly, showing her ID, 'but we just have a few questions, if you wouldn't mind.' Anik held up his own ID as he also reintroduced himself.

Harold was not eager to let them in. 'At this time? On a Sunday? I've just given Joyce her supper, you know. It's not a very convenient time.'

Laura kept her pleasant smile in place. 'It won't take long, I assure you. And it is important.'

'You have already been here and have taken personal items, as well as my mobile,' Harold grumbled. 'I just don't understand why you have to come unannounced on a Sunday. My wife isn't going to be happy about this at all.'

Anik decided to take the reins. 'You could always come back to the station with us, if that would be more convenient,' he suggested.

Harold stepped back, and Anik and Laura stepped further into the hallway. He then closed the front door behind them.

'I've been under a lot of pressure, and I don't want any trouble. My wife won't want you in her room. She's having her supper and doesn't like anyone with her; this is very distressing for her.'

Laura smiled. 'If you'd prefer, my colleague can sit with you in the kitchen while I talk to your wife.' They had actually already discussed this between them before they arrived and felt it would be more beneficial for them to ask their questions separately.

Harold knocked on his wife's door and opened it a fraction. They could hear him saying that a lady detective wanted a few words, then Joyce angrily saying she was not going to talk to anyone.

Laura moved forward, pushing the bedroom door open wider.

'It is imperative that you do give me a few moments of your time, Mrs Miller. Step away from the door please, Mr Miller. The sooner I talk with your wife, the sooner we'll leave.'

He slunk away, and Laura closed the bedroom door behind her. Anik then accompanied Harold to the kitchen.

Despite having seen Joyce Miller on a previous occasion Laura was still taken aback by her extraordinary bulk. The trolley beside her was stacked with cartons of Kentucky Fried Chicken, bowls of macaroni cheese and plates of chocolate cake, as well as ham rolls. A gardening show was playing on the huge plasma TV screen and Joyce picked up the remote and turned it off.

Laura moved closer to the bed, pulling up a small hard-backed chair. Joyce was using a plastic fork and spoon, as well as her fingers to split apart the fried chicken sections. She ate remarkably daintily, with her tiny hands and painted fingernails, popping sections of the chicken into her mouth. Her lipstick spread over her chin as she dabbed her lips with paper napkins.

'I want to ask you about your nephew's mother,' Laura began.

Joyce appeared not to be listening as she started eating forkfuls of macaroni cheese. Laura waited a few moments before she repeated the question.

'I've been asked about her before, but I can't tell you anything,' Joyce said eventually.

'Do you recall her name?' Laura persisted.

'No, why would I? But she was no good, let me tell you. My brother was a very handsome man, with a good job and earning good money.'

'She was never married to him?'

'No, thank goodness. But she got him because she was pregnant and he, like a fool, let her move into the house. The whole family was against her because it was obvious she was using him.'

'What if I was to tell you that her name was Abena Mensah?'

'Well, if you know her name, why did you ask me?' She took another forkful of macaroni cheese.

'I just want you to confirm it,' Laura said.

'It could have been,' Joyce said non-committally. 'Her nickname was Beanie, that was what Anthony called her. She was out for what she could get.'

'She was very young, wasn't she?'

'Old enough to know an easy target. It broke me and my brother up because he was such a fool about her. Then when the baby came, she couldn't look after him, not to mention cooking or doing any housework. She was a right slut.'

'How often did you see her?'

'As little as possible. But I worried about the baby, and sometimes I'd take him and give him a bath and cut his nails. She never changed his nappies and he'd be stinking.'

'So Abena was with your brother for quite some time?'

Joyce plucked off a bit of the chicken wing and sucked at the bone.

'I don't remember. Like I said, I never went round there much. A few years, maybe five or six . . . Until he met Karen, anyway. Then it was clear to him what a big mistake he'd made. Karen was a lovely girl. Why are you asking me about that wretched Abena? He threw her out.'

'When was that?'

'I don't know, but I had Rodney here for a while. Harold wasn't comfortable with having a youngster around, and he was a bit of a handful.'

'We've not been able to find out when Abena left the UK, so if you could try and recall the dates when you say your brother threw her out.'

'Went back to Ghana, that's where she went.'

'You say it was after five or six years of living with your brother?'

Joyce had begun to sweat profusely and was using the paper tissues to wipe her face and neck, leaving grease marks from the fried chicken.

'So, it would be around 2006, is that correct?' Laura asked.

Joyce shrugged, so Laura continued.

'Your nephew is now twenty-four, isn't he? And we have been told he was seven years old when she left.'

Laura was beginning to lose her cool, as Joyce had now started enthusiastically on the chocolate cake.

She took a deep breath. 'It must have been difficult for you to take care of him, considering your situation; you're not very mobile, are you?'

'Listen, I was never like this in those days. I was always a size twelve, dear. What happened to me is not your business. I had a band fitted and it was the worst thing I could have done. I had a terrible time, and it got infected, so I had to have it removed. I was bedridden and depressed about being so poorly.'

'I understand that often your condition can be caused by experiencing a tragedy or witnessing a violent act?' Laura said, hoping that might trigger something.

But Joyce just continued eating without taking the bait. Laura began to feel nauseous at the amount of food being consumed, albeit in delicate mouthfuls.

'So let me get this straight,' she said. 'Abena Mensah left your brother around 2004 to 2006, when her son Rodney was seven years old. Is that correct?'

Joyce reached to her bedside to pick up a large bottle of Coke.

'Mrs Miller, would you please answer my questions? I need to know exactly when Abena Mensah left your brother's house.'

Joyce unscrewed the Coke bottle and took a long drink. The sweat was now rolling down her face.

'I was told she did come back, and said she wanted to take Rodney.'

'When was this?'

'I can't remember. I was ill. But that's what I was told.'

'By your brother?'

'Yes.'

'Was he with Karen when Abena returned?'

'No, he was living on his own with Rodney. Then he bought a new house.'

Laura decided to change tack. 'Did your brother love Rodney?'

'Yes, of course he did.'

'Did you love him?'

'Yes, of course.'

'Did Rodney like Karen?'

Joyce shook her head, and for the first time appeared caught off-guard. Laura decided to go for the jugular.

'His own mother left him and his father then marries a very pretty young blonde woman and they move into a new house. How did he react to that development in his life?'

Joyce started to eat again, as if she hadn't heard.

'His two half-sisters, those adorable little girls, burnt alive . . .' Laura said, in a desperate attempt to regain Joyce's attention.

She stood and picked up the chair, putting it back against the wall.

'You know what I think, Joyce? Something happened that was so awful, so hideous, that it's made you hide in here. I believe it's connected to your brother, and I think that's why he pays to keep you in this state.'

Joyce drank from the Coke bottle again, then screwed the top back on.

'Or it is connected to Rodney, who is going to be charged with three murders. You have an opportunity to tell me what drove that young man to kill three innocent girls, Joyce.'

She unscrewed the Coke bottle again and took two gulping mouthfuls.

'Something happened at the house with Abena, didn't it? Were you there? Did you witness what happened? Was Rodney with you? Why don't you answer me?'

Joyce pursed her lips. 'Leave me alone. Go away. I have nothing to tell you.'

'Detective Jack Warr, who you met, spoke to two different psychiatrists, who both described Rodney as a lost soul. Perhaps at one time he was, but I think you know what turned the lost soul into an evil one. Now I will leave you in peace to finish your supper.'

Laura walked out as Joyce sat with tears streaming down her cheeks, still unable to face what she had buried in her bulk for years.

Laura stood in the hall, her hands clasped together in frustration. Anik saw her from the kitchen and closed his notebook. He thanked Harold for his time and walked out as Harold scurried behind him to open the front door. Laura hurried out and he followed her to the car.

'You alright?' he asked.

'Not really. I tried every possible way to get her to tell me the truth, but I couldn't make her talk. She knows something, though. I have a feeling her brother did something horrendous to Abena Mensah, or maybe Rodney did something to her, or he was a witness. I just found it so obnoxious watching her eating and refusing to answer.'

Anik opened the car door for her, then walked round to get into the driving seat.

'So, how did you get on with Harold?' Laura asked. 'If you had seen what he had given her to eat . . . talk about being a – what's the word they use to describe someone who is giving an alcoholic drink? An enabler. She's eating herself to death with his help.'

Anik started the engine. 'Her brother pays Harold to care for her, and the rest is claimed on benefits. Two carers split the washing and dressing chores, but not on Sundays, when he has to do it, and that includes changing her incontinence pads, which he hates doing, as you can imagine.'

'Did he say anything useful about Rodney's mother?' Laura asked as they drove out of the car park and headed back to the station.

'He couldn't remember her name,' Anik told her, 'as he only met her a few times, but he said she was very pretty, but very young and naïve. She'd been a student, but her family, who weren't living in the UK, ran out of money to fund her education, so she got a job in a café and that's where she met Rodney's father. He got her pregnant and moved her into his old house. But she wasn't used to cooking or housework and by the time she had Rodney, she was basically unable to cope.'

'Yeah, Joyce brought that up,' Laura said.

'Apparently the Middleton family hated her, said she was a free-loader. According to Harold, Joyce took on a lot of responsibility with the baby. He also said that back then Joyce was attractive and had a good job as a secretary. She and her brother were very close at this point.'

'Yeah, I gathered that from Joyce, too.'

'Harold basically said Rodney was dumped on them. He also said that Joyce later miscarried, almost at full term; they knew it was dead but she still had to go through a proper birth. Harold said Joyce was convinced the stress of having to look after Rodney was the cause.'

Laura looked thoughtful. 'She never mentioned that. She told me she had to have a gastro band fitted and it went wrong, but must have been a considerable time later.'

'Yes, apparently after the stillbirth she put on a lot of weight. He said after she had a band fitted, it was impossible for them to have Rodney anymore because it became infected, and she was bedridden.'

'Seems you got along with Harold,' Laura said. 'He certainly told you most of what I got out of her.'

'It took a lot of patience,' Anik said. 'But eventually I was able to steer him to when Abena went missing. He couldn't remember the exact date, but he didn't think she'd gone back to Ghana because he remembered a big row on the phone. He said Joyce was shouting at her brother because Abena never really left but had turned up again, wanting to take Rodney back to her family, as they had sent her money.'

'Wow, this is good . . . go on.'

'Harold got a bit anxious at this point. He reckoned Joyce's brother would gladly have let Rodney go, because by this time he was in a relationship with Karen, and planned to marry her.'

Anik stopped at a traffic light.

Laura nudged him. 'Don't keep me in suspense, what else did he tell you?'

'It was a bit sketchy, but he remembered Joyce going round to her brother's. Afterwards she came back and told Harold that Rodney's mother had gone back to Ghana. He thought it was strange because instead of going with her, Rodney remained with his father, even though he'd seemed eager to get rid of him.'

The lights changed and they drove on. Anik explained that Harold had become very anxious again and kept repeating that he didn't want to get anyone in trouble. 'He said that when Anthony married Karen they had moved into a new house. Karen didn't like Rodney, but Joyce wouldn't have him stay again, so he only saw him infrequently. After the still birth Joyce started to gain weight and was eventually bedridden. She was in a very depressed state and couldn't attend the christenings of the two little girls, but they were always made welcome at their flat. Joyce adored them but Anthony always stayed in his car when he dropped them off and collected them. He then started paying Harold to look after her.'

'Why did he do that?'

Anik shrugged. 'It felt to him that there was some secret between Joyce and Anthony and Rodney, something that tied all three of them together.'

'Did he talk about how things were before the fire?'

'No, I tried but he wouldn't talk about that. All he said was that after the fire Joyce's brother was out of control and by that time Karen was back on drugs. He remembered that they were called by the hospital as near-relatives for Rodney as he had severe burns. Joyce refused to let him come and stay to recover and she never saw him again.'

'But Harold remained in touch with him, because he collected him from Brixton and drove him back to his flat. Plus, he bought him a mobile.'

'I asked him about that and he said that was the way he kept in touch, because Joyce wouldn't let Rodney into their flat.'

'Did you get a feeling that they blamed Rodney for the fire?'

'Well, Harold said Joyce has always had the little girls' photographs pinned up where she could see them. They are the first things she sees in the morning and the last thing she sees every night, but there are no photographs of Rodney; there used to a couple, but after the fire she tore them up, and she hated even hearing his name.'

They arrived at the station and made their way through the press, who were still hovering around the front entrance. It was almost 10 p.m. and they got straight down to typing up their report for Jack.

'I'm going to give him a call to give him the headlines,' Laura said.

'Which are?' Anik said.

'That Abena Mensah was possibly murdered, either by Rodney or by his father, and Joyce knows it. That's what binds them together. We have no proof, but I think Jack can still use it. In the meantime, we can continue checking into immigration and passport control, and if we still get no result, we should check out the house and garden where they used to live, the one before the fire, to see if her remains are there.'

'Bloody hell, this just gets worse at every turn,' Anik said, shaking his head.

'Too right, and you know if Jack hadn't been so diligent in investigating Middleton, he could have got away with it.'

* * *

After Laura's call, Jack sat in his office and thought about how he would use the information. He had intended to be home earlier to spend time with Maggie, but as usual, he'd been so immersed in preparing for the interview, he'd not arrived back in time to even see her, let alone take her for a ride in the Tesla, as she had gone to bed to be up early for her morning shift. After a while he turned off the light and went to bed himself. Maggie had left a mug of hot milk on his bedside table, along with a sleeping tablet. He wanted to wake her and kiss her, but instead he just sipped the warm milk and took the sleeping tablet.

He was ready for the showdown.

CHAPTER THIRTY

Jack had shaved and showered by 7.30 a.m. He had asked Maggie to show him how to use her makeup to cover his black eye and it now looked almost invisible, the swelling having gone down completely. He doused himself with cologne and chose a white shirt with a starched collar and cuffs, which Penny had ironed. He then picked out a tie, trying a few before he was satisfied, and put on a pair of his smartest trousers, with a good sharp crease, and lastly a pair of side-zip boots. He tried on a couple of jackets and eventually chose a good quality tweed he had purchased from a charity shop. He combed back his thick curly hair, using a little bit of gel. After checking in the wardrobe mirror, he reckoned he looked the business.

Collecting his briefcase from the office he found a note on it with a big red heart and a row of kisses, wishing him good luck. He was about to walk out when he remembered about booking a restaurant for dinner. He thought for a moment, then decided he'd try to get a table at the popular Firehouse as soon as it was open to take bookings.

He knew today he would need all his wits about him, and just driving in his new car made him feel more confident. The press were waiting outside the station, but Jack had called ahead for the gates to be open and ready for him to drive straight into the backyard. One of the morning's newspapers had a new headline: Suspect in Hammersmith killings to be charged.

Waiting on his desk in the incident room was a fresh mug of coffee and the files he had requested, all neatly numbered with large, printed cards on the front of each. He double-checked the order and then stacked them in a cardboard box and placed them on his desk. He could feel the buzz in the incident room as everyone gathered, eagerly waiting for the prison wagon to arrive.

Glenda watched the lights come on in the main viewing room. She knew that any moment Middleton would be led in. Jack remained standing beside DCI Clarke, while Ms Bamford sat opposite them, nonchalantly inspecting her bracelet. She had a leather-bound notebook in front of her with an elegant gold pen beside it. No mobile phones were allowed.

Anik arrived in the viewing room and took a seat, shortly joined by Laura. Glenda insisted that no more people should be allowed in.

'She looks as if she's waiting for someone to bring her a glass of wine,' Laura said, nodding at Georgina Bamford.

'Don't let her appearance fool you, Laura; she is one sharp cookie,' Glenda cautioned. 'She's got quite a fearsome reputation, and believe me, her claws will be sharpened.'

There was a knock at the door as the officers accompanying Middleton arrived outside the interrogation room. They led him in and were given the nod to remove his handcuffs. He was wearing a worn black t-shirt, black trousers and black trainers.

'He's taller than I thought,' Glenda said quietly. She leaned forwards.

'He reminds me of OJ Simpson, a younger version obviously.'

'I think he's a cross between him and that Night Stalker, the one in LA,' Laura said. 'His hair is longer, but his eyes are similar. It looks to me as if he's been working out in prison, too. Look at those muscles,' she added, before someone told her to shush.

The intercom was turned on so they could hear each person in the interview room introduce themselves. Rodney Middleton said his name with his head bowed. Then Clarke read him his rights, speaking clearly and slowly. Middleton did not react.

Jack took out a file, laying it down on the table and opening it. He smiled across at Middleton.

'Before I begin to question you, Mr Middleton, I think it is important that I give you some information regarding the DNA evidence we have gathered. I want you to clearly understand what exactly DNA is, because I am aware that you have had no formal education, and have no GCSEs or A Levels. You have also not been able to gain any employment and have lived the majority of your adult life on benefits – although I am sure it has required some degree of intelligence to work the system.'

'I find all this unnecessary and insulting,' Ms Bamford said sharply.

Jack shrugged. 'I am simply attempting to inform your client regarding the complex subject of DNA.'

Jack had already caught the look in Middleton's eyes and noticed the way he tightened his lips. He knew that by focusing on his lack of formal education and his inability to earn a living, he was chipping away at his narcissistic self-image. Middleton clearly didn't like appearing inferior.

Jack produced a stack of documents and photographs.

'Now, even this tiny amount of blood' – he picked up his pencil and on a blank sheet of paper made a small dot – 'can provide vital DNA evidence, as the forensic scientists can tell us whose blood it is more precisely than a fingerprint. Now, to someone without formal education, this may be hard to grasp, but when our forensic scientists are evaluating DNA samples, they can also establish genetic relationships.'

Again Jack noted how Middleton stiffened at the mention of his lack of education. Jack now began to place photographs of the tools removed from the coal hole in front of him. He pointed to the arrows on each photograph, indicating where traces of DNA had been detected. Ms Bamford impatiently leaned back in her chair as Middleton looked at each photograph. He paid close attention to the wire brush as Jack explained that they had discovered DNA caught between the wires and had concluded that it was not skin or tissue from the outer body, but scrapings from a human heart.

With that discovery, they knew the victim could not have been alive.

In the viewing room, Anik shook his head. He could not understand what Jack was doing, going into such detail about DNA.

'You think he's trying to bore him into talking?' he suggested.

Glenda frowned, nodding towards the viewing room.

'Look what he's showing him now.'

Jack had been explaining how they had collected the samples from the bins in the basement, and about the extent of blood pooling in the coal hole. Then he leaned back in his chair. 'So, Mr Middleton, you now understand about the evidence collected from the basement yard and the coal hole. Let me show you the next section.'

'How long is this going to go on for?' Ms Bamford snapped.

Jack ignored her as he began to lay out the crime scene photographs from inside the basement flat. There was an enlarged picture of the hairs taken from the drain.

'This is very interesting regarding DNA. As you can see, four of the tangled hairs discovered in your bathroom, and in the drain of the bath, had the small bulb or root attached. This made it very easy for the forensic scientists to match them with the samples from the victims' hairbrushes. We gained further identifiable DNA from toothbrushes provided by the parents of the three victims. Now, another interesting point is contamination. This is important because we have two locations. We have the basement flat, where you lived with Amanda Dunn, and then we have the coal hole. So, it was imperative that we were able to prove, via DNA, that certain samples could not have been brought into that flat from the coal hole. This tells us with a high degree of certainty that no one other than yourself could have been responsible for those samples being there.'

Jack could sense that Ms Bamford was about to interrupt, so quickly slapped down photographs of the bed-linen, pinpointing semen stains and both pubic and head hair.

'Please can we forgo any more of your educational lectures, or I will be forced to end this interview,' she snapped.

'I am, Miss Bamford, simply making sure that your client, despite his lack of education, fully understands the nature of the forensic evidence.'

As if to show that he did not take the repeated jibe about his lack of education seriously, Middleton just shrugged. Jack now removed the second file from the box and pulled out the three photographs of the victims. First was Jamail. With one finger he pushed the photograph across the table closer to Middleton.

'Do you recognise the girl in this photograph?'

'No comment.'

Jack did the same with the photograph of Trudie.

'No comment.'

When he showed him Nadine's photograph, he got the same reply.

'So, Mr Middleton, you do not recognise any of these three girls? Yet we know that each one of them lived with you in your flat.'

'No comment.'

'You, along with your girlfriend, Amanda Dunn, picked up these three girls on different occasions from Euston Station and you both took them back to your flat, didn't you?'

'No comment.'

'After a certain period of time, when you were bored or when Amanda became upset by their continued presence, you got rid of them, didn't you?'

'No comment.'

'I think you killed these girls in your bedroom or in the coal cellar, where you later dismembered them. You then wrapped their body parts in bin liners and put them in the bins, ready for collection, didn't you?'

'No comment.'

Middleton was beginning to enjoy himself, rocking back and forth in his chair.

'I would like you to look at some CCTV footage which shows you carrying the bins to the pavement outside your basement flat,' Jack continued. 'Pay attention, if you would, to the way one item drops from the bin and you quickly put it back.'

The CCTV footage was shown. Middleton yawned.

'That is you, isn't it, Mr Middleton?'

'No comment.'

If Jack was becoming impatient, he didn't show it. He remained affable, smiling at Middleton as if he was enjoying himself too, as he recounted the two occasions on which Middleton had assaulted a shop owner.

'I am – or at least I was – confused by your actions. You seemed intent on being arrested, especially on the last occasion when you were arrested only a short time after assaulting the corner shop owner.'

Middleton glanced towards Ms Bamford as if he expected her to challenge Jack's account, but she gave a small shake of her head.

'Sorry, let me put things more simply to make it easier for you to understand. Both assaults were deliberately planned so that you would be taken into police custody, isn't that right?'

'No comment.'

'That would mean that you were absent from the premises for a lengthy period if any human remains were found. You were very clever to think of doing that,' Jack added, deliberately changing tack from his previous belittling of Middleton.

The narcissistic side of Middleton glimmered for a moment and he couldn't resist answering.

'I was in prison, like you said. Which makes me innocent, right?'

'Not really,' Jack said. 'How would you know when they were killed unless you killed them? And you almost blew it the last time, because the bins weren't collected due to a strike. This meant that the rotting body parts were left in the bin and could very easily have been discovered when they began to stink. Again, you tried to evade being caught by getting arrested, but something went wrong, didn't it?'

'No comment.'

'You told Amanda to get rid of your victims' clothing, so she made numerous trips to a charity collection point. Please look at the CCTV footage.'

They watched Glenda's edited footage showing Amanda putting clothes in the charity collection bin.

'Now, let me just freeze that section; you see the jumper? We now know that belonged to Trudie, and Amanda also kept a pair of pink socks belonging to her. Plus, she did not – as she had been told to do – get rid of your jeans.'

Rodney shrugged and gave a twisted smile. 'No comment.'

'We have your blood-stained jeans, Mr Middleton, just as we have the pink socks, also blood-stained; the DNA samples found on both these items were from two of your victims.'

The group in the viewing room were becoming restless. It was obvious that Jack was getting nowhere. Glenda asked if she should order in something for lunch, but Anik quickly said they should just call up to the canteen for them to bring it down.

'Are they going to break for lunch?' Laura asked.

'At this rate we could be here until his thirty-six hours are up,' Glenda said. 'He doesn't look the slightest bit concerned. On the contrary, he's loving it, rocking back and forth in his chair with a big grin on his face ... makes me want to slap him. And I find that woman really annoying, too. We should stop wasting time and just charge him with the murders. Get the bastard on trial; we've got enough evidence.'

'There were more victims, girls we haven't been able to identify. I think Jack's trying to get information about them,' Laura suggested.

'Hang on . . .' Anik said. He could see Jack was now leaning closer to Middleton, his hands flat on the table in front of him.

'Mr Middleton, you have claimed to be suffering from mental health issues in order to avoid being placed in custody in the past. You have been described as suffering from paranoia, but you are also someone with narcissistic and psychopathic tendencies. Perhaps it would be useful to explore this area further.'

Miss Bamford rapped her pen on the table. 'If you are inferring that my client is not mentally fit, then this meeting should be concluded.'

Jack shook his head. 'I am not suggesting that at all, far from it. I think Mr Middleton is completely competent. But I'd like to try and understand why he slaughtered the three innocent young women we know of. I wondered why he hadn't done the same to Amanda Dunn, also a very young runaway when he first met her. Instead, he kept her alive. Was it simply because she was a useful accomplice in drawing more innocent runaways to his flat? Or is there another deeper bond between them? What would you say to that, Mr Middleton?'

'No comment.'

'Isn't it because she had also killed, before she ever met you?'

'No comment.'

Middleton was once again rocking back and forth in his chair, smiling and shaking his head as if Jack was talking rubbish.

But Ms Bamford looked shocked, and so did DCI Clarke, neither of them knowing where this idea had suddenly come from.

'I am now going to show some photographs from Mr Middleton's childhood. He has no need to identify the people in the photographs; we know who they are.'

Jack laid out family photographs taken from Joyce Miller's home. They showed Middleton as a young toddler, with numerous shots of him sitting on his aunt's knee. There were some of him with his father, and finally one when Middleton was aged about seven.

'Happy families . . . an ordinary happy little boy with his daddy, his aunt and, last but not least, here is a photograph of your mother.'

For the first time Middleton showed some reaction. He stopped rocking and sat up in his seat, his eyes flicking nervously from side to side.

Jack picked up the black and white photograph. 'This is Abena Mensah in her Ghanaian school uniform, so pretty and so young. It's the only picture I have of your mother. There is something written on the back.'

He held it up towards Middleton, but he pressed back in his chair. Jack turned it over.

'The name is very faint, written in pencil. But there is something else written next to it in very childish handwriting. At first I found it very moving. "You should have taken me with you."'

Ms Bamford pursed her lips. 'What's the relevance of this?' Jack ignored her, staring at Middleton, who for the first time would not face Jack but looked away.

'Look at me, Mr Middleton, look at me.'

Middleton slowly turned his head, his dark eyes glaring at Jack. His body was rigid, his hands clasped tightly together, resting on the table.

'"You should have taken me with you." This is your writing, isn't it?'

'No comment.'

Jack shook his head and gave a soft laugh.

'I thought it was very sad because I was told she had abandoned you, leaving you with your father, who was already living with another woman, someone he wanted to marry. You were only seven years old. But this isn't really sad, is it? Not if you read it in another way.'

Jack and Middleton stared at each other.

'It's a threat, a child's threat. Written in anger, after she left you. After I read that note, I came to believe something happened in that happy family home, something horrendous, something brutal.' Jack knew he would not have much time before Ms Bamford stepped in. The existence of the photograph had not been disclosed so she had no idea of what was coming. But it was having the desired effect on Middleton, as he jerked his head from side to side, his mouth drawn in a thin tight line, his whole body almost rigid.

Jack removed two more photographs from the file and placed them face down. Jack quietly asked Middleton to look at him.

'Look at me, Rodney. Look at me. Your aunt rejected you, too. She weighs about thirty-five stone now; she's deliberately eating herself to death because of what she knows, because of the secrets she has had to hide, secrets involving you and your father.'

'OK, this has gone far enough,' Ms Bamford said, raising her voice. 'Either ask my client a further question connected to his arrest, or this interrogation ends now.' She made as if to stand, pushing her chair back.

DCI Clarke at last spoke. 'Please wait a moment.' He turned to Jack with a pleading look, desperate for him to get to the point before the interview was terminated.

'You had to wait a long time to take your revenge,' Jack continued. He turned the photographs over. 'Look at them. This is your youngest half-sister, little Susie. And this is Milly. Your aunt told me they are the last faces she sees every night and the first she sees every morning. You were the last face they saw, weren't you, Rodney, before they burnt to death in the fire? Your father beat you up because he felt so guilty about what he did to your mother. They just wanted rid of you, didn't they? They wanted you to leave the house, kicking you out. So you made sure they would feel the pain you had inside. Did you watch the fire eat up their tiny bodies trapped in the inferno?'

Middleton suddenly let loose with a howl like an animal. His face twisted into a terrifying mask of rage as he reached across the table to try to get hold of Jack. It was DCI Clarke who got round the table to drag him back into his seat, but the rage persisted as he screamed and cursed. Ms Bamford shot out of her seat in terror and Clarke then hit the emergency button, triggering two officers to rush in.

Middleton was foaming at the mouth as he raised both arms up in submission and was forced to sit back in his chair. 'Handcuff him,' DCI Clarke ordered.

'I don't need fucking handcuffs,' Rodney snarled.

Ms Bamford asked for a break and Middleton turned towards her.

'Just sit down, you cunt. I'm sick of you. Let me tell you, smartass Detective Warr, when I get out, I will kill you, understand me?'

Jack calmly returned to his second file and opened it again. He removed the photographs of Jamail, Trudie and Nadine and laid them out on the table one by one.

'Did you kill Jamail Brown?'

Middleton glared at him, eyes blazing.

'*Yes!*'

He gave the same snarling answer in relation to Trudie and Nadine, waving his hand over their photographs as if they meant nothing to him. The only images he could not look at were those of his little half-sisters. He laid his hand gently over their faces and started to cry.

The group in the viewing room were almost paralyzed with shock. They watched silently for the next two hours as Jack led Rodney Middleton through each of the murders. Middleton showed no remorse, and it was deeply disturbing when he laughed and admitted that there were more. He gave their names, seeming to enjoy the fact that there were so many. He also said that Amanda was like a slave to him, doing what he told her without question because she was in love with him, foolishly believing that he was the only person in her life who loved her. He claimed that she knew everything that happened to the girls they picked up. Finally Jack asked what Middleton knew about her past, but he wouldn't repeat anything she had told him. It was the only decent thing he did.

By the time it was all over, Jack and DCI Clarke were exhausted. There was no exhilaration. They would have many more weeks of work ahead as they identified the other victims Middleton had named, and contacted their families, and they still needed to prove that Abena Mensah had been murdered by Rodney's father. But they had the result they needed most. Rodney Middleton would plead guilty.

* * *

It was after 10 p.m. by the time Jack got home. All he wanted to do was to sit next to his wife with a glass of wine and order in a takeaway. Maggie was already waiting with a bottle open and two glasses.

'Is it over?' she asked.

'Yes,' he nodded. 'He confessed.'

'That's fantastic! Did you all celebrate?'

'No, it was a very tough and long day. I'm just glad it's finished.'

'Well, we can celebrate now.' She poured two glasses of wine.

'It's not something I want to celebrate yet, Mags, because we still have the trial.'

She paused. 'Well, there's something we – you and me – can celebrate. You remember a few weeks back when we had that night of passion; not the recent one, but . . .' She held up her glass. 'I'm pregnant.'

For a second Jack thought he was about to faint. Instead, he took a deep breath and burst into tears.

Maggie wrapped her arms around him. 'What are you crying for?'

'Because it's the best news ever.'

ACKNOWLEDGMENTS

I would like to thank, Nigel Stoneman and Tory Macdonald, the team I work with at La Plante Global.

All the forensic scientists and members of the Met Police who help with my research. I could not write without their valuable input.

Cass Sutherland for his valuable advice on police procedures and forensics.

The entire team at my publisher, Bonnier Books UK, who work together to have my books edited, marketed, publicised and sold. A special thank you to Kate Parkin, Ben Willis and Bill Massey for their great editorial advice and guidance.

Blake Brooks, who have introduced me to the world of social media, my Facebook Live sessions have been so much fun. Nikki Mander who manages my PR and makes it so easy and enjoyable.

The audio team, Jon Watt and Laura Makela, for bringing my entire backlist to a new audience in audiobooks. Thanks also for giving me my first podcast series, *Listening to the Dead*, which can be downloaded globally.

Allen and Unwin in Australia and Jonathan Ball in South Africa – thank you for doing such fantastic work with my books.

All the reviewers, journalists, bloggers and broadcasters who interview me, write reviews and promote my books. Thank you for your time and work.

ENTER THE WORLD OF

Lynda La Plante

ALL THE LATEST NEWS FROM
THE QUEEN OF CRIME DRAMA

DISCOVER THE THRILLING TRUE
STORIES BEHIND THE BOOKS

ENJOY EXCLUSIVE CONTENT
AND OPPORTUNITIES

JOIN THE READERS' CLUB TODAY AT
WWW.LYNDALAPLANTE.COM

Dear Reader,

Thank you very much for picking up *Pure Evil*, the fourth book in the DC Jack Warr series. I hope you enjoyed reading the book as much as I enjoyed writing it.

In *Pure Evil*, Jack not only has to hunt one of the most dangerous killers of his career to date, but also investigate a deeply personal case – a mysterious murder implicating his colleague DCI Simon Ridley. It is always such a joy to write about Jack – a brilliant detective with a burning desire to bring justice no matter the cost, who often blurs the lines of the law. But in *Pure Evil* I wanted to push Jack even further – to the very limits of both his skills and his morality. With a vicious serial killer who seems to have a cast-iron defence, and a colleague in the frame for a terrible crime, the story offers twists and turns aplenty.

If you enjoyed *Pure Evil*, then please do keep an eye out for news about the next book in the series. And in the meantime, later this year sees the publication of the next book in my Jane Tennison series and the next book in my Trial and Retribution series, which I am very excited to share more news about soon.

If you want to catch up on Jack Warr's story so far, the first three books in the series, *Buried*, *Judas Horse* and *Vanished*, are available now. And if you would like to delve into the Tennison series, the first eight novels – *Tennison*, *Hidden Killers*, *Good Friday*, *Murder Mile*, *The Dirty Dozen*, *Blunt Force*, *Unholy Murder* and *Dark Rooms* – are all available to buy in paperback, ebook and audio. I've been so pleased by the response I've had from the many readers who have been curious about the beginnings of Jane's police career. It's been great fun for me to explore how she became the woman we know in middle and later life from the *Prime Suspect* series. It's been a pleasure to revisit the *Trial and Retribution* series after its television success and I am thrilled to return to it in print – the first book in the series is available to buy now.

If you would like more information on what I'm working on, about the Jane Tennison thriller series or the new series featuring Jack Warr, you can visit www.bit.ly/LyndaLaPlanteClub where you can join my Readers' Club. It only takes a few moments to sign up, there are no catches or costs, and new members will automatically receive an exclusive message from me. Bonnier Books UK will keep your data private and confidential, and it will never be passed on to a third party. We won't spam you with loads of emails, just get in touch now and again with news about my books, and you can unsubscribe any time you want. And if you would like to get involved in a wider conversation about my books, please do review *Pure Evil* on Amazon, on Goodreads, on any other e-store, on your own blog and social media accounts, or talk about it with friends, family or reader groups! Sharing your thoughts helps other readers, and I always enjoy hearing about what people experience from my writing.

With many thanks again for reading *Pure Evil*, and I hope you'll return for the next in the series.

With my very best wishes,

Lynda

BEFORE PRIME SUSPECT THERE WAS

TENNISON

DIVE INTO THE ICONIC *SUNDAY TIMES* BESTSELLING SERIES.

And the new Tennison thriller . . .

DARK ROOMS

THE THRILLING NEW SERIES FROM THE QUEEN OF CRIME DRAMA

Lynda La Plante

IT'S TIME TO MEET DETECTIVE JACK WARR...
OUT NOW

THE
INSPIRATION
FOR THE MAJOR MOTION PICTURE

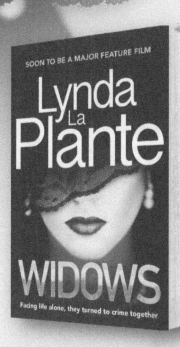

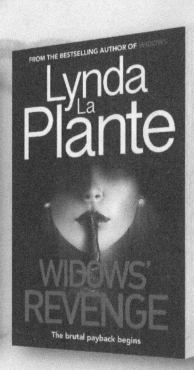

OUT NOW

WITHDRAWN

THE NEW PODCAST
THAT PUTS YOU AT THE
SCENE OF THE CRIME

AVAILABLE NOW